MARIO 1
Woman
In
Jeopardy

Works by George Hatcher

One Wilshire

Fiction by George Hatcher

<u>Ambulance Chaser Series</u>
Mario 1: Woman in Jeopardy
Mario 2: Coming of Age (2015)
Mario 3: Risky Business (2016)
Mario 4: Untitled (2017)
Mario 5: Flyboy (2017)

Independent Titles
Arabe (2017)
Pretty Face (2017)

MARIO 1
Woman
In
Jeopardy

George Hatcher

CasaHatcherPress books are available at special quantity discounts for bulk purchases, for sales promotions, premiums, educational use or fund raising.

For details, contact:
CasaHatcherPress.
http://casahatcherpress.com
800-416-6189

Woman in Jeopardy. Copyright © 2015 by George J. Hatcher
TXu001974269 / 2015-07-09

Designed by CasaHatcherPress
Cover Art: Mysterious Tunnel to the Light, Copyright © Mangojuicy/Fotalia
Ornamental blue doors, plants and windows,© Mangojuicy/Fotalia
201703
Library of Congress Cataloging in Publication data
Hatcher, George J.
Woman in Jeopardy/George J. Hatcher

ISBN 978-0-9965927-2-7

First Edition August 2015
10 9 8 7 6 5 4 3 2 1

Acknowledgements

This volume would never have been completed without the assistance and cooperation of a number of people who worked behind the scenes. I would especially like to knowledge first readers Kelly Heckart, and Ruth E Thaler-Carter, and, most notably, my personal assistant Jody Clinker, who is a master at finding errors that others miss.

To Allie, my pal, my editor, my collaborator.

To my family, friends, and colleagues, and especially Molly, through thick and thin.

By the time they find the bodies, I will be far away. As much as I'd like to see their expressions when they first walk in, it would be an anticlimax. I've pictured it already. First they find him. The maid knocks on number 13. No one answers. She opens the door, hoping to find the room reasonably neat so she can get away with just making the bed. Cleaning strangers' spit and shit, who can blame her? She's hoping careless guests left money out that she can steal. If she has a strong stomach , she screams. From the hall, there's a clear sight of him splayed out on the bed. My bet is she pukes first, then screams. I left him looking like he'd been chewed by a meat grinder. You'd be surprised how much damage a tire iron does in the right hands. I find it's much quieter than a gun, and I'm a hands-on kind of guy. What can I say?

She runs to get the manager who calls the police. They come and look at the body, and puke; then they look for the driver's license because there's nothing left of his face to identify. The stupid bastard should have known not to screw a married woman. She had her ring on, so it wasn't a secret.

Maybe they find her first. Luz. Such a beauty. At least she was this morning, before she pissed me off. I knew in my gut that something was up. I didn't need my ever helpful cousin to tell me my wife is a slut, but after he did, we planned the "consequences" together. He's really good with legal bullshit. As much as I enjoy getting hands-on, I'm good with other stuff. People don't tell me no.

I told Luz I was going to Tucson on business like always. My deputy went ahead to book rooms, and be seen. I waited on the far side of the out-buildings. Followed her straight to the motel. She never suspected a thing.

She got out of the car I'd given her and pulled her panties out of her ass. Hell, I watched her wiggle that ass all the way up the steps. She'd put on this sequined number, shiny and tight. I picked it up on one of my last buying trips. Still gives me a hard on thinking of her wearing it. Then I got pissed off. She hadn't worn it for me yet, but the bitch put it on for him. I followed my lawyer's standing warning not to go off half-cocked. I don't do what he says. In fact, it's the other way around; but I listened because he's had to clean up after me before, and contrary to most people's opinions, I do have a heart. I had to keep my cool, at least long enough to see where the fuck she was going. It wasn't her sweet old granny waiting for her in a room rented by the hour.

I waited in the car for a while, long enough to give them time to get started.

The longer I waited, the more steamed I got, knowing what was going on behind closed doors. I tried to be quiet getting out of the car, and going up the steps, to catch them in the act. I could have been a herd of elephants though, they wouldn't have heard, because they were making such a racket. Even outside on the landing, I could hear them, fucking. Bastard. I wanted to bash their faces in, but I made myself be patient, and knocked on the door. Said "Room Service." As if that piece of shit motel even had room service.

He's the one who opened the door. I'd never seen him before. Scrawny son of a bitch, holding a pillow in front of him to hide his puny ass. I got him a good one across the face with the tire iron. The pillow fell down, and he went flying. She saw it from the bed, the traitorous bitch, and launched into me, naked as the day she was born. I knocked her across the room with one punch. She was still. I put him on the bed, and then waited till he woke up before I started hitting him. No point wasting it on an unconscious man. When he passed out, I stopped, and drank one of their beers till he came to, then whaled on him some more. At some point, Luz woke up. She started crying, and I told her to shut her lying mouth. She brought this on herself.

He didn't put up much of a fight. I broke three beer bottles on his face, but he was already dead by then. I made her kiss him. You should have seen her recoil. Did my heart good.

She got worried then. She got all sweet, but I know her act by now. I let her suck me off. Like that would make me forget she'd been whoring around. I think it took her by surprise when I back-handed her. She started crying, and said she'd be a better wife. I told her to shut up. First time in her life she ever listened. I'm not saying I forgave her, but I got to thinking I'd let her live, make her suffer a long time for screwing around on me. She'd sure as hell know never to do it again. I guess I gave her one backhand too many. I heard her bones snap, and left her where she lay, with her eyes and mouth open in surprise.

The motel shower had shitty water pressure.

I left in my undershirt, drove with the window open all the way to Tucson. I think my cousin tossed the clothes in the hotel incinerator, and we went downstairs for a late dinner. The hotel fixes a good steak, and I'd worked up an appetite.

I had left the trip itinerary back at the sweatshop on my desk, so they'd know where to reach me if something came up. I expect my Uncle Rico will call in the morning to give me the bad news.

Prologue
1926
Nogales, Sonora

At the back door of the unopened cantina soon to be known as the Aztec Club, Luz stopped, used the brush she'd pulled from her bag, and tied her hair in a fresh pony tail. There were supposed to be jobs in Sonora, everyone said as much, and this new cabaret was going to have a restaurant too. Surely they'd need waitresses or maids to sweep up. The last time she'd eaten had been yesterday—an orange that had fallen, forgotten, behind a market stall. She'd been so hungry she'd saved the peel to eat later. On the way here, she'd washed up in a rain barrel, but after the dusty walk back to the brewery beside the restaurant, she was afraid she would be too dirty to convince them she was good for a job. She was down to a few coins, and had no idea what she would do after that, but she'd find something.

Yesterday she'd tried every business on the other side of the street. The last place they'd refused her was at the brewery, but she'd noticed the Aztec's OPENING MAY 1 sign next door, and had decided to come back today to take her chances. An immigrant family from Jalisco had been giving her rides back and forth to the abandoned barn outside of town where other immigrants from Mexico City, like Luz, were staying, but she didn't always make it back to their rendezvous point.

She hid her bag behind the steps and banged on the door of the cantina. Someone inside yelled that they weren't open yet, to come back tomorrow.

"I'm not a customer."

Booted feet crossed wooden planks. The door opened, and a waft of green-cut wood, sawdust, and fresh paint blew past. It was the only breeze she'd felt all day, too fleeting to be refresh-ing.

"Hola," a man said. More boy than man, really, with pink acne and greasy skin. His shirt was marked with paint, the sleeves rolled up. He looked her up and down. He couldn't see much thanks to her shawl.

"I need a job," she said.

"Yeah? You speak English? What do you look like under there?"

"Sorry, the sun burns me," she said, pulling her *rebozo* closer.

He said something, but she didn't know what it was.

"You have to speak English," he said. "Sorry, we got tourists from across the border. They're hiring maids here, but they want them to understand the American tourists."

"I'll do anything," she said, "Cook. Clean. I'll scrub till my fingers are raw. I must find work. I made my way from Mexico City where everyone says there are jobs here, and the streets are paved with gold."

"Yeah? I'd like to see that gold too," He grabbed her hands, and looked them over. Thick with callouses. She really had worked for a living. He gave her a sly smile and let her in. He was close to her own age, might have been eighteen, tops, not really attractive. "So what can you do?"

The back door opened to the kitchens, walls lined with stacked crates of produce for to-morrow's opening.

"I can cook."

"The cook staff isn't here yet, but they're all hired," he said. "I'm doing the finishing touches but they'll be here any minute. Can you clean that?" He pointed to a brand new sink, stained with paint. A bucket full of turpentine held several brushes. Luz dropped the remaining brush from the sink into the bucket and commenced scrubbing.

Some voices came from another room.

"Juan?" someone called.

"Hide!" he hissed. "It's my father."

"Is he the one hiring?"

He didn't reply, just shoved her into an

unlit closet.

"But is he?"

"You wait here!" he said. "Not a peep."

Inside, the new building smell of freshly sawed lumber was very strong. As the door swung shut, she saw the string. In the dark, she jerked it once. The ceiling bulb lit, wobbled, and dimly revealed row after row of full shelves piled to the ceiling, crammed with full canning jars. She grabbed one that looked like tomatoes. After she jerked a second time and the light switched off, she settled down on the cool tile to enjoy her bounty, whatever it might be. When she smacked the lid against the floor and unscrewed it, the top peeled off with a pop, and she dipped her finger in. Nothing had ever tasted so good. She savored the juice, and pulled out a tomato, enjoying it tremendously, then realized she was privy to a heated exchange outside the pantry door.

"You were supposed to be finished, and out of here by now."

"I'm almost done!"

"They'll be here for the pictures, and your

crap is still everywhere."

"I'll do it," Juan said. "Back off, and give me room, I'll get it taken care of."

There was more. Something about investors, and cooks, and the newspaper crew coming in to plan for publicity photos to be taken the next day. Something about trusting his useless offspring with this much responsibility.

Luz shook her head and whispered into the empty pantry, "If that's what parents are like, I'm lucky not to have any."

She stood to explore the shelves. If the argument continued, there might be time to enjoy another jar. But that was not to be. Juan stepped inside. He did not pull the door entirely closed.

Luz might have known better than to let herself get cornered, but having eaten for the first time in a while, she was full of good cheer. Maybe she was just full of tomatoes. Whatever the reason, she had let down her guard.

"You gotta go," Juan said urgently.

Voices filled the kitchen.

"Crap, they're here."

"What about the job?"

"Oh, the job," Juan said. "Hey, it's crowded in here."

She squirmed away, and he backed her against the door. He shoved his hand down her skirt, and fumbled between her legs.

The next thing she knew, the door flew open and she spilled out on her back, her legs splayed wide. Juan fell on his knees between her legs, his hand gripping his naked cock in plain view of a dozen cooks.

There was a lot of laughter, and a little swearing. The swearing came mostly from the heavier, older version of Juan.

"I give you good work and you embarrass me fucking off with your little chippies in here?"

He grabbed Luz by the arm and shoved her toward the exit.

"I'm no chippie! I came here for a job! Not what he had in mind," she said, trying to hide the tomato juice stains on her dusty *rebozo* and pointing at Juan.

"You want a job? Go down the tracks to

one of the Sanchez whore houses."

"Ha!" she said, "You think he scrubbed that?" She pointed at her perfectly clean kitchen sink.

Juan's father looked from her hands to the sink to his shamefaced son. "No, he doesn't know the meaning of elbow grease. You scrub like a cleaner. You don't look like one though. Too pretty. You speak English?"

"I can pretend," she said.

Juan the elder shook his head. "No English. No job."

He propelled her toward the door, but her shawl came unwrapped. Sunlight streamed through the new glass panes, and he stopped, dazzled by the light on her face.

He stared for a minute. He looked up and down her slim body, and back at her face, then pulled out some dollars and gave them to Juan.

"You got your day pass. Go across the border and pick up some more paint from the warehouse," he said. "They want another coat in the foyer."

"But I did three coats."

"Then do three more. No argument, " he said sternly.

He waited till Juan slammed off and was out of sight before he hauled her up the stairs to an empty room. He shut the door and turned toward Luz. There were still a couple of bills in his hand.

"I know where you can make some money," he said, reaching for his zipper.

It was a good thirty minutes before she got out of there. Before she left, she straightened herself as best she could, fixed the pony tail for the fifth or sixth time that day, tucking the *rebozo* back over her hair. She went to the steps where she'd stashed her bag, but someone, probably Juan, had made off with it. It contained everything she owned, except for the two dollars shoved between her breasts.

She recalled what Juan the elder had said about Sanchez. She headed toward the tracks, not knowing which way to turn once she'd arrived. She asked a couple of passing women if they knew of work, if they knew of this Sanchez.

"We all know that place," one of them told her. "You're going the right way. He's got some shops, they sew shirts. They've got lots of work. There's always something if you're willing to work your fingers to the bone. You work, you'll get paid, but it won't be much."

Sewing was better than whoring, but she wasn't counting her chickens yet. She made every possible detour, asking for work everywhere she passed. It was dark when she got to the place that belonged to Sanchez. The "shop" was not much more than an oversized corrugated tin shanty. The doors and windows were open, but when she looked in, she saw no one inside. There were stacks of shirts, pallets of fabric, empty benches ringing long tables.

"Hola!" she called, knocking on the open door. "Anybody here?" She stepped inside. A tall shape that was bent over a table straightened when she came in. She saw it was another young guy close to her age, not attractive, but different from Juan of this morning as day from night. Juan had been a bleating sheep. This one was lean and tawny, with the aura of a hungry lion. He was big all right, but too young to be in charge. A lion cub.

"Do you know where the boss is? I know it's late, but I can't walk another step."

She flopped down on a bench and put her feet up, unwrapping the shawl.

"I've been from one end of this town to the other, and no one is hiring. I hope you're not offended but frankly, I'm too tired to care. I've walked my feet flat, been sunburned to within an inch of my life, some creep named Juan at the new cantina stuck his dick in my face and stole everything I own. I think I'd give my soul for a cool shower and some clean sheets. Is your boss around? You think he'd care if I slept here, so I could be here when he comes in tomorrow? I swear before God and the Devil I am too tired to move."

"No need to wait," he said, in response

to this remarkable speech. He looked her over, top to bottom, circled the bench a couple of times. She was lying on her back, her slim legs crossed, her eyes at half mast, watching him circle her.

"I'm Francisco Sanchez." He put out his hand and hauled her to her feet. She was a light weight, slim and golden. "I'm not interested in your soul."

"Fuck," she said, dismayed.

"Exactly what I was thinking." He smiled.

She revised her opinion. Not a cub. He was practically slavering over her, exactly like a beast of prey over his next meal.

"I have a shower. I don't know how clean the sheets are, but if you're very, very good, I'll feed you afterwards."

It wasn't easy for full grown men to resist Francisco once he'd made up his mind, and an exhausted, and a starving Mexican orphan didn't stand a chance. She found herself in the passenger seat of a new Ford TT truck bumping back and forth across the border, down farm roads, dusty paths, and back roads no government agent had ever seen.

"I just have to deliver a few things," he said. "It's been five years since I personally made deliveries—I usually have drivers for this, but one of them quit unexpectedly, left me shorthanded."

"Was he a good driver?"

"His driving wasn't bad. He just didn't know how to keep his trap shut. He's not talking any more, that's for damn sure."

"That's foolish."

"What do you mean?"

"A good job is hard to come by," she said. "I'd drive if I knew how. I mean, it's a skill, but it's not hard. To just quit when work is so hard to come by—that's foolish."

"Yeah, well, he's in a better place now."

"Good he got another job," Luz said, shutting her eyes. "Funny though, that's what they used to tell us when someone died."

He laughed, then said, "Make yourself comfortable. This will be a while."

Luz hadn't been lying about being exhausted. She was dimly aware of the truck starting and stopping at a couple of places, but she gave up trying to keep her eyes open. It didn't matter to her that none of them were dress shops or stores, or that the cargo in the truck bed seemed to clink like bottles every time they went over a bump; such details were only blurry interruptions to her dreams. And why shouldn't she dream about American speakeasies? Eventually they circled back to Nogales, Sonora. She had a dim impression of a big wooden house, but she didn't wake enough to walk under her own steam. She heard him yelling for someone. They were in a tiled room full of servants. One of them undressed her; another ran a bath. She protested, but then Francisco was in the tub, huge and slippery, and rising underneath her like the healthy young animal he was; and then she wasn't asleep any more.

He had promised to feed her if she had been very good; and as it turned out, she must have been splendid. Good enough to be given a new dress off the racks of a Sanchez shop, and surprised with a seat next to Francisco at the mayor's table at the cantina on its grand opening the next day. She'd never eaten in such pomp and circumstance, but carried off the challenge admirably. Between the soup and main course, Francisco excused himself to use the facilities. In his absence, the mayor tried to charm her and filled her plate with stuffed mushrooms which she hated. Francisco returned with his knuckles skinned, carrying the cotton bag that had been taken from her the day before. He presented it to her without flourish or explanation, just dropped it in her lap. The mayor chattered on, oblivious while Luz gently touched Francisco's hand above the abrasion.

"No one ever did anything like that for me before."

"You have beautiful eyes," he told her, looking deeply into those eyes.

She didn't ask which Juan had produced it, only having the vaguest memory of telling Francisco it had been stolen. She had not brought up the incident that happened upstairs, and hoped that she hadn't told him about that too, but he had plied her with wine and got her to talk. She'd already confessed to him more than she shared with anyone else. How she'd lived in a charity home her whole life; how they put the orphans and foundlings to work during the day, loaned out to factories or farms or businesses in Mexico City that needed cheap unskilled labor. She'd been working at a textile factory when she was around sixteen years old, and one day, she had simply not returned home to her bowl of plain soup and threadbare cot. No one came looking for her. She was just one less mouth to feed. Since then she'd lived by her wits, not staying at any one job too long, mostly because the work she ended up doing was what no one else wanted to do. Lately even that work had dried up. Francisco's beneficence was the only hint that there might be any truth to the rumors of plenty up north.

Days at Francisco's house turned to weeks and months. In the evenings, he liked to come home and find her inside waiting for him. He'd often take her to the pool out back, where he liked to watch her swim naked. Unembarrassed by the gardeners, he'd strip down and join her.

Morning at the Sanchez compound began before dawn, when Luz would be seated at the kitchen table sipping coffee while Francisco polished off a huge breakfast: several breakfast meats, eggs, peppers, and a tall stack of tortillas. The kitchen was massive, with towering ceilings, large open windows with flow through ventilation, several ovens, work tables, and counters where the large staff ate before or after Francisco. Before Luz, he'd eaten only in his formal dining room, but she preferred the kitchen. They sat at a work table, stained and scarred with decades of chopping, their place settings across the table from each other, squarely in the center, their knees nearly touching. The head and foot of the table were covered in platters heaped with eggs, and various sausages and meats and fruit, enough to feed an army of servants when Francisco was done.

One morning Luz saw her own face staring at her from the back of the American newspaper. In the photograph, she was immortalized inside the cantina on opening day, sandwiched between Francisco and the mayor. Francisco wasn't looking at the camera; he was glaring at the mayor's hand on Luz's shoulder, and he had a fierce bulldog look she'd already come to know. The instant after the camera's flash, it had been all Luz could do to keep Francisco from tearing the mayor apart.

"We're in the paper," she said. "Together."

He flipped the page over to glance at it. "Too bad it's not in color. It doesn't do justice to your big brown eyes. We should have been on the front page. I'll get you something better to wear for the mayor's dinner next week."

"The mayor's dinner? I thought you didn't like him."

The edges of his mouth turned down. Not a good sign. He had a tendency to take his displeasure out on whoever was handy.

"The other mayor. Across the border," he said. "Arizona."

"I don't have a passport. I don't even have ID."

"Not a problem," he said smoothly. "My cousin Miguel is a lawyer, I'll let him know to take care of it. Until I get you a day pass, I can vouch for you. Dress pretty tonight. The cousin, he'll be here for dinner. Do you hear that Cora? Cook something he likes. Barbecue something big. Pig. Steer. I don't care what. Better get on it fast so there's time to cook it. There will be a dozen here, around seven."

"Yes sir," Cora said. She sat on a stool, heavily. Her mornings began at four, and ended at midnight, but she wasn't about to complain.

"I'll have to thank Miguel for handling the identification papers."

Francisco snorted. "Ha. No one calls him that. Call him Segundo."

"About the ID papers. I would not know what to do," Luz said. "I don't know why you're so nice to me."

"Because you're so nice to me."

"Can I come with you today?" She picked up a tortilla and began tearing it into tiny pieces.

"More tortillas, Cora," he said, sharply. Cora hopped up from the stool where she'd been sitting while writing out a list of ingredients for this sudden dinner, brought over a dish, and placed it on the table. When she lifted the dome, the tortillas were still steaming.

"These look wonderful," Luz said.

Francisco wasn't looking at tortillas. He watched the cook, and gave her a resounding slap on the ass.

"You're getting fat, Cora," he said. "Maybe you should be on your feet while you're working, eh? No sitting on the job."

"Yes sir," she mumbled. With him for a boss, it was hard for Cora to know if the slap was an expression of sexuality, anger, affection, or meanness. As for Cora, she was more embarrassed than she might otherwise have been because a couple of Francisco's body guards were eating at the kitchen counter. One of them giggled.

"Him?" Francisco asked.

Cora nodded.

Francisco picked up his steak knife, and turned his glare on the guard with the unwanted sense of humor.

"Pérez. Was something funny?"

Pérez stood. "No sir."

Francisco got up and walked to Pérez. "Sit."

Reluctantly, the guard sat.

Francisco stood behind him, held the steak knife to Pérez's throat, not unlike a barber. He moved close to Luz.

"Stand," he told her.

Obediently, she stood.

"Turn around." His big hand turned her clockwise. Francisco roughly raised Luz's robe from the back to expose a bare bottom, the crack of her ass pointing to Pérez and the others. Bared, her skin pocked with goose bumps, but Luz did not resist.

"Is this the finest ass you have ever seen, you asshole?" His face flushed red with sharp rage. Before Pérez could respond, he said, "Well this is my ass, and not you or anyone can stare at this ass, ever, unless you want to lose your eyes!"

Francisco spun Luz around facing Pérez, the robe straightening. With his big hand, he squeezed the cheeks of Luz's face. "Is this the most beautiful face you have ever seen, cocksucker?" He scowled.

Pérez was sweating. Francisco moved the knife, the tip pressing into Pérez's neck.

"Remember when you were on duty last week, and Luz was swimming? You remember the day? It was, I think, Wednesday. You were watching her."

"No sir."

Francisco moved the blade. A bead of blood appeared on Pérez's throat, an inch from his ear.

"That time, I saw you," Francisco said. "Watching. You can play with your prick on your own fucking time."

Sweat stood out on Pérez's forehead. Perhaps wisely, he held his tongue.

"You will not "watch" her again. Cora, coffee."

No one was eating. There was no sound but Pérez's harsh breathing, the tap of Cora's feet as she fetched the boiling tin pot from the stove, filled Francisco's cup, and handed it to him. Francisco pressed the flat of the knife harder with his left hand; and with his right, he dumped the coffee into the guard's lap. He shrieked—but didn't move.

"You're lucky it wasn't the whole pot." Francisco said.

Luz glanced at Cora, who shrugged, and bent to work. She slapped a handful of tortilla dough on the counter, and gave it two quick swipes with her *rodillo*, making a perfect round that she tossed on the griddle.

Francisco stabbed the point of the knife deep into the bench, between Pérez's thighs. Pérez shrieked. Blood from a shallow gash pooled on the seat and dripped down.

Francisco roared with laughter.

"Now that is funny. You should get that

looked at. It's just a flesh wound," Francisco said, returning to his plate. "Return to the bunk house at the hacienda and send someone else to replace you here. Someone who knows better than to hit on my woman."

Gripping his privates, Pérez stood. He looked as if he wanted to go after Francisco, but one of the gardeners stepped between them and offered to help him get to the ranch on the Arizona side.

"Try it again with Luz, Pérez, and I'll castrate you." Francisco sat down and finished off what was on his plate and told Cora he wanted more.

"Coffee too, for Luz," he said. "Fill her cup." He chewed and swallowed, then addressed Luz. "Why didn't you tell me about Pérez? Why did I have to hear it from someone else?"

Francisco looked at his plate and around it, and frowned. He gestured toward his knife still immersed the seat where Pérez had been, and the remaining guard pushed the bench within his reach.

He reached over and jerked his knife loose, and wiped the blood off on a napkin before he used it again, on a chop.

"Cora was there this morning. I handled it. I dumped my coffee on him, which you obviously know already," Luz said. Her fingers, as she held her cup, trembled slightly. "I didn't want to bother you. You expect me to run to you every time anyone makes a pass at me?"

"Yes," Francisco said. "Now what were you asking before all this? Something about going to work with me? You want to ride shotgun after midnight while I deliver hooch?"

"If that's what you're doing."

"Nah. It's boring. Besides, I've made arrangements. My cousin came up with a plan to squeeze some immigrants who owe him favors. They're going to be doing the driving from now on, and he makes a percentage. I'm dumping the local stuff all in his lap. It's small potatoes. We'll see if he's got the spine for it. I'm going to yell at the seamstresses today, got a couple new fabric suppliers to give us some deals, and check out a few new girls at the...." He shook his head. "No, you better stay here. Just stay here and relax."

Dinner with Segundo was uneventful. The American mayor's dinner went well. American newsmen took Luz's picture at that event and at another one a few weeks later. When not playing hostess, Luz walked around the property, swam in the backyard pool, and tried her hand at gardening. She had no experience with plants, though, and none of the seeds she planted grew. She attempted making friends with the servants, many of them pretty young girls not unlike herself. They were all standoffish. They did everything she asked of them, and more, but she was still an outsider. She still hadn't figured out if Cora was a friend or foe.

Newspapers at the breakfast table had become their routine. She read her Mexican paper, and he read an American one. After a month of this, she came across an article in her paper that made her laugh aloud. "You better talk to the reporter," she said across the table, showing him the column. "He's practically got your ring on my finger. Though I admit I figured by now I'd be sewing shirts for you."

"It's no mistake. I told the American reporters you were my fiancée."

She choked on her coffee, and placed the delicate cup in its saucer.

"Why would you say that to a reporter?"

He shrugged. "I like the way you handle yourself." He pushed away from the breakfast table.

"Get out!" he said sharply. Cora and a girl that had been chopping vegetables dropped what they were doing and made themselves scarce.

Luz pushed away from the table.

"Not you. You come here."

His robe fell open, and he pulled her on top of him.

"You can make this position permanent," he said slowly.

"This one? This exact one?" she changed position, once, twice. Faced the butcher block, grabbed the edge for balance. "Or this one?"

"Hard to choose," he said. "You like this life of luxury? Sitting on your ass all day with nothing to do but make me happy?"

"I'm not complaining," she said. "Is it over? Is it time to sew shirts?"

"Not if you play your cards right. See here's the thing: I gotta go to Chicago for a while. Might be days, might be weeks. I gotta leave you here. Hey, are you listening?" He pinched her on the arm.

"I'm listening," she panted. "Chicago. Weeks."

"No, don't stop moving. Do it just like that," he sighed in pleasure. "I can't take you with me, and I want to know you're all mine if I leave you here alone. I'll tie the knot with you. But you've got to be faithful. I won't put up with an unfaithful woman."

"Are you serious?" She stopped and stared at him. He had a big smile on his face.

"The deal's off the table if you quit moving."

She started moving again. The chair

creaked violently.

"That's better. So tell me, do I go to Chicago a married man, or do you pack your bags?"

So they were married. And before the year passed, Luz was dead.

1934
Nogales Arizona

"Ten-nine-eight..."

The huddle of children exploded from the playground into eleven giggling directions, bony knees churning, jackets flapping madly. Of all the kids playing hide and seek, Manuela and Carmen were the only pair. Together they shot toward Manuela's grandmother's apartment house because she was under orders to check in after school. Usually, Carmen's little sister—Manuela's classmate—would have made them a trio, but Elena was at home with a cold. As the eldest, Carmen was in charge, but Arturo was "It" again, so there wasn't much chance they were going to get caught, anyway. Whoever was caught would be 'It' tomorrow, a role Arturo rarely lost.

Carmen hid under the stoop while

Manuela slammed through the screen door and grabbed the sandwiches her *abuela* had left them; then they made for Bracker's department store, where they planned to get lost among shoppers. Unfortunately, Miltie had had the same idea and had already led Arturo there. Carmen spied him hot on the trail, not ten yards distant, his face pressed against the shop window. They were trapped! So they ducked into the alley where, behind a parked car, boxes were heaped by the store's incinerator, whose chimney belched waves of acrid black smoke.

Loaded with boxes, the elevator was an open platform that moved from the ground-level dock to the storeroom, and the doors leading from the freight elevator into the building were open, revealing stacks of pallets. The girls both looked in that direction and played a quick match of rock-paper-scissors. Manuela won, and got into the elevator, clambering to the top of the pile of freight to disappear into the department store stockroom. Carmen grinned; she wouldn't have chosen the elevator anyway. Likewise, she scorned the car—what if the driver drove off while she was hiding behind it? She looked between the boxes and an interesting pile of discarded apparel and dove for the cardboard, but that was too easy and boring. No cause for alarm, anyway. As long as she had shoes on, she could outrun Arturo. She glanced through the clothes, all still with their price tags, tugged a giant flowered blue dress over her head and topped the look with a floppy hat with a crushed brim. Thus disguised, she propped herself up next to a broken mannequin similarly arrayed. She balanced on one toe, mimicked several mannequin positions and chose the most comfortable, contemplated a pile of mismatched opera-length gloves, and wondered if she had time to put them on before Arturo made it around the corner. She took a moment to wonder about those mismatched gloves. There was probably not much call for opera gloves in Nogales, so where did the other half of the pairs wander off to?

When men's voices drifted through the stockroom door, Carmen braced to run. She expected to see Manuela charge out, chased by angry employees, but instead, the elevator groaned to life, moved up the six feet or so to the stockroom level, and slammed back down. A couple of men stepped on to the walk. Carmen stifled a laugh, and scrunched against the cold wall of the building, half-hidden behind the forest of broken mannequins. The elevator jerked a couple of times and stopped. Someone was playing with the controls.

In all, there were three men, one in a stockroom uniform, one a police captain. The third had stayed on the elevator where Carmen could only see a portion of his natty suit and hear him playing with the levers. For a moment, until he moved out of range, she could clearly see the captain, a man with the white hair and beard of an archangel.

A voice snapped, "Hey, what the hell do you want? What d'ya think you're looking at?"

The gig was up. Caught. Carmen took a deep breath and prepared to run.

"Ain't looking at nothing," Arturo's voice

piped up.

Carmen relaxed. She hadn't noticed Arturo's approach, but bless him, the men hadn't noticed her after all. They had moved out of her line of vision, but she could see their shadows. One of those shadows raised its arm.

Carmen heard an unintelligible noise out of Arturo, and the echo of his feet as he dashed out of the alley. She was relieved at his exit. Because the grown-ups were no real threat, she was so busy congratulating herself over her good luck that she didn't attend as the adult conversation turned to pleading, and some mention of money. She realized something bad was happening.

"I don't have it, don't have it, but I'll get it. I'll do anything."

The shadows scuffled. The bigger man pushed the other down, kicked at him, deliberately driving the whimpering heap in one direction.

"Tío?" The voice from the elevator questioned.

Carmen barely moved. Just enough to

see the speaker was big. Dark. Straining the seams of his fancy suit. His hand rested on the elevator controls.

"Up to you, Francisco. Handle it however you want."

The elevator man, Francisco, grinned. He was looking directly at her.

Simultaneously, as the elevator roared to life, the whimpers turned to screams. Carmen realized the shrill noise was coming from the beaten man. The motor squealed. The elevator bounced, wrenched upward a few inches and stopped. The screams continued.

Abandoning the controls, Francisco jumped to the pavement and dragged the broken man out from underneath. Carmen saw his shadow bend, reach down, and stand. Moments later, an open wallet hit the ground at her feet. A few dollar bills floated down.

"Holding out on us, eh?"

The screams worsened. Carmen shut her eyes, wishing she could close her ears, but dared not move. This was much worse than losing a game of hide-and-seek.

"Shouldn't hold out on us," the older man said.

The incinerator's metal door clanged. Boxes rustled and bumped as they were tossed in, and Carmen heard the crackle of fire. There was a loud thump from inside the incinerator. The scream became a wordless shriek. Then there was only the sound of fire, and a horrible smell.

As if nothing had happened, the two men exchanged pleasantries. Something like *Good job, boy, you'll go far. Do you want a ride?* and *See you at the house Sunday after church.* The vehicle started. Gravel scraped under tires, and underfoot.

Carmen did not move as the sound of the car receded, because only one door had slammed. Only one person had left. Her eyes were still squeezed shut. The instinct that told her to be very still also told her he was very close—something about the prickle of sensation in her skin—until finally she could feel his breath on her face.

"You can open your eyes, *chica*," he said.

She did not. Her heart pounded.

He pulled the hat from her head and tugged on her long braid, hard, until she opened her eyes to see that braid wrapped in his fist.

"Guns are so messy, don't you think?"

She swallowed hard and stared back. "How would I know? I'm ten."

He laughed. "Ballsy little *chica*." He looked up at a noise from the elevator. He pulled a gun out from somewhere, and pointed it toward the noise.

"What are you doing, Francisco?" Manuela demanded, clambering down from the elevator. She turned to Carmen. "Where's Arturo?"

Francisco pointed the gun back at Carmen, then relaxed his grip on her hair.

"He ran off." Carmen shrugged loose, and sauntered over to stand next to Manuela.

Francisco stared at the girls. "How the hell do you know me?" Awareness crossed his face. He pointed his finger at Manuela. "Aha!

Uncle Rico's get, the housekeeper's brat."

Manuela put her chin up. "So what?" She wrinkled her nose. "What's that stink?"

Carmen stared at Francisco and lied. "Didn't you hear the cat fight? One of the cats fell in the incinerator. It was really loud."

"Is that what it was?" Manuela made a face. "Stupid cat."

Francisco shoved the gun back into its hiding place.

"As long as it's all in the family," he said, inscrutably. He turned to Carmen. "The whole secret in life is to know when to be the mouse, and when to be the fox."

"What does that mean?" Manuela demanded.

"Ask her," he said, "but I bet she won't tell."

He bent down and picked up a couple of dollar bills from the pavement. He folded the money, shoved it in Carmen's shirt pocket. He caught her chin between two fingers, tilting her face this way and that.

Carmen spit in his face. He looked surprised, but not angry. He walked off, laughing.

Carmen was angry enough for two. She stared till he had turned the corner and still felt his fingers on her skin as if she'd been branded. She rubbed at her hot face with her sleeve. "Bastard."

"He's nuts. Mama says so," Manuela said.

Carmen nodded vigorously. "I believe her. She's right."

Carmen pulled the money out of her pocket.

"Do you want to spend that at the bodega?" Manuela asked.

"You can have it. I'm not hungry anyway. I'm going home. It's almost dark."

Until that moment, Carmen had thought the Arizona night was a peaceful place where the worst threat was the desert tortoise, Sonoran pronghorn, bighorn sheep, or *javelina*. Sure, there was the occasional jaguar and mountain lion, but otherwise, beasts of prey preferred to stay away from people. Even rattlesnakes gave fair warning.

It wasn't in her to fear the indigenous wild animals that came crawling through desert scrubs and Blue Grama, Tanglehead, and Sprucetop grasses, past the Acacias and Emery Oaks to bang at the door of a house in Nogales long after midnight. Now she knew to fear the two-legged kind.

Carmen had met the kind of snake that walked upright.

When the knock came, she was sure it was for her, even though she'd told no one what she had seen. The events of that afternoon weren't even why she was hiding in the cellar, hearing the banging at the door, the booted feet, the harsh voices. She was chilled to the bone at the voices, one of which she recognized.

It took some minutes for her mother to answer the door. Carmen waited an eternity in the dark, listened, and knew the full meaning of terror.

* * *

When the door opened, the police troop saw a comely woman in her forties, her lavish hair defying the confinement of the serpentine braid it was wound into. Her brown eyes were at half-mast, and her housecoat had been hastily flung over her shoulders, the belt hanging loosely from its loops. The bunched collar of a nightshirt poked up untidily. She held the door cracked only a third as far as the chain would allow, an inch at most.

"Señora Garcia," a young man said from the other side, "we must come in and search your house."

"Hello, Eduardo," Maria Garcia replied calmly. Carmen's mother was a midwife. Specifically, she was the midwife who had delivered him. She had known his family all his life, and most of her own. "How is your mother? I presume she is asleep at this hour?"

Eduardo flushed, his color telegraphing reluctance to answer in front of the squad, but she had delivered most of them, too. The ones she hadn't delivered, her mother had.

"She is fine," he said stiffly. "I assume she is asleep. We must come in and search. There is a...a fugitive."

"My husband only came home from the mine a few hours ago, and he must get up at sunrise. I would rather not disturb him," she said.

He looked behind him at someone she could not see, and then reluctantly pushed at the door, but she blocked it with her body.

"Just a moment," she said. "Who is it you are looking for in my house, and why do you think they would be here?"

"Just a migrant worker," Eduardo mumbled. The ranking officer selected that moment to push his way forward. Rico Sanchez might have a halo of white hair, seniority, look like St. Peter, and behave as if he had direct assurance from God himself, but that's where the resemblance ended. He was no angel. He knew it, and Señora Garcia knew it. Carmen, crouching in the basement, might not know his name, but she knew his voice, and had witnessed his evil first hand. Not all of his cadre were so informed. His loyalties were a lot closer to the earthly sphere and changed as the wind blew, as they depended on whatever benefited family schemes.

The public was Rico Sanchez's servant. His own interests were substantial, even though his older brother had inherited the family home—the biggest rancho around, encompassing land in Sonora and Arizona. His nephew ran bordellos and garment sweatshops all along the border. Rico's position with the police force was just a way for his family to keep the police in their pocket, along with government, politics, and every money-making enterprise in the county. It was a very crowded pocket. Little barriers like the law could not be allowed to come between the Sanchez machine and opportunity. Even his enterprising nephew Francisco, on occasion, took time off from his smuggling career to help the family business. He was the heir apparent, after all.

"Who is it you are looking for in my house?" Maria repeated her question.

"Just a migrant worker who is a thief that skipped out, leaving a big bill." Rico Sanchez tucked one finger in his lapel as he gestured expansively with his other hand.

"Off your family's rancho, no doubt," Maria said.

"That could be the case," Sanchez said. "So we are here to get him."

"First, I doubt he owes you so much as a peso. I've heard about the accounting at your company store. Even so, if such a one were a thief, which he probably isn't, he would have no reason to be here."

"He contracted to do a job. He can't leave until that job is done, and his store bill is paid in full. And we know he is here because he has a pregnant wife," Sanchez said, "as you very well know."

"Do I?" She dared much to keep the door open only a crack to Sanchez, but as the only midwife around, she dared because she was highly regarded in Nogales on both sides of the border—honored by wives and mothers, respected by husbands and fathers. It was only people who came from elsewhere, transplants, and the wealthy who went to the hospital in Tucson when their babies were due.

Unfortunately for Rico, Garcia women were not well known for doing as they were told. Much the opposite.

A few notes shrilled, then strains of a guitar tuning up came from inside the house.

"What is that?" Sanchez endeavored to see through the open slit beyond the midwife, but he was not a tall man. Señora Garcia was nothing if not tall. Stately, even. Sanchez, with all the authority of his police uniform and a troop behind him was still not enough to force her to open the door without physically shoving her aside. He shouldered the door hard enough to tug the chain to its limits and knock her back a few inches. The small success led him to ram into the door a second time, which caused it to smack her in the side of the face. She didn't budge, but she did rub her palm across her injured cheekbone. There was going to be a bruise.

She glared at him and braced her stance, even as he braced himself to shove harder. From inside, the guitarist began playing a soulful melody.

"Well, that's done it," she said, looking toward the sound. "You've woken him up. Now he won't get a wink all night. I suppose there's no harm in letting you in now. Mind you, don't wake my girls." The troop behind Sanchez lined up as if to charge in, but she raised her hand.

"Just you," she gestured to Eduardo. "I'll not have a bunch of locos traipsing through my house at two a.m. What would the neighbors say?"

"I'm coming in," Sanchez sneered, trying to take the upper hand and snapping his finger at Eduardo to fall in behind him. "This is police business."

"If you must," Señora Garcia sighed, as if resigned. The chain clinked softly. She waited as Sanchez was shifting his weight to slam into the door again and, at the last possible second, jerked the door fully open. To her disappointment, when Sanchez jolted forward, he only stumbled, but did not fall. His hat slipped over his eyes, then off.

Behind him, Eduardo and a few other

young officers stifled laughter.

"Wipe your feet first. If you get dirt on my clean floors, I'll be calling on your wives. Mary Christina, Dominga, Martine, Catalina..." As her eyes passed over the troops, each married man sent prayers heavenward that his wife's name not be mentioned. The police department might well be the muscle of Nogales, Arizona, but Maria Garcia was *La Reina*.

"And don't you wake my girls."

Sanchez righted himself. Lifted his hat from the floor. Smoothed his hair as if that had been his intent all along. He replaced the hat on his head. Gave it a little pat and shove to an angle he believed was rakish. With a swivel of his shoulders and a swagger, he stepped behind Eduardo, but only the sweetest optimist would say it was without losing more dignity. There was no other choice, as two wide-shouldered men could not stand abreast in the hall. Sanchez knew this from experience from the last time he had tried to muscle his way into the Garcias' house. He was not about to repeat that humiliation.

Eduardo performed a cursory search, glancing down the hall and opening a door he never looked into, but appearing diligent, at least while Sanchez was watching. Eduardo might have joined the police force, but he knew who wore the pants in his family. If he caused Señora Garcia any grief, he would catch hell from the family matriarch and his own bride.

Sanchez appeared satisfied with Eduardo's efforts and left him to follow his ears, which led to nothing of more interest than Mr. Garcia, still grungy from the mines, strumming his guitar in the small parlor. The arrival of the two policemen did nothing to interrupt his playing; he continued as if they were not there. Indeed, his eyes were shut as if he were asleep or mesmerized by the dulcet notes from his guitar. Eventually, they continued as if he were not there either. Señora Garcia refrained from saying "I told you so," but just barely.

Sanchez lingered at the front door as he gave up the search.

"I heard his wife is about to pop," he told

the midwife. "If they're not here yet, they'll be here soon. I'm leaving a watch." He quirked his finger at Eduardo and another man, and told them to stand guard till they were replaced at seven a.m.

"Thank you," Señora Garcia told Sanchez, "for protecting us from these dangerous criminals."

Sanchez preened. "We do our best."

His face disappeared behind her closed door. Inside, against the wooden jamb, Señora Garcia whispered, "Let's hope your best is not good enough."

She watched from the window for Sanchez and his men to move on, for exactly the right moment to open the door with friendly hospitality.

"Just something warm for you boys," she said to the guards left behind, handing them cups of a unique blend that she already had brewing, especially good for helping laboring mothers relax. "The night is getting cool. I made you some tea. Just a little something hot and relaxing."

Eduardo took a sniff of the infusion and gave the midwife a wry and knowing look. When his companion Paolo refused, Eduardo poked him.

"Don't be rude," he said.

She stood there till both of them had drunk their fill and offered more. Paulo put out his cup eagerly. Eduardo snatched it from him and gave a little bow, said his thanks, and returned the cups.

Paulo protested. "But you just told me to drink. Now you say don't?"

"You do want to be awake at seven, no?" Eduardo said, loosening his collar and looking around the agave, mimosa, desert honeysuckle, mountain yucca, and prickly pear in the Garcia garden for somewhere to sit.

As soon as she closed the door, Maria flew into a whirl of action, tossing off the sleepy routine and housecoat, beneath which she was fully dressed in plain, dark clothes.

She ran to a vantage point in the hall. Her husband would have joined her, but her frantic gestures stopped him in his tracks. She pointed to her ear and to the window.

"No, keep playing," she mouthed. He had started playing to let her know when the coast was clear. She peeked out a window and saw the two policemen sagging in her garden, neither quite as alert as they had been, but not quite asleep. Yet.

As strains of Spanish music filled the air, she found the trap door switch and tripped it. Her husband was a trifecta. Not only a tolerable miner and a splendid guitarist, he was also extremely good with his hands. He had a knack for making gadgets that worked. The trap door that swung open was one of his little gadgets.

"Mama! Are they gone?" Carmen's ten-year-old voice piped up through the opening, but even in panic after half an hour in the basement's pitch darkness, it was just a whisper. "The flashlight went out, and it's so dark down here! And the baby's coming!"

"Shhh *mija*," her mother said, "I'm bringing light."

She handed down lanterns. It was a good thing she hadn't let them search the girls' room. In the home's flickering gas light, they might have seen that only five-year-old Elena was still asleep, and that in Carmen's place, there was only a cleverly stacked bunch of pillows.

Until one looked closely through the trap door, the shadowy claustrophobia-inducing little room below appeared to be drilled from a single piece of solid stone, with three stone walls, a stone floor and a low ceiling that would not allow a tall man to stand upright. If one touched the wall just so, a trace of movement indicating a door could be detected, the door also carved of stone. If one opened that door, one would see it led off to another branch of the tunnel network. It could be noted that, where the stone had stopped, hard-packed dirt had been carved into, braced, and plastered over with a cover coat of mortar and crumbled stone, a near-perfect match to what had been nature-made and drilled out by miners long ago. The camouflage may have been deliberate; it may have been simply local artisans making use of what they had. Pedro had contributed in a small way to making the tunnel look like a small basement, as long as the curtain was up.

In the center of the cellar room, one thing was clearly not natural—a rickety aluminum examination table, complete with stirrups. It had once been a field-grade military-issue examining table, the cutting edge until some enterprising soul had devised a model that folded up into a briefcase.

It had been used by a hospital, then several country doctors, used and used until a backroom abortionist had left it in pieces. Pedro had found the pieces, put them back together, and carved for it stirrups of wood. A body-shaped wrinkle in the maroon-colored sheet indicated someone had recently tried the table. Still, the sheet was freshly spread, a startling color in the flickering candlelight. Terrycloth towels, clean but worn almost to transparency, were folded and stacked beside a tray of sponges, a pile of crisply folded newsprint, bottles of rubbing alcohol, tequila, shot glasses, some cornhusk wrappings, an assortment of sinister-looking doctoring implements, and an egg. The candlelight gave the room a red cast—the distinctive look of the entrance into hell.

One wall was only mended sheets strung from a spring device of Pedro's making, running corner to corner, barricading the space from whatever possible horror was on the other side. The mother-to-be, who had barely seventeen years under her belt, sat in a single chair wedged into one stone corner, the stool also seemingly plucked from hell, a three-legged affair, low, tilted, with a "U" shaped seat and looking as uncomfortable as the dickens.

On this Machiavellian instrument, a woman was sweating profusely, leaning back as gravity assisted her labors. The long dark hair pulled into a ponytail revealed a tawny face scarlet from exertion, loosened tendrils sticking to the skin of her wide forehead. She moaned, low in her throat, and panted, her hands furiously pulling at bands of cloth tied to the chair. Her arms and hands were lean and hard, speaking of a childhood of migrant labor. The moaning turned into a silent scream.

"Go to bed," Señora Garcia told her daughter, then knelt to make her patient comfortable. She checked the progress, then settled, her knees on a pillow until her legs had gone to sleep, waiting to "catch" the baby as it was born. When that event finally happened, she cleared the baby's mouth of mucous so she could breathe and rubbed her with a towel. The infant screamed fiercely at the intrusion and turned from blue to angry red. The red was good, indicating healthy circulation, a good heart, strong lungs.

Carmen, true to the nature of the women in her line, had not obeyed the command to go to bed, so she was able to help, diapering the newborn as her mother attended to the cord, the afterbirth, and her adult patient.

This was far from Carmen's first rodeo, even at ten. But it was the first time she'd ever felt the bad guys were coming for her. This was the first time she recognized the captain's voice.

An hour earlier, the mother-to-be had

been ensconced in a feather bed in the master
bedroom of the midwife's traditional adobe
house. A mad rush inside was cued by yelling
from outdoors. The natural proceedings of birth
were about to be interrupted by the rush of
booted feet. The rackety contraption of a col-
lapsible metal bed had been dropped through the
trap door, followed by the birthing chair that had
been around since Jesus, and the mixed bag of
supplies that ranged from superstitious baggage
that had outlived its origin to state of the art
medications. Next-to-last had been Carmen, mid-
wife-prodigy with scarcely ten years under her
belt, and five hundred years of folk medicine in
her head. While the wolves were wrestling at the
door, the last to relocate had been the young
mother. She had been hustled down into the dark,
and there labored by herself—with no one but
little Carmen to help—in absolute silence for the
duration of the half-an-hour in which the midwife's house had been invaded by police.

By now, Eduardo and his fellow guard
would be fast asleep, their slumber not to be in-

terrupted until Carmen woke them as she went to school in time to be replaced by the next shift of guards.

Still, the newborn had to be quickly hushed. The stone's insulation was marvelous, but there were tricky tunnel acoustics. In many locations in Nogales, on both sides of the border, people heard echoes of the baby's screams and were crossing themselves, heading to the church to speak of ghosts and spirits.

"She's perfect," Maria said. Her motions were quick, efficient, gentle. No one would know how deeply rattled she'd been by the raid. Here in the flickering light, no one noticed the slight shake of her hands or the way she jumped at the smallest sound.

She had already tied off and cut the cord, checked the afterbirth. She handed Carmen the baby and glanced toward the egg, part of a ritual the young mother had requested.

Carmen picked it up, and rubbed it, unbroken, all over the baby's body.

"Go on," Maria encouraged her.

Carmen whispered, "I believe in God the Father, Almighty, Maker of Heaven and Earth, and in Jesus Christ..."

The new mother leaned up as far as she was able, looking on anxiously. The Christian part of the ritual had been added by a Garcia foremother in Spain during the Inquisition, to guard against charges of witchery.

Carmen continued, still moving the egg and reciting faster as she went along. When used with the prayer, the egg was supposed to have absorbed any lingering evil the police had left behind. The egg was a defense against *mal ojo*, the evil eye. Eyes—and other body parts for that matter—did not get more evil than Sanchez.

The new mother relaxed against the back of the birthing chair. She was not the only one who believed that only direct intervention from God could guard one from the malevolence of Rico Sanchez.

Carmen finished diapering and swaddling the infant, placing the baby over her mother's heart. With satisfaction, the new mother averted her eyes from the egg, assured that it had removed any Sanchez-borne evil—or would, as soon as they properly disposed of the egg— and took her daughter into her arms with a joyful smile.

Carmen marveled. "Mama," she said, "look. It's like they already know each other."

"And why would they not, *mija*?" She moved her hands a short distance apart. "The baby has been this far from her heart for the past nine months."

She jammed the linens, towels, and tools into her bag, and wrapped the medical mess into a newspaper.

"Hurry," a voice said from the other side of the draped sheet.

The sound of a man's voice made Carmen jump, and she dropped the newsprint bundle that her mother had bound with string. It fell with a light thud that echoed, hollowly.

Maria whispered some quick directions and went to work on helping her patient clean up, racing against time. She handed over cotton packing, rolled a clean towel, and bound it tight to stem any bleeding. Little instruction was needed as this wasn't the mother's first infant. She pulled the new mother's dress, a simple cotton print, down to cover her knees.

"I'm sorry, I know you need to rest, but you must hurry, Rosarita." Maria noticed one of Rosarita's hands still clenched the rope. "You can let go now. The labor is over." She unfolded the girl's fingers and placed them flat on the baby's swaddled back.

"Sí," the young mother agreed. Exhaustion painted every angle of Rosarita's thin, young face, but there was relief there too. She wrapped both arms around the baby.

"You can come in," the midwife said, directing her whisper toward the sheet. "*Mamacita y el bebé hermosas*"

A burly man pulled down the sheet. Its support collapsed in the same manner as the handle of an umbrella and fell to the ground, revealing not the fiery entrance into hell, but a cavernous tunnel that disappeared off into distant black. In the last century, some Garcia ancestor had constructed the house over a much smaller tunnel, never dreaming one day it would be commandeered as a basement.

Carmen collected the fallen sheet, turning the birthing room back into the tunnel's dead end, as the new father knelt, gazing with love at his wife. Maria poured two shots of tequila, giving one to the father and one to Rosarita, who had had a head start to ease her labor. They drank, staring at each other and their baby, and gasping at the tequila's burn. Their daughter was now quiet enough that an indistinct sound of voices could be heard just outside or far down the tunnel. Given the acoustics, it was impossible to tell from where.

"We must hurry!" the husband said. His name, appropriately enough for the coming journey into darkness, was Dante. Carmen took the infant and cradled her in one arm as Dante helped his wife to stand. She was petite, short enough to stand upright in the cramped space, though she did not have the strength to do so.

"How can we thank you?" they both asked the midwife.

"No thanks needed. You paid me well. "

It was a lie but a kind one. The money had been very little. They could not afford more. Maria was tempted to give it back, but it was a proud couple, and she knew the coins they had given her would not get them very far. There was a local abortionist who took a lot of money, and did a lot of harm. Maria did a lot of good, but rarely had anything to show for it.

Carmen held out her hands and took the infant so the young mother could climb on her husband's back. She had already listened skeptically to the talk of germs and boiling baby bottles if she was going to use them. She was eager to be on her way.

Maria knew her audience, and continued with her usual spiel about avoiding the evil eye by isolating the baby away from people. "Just get to a bed as quickly as you can, and rest. Eat well and drink plenty. Lots of liquid, fresh water. Good food so you can nurse the baby." She wondered if they had somewhere to go, if they had paid a coyote or had relatives close by.

The father nodded impatiently, ready to be off.

"Cover the baby's ears," she said. Carmen obeyed.

Maria leaned over the medical table and gave a lever a hard thump. The table collapsed flat, with a metallic crack.

"*Dios!*" The young mother jerked at the noise. She hadn't liked the newfangled table and had opted for the birthing chair.

Señor Garcia reached for a lever in the wall. A huge rock in the ceiling moved on a well-oiled hinge, again revealing the opening to the house above.

"Carmen, you first."

After Carmen had climbed up, Maria put one foot on the birthing chair, and, with a tug from Señor Garcia up in the parlor, stepped up. With his wife on his back, Dante handed up the birthing chair and the medical table. Both had been selected for their portability. He wiped his hands off on pants that still bore the dust of miles of shafts and passages.

"Thank you, Señora," the husband said, looking down the tunnel. "Which way is south?"

"Aren't you forgetting something?"

Dante looked up questioningly through the opening at Maria. Maria looked at Pedro, who looked at Carmen. Carmen hugged the baby a little tighter and looked as if she might run into her bedroom and lock the door. But she sighed and gave the infant to Pedro, who handed her to Maria, who handed the infant down to her father.

He cradled her in his arm.

"She's so tiny," he said.

Maria watched him fall in love with his daughter. She saw his back grow straighter and the burden on his shoulders bear down on him a little harder. Whether it was the eye of experience or a gift, she could see the kind of father he would be––the kind of man the ilk of Rico Sanchez would never understand.

She pointed south into the darkness, finally answering his question.

"That way."

Dante grinned and turned north. "North or south, we have family. Big family."

"If you lose your bearings, try to make your way back and we can find you a guide. Go quickly before you are found."

The winding path turned people around. Not a dozen feet into the darkness, it branched out like a crooked spider, leading in many directions under Nogales—both Sonora and Arizona. The network of passages was old. By the beginning of the century, it had been impossible to tell what had once been cave and what was tunnel, but every generation made changes. People in these passages could have come from anywhere, go anywhere. They could also be intercepted at any point by men like Rico Sanchez, although in Dante's case, it was unlikely anyone else was looking for him.

"*Vaya con Dios.*"

Voices chimed from inside the house, but it was too late to offer well-wishes. The light of their candle had melted into the darkness. Carmen peered down into the dark hole.

"They're gone already, Mami."

"Our prayers will follow them."

Maria set the ceiling stone in its place, blocking the entrance to their cellar as Carmen finished the ritual, cracking the egg into a jar and placing the jar under the bed. In the morning, she would throw it away and not look back. Just as it had been for Lot's wife, the not-looking-back was crucial to the custom, lest the evil be drawn from the egg.

"Maria, why do you do that with the egg? It is just an old superstition."

Without missing a note, her husband shook his head at the foolishness of perpetuating the old ways. His fingers flew across the frets.

"Rosarita believes in it. If she believes, it will ease her mind. And how could the blessing hurt? And Carmen should know."

The notes stopped. Pedro stopped playing, put down his guitar and picked Carmen up. She was still shaking with fear. A look of concern crossed his face.

"Why did the bad men come, Papi?"

This was not the first time armed men had come. It would not be the last. Pedro was a good man, and with no way of knowing how big a dose of harsh reality Carmen had already swallowed that day, it was a struggle for him to try to interpret the world in a way Carmen would understand.

"They are not bad men, Carmen."

"Rico Sanchez is pretty bad," Maria yelled from the other room. "If he's good, I'll eat my hat. That whole family is one bad seed after another."

"...and you see, nothing bad happened," he continued as if there were no interruption.

"It was bad down there in the dark. It was a long, long time," Carmen said, shivering.

"My brave little girl," he said.

"I could hear your guitar, though," she said. "I knew you were there. It made me stronger."

"That is the backbone you got from your mama." He grinned at her, beaming with pride.

"Maybe one day you, too, will be a *partera*. You know, I hear they have schools for such things. As if they could know half as much as your mama about bringing babies into the world," he scoffed.

Maria left Carmen with her father. She stood at a window, observing the sleeping guards. They looked uncomfortable, huddled in awkward fetal positions on the cold earth. Neither they nor the guards who replaced them in the morning would ever see Dante or Rosarita going into the midwife's house, or anywhere else, for that matter. As far as the denizens of the Sanchez Ranchero were concerned, that particular migrant couple had dropped off the face of the earth.

She dug into the window seat and pulled out two old quilts. The door squeaked loudly enough to wake the neighbors, but not enough to rouse the two unconscious men in her garden. She followed the curves of her cobbled path to where the guards snored, oblivious. She grabbed a section from the bale of straw from under her rose bushes, shoved it behind Paolo's head, and shoved another behind Eduardo before covering them each with a quilt. Sure, they were grown men now, but she did remember the days they were born.

Chapter One

They were the Garcia sisters, a couple of beautiful girls struggling to survive obscure, small lives in an obscure, small border town forgotten by time. In another day and place, they might have been the Quiñones Garcia sisters, but their father Pedro, as all men who married the Garcia's eldest daughter, had given up his *apellido* Quiñones—a family tradition.

During the war, people around town always said that if the United States were ever invaded, the residents of Nogales, Arizona, and Nogales, Sonora, would be safe because no one had ever heard of them. Not that any greasy-palmed official, fence, or marker between the two countries was a barrier to locals. Besides, these days most adults on both sides carried day passes to work on the other side. They were easy to acquire from Nogales officials, whose one claim to fame was their unlimited capacity for corruption.

Carmen, the elder, was twenty-three and worked in a nearby sewing factory as the book-keeper. As her mother had been, she was a mid-wife. The local women still preferred the old ways; they were suspicious of hospitals, which were too cold, too impersonal, and too expensive. Elena, the younger Garcia, was a high school senior who had just turned eighteen. When Carmen had still been a schoolgirl dreaming of nursing school, their parents had died, first their mother from cancer and less than a year later, their father. The doctor had told the girls that their father Pedro had died of a broken heart because he couldn't bear to be without his beloved Maria. All their father had left them was a little pouch of money in a dresser drawer and a little adobe house on the American side.

They weren't just poor. Even for poor people, they were poor. The house and five hundred sixty dollars were all that remained of Pedro's twenty hard years mining copper. That money would never go toward putting electricity into their traditional adobe house, probably the last of its kind still standing in Nogales. The property, like their last name, had been handed down from mother to daughter for more generations than the girls knew. The home was primitive, but the gardens were wonderful. Maria had had a green thumb. The girls felt their home was perfect as it was, although even in these modern days, they had a pump in their kitchen, hot water was heated on the stove, and some of the whitewash outside had started to flake. At least their father had connected their bathroom to the public sewer line; a prior generation had hooked up to a gas line, giving them museum-quality gas lighting; and they had a flush toilet, albeit one that also belonged in an exhibit archive.

When their parents left the girls orphans, Carmen, who was fifteen, catapulted into adulthood. She finished tenth grade, feeding herself and her sister by moonlighting at night doing the books for the bodega in return for groceries. She told her boss, Mr. Pasquel, that she was going to apply for work at the factory, the only place around that might hire a young girl like her, and give her a real job.

"This is a real job," Mr. Pasquel insisted, though he had little need of a bookkeeper, and money for wages was scarce. "You cannot work at that factory." He railed against the factory's owner, Francisco Sanchez, but Carmen was at an age to be immune to advice. Since she'd been ten, she'd lived with the knowledge of what the Sanchez name meant. It was like living with a wasp nest on the porch, guiding her every careful move to stay out of the vicious creature's radar.

"I forbid you. Sanchez is a junkyard dog. Lower than a dog." It was the worst kind of language he would use in front of Carmen's innocent ears. He said much more, but with the selective hearing of a teenager, Carmen managed not to heed it.

"You're not my parent," Carmen said. It was the last time she would say such a thing, the last blush of childhood's luxury of rebellion. Bound and determined to do as she wished, she believed there was no cost too dear to get a better wage. She was the only breadwinner now. Many local women supported their families on a seamstress's salary. From her new mindset as the provider responsible for supporting Elena, anything producing a real income was the ultimate objective. Her onetime goal of nursing had become a pipe dream.

She was barely sixteen, an innocent, when she applied to work at the factory. When she came home, she was no longer innocent, with a better understanding of Pasquel's warning, but too proud to go running to him. The truth was that she had mismanaged a sewing machine, ruined the cheap shirt she'd been sewing, and had been fired on the spot. Her pleas to do anything for a second chance led to Francisco Sanchez taking her behind closed doors to "discuss" the matter, where he had her over his chair, then on the floor on a trophy bearskin rug from his own kill. He was on her a third time, over his desk, when she found and pointed out a mistake in an open ledger. Nettled, he slammed the ledger shut, finished what he was doing with a grunt, and pulled away.

Watching as she struggled to straighten her clothes, he looked her over in a new light. He opened the ledger and checked. She *had* found an error.

"You think you're some kind of book-keeper? That's a real job. You can't even work a sewing machine."

"Neither can you," Carmen said. "And you're the boss. You don't sew and it doesn't stop you."

She thought he might hit her. He had that mean look in his eye, but his expression changed to one of incredulous recognition. He put his thumb under her chin, tilting her head up.

She slapped at his hand.

"I remember you." His eyes narrowed, flickered to her breasts, and back up. "You've grown."

Abruptly, he shoved her in his chair behind an Underwood adding machine and tossed down a closely written page of numbers.

"Add it up," he said.

Carmen fixed her eye on the numbers and, with a lightning hand, churned through them flawlessly.

A brutal initiation. Instead of sending her home unemployed and ruined, he apprenticed her to the bookkeeper, a nervous young man with an addiction to pep pills that got in the way of his efficiency. She was ruined, but at least she would have a paycheck coming in.

Sanchez personally escorted her down the stairs to the main sewing room, sending her off with a carnal slap on her backside. The slap was a statement of proprietary rights, and Carmen knew it. He turned away and ascended.

"I hate you," she yelled over the machines, freezing his foot on a stair. At her words, the rumble and creak of old industrial Singers, Pelhams, and Necchis ceased. Voices froze in mid-word. The sewing room fell as silent as a footpad at midnight. The only movement was from a symphony of dust motes dancing in the air, microscopic threads happily floating in the atmosphere, redolent of the eye-burning vapor put out by fabric dye.

A pen dropped from Francisco's pocket as he turned. Its roll and bounce down the last few stairs were the only sounds. All eyes turned in the direction of the landing where he stood. Some of the seamstresses had their mouths covered. Others stood in sympathetic alarm. Energy tensed the atmosphere like a lightning bolt about to snap.

"But you want the job," he taunted back.

Not much amused him, but he appeared to find her defiance amusing. No one defied him. Instead of being angry, he enjoyed the audience and her public embarrassment.

He smiled into Carmen's glare, feral like a cat, and pointed toward the bookkeeper's desk. She held his gaze for maybe a minute before she obeyed, but her chin was held high. He thumbed his lapel and reached into his pocket for a cigar, which he twirled under his nose and sniffed before gripping it between his teeth. He followed her departure with the greedy lechery of a sated yet ravenous satyr, plucking at his suspender. It wasn't until she was out of sight that he tore himself away to survey the room full of transfixed seamstresses. He tugged on his watch fob, dramatically glanced from his pocket watch to the stacks of completed garments, and put the timepiece away with a flourish. When he looked up, he met the eyes of every woman in the room, and snapped his fingers. The workroom burst into activity, loud enough that no one heard his chuckle as he climbed the stairs. Even in retreat, Carmen was the lone lioness in an acre of scurrying mice.

* * *

For Elena, Carmen cleaned up the truth. The tawdry details stayed in the factory, far from the ears of Elena and her pal Manuela, who had come over to play and stayed to eat. Manuela, a big, dark, moody girl, ate at Carmen's frequently because her mother was the housekeeper way out at the Sanchez rancho, and took more care of the Sanchez family than her own. Manuela could have stayed in the housekeeper's quarters, but her mother insisted she live in town with her grandmother. Her father's identity was a mystery. Manuela's mother, also called Manuela, had never married.

"You should have seen the shirt I sewed," Carmen laughed as she set a plate of savory tortilla fillings on their table. "They fired me on the spot. I was so nervous I sewed the arms together, and the buttonhole to the back of the shirt."

"So you didn't get the job?" Elena asked. She tried to look appropriately sad but it was hard not to laugh at the image of the shirt, just as it was hard to look attentive while jostling for her half of the kitchen chair she and Manuela were sharing.

As always, Manuela ate like a bird. Elena, on the other hand, put way too much filling on her share of the tortillas Carmen had made earlier in the week. When she took a bite, bits of grilled chicken, lettuce, and tomatoes spilled out. Carmen didn't correct her, as she normally did. She didn't say not to eat everything in one bite, and not to talk with her mouth full.

"Fired as a seamstress," Carmen explained

carefully, "hired as assistant bookkeeper." It took a few seconds for that to sink in, and a few more for Elena to swallow enough of her huge mouthful to say something intelligibly without spewing food all over her pinafore.

"Bookkeeper! On your very first day," Elena marveled, even though she was not too sure of what that really meant, except that it sounded important, and involved numbers. She leaped up and hugged her sister, and did a little dance with a mystified Manuela, who didn't really understand what was happening either, but would go home and fill her mother's and grandmother's ears with the news. This time tomorrow, all of Nogales would know of Carmen's exalted position. Tortilla bits, lettuce, and chicken did go everywhere, but Elena's joy was like sunshine, and Carmen was determined not to cast a shadow over it.

She need not have worried. Elena sensed nothing amiss, and was soon deeply embroiled in far more important issues, like discussing the Career Girls paper doll set that Carmen had brought home as a celebration gift.

With the paper doll freed from its page, Elena thumbed through the different outfits, contemplating them with all the seriousness of her eleven years. The doll was in her underwear, a bad likeness of Betty Grable in a cheesecake-pose sitting position. Everything this year was Dorothy Lamour or Betty Grable, in red, white, and blue, posed with one of her hands held to her head in a salute.

"I can't decide if I'm going to be a nurse, schoolteacher, model, business girl, or airline hostess. So many choices."

"I vote for the nurse," Carmen said.

The colors of the cut-out dresses were all patriotic, as were the backgrounds. Elena studied each one carefully until she turned to the movie-star outfit, a red and blue A-line dress worn with spindly high heels and a careful line drawn up the back of the leg to represent the silk stockings that no one could afford, and a glamorous white fur throw to complete the ensemble.

"This is it!" Elena declared. "I'm going to be a movie star!"

She never realized that to Carmen, the at-home celebration over landing the job marked a day of mourning. Carmen had learned what was, for her, an important survival skill: not to dwell on damage done, but always to move forward.

Each day, when she passed his shop on the way to work, she avoided eye contact with Mr. Pasquel.

Luckily for both girls, Carmen's math was better than her mechanical skills and Elena's acting. Within weeks of Carmen's hiring, the bookkeeper she had been apprenticed to failed to show up. He was found in his shabby apartment, dead of an overdose, no doubt due to Francisco's generosity now that he had a cheap replacement. Carmen took over his job, making significantly more as a bookkeeper than she would have had as the best-paid seamstress. If that blessing had a high cost, she told no one.

Chapter Two

For the past seven years, Carmen had walked to work on most days. It wasn't far, and she enjoyed the sunshine. When she turned the corner this morning, she pretended not to notice the massive Cadillac keeping pace with her, followed by a second car packed with thugs. The pretense never worked, but a girl could hope.

The Cadillac's driver, Blasio, rolled down the window and yelled across the street. "Hey, Carmen. The boss wants to see you." Blasio gave her a cocky look, knowing she couldn't say no.

Mr. Pasquel was a man of the old school. He chose that instant to come out of the corner bodega, but it took her a few seconds to see that, instead of his cane, he was carrying the thirty-five-inch Louisville Slugger baseball bat kept on display in his front window. At times like this, Carmen recalled that he had been a friend not of her father, but of her grandfather. Eighty-eight years old if he was a day, and he was using the bat as a cane. From the days when she had been too small to remember, he'd given her *pepitoria*— candy brittle with pumpkin seeds, spicy dried mangoes, and little Day of the Dead candy skulls. Later it was school supplies, and still later, the job that had kept Elena and Carmen alive until she started working at the Sanchez factory. He looked as if he were going to hobble out into the street like some kind of senior Sir Galahad. She could not let that happen.

Carmen put up her hand to stop his approach. He ignored her, but his great-niece little Pilar was quick to run inside and fetch her big brothers—the two young Mr. Pasquels—who dragged him back across the sidewalk and shut the door. He could do nothing to defy the young Pasquels, both built like Mr. Universe. They knew there was no point in their grandfather getting hurt over some neighborhood girl who wasn't even a cousin. Carmen saw them inside, arguing through the window.

It may have only been her self-consciousness, but to Carmen, it felt as if all of Nogales had stopped dead just to watch her. Maybe they were concerned for her. Maybe they thought she had morphed into some kind of wild thing. Maybe they were just glad it wasn't their daughter or little sister out in the street with that big car rolling slowly beside her. As bad as it was for Carmen, it would have killed her for this to be happening to Elena.

"Hey, *chica*," Blasio said, "I c. ...c. ...can help you in, like before." Blasio hadn't been driving for Francisco long, but he did relish the borrowed power of his position.

Which day did he refer to? It was one of many. She wanted to run home and lock the door. Such tactics always failed. She fought him tooth and nail, but it was like being pitted against a devil. Opposing Francisco was like being a defiant cow herded to the slaughterhouse. He would leave her alone for a while—just long enough to feel a little safe. Then she'd find herself like one of those doomed slaughterhouse cattle. Herded up to the exit. Gates falling into place. Chutes blocked. One by one, all avenues of escape eliminated. Francisco knew how to manage his world to get anything he wanted. And sometimes, what he wanted was Carmen.

She clutched her little purse in front of her, and swallowed, trying to quell the sharp nausea. She had no choice. She looked both ways and slowly crossed the street, as if slow walking would put it off. The sympathetic eyes of her neighbors made the hair on the back of her neck prickle, and her face flush hot with embarrassment. At least Elena was already at school at this time of day, and would never see this most recent humiliation.

"Get in." Blasio jerked his head, indicating behind him. "You know how to open a car door, don't you?" He adjusted the angle of his mirror so it reflected the backseat, and grinned lasciviously.

Elena slowly opened the door. The back seat was empty, but not for long. Her boss— everyone's boss, at least in this part of town—

got out of the front passenger side, and into the back. He was surprisingly quick for such a big man.

To Carmen, he was nothing but a big blur. She would not look up to see his eyes. He patted the seat next to him. She was transfixed, standing in the door.

"Blasio, help the lady in."

As if she were not already standing in the open door.

Blasio got out and gave her a shove. She plopped onto the seat, one foot still on pavement, but she got her leg out of the way before Blasio managed to grope her or catch her leg in the door. The force of the slam rocked the car, a portent of things to come. Worse, momentum had brought her too close to Francisco. She would have scooted away, but Francisco grabbed her knee, slid his hand up, and squeezed hard enough to let her know he meant business.

"You want I should go sit in the café or something?" Blasio asked, standing just outside the driver's side.

"What for?" Francisco said, carelessly. "Get the fuck in. I don't want to be late for work."

She heard his zipper slide. Saw out of the corner of her eye his right hand at the crotch of his trousers, tenderly moving up and down.

Blasio resumed his position behind the wheel. He fiddled some more with his mirrors. Carmen saw his excited eyes glint in the glass. But he was nothing. The real ticking bomb was beside her, breathing heavily. The seat creaked.

Francisco patted his lap.

Carmen realized she couldn't do it, and lunged for the door, but he was quick again, and dragged her over him.

"What the fuck?"

The pencil skirt she'd put on this morning was an obstacle. When she was walking in it, she couldn't take large steps, and now its narrow width kept her from spreading her legs wide enough to straddle him. Not for long. He jerked the skirt up over her hips, revealing that she was wearing stockings and a garter belt.

"Ah," Francisco said, "For me? Honey,

you remembered." He laughed, pulling her legs apart so she was on her knees straddling him, facing him. He adjusted her angle and leaned back as far as the seat would allow.

"That's better," he said, running his hands up the silk stockings to bare flesh.

There was nowhere to look. She wouldn't look at his face, and she wouldn't look at that massive cock she'd seen already too many times before, at Francisco's whim.

She shut her eyes.

"Not here. Please, not here on the street," she whispered.

"What did you say? Here? Of course, let me oblige. You know what it does to me when you ask so nicely."

He adjusted himself and with a flex of his hips, probed. Grasping the cheeks of her buttocks, he pulled her forward.

She panted sharply when he wedged his way in. Her eyelids were down. In her head, she was in the dark, but she could feel the driver watching, his intrusion as harsh on her skin as the one below.

"Blasio, get us to the alley behind the factory."

The springs squeaked and rocked.

Blasio started the car up resentfully, making it clear he preferred watching the backseat action rather than the traffic merging on the road.

It wasn't far, and in a few moments, the Cadillac was nestled in a narrow brick corridor. Even with her eyes shut, Carmen recognized the hard double-bump as they rode over the crumbled pavement where the roots of a cottonwood across from the factory had torn up the concrete, recognized the acoustics of the alley and the familiar eye-burning stench of fabric dye from the tarp-covered cotton bales stacked two stories high. She heard the series of bumps of the entourage vehicles. She heard the rip of her panties.

"Ah, Carmen," Francisco panted. "You have the face of an angel. That skin of yours, it looks and tastes like honey. Those happy green eyes. They pierce the heart I don't have, can you feel it? Like I'm piercing you?" He panted, grabbed the cheeks of her backside, and began moving her up and down. "You do the work, fuck me. Move your ass. Come on. That's it."

Carmen braced her hands on the seat on either side of his head and rode him, driven mostly by his cupped hands. It felt like hours and her legs were shaking from the strain and her awkward angle. Twice she heard footsteps in the alley, approaching close, probably someone looking in the window, then running away. She could hear Blasio in the squeaking front seat. He must be jerking off. Sweat was dripping off her, but Francisco's erection didn't falter. He didn't care she was crying, either.

"I won't stop till you come on me. No whining like the factory girls. You don't want to do it, but you always do, don't you? So fierce." He reached between their bodies and played with her. "You fight me all the way there." He was breathing hard.

She didn't want him to know, and tried to keep from showing it, but he knew. He half-shouted in triumph, half-groaned, the hot gush of his seed erupting into her. "Much as you hate me, you can't help it, can you?"

Carmen said nothing, could still feel the blast of the unwanted orgasm as if she were coming apart. Each time, it felt like he'd stolen a little piece of her. He pulled out and shoved her aside. She heard the rustle of clothing, heard the crack of a match, the sulfur as if from the devil himself. His cigar smoke circled her.

"If you're not clocked-in in four minutes," he said, "I'll assume Blasio here is fucking you, and I'll dock you fifteen minutes. See that you put that on your time card."

She knew what that was about. He knew she wouldn't have anything to do with that idiot Blasio. He just wanted to make sure she didn't have a chance to clean up. He wanted everyone to see her running in with her hair askew, her dress wrinkled, smelling and dripping with sweat and sex, trailing the dark fragrance of a hunted animal with him close behind her. Everyone would know he'd had her again.

She scrambled out of the car, not even

checking if anyone saw her bare bottom and twisted garter belt. She tugged the narrow skirt down from where it had been bunched at her waist and headed for the factory entrance, trying to smooth the telltale wrinkles from the cloth as she ran. She bumped into him, or maybe he'd moved in her way on purpose. It was like running into a wall. The impact knocked her to her knees. She picked herself up, racing awkwardly, all heels, skinned knees, and pencil skirt, for the time clock. Thanks to the acoustics in the alley, she could hear them both, Francisco and Blasio, damn them both, laughing, as well as the raucous amusement of Francisco's retinue as the herd of automobiles that followed him leisurely spat out their occupants.

Francisco said loud and clear, "Hell of a piece of ass."

There was nothing in the world Carmen hated as much as Francisco. She knew she was nothing special to him—he preyed on all the girls. She had done everything she could to keep him away from her little sister, and so far, she'd managed to do so. But she had resolved one thing, if she knew nothing else. She'd never let him harm Elena.

Chapter Three

Elena was exquisitely beautiful, with facial features much like Carmen's—without the extra pounds. Everyone in Nogales expected that, after high school graduation, Elena would move to Los Angeles, become a movie star, and make the town proud. It was gossip Carmen had heard every time they went to the town's one movie theater, the one that ran the same movies over and over on its one screen. Carmen had made it clear to Elena, and to everyone in their small world for that matter, that it would be a cold day in hell before she moved to Los Angeles. It would be the last place on earth she'd ever choose to go. They were not moving anywhere. Nogales was home.

Carmen had taken her protective mother-hen role for Elena very seriously, and tried to guide her as best she could. The thought of living in a big city gave her chills. The only thing that had ever made her consider moving was her boss, but she reasoned that if there was one bully, one *peleón*, like Francisco in little Nogales, there'd be more just like him in wild and woolly California. Better the known enemy, as the adage went. The two of them living among strangers without the small-town safety net was a very scary image to her.

She never stopped to notice that that safety net she imagined at home had never saved her from anything.

Nogales was just Nogales, but at least everyone knew them, and everyone liked them. Garcia was a respected name. They had a standing in the community that went back generations. It's just that Francisco Sanchez was like a cancer one had no choice but to live with.

Not only did he own the factory where Carmen worked in Arizona, but if there was a successful enterprise in the county, he had a stranglehold on it. In his early forties, he was a huge bear of a man, a widower with no children. He lived like a *señorial* in a big ranch house on property straddling the border. It was only one of his properties, special because he had not won or purchased it, but had inherited from his father. After his wife's death, he'd left the Mexican house, letting Segundo rent it out and keep the proceeds. Their uncle Rico had lived and died on that ranch, corrupt till the day he died, and his demise under shady circumstances had been hushed up by his nephews: his sister's son Miguel as well as his brother's son, Francisco. On his inheriting it, Francisco had the original modest dwelling torn down and replaced with a grandiose replica of the *Dives-Sur-Mer*, a French hotel he'd seen pictured in the August 1943 *National Geographic*. Now the textile mill and sweatshop where Carmen kept the books were just two of his "factories." After he acquired a business, inevitably it became a sweatshop. He owned many outright, and many more were under his thumb or protection.

It never paid to ask too many questions about the way Francisco ran his world. In addition to his legitimate enterprises, he had fleets of trucks, fleets of runners, and a network across two countries that enabled him to distribute whatever he chose to sell. He used his physical presence like a weapon. Unusually tall, tawny like an Indian, black eyes in an Anglo face, commanding manner, volatile hair-trigger temper he took great pride in as part of his machismo: he was rarely challenged.

In the forties before World War II came to an end, Francisco had added contracting with the US government to manufacture uniforms for the military to his other, shadier agreements. His factories were more than a front for delivering bootleg liquor. They became established, and now they were kicking ass with work, fabricating all sorts of garments. The deal had resulted in his becoming untouchable in the legal world, a façade behind which he could do anything. From that beginning, he had branched out at every opportunity. Recently he'd bullied his way into ownership of a tool and die factory, and had already increased projected profits two hundred percent by switching to cheaper raw materials, adjusting the mix, cutting staff and wages. Though dark alleys were more his style, the factory was the site of a number of shouting matches that resulted in his firing managers he thought he'd bought along with the company, but who defied him. Fight by fight, he replaced or eliminated management.

Segundo was second in command. Anything Francisco did not wish to do, he delegated to Segundo.

Carmen only saw the books they put under her nose. She didn't know the fine details of anything. She saw Segundo in passing. He reminded her of a weasel, with his narrow, pointed features; beady eyes; oily hair; insinuating mannerisms. As a girl in school, she had read the book *David Copperfield*, and recalled the obsequious Uriah Heep. When she first met Segundo, the fictional Uriah had immediately come to mind. Carmen did not have to avoid him, because Francisco liked dealing directly with her, and saved Segundo for dirty work he didn't enjoy. Segundo, in turn, had a tier of bullies to keep things running as Francisco wanted.

The sewing factory and now the tool and die shop were legal. Those details she knew. However, Francisco had fingers in a lot of illegal pies. Some of the number columns she handled were encased in ledgers wrapped in brown paper. She had no idea what businesses they reflected, nor what the cryptic notes scribbled in the margins might indicate: quantities and costs of "fabric," supplies, sale records or percentages that might be someone's quota, payoff, or piece of the action. What was written was code for something else, and she knew not to ask.

She'd been interrupted while doing payroll in her office—more of an upstairs closet, but at least it was hers, away from and literally over the sewing machines. It had a tiny window, which she kept open, and a door, which she kept closed whenever she could. The door opened to a hall called the overlook, which wormed its way around the upper story so Francisco could peer from its height into the workrooms and storage areas. To reach Francisco's office meant climbing the stairs to the overlook and walking by her office.

Other than Francisco, visitors to Carmen's office were rare. On this day, persistent knocking drove Carmen to snap with frustration, "What is it? Why knock? The door is open."

Her concentration was broken, making her lose track of a six-inch string of numbers. Irritably, she ripped the ruined strip of paper off the adding machine and tossed it in the trash.

"Miss?"

"No formalities here. I'm just Carmen. If you need to talk to the boss, his office is down the hall."

"No, I just need to check on these figures."

Carmen's exasperated glance revealed the speaker was a working man in beige canvas dungarees. Although he was dirtied as if he'd been coming from a job, he'd slipped on a jacket and clean button down shirt for his venture into the office.

"Tomas Turcios," he introduced himself.

Carmen recognized the name. The plant manager of Francisco's latest acquisition. He was the highest remaining honcho on the totem pole now, as everyone above his rank had already had their yell and been fired. He held a cap at his waist, and his sweaty dark hair had dried to the shape of the hat. It had been a long time since she'd seen politeness inside this building—maybe never. He was stocky and burly, and furry on his exposed edges, like something in the *Ursidae* family. The manners made her look at him more sympathetically, but this politeness was an indication of how new Tomas was to Francisco's employ.

He'd learn.

He stepped up to the desk and dropped a list in front of her.

She glanced at it. "So?"

"That's the supply list for the tool and die factory."

"And?"

"I don't have the money to pay for it. I took in two trucks today and paid for them out of my own pocket." He spoke slowly to her as if she were a small child. "These supplies aren't optional. It's not like we can stamp these tools out of aluminum. Aluminum is too soft. We have to mix the steel to get the right strength. We can't cut short the carbon, or any of the other metals, or the amount of fuel. The foundry can't reduce how long the mixture must be processed. It just can't be done."

"Mr. Turcios, I'm sorry, I—"

Tomas waved the list in her face. "Look, Carmen, this can't be ignored. There are standards at stake here. Safety. If we skimp on the metal, the tools will be no good." He bumped her desk, knocking a brown paper bag to the floor where it landed with an aluminum thud.

"I don't make choices, Mr. Turcios." Carmen thumped herself on the chest, once with each statement. "I'm just a number puncher."

He bent down and picked up the little brown paper bag. A brass door chain guard, now slightly bent from where it had struck the ground, had fallen out. He bent it straight with his thumb and started to put it back in the bag. She wiggled her outstretched hand for him to give it back. The lock was a whim purchase, something to put on her office door. None of his concern.

"This is exactly what I'm talking about," he said, slamming the lock down on her desk. "I'll show you what I mean!" He stormed out.

Carmen dropped the lock back in her bag and didn't think any more of the lunatic. His little tantrum was nothing.

The day before, Francisco had pulled a fit over government red tape. He had dozens of enterprises south of the border which he'd taken over. Like a prowling wolf, he sniffed out failing mom-and-pop shops and wildly successful outfits alike, intimidated his way in, put his bullies in charge; but his methods weren't so easily accepted in the US Today he'd been swearing and stomping around his office for an hour over the "lazy bums," "cheeseheads," and "two-bit chiseling punks" he'd had to deal with in his takeover of the local machinist shop. All he wanted was for them to do as they were told. Was that too much to ask?

Carmen had heard the rant a dozen times

today.

The idea behind getting the machine shop was to cut back on what he spent on repairing his cheap sewing machines. He'd thought it might be convenient to be able to machine parts for his industrial sergers and overlock machines. Industrial machines of good quality cost a bundle unless he got them third-hand, ready to fall apart. He had trouble finding maintenance men handy enough to keep everything running. He already regretted the purchase, and swore loudly up and down the halls that it was the last straw and he would never take over another business—not in the US anyway. Francisco's anger was not a pretty thing. Heads rolled.

What did it matter, anyway? His real income came from the host of illegal enterprises. She kept a blind eye, as best she could, to his doings, even when he handed her numbers that she realized had been creatively edited and handed back, whose company names had been taped over with masking tape, or tracked shady deals that had no names at all. As far as Francisco was concerned, this was all business as usual. She didn't spend an extra thought on Turcios, but returned to her work.

Tomas Turcios was a determined man. When he stormed back a couple hours later, his hat was nowhere in evidence, not in his hand, nor on his head. He had also apparently misplaced his former politeness more quickly than she had expected. This time, he didn't knock, but came straight in, and poured fifty pounds of metal hardware on her desk, directly on top of the ledger she was working on.

Carmen shoved away from the cascade of locks, her task chair grinding against the uneven wood floor. She stood.

"Mr. Turcios, I'm trying to work here. Do I need to call security?"

"This is a door guard," he said, picking up a smaller, sturdier item. "But this one is the real thing. And this. And this." He grabbed a couple different types and shoved one of them in her hand.

"Bend it. Go on, do it."

She tried ignoring him, but he was insistent. Of course she couldn't bend them. He made her get the one out of her purse, and proved that even she could bend hers easily with just her bare fingers.

"Hah!" He snatched it from her and folded it in half. The mechanism folded and snapped. "How could that keep anyone out?" He squeezed and dropped the twisted chunk of metal in a loosely fist-shaped wad.

He picked up a massive deadbolt from the pile he'd dumped on her desk. "Now this— *this* is a lock." It slammed down with a meaty thud. He picked up an even bigger one. "And this is a lock. No one's getting past this baby without a chain saw or unscrewing the door." He leaned back against her doorjamb with his arms crossed. "That's why I gotta get the full list of supplies. So we make real tools. Not toys."

Carmen could have wailed her frustration, but she wasn't a wailer. She was a fighter.

She leaned over her desk—she'd inherited her mother's statuesque frame—and poked him in his shoulder.

"Look, you, that might have been a toy, but it was *mine*. It's too bad the little chain guard was cheap, but it's all I could afford. Your beef is not with me, but that was my property you just squashed."

She picked it up, holding it delicately between two fingers.

"What does it look like now? Not even a toy. It looks like a...a smashed roach. How can I take this to the bodega for my money back? I can't even tell what it used to be, and I watched you manhandle it into a lump."

She dropped it to the desk, where it bounced lightly, with a tinny ring like a little bell.

"So, thanks a lot for the lesson on locks. With your temper, you should fit in here nicely. Will you please go?"

He gave her a cold look, gathered up his list and locks, and left.

She thought that would be the end of it, but he'd taken her lock, too. She'd have to track him down because she intended to get her money back. Maybe she could straighten it, and talk old Mr. Pasquel into an exchange.

She returned to her math problems. She finished with the payroll for the sewing shop, and had moved on to a packet of tattered ledger sheets a nervous secretary had left on her desk. It seemed that she was, in fact, expected to halve the tool and die budget after all.

Carmen squinted at the numbers. None of it made sense to her. She wasn't a metallurgist and didn't know the proper proportions. Maybe if she cut everything exactly in half, it would at least keep the ratios that Mr. Turcios had been so enamored with.

She heard something go "boom" down the hall, something that reverberated the rafters and shook dust on her head. Probably a desk being knocked over or a man slamming against a wall.

"Segundo!" Francisco yelled. He was in a rage again.

Raised voices. That wasn't unusual, but it *was* unusual for him to meet opposition. Francisco couldn't yell loud enough for Segundo to hear, today. He must have forgotten. The gossip mill had it that he was off on a fabric-buying trip to Mexico, which was bad news all around, since a thwarted Francisco was even meaner than usual.

The other voice was definitely male. She peeked out the door, seeing nothing in the hall, then looked through the floor grating to the sewing room below where the occupants were dripping sweat from convection, as fans circulated trapped hot air and thread fibers. Half of the seamstresses had stopped working as they listened to the fourth shouting match of the day. At least this one was behind closed doors between the boss and some unknown intrepid male soul. The other half soldiered on, pretending they only had eyes for their work but their ears were tuned to the brouhaha, welcoming any break from their drudgery.

When Francisco's door slammed open and Tomas came flying out, Carmen flew to her seat and started scribbling numbers, trying to look busy and oblivious. Tomas and Francisco thundered past her open door. Another shouting match. Another firing. Ironically, Turcios's cut position would provide juggling room in the budget.

Hours later, well past closing, Carmen was burning the midnight oil. She'd missed the opportunity to leave with the crowd of girls. Usually they tried to leave together, but she, a secretary, and two of the seamstresses had work remaining at the end of the day. They had all stayed late so they could leave together, something Carmen had done a hundred times. Tonight, though, the darkness seemed darker, and the creaky noises in the old building were more menacing than usual. More than once, she thought she heard footsteps on the stairs. She even got up to check the empty hall. Then, unexpectedly, Tomas the madman, the one who'd been tossed out already once this afternoon, was back. He was much the worse for wear. His pants sported fresh rips and dribbles of crusted blood. Black eyes, a purpling broken nose, split lip. Beneath his torn jacket, the formerly pristine white shirt was spotted with filth. He still carried the canvas bag of locks.

"Hey, Carmen." Some of the salt seemed to have gone out of the lunatic. He gave her a sideways smile with his swollen mouth. She'd been so wrapped up in work earlier that she hadn't realized he was young and charming. Then again, she'd have liked him if he were ugly and rude, pockmarked, squinty-eyed with bad teeth and a skin condition. He'd stood up to Francisco, and that made him okay in her ledger.

"Mr. Turcios, I've been led to believe that you are without employment. I am supposed to tell you that you can apologize to Francisco and get your job back with half salary, or apply to him directly for your final paycheck." She gathered ledgers to put them away. The former plant manager was walking with a limp.

Tomas shook his head.

"I'm done with Sanchez and his crazy rules. But I was thinking after I busted your door chain, who do you need to keep out? A nice girl like you."

Seconds dragged. Carmen stared at her

desk, not saying a word. Put ledgers in the top left drawer; account books in the right center.

"Son of a bitch," Tomas said quietly.

Carmen saw the knowledge in his eyes, and her face grew hot. He was too polite a man to say anything. He was also the kind of guy who rattled when he walked, he had so many tools secreted on his person. Right then, right there, he knelt at her door, pulled out a screwdriver and started removing the closet-style door knob that had no striker plate of any kind.

"I just happened to have my awl with me." The implement appeared like magic out of one of his pockets and he dropped it on the floor beside him. "You never know when you'll need one of these things."

In a low voice, he said, "At the plant, I have...had guys who do hardware. Any maintenance guy worth his salt can change a lock in his sleep." He glanced around her office. Carmen could feel him looking at the lopsided window shade held in place with a push pin. The walls of her office had only been framed to eight feet. Unlike Francisco's highly decorated office with its high-beamed ceiling, Carmen had no barrier to the underside of the roof two stories up. Ductwork swung loosely overhead. Dents, water marks, and scars pocked her unfinished plaster walls. The flooring was composed of sketchy floor slats through which, in places, a seamstress sewing room could be seen and heard below.

"If you got maintenance guys here, you got me fooled. The shape the shop is in, they must be taking a twenty-year nap. This place is held together with tape." He pulled a piece of cellophane off the door. A flake of the door came off with it. "Cheap tape, at that."

The door, at least, was solid.

"About your job…"

"Look, hon. Don't sweat it. Someone will get promoted in my place. Someone real good at saying 'Yes, boss.'"

"You'll never get your money back," Carmen said. "Not if you paid your own dime for those supplies."

"That black eye your boss is wearing now

is worth every penny." He paused for a second and rubbed his bruised knuckles. "It's okay. I've already lined up a lawyer."

Carmen shook her head. "If you live that long."

"Is it like that?" Tomas hesitated, then slipped on the rose, cylinder, and shank. A doorknob was taking shape. "I've already moved on. There's a lot of demand for a manager with my experience. Got my pick of jobs anywhere in the country. I could start at the bottom somewhere, too. It would be better than staying here." He said this to her as if he were speaking of himself, but Carmen wondered if it was meant as advice.

"I can't afford that lock," she said quietly. "I saw the price tag. That would be more than a week's salary."

"Consider it a gift from an asshole. I had no business taking out my temper on you."

Carmen was tempted to hide the tool and die budget that was now sitting out in the open. She let it stay where it was. She barely heard the clink of his tools as he fitted the pieces. Maybe he was working extra quietly so Francisco didn't hear. It was probably safe. At this time of night, if Francisco was around, he'd already had some rounds of beer or tequila with the boys, and would probably be sleeping it off somewhere. The careful silence was heavy in the moments he replaced the knob and assembly, and augured the hole for a deadbolt that King Kong couldn't budge. She could tell he wanted to say more, but was bound by politeness not to refer to her situation. He was a complete stranger, had never seen anything that implicated how Francisco had treated her, but even he knew. Carmen stumbled to a filing cabinet and turned her back to him so he couldn't see tears she couldn't control. She was so trapped. She opened a drawer and fiddled with the folders and papers, waiting for him to go.

"I wouldn't want a daughter of mine working here. Or a sister. Or a wife."

And then he was gone.

He'd written his name, address, and a phone number on one of her ledger pages. On an impulse, she tore it out, folded it into a tiny square, and put it in her wallet. Might be something worth keeping.

The lock had consequences, of course. The first time Francisco found the door locked against him, he beat on it with his fist. Carmen cowered in silence, pretending to be elsewhere. She stayed late and sneaked out at midnight, slipping through the corridor's night shadows like a wraith. But the next day, Francisco was there to greet her with a silky voice and vengeance on his mind. In his office, he demonstrated to Carmen the error of her ways. Although he never tried her closed door again, he took to ambushing her in capricious and vengeful fashion, or simply knocking on the wall between their offices to summon her to his lair.

Chapter Four

The Cadillac Francisco had now was just one in a long line of flashy cars, and he always had a driver. Having a driver made him feel like a big deal, plus it freed him up to bully deals in the backseat. He had enough gold around his neck, wrists, and fingers to add several kilos to his body weight. Not only Carmen, but all his workers hated him. But he was a perverse man and reveled in his reputation, like a reigning Loki of both Nogales towns. He liked the reputation that there was not a teardrop's worth of kindness in his whole body, and he cultivated behaviors that contributed to his reputation of being a devil incarnate. The seamstresses laboring in his sweatshop were there because Nogales offered so few ways of making a living. The only thing between starvation and the street was factory work or a brothel, all of which he either ran, backed, or "protected."

Carmen was far from his only victim, just the victim of the moment. What Francisco wanted, Francisco got. Earlier that same week, when his office door had been shut and a sewing machine unattended, all the seamstresses knew what was going on with the girl. It was usually the young girls he targeted, but married women weren't immune. It didn't matter to Francisco if the girl was married or not, slim or not, pretty or not, willing or not. The married ones didn't tell their husbands. Husbands and boyfriends who got in Francisco's way tended to have terrible accidents. The girls—widows—who had been there ten years or more knew names. They weren't telling, but rumors persisted. Carmen wasn't the only one feeling relief when she wasn't the one in his office behind his closed door.

As much as Carmen hated the man, she never explained to her sister what went on at the factory. She was sure that Elena would have been horrified at what the work cost her, and would surely hold herself responsible. There had been no other way of providing for her little sister. Carmen went out of her way to avoid spreading or even acknowledging the rumors about Francisco. She might have been successful if so many of the factory girls had not been Elena's age, talking more than was wise. Sex stories about insatiable Francisco were the buzz of the town. He reveled in his notoriety. Elena heard just enough to make her curious.

Francisco's gang was a collection of thugs patterned loosely after what he'd seen in his early years of bootlegging for Capone. He'd managed to attract every thick-brained, bull-headed, hard-hearted bully on both sides of the border, and they managed to make Francisco's life easier and everyone else's life harder. To an extent, they did his bidding, but being as vulgar and selfish as he, their own interests came first. This meant they did their duty to Francisco only as far as he could see. Not being a man who comprehended loyalty, he did not expect it in others, but ruled by fear, and allowed them to do the same as long as they kept out of his way.

For the women in the factory, life was

not good. Carmen tried to keep this a secret from her little sister, even though there are only so many broken arms and black eyes coming out of Francisco Sanchez's businesses that she could explain away.

Two nights after the Turcios incident, Carmen came home exhausted, but as she always did, shook the dust off her shoes and put them by the door. The last block to her house, the path was less of a street and more of a raw cut into the Nogales earth. They used it as a stairway, but the incline just outside her door was a wall of piled rocks keeping the upper road and their house from crumbling into the tier below, where a family of five lived in one little room.

Their little house that had belonged to her mama's family for generations was a home to take pride in, even if it wasn't one of those fast-built clapboard houses springing up all around as the older houses were bulldozed. In 1948, quickie developments were being thrown together for veterans soon to be coming home in droves to enjoy the benefits of the GI Bill.

The Garcia home had been built of long wooden beams and adobe, cut deep into a hill, in a vein of stone of a forgotten mining tunnel. It would be standing long after the cheaply made new clapboard had fallen to moths and mold. Except for the garden, it was nothing special from the outside, but inside, from the terracotta tiles to the woven tapestries, to the hand-tooled old-style pump by a hand-carved soapstone kitchen sink, it had an Old World charm and beauty. Their papi had been a man of great pride, and he had faced their house outside with plaster and whitewashed it besides, although he'd been gone enough years that the paint and plaster were chipping away. The whole thing made Carmen want to weep, then sweep; so she did both. She was in a mood because Ambrose had followed her home again, and she'd walked so fast it was a miracle anything had stuck to her shoes. It was not just that Ambrose was uninteresting to her. The years working where she did for the employer she had had taken their toll. She felt herself beyond reach of a relationship. How much easier her life would be if she could keep her heart wrapped in ice.

Too tired to cook, Carmen had gathered cold cuts, bread, and cheese for sandwiches. She hadn't eaten but elected to wait for Elena, staring at the little kitchen's black-and-white tile floor and whitewashed adobe walls. The counters were of red tile, bordered with cheerfully painted Talavera tiles that were available on the Mexico side for pennies on the dollar if you weren't a tourist and knew where to go. They had given away the massive old family table that had always been too big for the little room. It had never sat squarely on the floor anyway, although that might have been the fault of the floor as much as of the table. Last summer, they'd found a tiny secondhand cafe table with a wood top. Later, they'd covered the tabletop with colorful broken tiles. Initially, it had been a fun project for Elena's home economics class, but it had become their main table. Elena had made a little mosaic in the corner with her name on it.

Elena was sitting at that table an hour

later when she said, in the middle of her eating her sandwich, "There's never anything to do here." She stood up, put her hands on the back of her chair, and started dancing with it.

Carmen watched critically. The style of dancing had changed since she was in high school, but their father had taught them to Jitterbug.

"Try doing your homework!"

"Did it already." Elena's music was playing, tinny and loud, from the little Air Chief battery-operated radio in her room.

"Pecking!" She giggled, and did the move.

The style of song was not Carmen's favorite, but she wasn't going to complain, as long as the music kept Elena happy. And she knew the lingo. She jumped up, grabbed Elena's hand, and did a little jerk, pulling Elena from the back of the chair. Elena rolled into the dance, and they kept it up to the end of the next song, when Carmen flopped back down, breathless and giggling. "Get a load of us cats. We're solid."

"More! C'mon, let's hit that jive." Elena laughed, and tried dragging her up, but Carmen wouldn't budge.

"I miss Papi," she said.

"Me, too."

"He could sure dance."

"Cut a rug, he called it," Carmen said.

"I remember."

"You take after him that way."

Elena did a couple moves in quick succession. Make with the toes, swing the wing, whip the hip. A couple of discordant thumps sounded, but a kink in Elena's wing made Carmen laugh out loud. "This band can't keep time!" she yelled, forgetting her good intentions not to tell Elena what she really thought of that jive music.

"That's not the band, that's the door. There's somebody at the door!" Elena yelled back.

In a panic, Carmen shot out of her chair, her plate clattering to bits on the tile floor. Her first thought was that it was Francisco.

"Hey, I'll get it." Elena rolled her eyes at Carmen's clumsiness and crossed to the door before Carmen could stop her.

The door opened, and for the fraction of

an instant, the height of the guest meant only one thing. Then Carmen saw it wasn't Francisco, and her heart slowed to a more normal pace. It was some skinny boy from Elena's class.

"Hey, Elena." It was so cold outside, his breath froze in the air.

"Carmen, it's Miltie," Elena said. "Maybe we should go on a double date. How about I call Ambrose…"

"Forget that, Missy. You know how I feel about Ambrose." She felt nothing for Ambrose Guzman but friendship of the mildest sort, and she had been avoiding his advances since school days. He was a year her junior. She'd heard he was dating a hairdresser now, anyway, though he still followed Carmen home sometimes.

Carmen turned away. When she looked up, she could see the shape of Elena and that boy sitting side by side on the rocky incline outside the kitchen door. It was night but not very dark out, something that was easy to tell from inside their gaslit house. The oil lantern smoked some. Carmen turned the light down and left it in her room so her eyes could get used to the dark. After a moment, she could make out the sweater Elena was wearing. Maybe she should have fetched her a jacket.

"Do your homework first!" Carmen yelled out the door, louder than was necessary. She ran into Elena's room and switched off the radio, not just to conserve the battery but to eavesdrop on what her sister and Miltie were saying. By the time she was back, Elena was already down the rocky path, not walking away, but standing there, looking toward the kitchen, waiting for Carmen to stick her head out and complain.

"It's Friday night," Elena yelled, "I'll be back before midnight. We're going to the game." She turned to Miltie. "Okay worm, let's squirm."

Miltie responded with a confused "Huh?"

Carmen stood outside the kitchen door for a long time, thinking of the high school games and Friday nights she had missed out on. At least Elena would have that. She watched Elena and the boy walk downhill past the other adobe buildings and the shanties, and finally past the newer clapboard buildings at the end of the road, to fade into the night. At least Elena would have a chance to have a childhood.

Chapter Five

They did go to the game, but only technically.

Elena was glad to get out of the house. Carmen was such a wet blanket sometimes; all she ever wanted to do was stay indoors with the doors locked. She was more like an old mother hen than a big sister. It was rare that she kicked up her heels as she had tonight, acting in a way that reminded her Carmen was still in her early twenties.

By the time Elena and Miltie got to campus, the players had left the field, and the bleachers were scattered with necking kids. They crossed the field holding hands, walking on crisp shards of frozen grass that crunched underfoot. As Elena passed one couple, she saw that the girl was her friend Manuela. Manuela winked over the shoulder of the boy who was stretched out and moving on top of her as if they weren't both dressed for a blizzard with what looked like a foot of fabric between them. Elena waved almost imperceptibly with her free hand and knew she would give Manuela the third degree during fourth-period study hall.

When she sat down, the metal was bitterly cold under her bottom, like a block of ice. Miltie wasn't much warmer, either, but he was kind of good looking, a little shaggy, and skinny-tall—the kind that hadn't filled out yet. Elena wrapped her arms round him, copying what it looked like everyone else was doing and gave him a good squeeze. Maybe too good a squeeze, because he made a sound like a squeak. He wasn't even as solid around as Elena, and his skin was the temperature of the cheese she'd pulled out of the icebox for dinner.

He was still just a kid. She felt like he might break. She wasn't interested in kids.

Milton put his mouth somewhere around her collar, tangling up her earring.

"Hey," she interrupted him, shoving him

back and freeing her ear. She couldn't help wondering what was supposed to be so great about this necking stuff. Miltie was tolerable but she was no more interested in him than any other kid in school. At least she'd have something to talk about in fourth period.

"Watch out," she whispered, seeing the coach coming across the field, rousting other couples who were hanging out on the bleachers.

"I've got a car," Milton said. "It's got a backseat."

"Why not?" Elena shrugged.

They dashed off before Coach could yell at them too, and settled in the back of the old beater Milton had bought with after-school work money, which couldn't have been much. The vehicle was ancient, the upholstery worn down, and the backseat smelled like the basement of the Catholic Church on Third Street. Milton shoved her down and spread her legs. Whatever he was doing down there hurt, and though he seemed to like it, Elena didn't care for it. Then it didn't hurt quite so badly, but he was done, apparently.

Milton made another squeaking noise and gave her a big wet kiss.

"I love you so much, Elena."

Elena didn't say anything at first. She wasn't sure how she felt about him. She only knew she didn't want to end up a virgin old maid like Carmen.

"You're a nice guy, Miltie."

She wasn't all that sure he was a nice guy. She patted him on his hand, and wished he'd move off her so she could breathe and get circulation in her right leg, which was asleep. Something was jabbing her. Maybe the door handle.

He climbed off of her, flexed like a giant daddy long legs, and got in the front seat. The door on his side didn't have a latch. Elena fumbled at the thing at her back, which, to her good fortune, did turn out to be the handle, so she used it, opening the door with a creak and a snap. The door handle came off in her hand, and she put it in her pocket. She slid out of the car, breathed the night air, fiddled with fixing her skirt, and stamped her foot to get the blood moving. Pins and needles. Not exactly an improvement. The high point of the night had been cavorting in the kitchen with Carmen. She wished she had stayed home. Would this date ever end? He was still talking. He had been talking non-stop since he'd showed up at the door.

"Was it your first time? It was my first time. Maybe we should get married. People get married after they do it, right? I wish you'd get in next to me."

Elena nodded, not sure what she was agreeing with, and wondered what he was feeling. It certainly seemed like it meant more to him. She looked over his shoulder, not meeting his eyes. There wasn't anything romantic about this parking lot by school, and there were other cars around with their windows steamed up. She thought she saw a familiar looking older guy watching them from behind the bodega sign, but it was too dark to see clearly. It was still cold and getting colder. She wasn't sure that getting back in the car was such a good idea, but she didn't want to walk home on such a cold night. When

Milton walked around to her side to open her door, she got in. He seemed to want to start kissing her again, but Elena had had more than enough. She wanted nothing more than to go home.

"I have to get back to the house," she said, pushing him away. "I promised Carmen I gotta finish my math homework. She's real concerned about math, since she's a bookkeeper."

"But it's Friday night."

Elena shrugged. "She thinks she's my mom. I better do what she says or she'll never shut up.

After he drove her home, she tossed the handle and made a fast exit.

It might have been better if Carmen hadn't noticed the bloody spot in her laundry, but Elena lied, and told her that her period had started. Carmen brought her a cup of tea and a warm towel to put on her belly—the ending to Elena's first sexual experience. A clumsy experience with a classmate in a very old car in the high school parking lot, cold as could be. She found the whole business quick, bloody and disgusting.

* * *

Milton was in the clouds. Elena was his girlfriend. The next day, she acted as if she'd never seen him before, not even as a friend. He wanted to talk to her, but when he would walk up to her, even if he'd so much as look over his shoulder in her direction, she'd be gone, vaporizing out of sight like smoke.

He found himself following her around like a lost puppy. She didn't seem to notice he was alive. With his bony height, he was already halfway a laughingstock, so he was accustomed to giggles and stares that followed him down the halls of the high school. He held his tongue and didn't confide in anyone, at least not until he had a chance to get to his sister's house after school.

Milton walked over to ask what to do about Elena. In school, Delores had been bubbly and one of the popular girls. Before Delores married, she and Elena had run with the same crowd. Now Delores lived in half of a duplex with her baby and one of the factory girls; her husband had died in a mining accident. At least, his body had been found in a mine. She'd have moved back home but there were eight siblings still in the nest, and they needed the space.

When Milton went looking for her, she wasn't in her apartment. He decided he'd catch up with her outside the factory where she was working. At six, he heard a bell ring and shortly afterward, a knot of girls rushed silently from the building, passing him on the sidewalk. He almost didn't recognize Delores, who had become a quiet stranger. She couldn't summon much energy to be interested in anything. She wasn't at all encouraging about Elena. She told him to just forget about it. If Elena was ignoring him, her heart wasn't in it. He tried convincing her of his sincerity, but his protestations made her snap at him in an uncharacteristic fashion.

"Why won't you males ever listen?"
She refused to hear another word.

☒

Chapter Six

Elena graduated, firmly in the middle of her class. She'd never really taken an interest in school. When she couldn't convince Carmen to move to Los Angeles and had no funds to take off on her own, she did what many graduates went out to do. She looked for a job.

There were no jobs, anywhere, at least not in Nogales. JCPenney had nothing. Newberry's had nothing. Job hunting was fruitless, even though she had experience—she had started working at the ticket booth of the only theater in town while in her senior year, but it only paid minimum wage: 40 cents an hour and all the movies she could watch. Films like Errol Flynn in "The Adventures of Don Juan," Judy Garland in "Easter Parade," had been okay, and she'd have watched a toaster if Johnny Weissmuller was on it, but Hitchcock's movie "Rope" gave her the creeps. If she'd seen it once, it would have been one time too many, but working at the Rialto, she'd seen it twenty times at least, and finally quit. She still had nightmares of being shot and shoved into furniture next to Dick Hogan while Jimmy Stewart and Cedric Hardwicke ate dinner over her.

Sometimes she dreamed it was her math teacher who did the shooting. Sure, Dick Hogan was cute as bee's knees and swanky as a new hot rod, but in her dream, she was dead right beside him, tight as a couple of carrots doing the tango in Tupperware.

"I can make a dollar an hour if I work in the factory," she begged Carmen at least once a day. "I can learn sewing. How hard can it be? You can get me a job there. You practically run the place."

"You don't need to rush into a job. I can support us while you find something with a future," Carmen insisted. "You will not work there for that man! You have no idea. You're better off finding work anyplace else. And sewing is drudgery. And the man is evil. He's a hoodlum."

"Like Dillinger?" Elena mocked.

"He's no Lawrence Tierney," Carmen shot back. "He's no actor. He's a real, bad man."

"I know all about Francisco. He's rich. He's powerful," Elena shouted back. "It's all over town. The only place he's not talked about is in this house. You don't have to worry about me. I can take care of myself. Besides, you do okay there, why can't I?"

"No! I do not," Carmen said without thinking.

"You mean...you and him?" Elena was shocked.

"No, nothing like that," Carmen said.

"What's so bad about him anyway?"

Like Mr. Pasquel before her, she couldn't put it into words that Elena would hear. It was an extra challenge to warn her off when she didn't really want Elena to know exactly what she was warning her from. "Take my word for it. He's a monster. Even his wife, his Luz he was supposed to be so crazy about, he kept locked up in his house like in some kind of harem until she had to die just to get out. He was crazy jealous. He's trouble you don't want, Elena. You don't need to work there."

"I'm not marrying the man," Elena protested. "I just want the work."

Carmen wasn't going to change her mind. Neither was Elena.

Elena was determined to get a job, and Francisco was the only one with jobs. One day, after Carmen had already been at work for a couple of hours, Elena dressed in her Sunday best and went to the factory. In the years Carmen had worked there, Elena had only been there twice before, both times shuffled out quickly before anyone could notice. This time, Francisco spotted her long before Carmen did, closeted away as she was in her tiny second floor office. He recognized her from his close surveillance of Carmen. It was a small town.

"My God," he said in Spanish, "you've grown into a beautiful angel."

Elena's big smile glowed. "Don Francisco,"

she said, "you are much too kind."

Nobody smiled at him like that. Not ever. Not Luz. Not even his mother. And the "Don" was a nice touch.

Francisco's ego was tickled. He had practically made a career of his encounters with young girls. Pretty women, young, inexperienced, knowing the stories about him, timidly made entrance to his hellish factory. They did not hold his attention. This one, like her sister, didn't have a meek bone in her body.

He spent a long time actually interviewing her, which he never did—in his mind, an interview was a euphemism for something else entirely—though mostly it was to keep her talking so he could look at her face and the rest of her. He even tried to be subtle when he was looking down her dress. None of the other girls had affected him this way.

When Carmen got back from her fifteen minute lunch break, another desk had already been squeezed into her office. She churned through her daily paperwork as it was delivered to her, sneaking glances at the other desk. Almost up to closing time, she wondered who would be there. Then Elena walked in with an empty folder and sat down. Carmen was about to unload on her when Francisco came in after her, carrying a tiny flowerpot with what looked like a dead stick coming out of it.

"Thank you," Elena said, as warmly as if it were a dozen roses.

Francisco mumbled something about cuttings and a rosebush, made moony eyes at Elena, glared warningly at Carmen, and walked out.

Elena sat behind the desk, smoothed her skirt, glanced at her sister, and pulled the dead stick from the flower pot.

"Cottonwood," Elena said, giggling.

"From across the street?" Carmen asked. "He couldn't even find you a dead rose?"

Elena was ecstatic, Carmen tight-lipped. "We will talk about this when we get home."

"The cottonwood?"

"The job. "

It was definitely a shard from the irrepressible cottonwood from across the street, the one that kept sending up shoots everywhere, no matter how many men Francisco sent to mow, saw, pave over, and hammer away at the shoots. More kept coming.

Elena went to work in the office as Carmen's helper. Francisco said she was too special to work with the herd of seamstresses in the hot room. Not that Carmen's office was cooler.

For a few weeks, things at the factory were a little different. When Elena was there, the seamstresses and Carmen were safe. Francisco was on his good behavior—which, in his case, meant that every second not spent on business was engaged in watching Elena like a hawk. Carmen's worries took an extra turn at the way he was paying her little sister so much attention. He'd never done anything like it.

He snuck into her office and replaced the stick with an actual piece of a rose bush, though whether it quickly died or had been dead to begin with was anyone's guess. He found excuses to come into the little office, bringing papers that didn't need anything done to them, and consulting with Elena as if she'd been bookkeeping for years, instead of screwing up high school math exams a few weeks ago. He sent her on chores, delivering packages to other offices in the factory or signing off on supplies, a thing which he normally allowed no one else to do. He would follow her and stand around the corner, peeking through windows so he could watch and see if she ever flirted with other men in the factory, drivers, or delivery men. She never did.

Of course, he never caught her watching him watch her. He never saw her sneak hidden glances back at him when he looked away as he followed her. She'd giggle to herself when it was happening, and later she'd giggle over it all to Carmen, and tell her it was just like how jealous Milton had been with her in high school after their one miserable date.

Carmen wasn't giggling. Francisco's attention was nothing to trifle with.

Elena and Carmen had started walking to work and clocking in together. The only benefit of having Elena working with her, as far as Carmen was concerned, was that it deterred Francisco's attentions to her. Once inside the building, they usually found a line waiting to clock in. Francisco expected all the forty-two seamstresses in the building to clock in between 7:59 and 8:00 a.m., something that was frankly impossible. It had them all jumping around like racehorses at the gate, punching in in rapid succession, a circus he frequently watched with great amusement. When he wasn't hovering, the minutes leading up to 7:58 provided most of the seamstresses their socializing of the day—a chance to chatter about their husbands and boyfriends, their babies, the neighborhood gossip. In the minute following their arrival, from 8:00 to 8:01, the factory's male employees were expected to clock in, and their shift ended on the minute as well.

    With Elena there, Carmen kept to herself, but Elena was bubbly and irrepressible. One day, Elena saw Milton's sister, Delores Vecchio, and made a beeline for her. She was not that much older than Elena and they'd had a class together once. Carmen grabbed Elena's sleeve and tried to drag her away, but Elena was nothing if not stubborn. She may have wondered what could be wrong with talking to an old friend. Carmen still wanted to protect her little sister.

Delores had plenty of her own Francisco horror stories to tell, and the telling of those wouldn't faze Carmen a bit; but first she wanted to extract from Delores a promise not to share Carmen's secrets. It was with great alarm Carmen failed to keep them apart.

"It's better with you here," Delores confessed. "Since you're here, he's left the girls alone."

"Why would they want to be left alone?" Elena asked, knowing Delores meant Francisco.

Never quite grasping the darkness of Francisco's reputation, Elena was always digging for more. It was that moment that Francisco walked by, causing silence to fall like in a tomb. Ignoring forty-some-odd women he'd slept with one time or another, he spoke only to Elena. Behind Elena's back, he'd gestured to a startled Delores, who followed him back to his office like a cowed puppy going to its doom. That the door was open meant nothing, but all he did was ask what Elena wanted and to tell Delores to keep her mouth shut.

Delores was more than happy with the reprieve.

Chapter Seven

In passing, Carmen heard Francisco tell Delores, "I have a favor to ask of you."

He'd had to detour past four offices and one flight of stairs to run into Delores that way.

Carmen knew in her bones that the conversation had something to do with Elena. Curiosity and concern were eating her alive. Before the day was out, she meandered accidentally-on-purpose to the factory floor, supposedly to get the previous day's production numbers from Berto the shop head, a none-too-sharp man whose duties, among other things, included counting piece goods. She timed it to catch him in the workroom. Standing beside Delores's sewing machine, Carmen kept talking to him and recycling his pile so he kept losing count of Delores's stack of work, giving the two girls time to communicate undetected. Delores's eyes were red, and her hands moved as if she were in her nineties instead of barely out of her teens. Their conversation consisted more of pantomime than actual words. The only one who was unaware of both sides of the conversation was Berto—all the seamstresses were following avidly along, though Conchita accidentally sewed a sleeve shut and had to rip out the stitches, and Donita was trying to figure out how to correct accidentally cutting three armholes without anyone noticing.

"Did he..." Carmen mouthed, and made a graphic gesture. Not that Berto would have noticed. He was busy trying to count the five extra pieces that Carmen had just slipped from the counted to the uncounted pile.

Delores shook her head. "No, he didn't touch me."

"So, why the tears?" Carmen wiped her eyes, and squeezed out an imaginary handkerchief.

"He said I have to watch her. I have to tell him if Elena is alone with a guy. If she talks to a guy. If she looks at a guy. If she even thinks about a guy. How am I supposed to know what she's thinking?"

"Or else?" Carmen suggested by shrugging.

"Or else I get fired. I can't be fired. I got a baby to feed. Tell her not to fuck around. He's loco. Can you maybe just send her to a convent?"

At home, Carmen commanded, asked, and finally begged Elena to quit. She started making what were—for her—wild promises.

"I'll even go to Los Angeles if you would just quit!"

Finally hearing something she wanted, Elena capitulated. "With me working, we can save money to leave," Elena promised. "Don't worry about Francisco. Till we go, I have him under control. Besides, it's not like I'm a virgin."

It was the first time Carmen had heard that revelation, but she didn't have the heart to ask for details. She had a feeling she wouldn't like the answer.

* * *

Time crawled for Carmen, but the same

two months passed quickly for Elena, who was happy, and busy planning how to say yes to Francisco. Despite her sister's warnings, she was totally infatuated. She was starting to think there was something wrong with her, as she heard rumors that Francisco went after every woman he could. Except her. She was under his nose every day and, though he watched her like a hawk, he'd been a perfect gentleman. Well—a perfect gentleman who looked down her blouse and had drilled a hole in the ladies' room wall.

Elena was at her wit's end, so she decided it was time to tap someone else's wit. Delores was a widow now, but she had managed to bag her sweetheart back in high school. She might dress like a frump now, but once she'd been the closest thing Elena knew to an undergraduate femme fatale, always in the principal's office for wearing red lipstick and skirts that barely covered her knees. It took Elena four days of coming to work early to find the right moment to make it look casual, but eventually she managed to run accidentally on purpose into Delores when she grabbed her time card to clock in, and took that opportunity to invite Delores to share some of Carmen's famous empanadas.

At noon, Delores must have charged off at a run, because by the time Blasio clanged the old school bell (once to start lunch, twice to end) and before the reverberation had ended, she was already across the floor, up the stairs, down the hall, and in the office Elena shared with her sister.

"Where's Carmen?" Delores asked.

"At a meeting." Elena shrugged. She reached in her purse and pulled out the empanadas. They had to eat quickly. Francisco's girls were lucky to get the full quarter-hour. Elena didn't know what was behind Delores's speed—whether she had missed Elena's friendship, or her appetite for Carmen's cooking. She never considered there could be a third reason.

"I've missed you. We used to be good friends before that date you had with my brother," Delores said as she licked crumbs from her lips.

"Miltie is a nice boy," Elena said mildly.

She did not ask how he was doing, though.

Delores looked at her, but it was obvious to her that Milton did not inspire Elena in any fashion.

"Carmen is such a good cook."

"She is," Elena agreed, still unsure of Delores's motives, but she had motives of her own.

"Carmen is good at everything," Delores said.

"Not everything." Elena sighed, getting to the point. "She can't give me advice...on romance. On love."

Delores rolled her eyes, but avoided answering by taking a massive bite and chewing energetically.

"But you've been married. I need advice. On men. So tell me—how do I get a man?"

Delores choked. She started coughing, spraying crumbs everywhere. "I wasn't married long. You know my husband died in a mine accident. I didn't get to fool around so much, so I don't know anything about that stuff, not really."

"You were one of the most popular girls

in high school. You'd know, for example, if there's a boy I want to get to third base with, how I could get his attention. He doesn't seem to notice I'm alive. What am I doing wrong?"

Delores stopped in mid-chew. She shook her head. She took a huge bite, then said with her mouth full, "What boy? No, don't tell me. Don't talk to boys." She repeated it four more times, each time emphasizing a different word, "Don't talk to boys. Don't talk to boys. Don't talk to boys. Don't talk to boys." She set down the remains of the empanada—admittedly leaving only crumbs—and ran out.

A minute later, Carmen showed up with a box of receipts to calculate.

"I just passed Delores running down the hall crying. Is Francisco back to his tricks?"

Elena shook her head and looked interested. "What tricks?"

Carmen gave her a hard stare. She got that stubborn look she could get sometimes, and put up her hand like a traffic cop. There would be no more said on the subject.

In spite of getting no advice on how to proceed, Elena's romance with Francisco blossomed.

He asked her to dinner, finally. Straight from work, he took her to a nice café where Elena and Carmen had never had enough money to go.

Francisco ordered from the menu for her. Elena picked at the food, so anxious and excited she didn't care what was on her plate. Francisco ate everything on his plate and finished what was on hers, too. For a moment, Elena thought he might go for what was on Blasio's plate. Fortunately, Blasio had been seated at the other side of the restaurant at a small table by the back door. When they left, Francisco seemed to have forgotten he was there and left him standing on the sidewalk, yelling a question about how he was going to get back to the ranch.

In the passenger seat of Francisco's big Cadillac, Elena sat with her hands folded in her lap as Francisco personally drove her to his ranch house. She knew before they got there that they would do it.

When Francisco pulled up, a pair of guards ran out of an adobe gatehouse. Elena watched curiously as one unlocked the wrought iron gate and swung it open, while the other stood at attention.

"Why do you need guards?"

"Why not? I have enemies." He shrugged.

The car topped a hill and followed a paved roadway to the house. On one side, a barbed wire fence separated the property from the desert. The paved drive was bordered with crushed shells and cut through a garden of cactus, piled rock walls, dry fountains, pond beds, and freestanding boulders covered with moss. He got out and opened the door for her. Then he opened a gate that led to an open courtyard. He all but dragged her into the foyer. Then, finally, he kissed her.

She'd planned to nose around the house. It was the biggest house in town, and for weeks now she'd been thinking about him walking her through it, but she got distracted by his mouth on hers and forgot to look.

She flung her arms around him. He was big around, barrel-chested. After skinny Milton, she loved the solid feel of his big body. He didn't feel like he was going to break when she hugged him. And when she squeezed, he didn't squeak. Her nipples got tight and pointed. An ache started between her legs.

He stared into her eyes. "I feel something special for you," he said, smacking himself in the chest. His fist made a meaty sound. "You know I was married before. I never thought anyone could take the place of Luz. Luz was my angel, but maybe, you. From the first minute I saw you. I had never hoped to find a replacement for her. Until you."

She wanted to stop him. She wasn't a battery, or a tire, or a new pair of socks. The idea of being someone's replacement didn't exactly light her fire. She was about to call off the whole date.

He bent his face to hers, giving her a kiss. His whiskers were rough against her skin, and then suddenly nothing else mattered except the feeling of him against her. She got another electric jolt from her nipples and between her legs. Whatever it was, it felt good. She wanted more. She was intoxicated. He smelled of the beer he'd had with dinner. Unexpectedly, that scent filled her head, turned into something different, almost an aphrodisiac.

His mouth on hers wasn't sloppy-wet as Milton's had been. His lips were almost dry, and deft, seeking entrance into her mouth, teasing, but not quite entering. She found herself not only responding playfully, but trying to anticipate his moves, even as he managed to surprise her. He swept her up into his arms, and the next thing she realized—at least the next thing beyond his mouth, which had captured all her attention—was that she was on his bed, on soft-silky sheets no doubt manufactured at his factory. Somehow she was naked as he hovered over her. Where had her clothes gone? How had he undressed her without her noticing?

His mouth found one nipple, and he sucked hard. She heard someone moaning, and was shocked to realize she was making that sound, but all she could do was writhe and feel him against her. He whispered about how beautiful she was. She was so far gone in sensation that he could have been reciting the alphabet. His big body and his obvious admiration made her feel womanly. No. Sexual. Was it the words? Maybe it was his breath against her skin. He was big, and his maleness was so foreign, hairy as she had not imagined but not unpleasantly so. Milton had been about as hairy as a two-week-old baby, and he had not been at all interesting. Maybe it was because Francisco was forbidden. His differences were erotic.

He kissed her toes, then the bottom of her feet. She was ticklish and tried to jerk away. She noticed he was almost methodical about it, as he worked his way up one leg then started kissing the other, making note of what she responded to and what she drew away from. She seemed to have a sensitive spot behind her knees, and he kissed her there a couple of times as if to make sure, as if he were saving that knowledge for later. When he found her wetness with his fingers,

Elena tried to push him away.

"I'm too wet down there," she told him.

"You're supposed to be. It means you're ready for me to come inside." He hovered over her, barely pressed into her with a finger.

"Inside." He drew the word out as he pressed in.

She went wild with ecstasy, bucking her hips and moaning.

"Oh." She breathed at last. She grabbed his hand and looked over his magic finger.

His expression betrayed his fascination with her. She never reacted as he expected.

"How exactly did you do that? No wonder people do it like jackrabbits. Let's try again. I'm not sure I got it right that time." She hesitated. "Okay, I lied. Whatever it was you were doing, you are damn good at it."

He liked that. He laughed. "I need in you now, woman, or I'll go off like a schoolboy."

"In sounds good," Elena agreed.

When he finally got on top and entered her, it was over as fast as it had begun. It didn't matter. Both of their bodies had figured out what went where with remarkable expediency. She purred with delight a second time.

He was still on top of her, but growing softer, at least that part inside her was.

"I've been with a boy," she confessed to him. "I thought I knew about sex, but I never dreamed your lovemaking would put me on cloud nine. I had no idea. I never even imagined. Maybe we can do this again some time."

"Maybe," he chuckled, then got serious. "I love you," he told her. "Marry me. I want you to have my children. We will build a house on the US side, a big house. I will make you happy."

"And we can do this a lot," Elena said.

"But..."

"But what?" Suddenly his weight on her was scary and oppressive, and not so nice.

"No more boys."

How did he do that, she wondered. How did he go from sexy to ominous, without moving a muscle? It wasn't about just this moment. She realized she had stand up for herself or she'd be under his thumb the rest of her life.

"Okay. Your one thing for my one thing," Elena said, wondering if she was doing something more dangerous than negotiating her half of a marriage proposal. He had physically tensed at her words. He felt bigger and meaner, without having said a thing. The expression on his face was terrifying. She realized in that instant that all the rumors about him were true. The ones she thought were impossible did not even hint at the depth of what he was capable of doing. She thought of all of Carmen's denials. Although somewhere deep in her intuition she knew there was some spark of truth in all the smoke, nothing mattered any more but Francisco. He had become her world. She would risk anything, dare anything, do anything. She took a shot in the dark and made a stand. She hoped he would deny the connection, even as she made her demand. She had to make some kind of stand, or he'd walk all over her. But mostly, she hoped there was nothing there for him to give up.

"And that one thing is...I'm not sharing

you with Carmen."

"Carmen?" He looked at her in surprise. "You know about that?"

Her heart sank a little. *Know about what, exactly*, she wanted to ask, but instead enunciated carefully, "Of course. I know everything. She's my sister. *And* I know all about how you're a badass with a hard-on."

He looked shocked, then gave a harsh burst of laughter.

"I don't know whether to kiss you or wash your mouth out with soap."

"You can try," she said, archly.

"Maybe I'll wash your mouth out with something else. But first, how do you know about Carmen? Did she tell you?"

"Carmen never breathed a word. But people talk a lot. And I seem to be the only woman in Nogales that you haven't had sex with. I don't even care about the other women, so long as you come back to me."

"Okay. Carmen is off limits," he agreed. "Why would I want her, anyway, when I can have..."—he flexed where he was still joined with her—"...you," and laughed when she moaned and moved. "You and everybody else."

"But you gotta tell me."

"Tell you? Tell you what? That I love you? I already said that."

"No, you gotta tell me when you do it with another woman."

"I'm not getting permission," he growled. "I do what I want, even if I do love you."

"No, you stupid oaf." She mock-punched him on the shoulder with the heel of her hand. He didn't budge, but that daunting line of his eyebrows rose.

"I want you to tell me when you do it with another woman. *¿Me entiendes?* No lies. I just want you to be completely honest."

He seemed to understand what she had said, and sprang to hard attention. They were still joined, and the joining resulted in some hard, athletic sex that, after so many performances, took real work to reach a conclusion. But when the lust was out of his eyes, instead of being calm and exhausted, he was back to his demands, back to the other Francisco, back to being Mister Scary.

"No more boys. *¿Me entiendes?*"

She felt an unexpected flash of fear, but she had made her point. "You get no more Carmen, me no more boys, and I'm all yours," she agreed.

Chapter Eight

Francisco should have been exhausted after the night he'd had with Elena, but he was energized. He had several of a stack of government contracts Segundo had left for him to sign, and a list of projects to read about and okay or refuse. He whipped through the documents in a vigorous frenzy, scarcely looking up when someone opened his door and entered without asking permission. He snarled, prepared to bite someone's head off; at last he did look up, and was transfixed to find Carmen standing there. The rage fell away. Carmen, who had in all the time he'd known her, never once come into his office under her own steam. She closed the door firmly, and turned to face him. He was fascinated. His rage turned immediately to lust. She was ferocious, this Carmen, a lioness on the hunt.

"She told me," Carmen said. "I tried to stop her, but she has a mind of her own. Is it true?"

"Is what true?" Francisco leaned forward, putting both elbows on his desk.

"Is it true that last night you asked Elena to marry you?"

He hesitated before responding. Each second of delay he could feel Carmen pulsing with more passion. He immediately regretted his promise to leave Carmen alone. He was not accustomed to depriving himself.

She bypassed the desk, and walked up to his chair, standing closer to him than she ever had under her own steam. She leaned closer to him. He inhaled the scent of her, nothing sophisticated from a bottle; but something fresh and spicy and green, and out of a garden.

He could not help it; his eyes flickered up and down her body, a body he knew well but that still remained a mystery. In all these years, he'd never gotten any of her. She was impervious, unreached. He wanted her now, as much as he ever had, and thought about how he could drag her to the desk, pull up her skirt and take her again. How she'd fight; how she'd come. She always did. He grabbed her forearm.

She did not shake him off. She did not pull away.

"Carmen," he said. He was a breath away from tossing her down and fucking her.

She looked him straight in the eye. Grabbed the letter opener off his desk.

"You want to marry her. Elena consented," she said. Her face had a new leanness to it, a strength, a determination he found gripping.

"Yes," he said.

"We have no brothers," Carmen said. "Our father is dead. No menfolk stand for us. So this job is up to me. I am telling you now." She held the letter opener in front of her like a rapier she very much wanted to stab him with. "If you marry her, you will make her happy. If you cause her one moment of grief, cause one single tear to fall from her eye, if you give her one sleepless night, I will make you pay. If you so much as think of hurting her, I will destroy you, if I have to come back from the dead to do it."

Francisco moved slowly. He released his grip on Carmen's forearm, and reached for his top button. He pulled his tie loose, unbuttoned his shirt, slowly, button by button bared his chest. Grabbed the blade of the letter opener with his bare palm, and pulled it toward him, till it was touching his sternum.

"Why wait?" He strained upward toward her, his face inches from hers. "You know you want to." He could not himself have said what he wanted her to do. He might be daring her to kill him, but there was a sexual edge to his challenge.

Someone knocked.

"More contracts for you," Segundo said.

"Bring them."

By the time Segundo was inside, he saw what he had seen so many times before, Carmen in high color, Francisco with his shirt half off.

Carmen tossed the letter opener on Francisco's desk, and walked out.

"Hand me my tie." Francisco said. "I swear, jalapeños run in that woman's blood."

Segundo picked up the tie from the floor. Francisco wrapped it around his bleeding palm, and made no explanation, but then, he never did. "Now, what are these new papers about?"

* * *

Milton had decided he was in love with Elena. After he heard rumors that she had started dating Francisco Sanchez while working at his factory, he began to meet Delores after work every evening to escort her home so he could ask her about Elena, but Delores never wanted to talk about the subject. On one of the nights when she worked late, he was approached by Blasio. He had never really known Blasio, not beyond being talking acquaintances. All he knew was how badly Blasio stuttered. Blasio told him Francisco was looking to hire some m-m-m-men. Was m-m-m-m-Milton interested?

Milton was impressed with himself, wondering what he'd done to get a personal invitation almost directly from the big man. He was interested, and when he first heard the question, restrained the impulse to respond "M-m-m-me?"

Of all things, dreaming was what he was best at, and Blasio's proposition started an instant dream buzzing in his head like a humming of a hundred sewing machines racing at full bore. He would get a job working for the boss; he would rise to the top; he would win the girl back. Milton went breathless, dizzy with the possibility of it, and dived in to capture the dream of himself in silk shirts and linen pants, smoking cigars and being followed by an admiring entourage of mob punks with guns, and Elena by his side. He saw it so clearly he had the taste in his mouth; his mouth was full of it, and full of the memory of Elena's kiss.

"Yes." It came out of him too loud, too enthusiastic. Blasio gave him a funny look. When his sister came out later, he didn't tell her. He was pretty sure Delores had figured out the reason he was walking her home was to get the occasional glimpse of Elena, but Delores had gotten so crazy on the subject of Elena that he'd stopped mentioning her. Even so, just the fact that Elena was working at the factory was incentive enough. He was ecstatic at the possibility of a job under the same roof as his would-be sweetheart. He set out to do anything he could to bring himself to the eyes of the boss, to be seen in a favorable light.

* * *

Unfortunately for Milton, after that night with Francisco, Elena did not work at the factory any longer. She stayed home in the little adobe house and waited for Francisco to pick her up after closing time. They drove to Tucson and twice to Phoenix. He took her to big stores where he bought her dozens of shoes, dresses, lingerie the likes of which she had never seen before. He spoiled her to death. He told her lots of stories about his beloved wife Luz, who had died much too soon. He told her how his life had been so empty without her. But now at long last, he was no longer lonely.

"I love you," he said, time and again. "I have been good as an angel, and I expect you to be the same. I'm very possessive of what is mine, and you are mine now. All I ask is that you be faithful. I'm a very jealous man."

Little did she know how jealous.

* * *

Francisco knew many people in these cities because his factories contracted work for so many stores. During their trips, Francisco made his rounds and collected checks from those who owed him. Then they cashed the checks. This meant visiting every bank that every check was drawn on. Elena was impressed that the bankers all knew and deferred to Francisco. She had never seen so much cash. He was so thoughtful of her that it seemed unbelievable that this man was hated by almost everyone she knew.

They walked around the city holding hands like young lovers. Sometimes Elena looked at her slim, pale hand swallowed up in his much larger, darker one and felt deeply moved. Many called him the devil but Elena knew better. He was so kind. She knew him better than anyone. She was committed to showing everyone the Francisco that she knew—the way he really was. A changed man. A good man. Before her arrival in his life, he had just been misunderstood.

Elena had fallen in love with him. Carmen and many of her friends voiced concern. Every day it was something new. He was too rich. He'd made a pact with the devil. His friends were criminals. He broke the law whenever he could. He was unprincipled. He bribed police. He was a crook. He had thugs. He didn't go to church enough. He didn't support charities. He was a sexual dog. One day, it was the age difference. Elena never considered that anything but an asset. She was comparing him to her one other experience, with string-bean little-boy Miltie, after all.

She believed that if she took good care of him as she now did, he would be faithful to her. Now that she had asked him to tell her about his unfaithfulness, he would never again fool around with his women employees or even look at another woman. It was all up to her. If she took care of Francisco, he would be a good husband. When she tried to convince Carmen of this, her sister only rolled her eyes.

"You're so naïve," she said, and grunted in disgust at her sister's monumental stupidity.

Carmen could not regret keeping Francisco's treatment of her out of Elena's eye. And now it was too late to do so.

"When you marry the dog, he stays a dog," she warned, but the warning fell on deaf ears. Elena was enraptured by planning the wedding. After the announcement, she appeared on the front page of the newspaper and on the society page. Even up to the last moment when Elena was walking down the aisle, Carmen prayed that the plans would fail, Elena would get cold feet, or Francisco back out, but everything went like clockwork.

The wedding ceremony took place in March on the Mexican side of the border at a church that wore bullet holes from the Battle of Nogales. The fiesta that followed was for the entire town in the park across the street from the church. A hundred picnic tables had been brought in, and when those were full, Francisco called for more.

Some of them were covered in food. The rest were set with enough place settings for everyone who was anybody on both sides of the border. The wedding cake was bigger than a dream. Hundreds of people descended on the wedding supper to eat and drink and feast to the newlyweds' good fortune. Everyone except Carmen loved the wedding, and she kept her opinion to herself, for the most part. Everyone else pretended to love the man no one dared to offend.

Not only were there hundreds of locals from all walks of life, there were also strange men in suits, speaking in strange accents. They all seemed to know Francisco. Tequila and gin flowed like water. Guests gorged themselves, and guzzled wedding punch. When the punch was gone, they started on the gin, and ate again. Twelve hours later, after Elena threw her bouquet, and she and Francisco had left, the mariachis and *bandas* were still playing music everywhere. People were still eating, drinking, and dancing. Some of them passed out in their plates, woke up, and kept on partying.

Francisco drove them to Los Angeles for their honeymoon, leaving Segundo in charge at home. They checked into a grand hotel called the Hilton at Seventh and Figueroa at first. A few days later, they moved to the Beverly Hills Hotel, to try out the new Crystal Room and the Lanai Restaurant just for the heck of it. They visited Hollywood, and rode around in tour buses for several days, sightseeing. Elena had never told Francisco about her onetime dream of becoming a movie star or a model or about wanting to move here after she graduated, and realized that now was not the time. Besides, she was perfectly content with the life she saw unfolding with her Francisco, and one day with their children. Her husband was already like a new man. He made certain that she was elegantly dressed at all times and managed not to punch out every random man who crossed their path or who looked at Elena with his jaw gaping.

    Elena found herself changing clothes several times a day, just to wear the different outfits in front of him, which then made him crazy to want to go out in public somewhere just to show her off as his and his alone, and even crazier if some man actually noticed her. Where the public was concerned, he was as sensitive to their age difference as Elena was immune to it. He complained that didn't want people to think she was his daughter. She laughed at him and called him her handsome hero.

Her handsome hero took her to shop. She modeled clothes for him, but after days of this, he was impatient. He had gotten the owner's business card as someone to add to his buyer list, but with no more business to transact, he was pacing; he was grinding his teeth behind his smile. It was not as if Elena were modeling lingerie.

Now that would keep his interest. He pictured her in the nightie she'd worn last night, the one that bared those sleek, long legs of hers. He'd have to make sure there was something comparable to interest him in that pile of current purchases she was building. At least she seemed to be enjoying herself. She could have been wearing a potato sack. Everything she wore suited her as far as he was concerned. The current outfit did, in fact, look a little like a potato sack, except for a wide belt cinching her slim middle. He still wanted to punch out the guy on the sidewalk who was looking in the window. Francisco slammed his hand into the plate glass, and the guy jumped and bolted off. He smiled, satisfied, and turned back to see the faces of four store employees looking at him as if he'd just grown horns and a forked tail. He leaned against the wall and crossed his arms, exhaling a lung full of smoke at them, like a lazy dragon.

The shop girls kept their distance, as if he'd been dipped in the Nagasaki dust cloud. Before Elena, their nervousness around him would have been justified, but now they interested him as much as pesky little houseflies buzzing around his head, other than to amuse himself by alternately leering and glaring at them whenever Elena disappeared behind the curtains with her next stack of potential purchases. The shop girls skittered away like a flock of birds. He loved that Elena was oblivious. She saw only his pleasure in her and how he loved everything she wore. Once he tried to select something for her, but she said he was trying to make her look like a schoolmarm or a nun.

"You do not look like a schoolmarm. No school teacher ever looked like you, my wife."

"I will not fight with you. Not on my honeymoon." She stuck out her tongue at him. "I'm here to shop, so let me." She turned away, pouting.

One of the shop girls slipped behind Elena, and took away the nun dress. She whispered something in Elena's ear, and flitted away. Elena leaned forward, as if confiding a secret. "You make them nervous," she told him, and giggled.

"I don't know why." Francisco pulled at his collar. "Shit, it's hot in here." The suit and tie he wore were from his own factory, though he'd had them professionally tailored. He felt rich, and knew he looked rich. The suit fit him well enough, but he had no one to impress here except Elena. He should have just worn shirtsleeves and left the jacket in their hotel room. Last month, he'd gone to the only place for a man to buy a suit in West Los Angeles, the just-opened Carroll & Co. on the second floor of a Beverly Hills medical building. He'd gotten three suits in different sizes. One fit. The others were for his seamstresses to rip up to make patterns for cheap knock-offs.

"Go get a beer," Elena suggested. "I could spend hours here." Pulling out two dresses, holding first one then the other in front of her, she checked them out in the mirror and turned to Francisco. "What do you think?"

Francisco looked at his watch, and glanced at Elena surrounded by fidgety shop girls. She was like the centerpiece of a human bouquet. He'd have liked to have a picture of that moment. With all the women naked, of course.

"I'll take you up on that beer," Francisco agreed. "I'll be back in an hour."

"Better make it two."

"Two beers or two hours?"

"Yes." Elena's voice was muffled, as she headed back to change again.

"There's more than one shop in Los Angeles," he yelled back. But he was out the door quickly, before she could change her mind. He opened his wallet and stepped inside the phone booth at the corner, pulling the door shut. The new wooden shell of the booth was painted red, but it already smelled of traffic, urine, and city dirt. From the wallet, he dug out a business card, dropped a nickel in the pay phone's slot, and dialed the number scribbled on the back.

Ten minutes later, his coat was folded over the chair, his tie was in his pocket, and a frosty beer stein was in his fist. The backstreet pub was a block from where Elena was enjoying her shopping spree—a smoky, crowded watering hole indistinguishable from hundreds of places all over the country. Coming in, he'd passed a long bar with a dozen bar stools, all occupied. It was too dark, too crowded, and too smoky to see much going on in here. The bar had pretensions of decency, but really was a sleazy joint, the kind of place he would never take Elena. To call it dimly lit would be an exaggeration. It was packed with people who minded their own business, and their business was getting drunk. Plenty of deals of all kinds had been made under the low ceiling, as many of them legal as illegal. The crowd was not quite shoulder to shoulder, but it was pretty much packed, mostly with sweaty shirt-sleeved men, and a few lady birds. All of them were strangers to Francisco, except for two men whose arrival had pierced the crowd with a brief arc of blinding sunlight before the door closed. Now they were zigzagging across the crowded floor to meet him.

Francisco rose in welcome, but only briefly, to show his location, rather than the minimum of courtesy. He nodded at the server, who rushed to get their orders before the men reached the table. Francisco had already given him a twenty and promised him another depending on his service. The men pulled up two chairs, and sat.

The rosy-cheeked older man whistled at Francisco's suit. "That's some chrome plate you're wearing."

Francisco puffed his chest and thumbed his lapel. "Yeah? It's a knock-off out of my Nogales factory."

The conversation shifted to Spanish, rapid-fire and low-voiced, and back to English when the server came with two more beers.

"Ain't exactly private," Johnny Pinto, the younger of the two men, complained. His hair was dirty blonde, his eyes dark. He exchanged glances with his older companion, who had a face as round, red, and shiny as an apple. Appleface nodded and put a hundred dollars on the table. Francisco recalled that his first name was Mando, but that he went by his last, Armas. He chuckled to himself, thinking one day he was sure to call him Apple instead.

Francisco shrugged and pocketed the money.

"Quit whining. It's better than the place you took me last time," Francisco said, and pulled out a medicine bottle, which he set in the middle of the table. "This is the stuff."

Johnny, younger, and impatient, started twisting off the cap.

Francisco snatched back the bottle. "Not

here, stupid."

"Don't call me stupid!" Johnny flashed
directly to anger, which was cut short when Francisco pulled out a gun and shoved it into Johnny's
armpit.

"I'll call you any fucking thing I want to,"
Francisco said. "What's more, you'll like it."

Armas tried to smooth things over. "Cut
the gas, Johnny. Don't have a cow. And don't
make me regret bringing you in. He's been at this
a long time. He knows how to survive. If he says
hold off till later, we hold off till later."

"Damn straight," Francisco agreed, shoul-
dering the pistol and handing the bottle to Armas,
whose expression did not change.

"Gotta excuse the kid. He's still jacked
up after getting burned last week. He was delivering some..." he cleared his throat, "...folding
green paper and the seller pulled a fast one. The
kid here had to burn rubber to beat the cops."
Appleface Armas was calm, bland, undistin-
guished in mien. Round-faced, stocky. He could
have been an accountant or a ticket taker. No one

would take him for a drug dealer.

Johnny's face darkened with rising blood. "If I ever run into that Blackstone again, I'm feeding him a knuckle sandwich and taking my cash out of his hide."

"Yeah." Armas threw his arm over Johnny's shoulder. "The boy here had to cover his losses out of his percentage."

Johnny shook off the arm and snarled, "I'll get it back. He's just a local scumbag."

Johnny eyed Francisco's coat, wary of a reappearance of the revolver. He rubbed his armpit where the muzzle had recently been jammed.

"So how'd you get your start?" Johnny asked, as politely as he was able.Even after Francisco's lesson, every word dripped with defiance before it bounced off the chip on his shoulder.

"Rumor is he got his start—" Appleface began, but broke off with a cautious glance.

Francisco gave a curt nod of permission.

"You tell him, Mr. Sanchez, if you want the story told," Armas continued smoothly.

Francisco glanced around the room full of men getting shitfaced. No threat here.

"Okay, Armas, why not?" He didn't advertise his activities but, when none of his usual crew was around to carry tales, he was certainly not immune to boasting. "Remember that guy who died last year, in '47? The famous bootlegger out of Chicago?" Francisco asked.

Johnny shook his head.

Armas poked him in the shoulder. "You're just a kid. You don't know nothin', do ya?" He laughed.

Francisco's hand was wrapped around the mug, which was sweating profusely with condensation. He pushed it away and made as if to wrap both his hands around the barrel of an imaginary machine gun, pretended he was gunning down Johnny with it. He made the appropriate noises. RAT-TAT-TAT-TAT. No one around them bothered to look up.

"Even *you* had to hear about prohibition. I was just a kid when I started with Capone. I ran shipments of hooch out west for him. And when that all ended in '33, I kept running shipments, just changed products. Took over some speakeasies here and there," he said vaguely. "Put some girls in. Kept the network going. It's bigger now than it was then, and it's all mine."

Johnny was a little shaken but tried to look unimpressed.

Francisco took a gulp of his beer. He waved his hand at the server, indicating another round.

Armas asked, "Where are your people? You always have a guard, a driver, a retinue."

"Is that any of your business?" Francisco asked. "Don't tell me you're concerned about my safety." He gave a short, harsh laugh. "I'm touched."

He reached inside his coat, pulled out the gun again, and rested it on the table, aimed at Johnny—poor Johnny, who was a hair's breadth from losing it. He laid his hand over the gun so it could not be easily seen. "I had no idea you were so concerned over my welfare. This week I'm on vacation. Celebrating my nuptials, boys. This is all the retinue I need." He put the gun away.

Francisco mock-reached in his coat once again, watching Johnny startle and jump a little in his chair. Francisco laughed. At each move, Johnny looked closer to coming apart at the seams.

The conversation drifted a bit, with Armas conjecturing about how much product he might need, and how much it would cost. They did not shake hands on a price, but floated the idea of half up front.

"Let's hold off on the details," Francisco said. He took out a pencil—not the gun this time—and wrote down a number on a napkin that he shoved over to Armas.

"Call me if you're interested. That's the number at the hotel where we will be until Thursday. After that, you know where to reach me. If you miss me, you can run this through Segundo at the usual number."

Francisco checked the time and stood. "I have to leave you gentlemen before the little woman buys every stitch of clothing in Hollywood. I'll be expecting your call."

Francisco stopped at the same phone booth and dialed his own office. He told the girl who answered to get Segundo. He didn't have to say it twice. He heard her feet tap off into the distance, then another phone picked up.

"Yes, boss?" Segundo had taken the call just outside of one of the sewing rooms. He yelled into the phone to make himself heard over the hum of the machines.

"Armas's operation had some trouble with a guy named Blackstone. Put some feelers out. I want to know everything about him. He's got a rep for pulling a double-cross and he's working Los Angeles. I wouldn't mind doing Armas a favor and getting him his dope or cash back. Minus our cut, of course. But a favor for Armas, that'd be big."

"I'm on it."

Francisco was confident that, by the time he got home, there'd be enough answers to get and stay ahead of Blackstone, with a chaser of healthy gratitude from Mando Armas.

Chapter Nine

Francisco was a little glum after a footman took Elena for his daughter. That evening in their hotel room, Elena cheered him up by modeling, but mostly removing, some clothes he liked very much. She kidded, "Daughters don't do to their fathers what I do to you." She reached for his zipper to prove it.

He loved her, no doubt about it. There was so much joy in her, her laughter, that beaming smile, her perfect white teeth. Her long legs. Her rosy bottom.

"Such a precious jewel. You're mine. I walk down the street with you on my arm and everyone I pass is green with envy," Francisco said. "A woman wild with passion, my woman. Someday, the mother of my children."

He loved showing her off. They returned home, but he brought her along on some of his frequent trips to Tucson, to Los Angeles, to all the cities in between. They were business trips, but it never felt like business with Elena along. Trips to Nogales with Elena were fewer and fewer.

* * *

For Miltie, life had taken a bad turn. He had never heard the rumors about Francisco's proclivities or, if he had, he'd never thought of them in relation to his family members who worked for the factory owner. He could not picture Delores as anything but his sister, the family *wisenheimer*, and she lived in the context of his family. He never thought about how subdued she was now out in public or what had brought about that change. She'd just grown up. He thought that was it. It never occurred to him she had camouflaged herself to be concealed from a predator.

The job he thought would change his life had turned into a nightmare. As if it hadn't been bad enough when he heard Francisco and Elena were getting married. He should have known not to ever mention Elena to the boss. He couldn't even remember what it was he said. Maybe something about being in the same class in high school. Maybe he mentioned he dated her. Maybe he had mentioned her more than once. Or twice. Or three times. But it all led to a day in Francisco's office too horrible to be believed. On that day, he let down his sister and himself. He could never see himself as a man again. He tried to quit, but Francisco wouldn't let him. Segundo hauled him away from the factory, though, to work on the ranch, an exile from Nogales. It was hell for Milton knowing Elena was living there with Francisco.

* * *

After Carmen drove her back from a secret visit with a doctor in Tucson, Elena was dancing with joy. Even Carmen's refusal to come inside didn't get her down. She came jitterbugging down the long hall, passing maids and making them smile. She hoped Francisco hadn't noticed she was gone, but it didn't worry her enough to keep her from doing the *Jarabe Tapitio* around a maid, who was dusting the chandelier in the dining room, and the *dance of the little old men* around

the little old man sweeping up the patio. She jit-
terbugged into the kitchen where Manuela was
doing dishes.

Most of the staff called Manuela
"Manuela's daughter. " It was courtesy title signi-
fying she had inherited her position from her
mother, and that she'd been around the rancho
off-and-on since she'd been in diapers. For Elena,
the relationship turned strange. A barrier had
come between them since she'd gotten married.

The cook had already gone. The mess she
left indicated she must have been making jam,
and had prepared a big tray of enchiladas which
were baking in the fancy new oven. There were
dishes everywhere, and an out-of-place stepstool
that the long-legged housemaid did not need.

"Let me do that!" Elena chirped, snatch-
ing an armful of dishes and dumping them into
the sink where her ex-friend had run hot water
while staring idly out the window at a cute gar-
dener.

"I love this hot water," Elena said. "At
home, we still boiled it on the top of the wood

stove. Remember, Manuela?"

"Yes ma'am."

Elena's actions snapped Manuela to attention to the job she was supposed to be doing. Manuela flushed, grabbed the stepstool and righted it, and started grabbing dishes to set the table.

"*El jefe*...he doesn't want you to work!"

"*El jefe* my ass," Elena snorted disrespectfully. "I have to do something! There's nothing else to do!" Elena splashed happily in the water, soaping a sponge while her feet were busy with a little dance step. "I know what. You go tell Arturo I want rosebushes on the west wall. Maybe you can help him..."

Manuela flashed her a shadow of the old grin and was outside in a flash of skirts to cavort with her boyfriend.

Elena giggled as she watched them through the window, then sighed. Last year she and Manuela had been in the same high school graduation class. She remembered being in first grade with her, lining up to go outside, at the head of the line as the tallest girls. This year, as Mrs. Sanchez, she was a lonely and voiceless exile from everyone she'd known. As the inheritor of her mother's domestic role, her best friend wasn't supposed to acknowledge they'd ever been equals, but for Elena, their friendship, even what little remained of it, was a lifesaver. The isolation Francisco had decreed would have been intolerable without Manuela.

But Elena was a sunny spirit, and nothing kept her down for long. She attacked the dishes with a zealotry that would have shocked the pants off Carmen, and soon a pile of sparkling plates were stacked on the sideboard. She was working on a recalcitrant iron pan when he arrived and grabbed her hard about the waist.

"Francisco! You're home!"

He stood behind her, his grip fierce, pulling her against him.

"No, don't turn around!" Francisco said. "I want you like this, now."

Elena moaned and leaned backward. Francisco moved his hands under her clothes.

Buttons popped, and pinged, and clattered around the room as her shirt accommodated him, and he cupped her breasts, pulling her hard against him, his chest at her back, his big erection already seeking entrance.

They might call him a devil. Maybe he was, because he had a devilish chemistry with her. Always, she wanted him. She couldn't help but focus on the sensations he caused as he found her entrance and moved deep. She didn't care if anyone was outside the window, seeing her perched over the sink. She was caught up in his spell, sighed, coming as soon as he was inside her. With any luck, she'd come again.... At some point, she realized what he whispered into her ear as he pumped steadily into her. Heard it with a sick fascination.

"... did what you said—the other woman. I did her." He had bent his head so that his mouth was close, nuzzling her neck. He moved his hands to her hips, then hugged her to him by one arm wrapped around her waist, the other moving between her legs where they were joined.

"Wh...what?" Elena was confused.

"You said to tell you. So I did it. Today. I didn't even want her. I wanted you. I wanted to tell you about it." He gave a nasty laugh. "One of the sewing girls, in my office. The dumpy one named Delores. I think you know her. It didn't take five minutes and the whole time I was thinking of you, of coming here, doing this, and telling you about it..." He described the office encounter, in great detail crudely. His own words excited him.

He grabbed her hips and pistoned into her hard, his hand rubbing her fiercely, demanding. "I put her on the desk. Like this." Unexpectedly, he pulled out, swung her around, and plopped Elena's bottom squarely on the counter.

Dishes clattered. He swept them aside. Francisco was caught up in his memory, maybe in some cross between memory and fantasy. He caught Elena's gaze, hypnotizing her like a cobra, stood, breathing hard, kissing Elena's mouth, pulling her with him into his darkness. His hands gripped her thighs, spreading her, braced wide by his torso. "You can't come till I say." His fingers paused above her, a hair's breadth away.

Then, as if he were being subtle, he changed his topic. "Where the hell did you go this morning?" he asked, sliding down her body. "I bet your scrawny little Milton couldn't do this." He placed his tongue flat against her spread body, and gave her such a long, slow lick she'd have sworn on a stack of bibles before God himself that his tongue was a foot wide. He stood, whispered again more details of dumpy Delores on his desk, her reluctance, succumbing to his power, Blasio and Milton in the room as witnesses to everything. Blasio leering, enjoying it, Milton excited but looking like he might be sick, like a girl.

Francisco abandoned his confession, and moved against her but not in her, then again, like a cobra, he dropped to his knees and struck, buried his face in Elena until she begged him for release.

"So, where were you today, wife?"

Elena, so far gone, didn't even think about his question. Begged.

"Please, Francisco—"

"Tell me. Where were you? Tell me and I'll give you all the cock you can take."

Elena's eyes never opened. He had not stopped teasing her body.

"With Carmen. There was a doctor's appointment in Tucson. We borrowed Papi's old truck that we had sold to the neighbors."

She shook with need. He took his time, thinking about what she said.

"You will tell me the doctor's name."

"I'll ask Carmen."

"*I* will ask Carmen," he said. She didn't argue, just grabbed at him.

He gave a harsh laugh and stopped his interrogation.

"You may come now," he said, and pressed himself deep.

They both came, explosively.

Elena's head fell forward on Francisco's sweaty chest. She noticed vaguely that the sun had set, and realized that none of the servants had bothered them, not to ask a question, not to blunder in, not even to make an appearance from the kitchen window. They were both breathing hard. Her body was still pounding and throbbing from what they'd done.

"What am I going to have to do with you?" He looked at Elena's slim hand, the soapy bubbles only a memory. "To come home and find you gone; to come back and find you doing dishes. Why do we have all these servants?"

"Little good that did." Elena glanced at the shining plates shattered on the tiles. "All the work washing and look what you did to them."

"You can buy more dishes. But you better swear to me, promise not to wash them."

"It's not the dishes. I don't care about the dishes." One dish remained on the counter. She picked it up and waggled it in his face. "See?" She tossed it on the floor, defiantly. "I have to do something. Not sit here all day doing nothing."

"Something is not servant work. Something is pleasing me." He picked her up, carried her into their bedroom, and dropped her roughly on their bed.

"Wait." Elena put up a warning hand. "What did you mean about Milton? You said Milton couldn't do this... You said Milton was in your office... Did that thing with Delores really happen? What was he doing in your office? How the hell do you know Milton? I went to school with Milton."

"Milton. I heard he 'dated' you. I have to keep an eye on him." Francisco smiled, but it was a particularly ugly smile. "The little boy needed a job. You know he's working at the ranch here, but doesn't even pull his own weight. He's all bones, like a palm tree. Maybe he'll get big enough to be useful, but he don't listen too good. He's not so smart, and he can't do what I can."

"I know, and you don't see me with Milton, do you? Of course he can't do what you do. He's just a boy. You're a man. But what do you mean? How do you even know..."

"I know because I had Blasio watching Carmen. And when you went to bed with Milton, Blasio was watching, and told me all of it."

"Well, that little shit. I didn't even know

you then. I was still in high school. He's a nasty voyeur! He didn't tell you right, then, because we never made it to a bed. We did it in a car, my first time, my only time before you, in the high school parking lot, and it was awful. I wouldn't ever do it with him again. It will be twenty years before he's as good as you."

That shut him up, but not for long. The thoughts of Milton being first with his precious Elena began to eat at him. A moment later he was at it again.

"You better not be with him in twenty years, either."

Elena narrowed her eyes at him. "I remember what you said. You said he was watching you in your office. With Delores. What are you doing, giving him sex lessons?" She leaned into his face. "He could use some lessons."

"He's such a little girl, he started crying," Francisco said scornfully. "I was just showing your little boyfriend who's got the power."

"Of course he was crying. Delores is his sister."

Francisco looked shocked, then appalled, then even he was disgusted.

"I didn't know." Then he laughed out loud, harder than Elena had ever heard him laugh. It was not a nice laugh.

"What a little shit. Didn't even have the balls to stand up for his own sister." He growled, then laughed, but like a dog worrying a bone gnawed white, he came back to it once more. "You better not do it with him again."

"Are you impaired or something? I'm not fucking interested in fucking stupid fucking Milton!" Elena yelled at him, punching him in the shoulder.

At the punch, his lips pressed together, which Elena took to mean something bad. It sure looked bad. He flipped her over across his lap, her bare bottom facing up.

"Francisco, I don't know what you're thinking, but no."

"No? Maybe you need a spanking to remind you... the husband is the boss."

"Francisco," Elena warned.

Francisco gave her bottom a soft slap, then touched her.

"Francisco, you devil," she said again, moving against his hand, all the warning gone from her voice. He turned decades of sexual experience on her, and she forgot entirely about telling him she was pregnant.

It was hours before Elena remembered poor Delores and Milton, and then the thoughts tormented her. She wished she could have left the thoughts in the kitchen, where she'd heard the story, but the memory of Francisco's description followed her. She wondered how he could have so misconstrued his promise to her. He had turned her desire for honesty from him into some kind of wanton sex game. And she'd never given him Milton's name. Something had changed, as if by telling her another woman's story, he'd poured some of his darkness in her soul.

Elena never heard from Milton again.

The next day, Francisco came in and tossed a set of keys into her lap.

"For your sister," he said. "It's not new or

fancy, but it runs. She's still walking to work. I can't have that—she's my sister-in-law. And I can't have her driving you around in that rusted-out piece-of-shit jalopy your father used to drive."

It was probably the closest in his life that Francisco had ever come to an apology.

Chapter Ten

He was thrilled about the baby. The heir to his kingdom. He watched Elena like a hawk. She thought she had learned the meaning of solitude, only now she learned its breadth and width. Alone in the hacienda except for the servants, her only outlet was when he took her on shopping trips in Nevada, California, or the bigger cities in Arizona like Tucson, where she could buy whatever her heart desired.

He had outright forbidden her leave the property without him, mostly in the name of safety, but allowed her to wander the grounds. He was paranoid about mob guys coming after him and anything precious to him. "I'm a target," he said baldly, "and because I am, you are too." He did everything he could to assure she had whatever her heart desired, but she was practically a prisoner. In Nogales, no one but his household staff and her sister ever saw her growing pregnancy.

And yet, part of her played into his mindset. She did not want anyone to see her burgeoning belly. She didn't even like the field hands to see her as she grew. It was a lucky thing for Elena that Manuela had unbent and was her friend again, as long as Francisco was not around. Only Manuela was there when they would skip stones on the muddy lake behind the house, walk the paths in the pastures, and, when Elena was too big to get around much, watch "Arthur Godfrey's Talent Scouts" and Morey Amsterdam on the little Bakelite television Francisco had brought home from a New York trip. When there was nothing on, which was most of the time, they played backgammon, listened to Sam Spade, Superman, or Abbot and Costello on the radio.

A rift threatened the day Manuela secreted Francisco's new Kodak Tourist camera in her big floppy purse, although the camera was a cumbersome device. Francisco was gone as usual, and not expected back for another day. Manuela had taken advantage of his absence to take the camera and practice putting in the 620 film, pretending to frame and shoot pictures, work the focus, and correct settings for daylight. Elena had wanted to pick wildflowers before they dried up, so they had undertaken that long walk. It was late enough that a chorus of cicadas and night creatures buzzed and chirped and croaked. They were on the way back to the house before light and opportunity converged. Manuela was well in the lead, and turned to look back. Elena was barefoot with mud to her ankles, armfuls of flowers in her arms.

"Damnit," she swore. "I've stepped on every burr in Arizona." But she made a charming picture in her white cotton shirt, one hand holding a sunhat on her head against the breeze, flowers nestled in the crook of her other arm. The hard wind flattened the fabric around her pregnant belly.

Manuela started taking pictures.

Elena went ballistic and chased her, pregnancy and all, back to the house.

"I want pictures of you," Manuela said.

"Not like this! When I'm looking like a baby elephant!"

When Elena vaulted out of the mud sucking creek, she came tearing after Manuela, as fast as she was able. Who knows what would have happened if Elena had caught her, but Francisco returned home earlier than expected. At the sound of the car, Manuela froze like a deer in headlights.

"Payback," Elena said.

She caught up, and knocked the camera out of Manuela's hand. It hit the ground hard and fell apart.

Manuela shrieked and dropped to her knees. She fumbled with the camera halves, but the back was off for good.

"He's gonna kill me."

She glared at Elena and ran into the house.

Elena heard the car door slam, and then the garage door. Inside, Francisco roared her name.

Also inside, Manuela answered something barely audible.

There was no time to spare. Elena clambered down, pulled out the film. It uncoiled like a carpet all the way down to its spool, exposing it. She half-heartedly rolled it back on its roll, and tried wadding it inside, where it did not quite fit any more. She solved that issue by putting the camera backside down and perching herself next to it on the split rail fence. It didn't quite lie as it should, but she hoped her husband would not notice.

The iron gate from the courtyard creaked. Francisco appeared, looking angry.

"Where were you?" Then, seeing her atop the fence, the anger turned. "What the hell are you doing up there? You could get hurt." He stomped in her direction.

Holding it carefully, Elena picked up the camera and snapped a picture, and another and another. At least, her fingers moved as if she were taking pictures. She set the camera down just as Francisco reached her, dragging her off the fence.

Elena wrapped her legs around him as the camera hit the ground and splayed into pieces.

"Your camera—" Elena said.

"Fuck the camera," he said. Realizing there wasn't anything under Elena's cotton dress, Francisco growled, and kicked the camera aside. "Take a picture of this."

* * *

On other days when the gate creaked open and Francisco's car came down the driveway, Manuela and Elena giggled like schoolgirls, jammed the evidence of their games under the sofa cushions, and retreated to opposite ends of the house before Francisco made it inside. Francisco only had to impress on them both once that he didn't approve of Elena fraternizing with the town or the help, either, but that never stopped Elena and Manuela.

They were often up till late at night when Francisco was on a trip without his wife.

One day, they had watched the ABC feature film, something with Shirley Temple. Now it was after midnight, television was off the air except for the Indian-head test pattern, and there wasn't much worth listening to on the radio. Manuela was still in her maid uniform, but the belt was unbuckled and the scuffs she'd been wearing were on the floor at opposite sides of the room. Manuela herself was splayed out on the couch like a rag doll, a crumpled grocery bag at her side. Her head was propped up on a pile of pillows, and a silk crocheted throw was tucked around her to her neck. Beside her was a beer, a tea cup and saucer, and a teapot. All were empty. Neither of them had actually been drinking tea.

Elena was perched at the edge of the ottoman, curved like a vulture over the Chinese checkers board on the coffee table. Her hand slid over to one of Manuela's checkers.

"Don't even think about it," Manuela said without opening her eyes. "If you cheat, I'll spit in Francisco's tea."

Elena laughed and stole one of Manuela's pieces before making her own move.

The sound of tires crunching over gravel snapped them to attention.

"Shit." Manuela exploded off the couch in a burst of pillows. The shawl dropped to the ground. She bounded across the room, leaped into her slippers, grabbed the grocery bag, and swept the checkerboard into the bag.

"Hey!" Elena protested, but not very vehemently. "Belt," she said, pointing with the narrow end of her beer bottle toward Manuela's middle.

While Manuela fastened her belt, Elena took a last swig, downing the last half of her bottle in one big chug, and dropping it into the bag Manuela held open for her.

"C'mon, c'mon," Manuela urged, and Elena reluctantly dropped in the unopened beer she had tucked behind her.

The sound of keys rattled in the hallway. Elena rolled into Manuela's spot and grabbed the tea cup as Manuela jammed some pillows into place conspicuously behind her head and chucked the shawl at her. By the time Francisco reached the hall, Manuela was the perfect servant, pouring invisible tea into Elena's cup as Elena was finishing it. Elena had almost succeeded in looking comfortable.

"Just one more pot of tea," Elena said. "I'm so chilled."

"Yes, mum."

Elena stifled laughter at Manuela's perfect imitation of Arthur Treacher's butler character in the Shirley Temple movie. Manuela trotted off with the teapot toward the kitchen, grocery bag secured under her arm, the short Goebel beer bottles within clinking slightly.

Francisco brushed past without acknowledging the housekeeper and collapsed on the couch, leaving behind him a pungent smell of smoke and spirits. He tended to sweat regardless of the weather, and was rumpled and exhausted but not enraged, which meant his backroom dealings had gone well. He winced at the sound of someone gargling on the radio and unbuttoned the top buttons of his silk floral shirt, glued to him by a thin layer of perspiration, like a superfluous, rainbow-colored onion skin. He peeled it off.

"What the fuck are you listening to?"

"I think it's the 'William Tell Overture' by Spike Jones. How was your day?"

Elena reached to turn off the radio.

He shrugged. "No, leave it," he said, chuckling as Spike Jones started narrating a horse race. His laugh turned to a grimace as he pulled his leg over his knee to unlace a shoe. Elena got up from her spot to kneel at his feet. She stopped him with a touch and untied his shoes, tugging them off and tossing them aside. He watched her fingers with some fascination as they handled the laces, and looked down at her bent head against the backdrop of his coarse linen pants. He dug his fingers into her hair.

In the distance, the tea kettle whistled.

Elena was motionless between his knees when Manuela returned with a full teapot.

"That will be all tonight," Francisco said.

Manuela set down the teapot and retreated without a backward look.

Chapter Eleven

After doing nothing while his own sister was raped in front of him in Francisco's office, Milton had killed Francisco a thousand times. He walked into the office, slammed open the door, and fired a gun into Francisco's smug face. He waited in the parking lot, ambushed him from a window. He stood on the street, waiting for the car to turn down the alley by the factory. He shot Blasio, undressed him to put on his monkey suit, and used it to pretend to be the chauffeur, driving Francisco halfway to nowhere, stopping the car, and when Francisco asked what the hell he thought he was doing, shooting him from the front seat with a pistol. He had killed Francisco Sanchez so many ways and so many times, there had to be nothing left in his soul. But in the end, he had been even too fearful to quit, even too traumatized to open the door and say he was leaving, much less harm a follicle on Francisco's head.

Milton was just one sibling in a big family. There were too many people to lose. The danger was not just if he failed, but that, if he were successful, Segundo or some other flunky would take revenge on his family.

He was nothing against Francisco, so he'd cried, and became less of a man. He had done nothing, passively accepting when dropped off at the ranch to become a field hand. There were sheep to herd, stalls to muck out, hay to toss in bales to various animals on the ranch except for the longhorn cattle, which mostly fended for themselves. A group of young men had been hired to help drive the sheep in and help with branding them. Not that this was something Milton knew much about, but he, like most of the local boys, had done ranch work at some time in his life, the way boys in bigger towns joined Boy Scouts, threw newspapers, or mowed lawns.

It seemed routine. Not very interesting, but the job in the fresh air built him up a little bit. Elena was a lost cause, even in his head, ever since his failure in Francisco's office had proved him in his own eyes to be less than a man.

He'd grown overnight from admiring to hating Francisco as much as everyone else. He'd heard that Francisco never actually worked the ranch, he lived there. He never showed up at any of the work calls, never did any manual labor. With his own eyes, Milton watched Francisco come home from work, ignoring any activity around the barn and confining himself strictly to the big house.

He had been ejected from the sidelines of a life he'd wanted. Now there was nothing. He became a watcher.

Before Elena had moved in, remodelers had doubled the size of what had already been the biggest house in town, putting a massive stone courtyard with arches and frescoes, fireplaces and fans, gardens, and a lookout tower in the back of the original house, from which distant Nogales could be seen from one side, and miles of barren desert from the other. Not even Francisco could change the view. Then they'd blocked the opening with what looked like a mirror of the front of the house, entirely enclosing the courtyard. There was a gate, Milton discovered, and through it, and through glass windows and arches, if one were in exactly the right spot, one might see inside. That became his focus—the single wrought-iron gate that opened from the courtyard to the crushed-shell drive. There he watched.

Milton was branding sheep late into the night. After that was done, he went with his binoculars over to his corner of solace: a spot between a couple of cacti, where he could see straight through the hacienda's courtyards. He tended to retire there after work instead of to the bunkhouse, where he drank tequila until he forgot who and where he was. He had already reached that point of oblivion, so he didn't know how the ambush happened, but one minute, he was in a mindless stupor in his voyeurism spot, and the next he was flat on the ground, hogtied, and someone was brandishing a branding iron at him, white-hot from the fire. They seemed not to realize he wasn't a sheep and tossed him around between them—a group of them, big men, all stockier than he. They had bandanas around their faces, like out of some "Perils of Pauline" movie. He was terrified, but between the terror and bouts of vomiting, in his heart, felt he deserved it. He wondered if this was the terror his sister had felt when Francisco had taken her in his office.

One of them waved the iron around, expressing himself as he talked, with the red light from the tip writing gold lines into the air. There was something familiar about his size and voice. The world spun, and Milton found himself face down in the dirt, someone's foot pressing down on the back of his head. He could not place the voice, and was too terrified to notice anything but that white-hot tip close enough to singe him. It glanced against his back, and he shrieked. One of them reached into his shrieking mouth with a bandana-wrapped hand and grabbed his tongue.

Then he knew. The voice he'd always remember told him to forget about Elena. He saw close up a fist he'd never forget, smelled his beard shriveling into ash from the proximity of the white-hot iron that scored his tongue. Somebody said something about his talking too much.

    "I'm sorry... I'm sorry." The last intelligible words he said met only laughter and fire.

Chapter Twelve

Manuela sent Ana, the junior maid she'd just hired, to the laundry room to iron sheets under the direction of another woman who used to be the cook, but who had been demoted after Francisco found fault with her bean dip. The new girl was eager to work, and that was a good thing. After the girl left, Manuela continued standing in the center of the hall, blocking the way in case anyone else was inclined to head in that direction. She'd already sent Segundo packing, as well as a couple of ranch hands.

Her Captain America comic book was open on top of the stack of towels she was balancing. She turned a page. Every so often, she looked toward the linen closet door, from which a steady thump was emanating and, every so often, a moan or shrill cry.

"Hurry up, for God's sake," she whispered

to herself, "I don't have all day."

Another half-dozen thumps and a crescendo of moans and yells were followed by laughter and voices that were anything but low.

Manuela heard the doorknob turn and snapped into gear. She nearly dropped her towels as she galloped into an open bedroom—the empty pink guest bedroom. The furniture was painted white, princess-style, and a mirrored glass on the dresser held a crowded array of perfumes. Everything else was in shades of pink, from the hot-pink dotted Swiss bedspread to the cool-pink walls, dainty pink bedside lamps with clear globes with a dotted Swiss pattern, and lacy pink curtains. She hid behind the door and held her breath, shoving a ruffle out of the way so she could peek through the door slit and know when the coast was clear. She made it just in time to glimpse her employers streaking to their bedroom. She heard the heavy footstep of Francisco as he led the way, and the slower, pregnant patter of Elena. Bare feet, both.

"Thank God for small favors."

Manuela waited till the master bedroom door slammed, but still poked her head out with caution before daring to move into the hall. Full frontal nudity in the person of Francisco was a hundred acres more skin than she wanted to see. Fortunately, the master bedroom door was shut. She walked confidently to the closet, which was in the opposite direction, and pulled the door open, finding, as she expected, every blanket, sheet, and towel in a wad on the floor. The linen closet shelves could not have been more empty. Not only was it not a surprise, it was the reason she'd hired more help. After the first time this happened, Manuela vowed she'd quit—just walk out the door and panhandle on the streets of Nogales before she'd allow herself to spend any more time folding and refolding the same laundry, now that the ridiculously huge linen closet had become one of Elena and Francisco's favorite playrooms.

Manuela said with disgust, "I'll be glad when you people rediscover beds," then glanced out to make sure no one had heard her.

She heard a few doors slam, and one of

Francisco's cars started up. He was off to work. Manuela headed into the pink room, grabbed a couple of fuchsia hampers and a bottle of *L'Air du Temps* off the dresser. She sprayed the closet heavily with the perfume to mask the smell of sex. She found Elena snoring, alone in her big bed, asleep on her side, her bare pregnant belly surrounded by pillows, and more pillows propping up her legs. There were bruises on her arms, but a sleepy smile on her face. Manuela shook her head, caught somewhere between envy and pity, and covered Elena first with a sheet and then with the ridiculously opulent beaver-fur blanket Francisco had brought home from, of all places, Dayton, Ohio. She snagged the laundry hamper from the master bedroom—the closet was a three-hamper job—and pulled the door shut so she wouldn't wake Elena when she hollered for Ana to come practice her ironing on three more hampers of rumpled linens.

Chapter Thirteen
December 29, 1948

A gust slammed the window open, blasting a breeze through the hot kitchen. Carmen had been baking. As she closed the window, securing it this time, she saw clouds hanging low in the sky, so low she could touch them, gray as worn flannel, heavy with rain. She could feel the moisture and electricity they carried, the ominous, dark weight of them darkening the day till it looked like dusk, though the clock had only struck noon. It was the dead of winter in Nogales in this depressingly empty house. The gloom made her superstitious and unaccountably sad. Silly of her—it was only rain. She made a dozen trips outside, stacking wood beside the fireplace and trying hard not to think of how quiet the place was without her little sister's presence. The wind outside was bitterly cold, whipping up the tarp's edge as she tried to secure it over the stacked firewood, and she had to weigh it down with a concrete block. Maybe some of it would remain dry. At least she would never run out. She'd been paid with firewood and the promise of more by too many grateful families who had nothing else to pay her with. Her woodpile never came close to being low, but was replenished when she wasn't looking, almost like magic.

While she was fighting with the tarp, she thought she heard the phone Elena had insisted on installing, and it rang again when she dropped her latest load of tinder by the fireplace. That time she answered, but no one was there. She laid out the logs to have the fire ready to go that night when the temperature dropped. It was December, after all, and the nights were often freezing. Now that she was "family," getting a real wage from bookkeeping and had no expenses expended in taking care of Elena, she had already saved enough to put in a new roof. Next she might even splurge and get an overhang built over the woodpile so she could abandon the tarp. Maybe she would even get electricity installed, although she'd lived so long without, she didn't feel she needed it.

The phone rang again.

"Hello?"

"Where have you been? I've called three times." Francisco's voice blared from the phone.

Carmen sank to her knees by the fireplace. Suddenly the tile floor felt very cold.

"What is it?" She breathed. Tried to breathe, but the room was suddenly bereft of air. A knot formed in her stomach. In her throat. Heart racing. She felt the urge to run. Felt again the presentiment of horror, even though Francisco had left her alone since he'd married her sister.

"She's having pains."

Carmen didn't have to hear a name to know who he was talking about.

"Where the fuck were you?"

"I was outside. Getting wood." The knot eased. Carmen's terror dissipated, changing to excitement of a different kind. "Why didn't you say so? I'm on the way."

"I already sent Blasio to pick you up. He's at the shop so it will only be a minute."

Unpleasant news. Blasio would leer at her, but at least he kept his hands to himself now that Francisco was her brother-in-law. She threw on a shawl. Blasio would arrive soon. He was minutes away and drove like the devil. She would be ready. Her nursing bag was always packed.

* * *

Francisco slammed down the phone. Blasio had been in town at the factory and would bring Carmen to Elena's side faster than if she drove herself. He had never been happy about Elena going to the doctor in Tucson. Though he'd always distrusted the closeness between the sisters, the idea of a man, even a doctor, ogling his naked wife was even worse. Six months ago, Elena had begged, pleaded, even had thrown a tantrum, smashing a perfectly good bottle of tequila, demanding Carmen be the one to deliver the child. Even pregnant, a bossy, pissed-off Elena still got Francisco hot enough to skew his judgment. After the argument that led to spontaneous sex in the patio surrounded by pieces of the broken bottle, Francisco unbent enough to say yes, albeit begrudgingly. The promise had been extracted from him, but he still left the house whenever Carmen was there.

At first the examination visits were monthly, but as Elena got closer to her date, Carmen came over every three weeks, then every two, then weekly. He always found something to do elsewhere before she arrived and, if her car was still there when he returned, he would go inspect the bunkhouse, start up a game of poker, or sit outside with a bottle until after the old car he had gotten her had disappeared over the hill. Why he did that made little sense as he saw her at work every day. Today would be an exception.

"Arturo!" Francisco's holler shook the walls. Normally Arturo was relegated to the gardens, but he had been delivering some TLC to the houseplants. None of the usual house staff was good with plants.

"Yes, boss?"

"Clear the house. Everybody out. Everybody out but my wife and sister-in-law."

"Yes, boss."

* * *

Francisco was there when Carmen cleared the rancho gates. Otherwise, the house appeared deserted. Housekeepers and grounds people—even Segundo—had been banished to give Elena her privacy.

Carmen ignored him.

She found Elena lying on the enormous bed she normally shared with Francisco. In preparation for labor, the room was a sanctuary of pre-baby order except for the marks Elena's husband had left behind. Gaudy cufflinks on the highboy. A stack of suitcases on a stand, the top one open and half-empty, as if packing or unpacking had been abandoned in mid-process. An unopened beer. A dirty ashtray. One of Francisco's cigars had been lit and abandoned there, burned to ash but appearing still intact, till Carmen bumped into the highboy and the ashes shivered into dust.

"We can manage by ourselves," Carmen said to Francisco, shoving him out of his own bedroom and shutting the door in his face. Carmen still hated him. She didn't care where he disappeared to as long as he was not around her. She heard his footsteps as he walked off. Probably somewhere in the empty house, drinking.

"Don't be so hard on him," Elena panted. "I wish you'd give him a chance. I just want the two of you to get along." The contraction eased and she relaxed.

"Shh... " Carmen patted her hand. Elena looked entirely too happy and comfortable to be very far along in her labor, but she didn't say so aloud. "How far apart are your pains?"

"Short pains," Elena said. "Long wait between them. About fifteen minutes. But my water broke." She smiled proudly, as if it was something she had accomplished on purpose. She beamed a huge smile up at her sister. "Just think, in a few hours, the baby will be here. I can hardly believe it!"

"Fifteen minutes," Carmen repeated, watching the window. "I heard the car start. Francisco just drove off. Your pains are fifteen minutes apart and he goes off? What's wrong with him? I don't want him underfoot, but he should at least be here."

"He'll be back."

Because she was looking out the window, Carmen saw the lightning strike close by, but still the thunder took her by surprise. It was deafening and powerful, so close it rattled the house, shivered the chandelier, and sent the crystals tinkling and swinging.

"*Dios.*"

The lights flickered and dimmed momentarily.

"It will be okay," Carmen assured her sister, "we don't need light."

The heavens split, and a torrent of rain engulfed the house. The light fluttered and came back full force.

"Let me check and see how far along you are," Carmen said, checking the clock. She made a cursory examination, then tucked Elena's gown back down around her ankles. "You've a long way to go," she said, illustrating with her hands just how much she needed to dilate before things started happening.

"No! I thought I was farther along."

"You were Mama's daughter, too. You know better than to be lying down, if you don't want it to take forever. If you want to speed it up, you can get up and walk around."

"Yes!" Elena said. "Anything!" She waited as Carmen walked around the bed and helped her up. Thunder shook the house again. "I hope he's okay in that rain."

"I'm sure he'll be fine," Carmen said drily, "but he should not have left."

"He had to. He's got work. He just got back from a trip and because of me, hasn't been to the bank or been locked away for hours with his dull accountants like he usually is. He's been a nervous wreck." Elena giggled. "It's funny to see him so... normal."

"Normal? Francisco?"

Carmen wondered what fantasy world Elena was living in, and who exactly her sister thought she was married to that Carmen just didn't see. She could think of a lot of things to call Francisco, but normal wasn't one of them. She couldn't be happier not to worry about the displeasure of a chance encounter with Francisco hanging over her head as she and Elena walked slowly down the hall.

"I don't see how you can stand him," Carmen said. "It eats me alive that you're here in this cocoon he built around you. You don't even know what he does to the girls. You do know he's still doing it? Still taking every girl he can get away with."

Carmen had expected shock, or horror. She wasn't expecting the strange light in Elena's eyes. She wasn't expecting the strange, dark laugh.

"I know. I know in great detail." She laughed. "Before we got married, I made a deal with him. He promised he'd leave you alone. Getting you out of the picture was part of the deal." She slowed, and focused on Carmen's eyes. "I know you denied you were interested in him, but I'm not an idiot. You were hiding something that was going on between you two. I never knew what it was, and I still don't," Elena said, waving away Carmen's objections. "Don't bother denying it. It doesn't matter any more, anyway. But that was when we got our wires crossed, he and I. I thought I asked him to ask my permission first. But he didn't understand. Instead, he tells me after, and gets a big kick from it, too. So I know a hell of a lot more than names and places. I know positions, and who was in the room, and how many times she⊠—well, I know all there is to know. And I know he loves me. Me. They can't have him. He's mine." She stopped pacing, and with a short gasp, jerked to a stop, shut her eyes, and bent over. "Pains. Escalating."

"Breathe," Carmen said. Now was not the time to talk about Francisco. She reached out and took Elena's hand.

Elena was able to stand straight again and showed Carmen the open door to the baby's room. The revelation over the other women hung between them. Carmen shocked that Elena wasn't shocked, Elena knowing Carmen didn't get it. She wasn't about to enlighten her, either.

"Did you see the room?" Elena changed the subject, still gripping Carmen, dragged her in.

Carmen followed, finding that the infant's room had been rearranged for what might have been the fiftieth time. In the whole house, this was the only room that looked real to her. The rest of the house was too full of things, as if Francisco could not bear to see a blank space on the wall or a corner without a piece of furniture in it. Carmen found the house as oppressive and pompous as Francisco himself, though Francisco himself blamed the New York decorator he'd hired for Elena.

"Did you hear that?" Elena cocked her head, listening to something only she could hear. "I hear a baby crying. Papi always said if a pregnant woman hears a baby cry before hers is born, it will be a genius."

"That's an old wives' tale," Carmen said. "And what you hear is the wind. But of course... no matter what you think you hear, your baby will be a genius. She'll be yours, after all."

A bright quilt hung on the wall, and a matching one was folded over a quilt rack at the foot of the baby's bed. Piles of diaper bags filled two matching rocking chairs and the crib. An embarrassment of excess.

"How many of these do you think you'll need?"

"I confess, I love these. They're all so cute, I just can't make up my mind. They have them in every color in the stores, in cloth and leather. In Tucson, I even saw one in fur."

Elena giggled, waving one around and tossing Carmen another, an enormous green quilted one with a peacefully sleeping lamb embroidered on the side.

"You could put a car in here," Carmen said, opening the bag and dropping in some of the pins and diapers, where they seemed to disappear in the cavernous emptiness.

"See this?" Elena pulled out a bright, strappy cloth that looked like its mother had been a diaper and its father a backpack. "You put your arms through these things and carry the baby on your back. That's when she's older." She tossed another one to Carmen. "This sling is especially for when she's little, for a size one. The baby is in front. Arms free! I got one in all the colors." She tossed another.

"What's wrong with a *rebozo*?"

Elena made a face. "You're so old-fashioned."

Packages whooshed past her head. Carmen caught one and dropped it in the bag she was holding.

"How much of this stuff do you need? Pick one and give the rest away. You're like some Hollywood woman obsessed with shoes," Carmen scolded.

"I like shoes. I like clothes. I like baby bags. It's nice Francisco has so much money so I can get everything for the baby! Our baby will not be like we were—one pair of shoes in the winter, holes in our socks, hungry till spring."

"Truly, Elena, was it so bad?"

"Maybe not. We had Mami and Papi. They were the best. But we still went without."

"We had everything we needed," Carmen insisted.

"My baby will never want for anything. Never be homeless or go hungry. She'll have Francisco and me and you. She'll have everything." Elena stretched her hands over her belly, in a big embrace, then blushed in embarrassment. "Now, Carmen, which do you like best?" The green bag was adorable, the lamb executed by hand with wonderful skill on a field of such a lovely soft green that Carmen would have liked to curl up on it as well, but Elena was right—they were all cute. How did one make choices when cost was no deterrent? She would have scolded more, but Elena had years of experience in distracting her from serious problems. She slung a diaper that struck Carmen full in the face. It was a perfect hit, and perfectly harmless. Elena tossed her more baby things, diapers, pins. Carmen caught them with the bag. Elena's humor was infectious.

"I couldn't make up my mind which one. They're all so perfect. So we got them all."

"Stop!" Carmen said, laughing.

Elena tossed another barrage of diapers, some on target, some not. "But it's fun!" She put her hand to her neck, and twirled the charm at the end of a long gold necklace.

Carmen shoved the diapers into the sheep bag.

Elena spun around in circles, clasping her huge belly.

"Enough of that!" Carmen laughed. "You're making me dizzy. You're making the baby dizzy."

"I didn't think of that!" She stopped spinning and caught Carmen's hands. "My baby is almost here! Your niece."

Elena leaned heavily on the changing table she'd spent days moving around until she finally decided to leave it across from the window and looked at another wall. "Maybe it should be over there..."

Her eye caught another diaper bag.

"Look at this one, so cunning! It has all these compartments." She pulled her wallet out of yet another baby bag. "I've got it all packed already."

She showed Carmen her recent driver's license picture. With the extra weight of her pregnancy, the license photo looked more like Carmen than it did Elena. She closed the wallet and dropped it on the baby's dresser.

"You shouldn't be so careless."

"You fuss more than Mama ever did. You keep it for me," Elena said, shoving the wallet into Carmen's pocket. "Francisco never lets me go anywhere anyway."

She caught sight of herself in the mirror. "Look how alike we are!" Elena said. "Like the Torres twins in second grade."

"Your second grade, not mine. You made me be the old grownup."

Elena stuck out her tongue. "Five years. I can scoff at your five years now, I'm almost a mama."

"I'm almost an auntie."

"Auntie Carmen." Elena found that hilarious and laughed till her face was rosy. "Oh, that reminds me! Let's me go get the jewelry box—" Elena grabbed the necklace she'd been playing with and, without undoing the clasp, slipped it over her own head and dropped it over Carmen's.

"No," Carmen said. "It's yours."

"I got it for you! Come see!"

Elena was off again, back to her bedroom, to her dresser. Thinking she knew what was going on, Carmen followed, and picked up a pretty carved box.

"Not that one," Elena said. "That's just got the cheap stuff. I like the box but there's nothing really good in it. He brought it back for me from one of his trips." She took it out of Carmen's hands and carelessly dropped it.

Elena turned to a big wooden box on her dresser, an old-fashioned key sticking out of it. She turned the key and opened the box, revealing tray after tray of rings, earrings, and a rainbow of gems in every imaginable color glistening on gold strands. The contents were probably worth a fortune, but Carmen didn't really know or care. All she'd ever had was costume jewelry.

Carmen poked at the jewels with her finger.

"*Dios*, Elena. Is this for real? This looks like pirate treasure."

"He's always bringing me things. This box is usually in the safe. Who am I going to wear it for? The help?"

Elena withdrew a necklace exactly like the one she'd put on Carmen. "The last time he took me to Tucson, I got this for you."

She snapped the box shut, dropped the necklace over her own neck, and held out the gold charm at the end. "See?"

Carmen lifted the one Elena had just given her. The chain was smooth, the bonds so fine the necklace looked and felt almost like a single piece. The links were barely distinguishable. The two charms fit together to make a single heart. On the back, their names were engraved.

"The *cadena*, this kind of link, it's called an omega chain," Elena said. "I picked out the charms myself."

Carmen's eyes were wet. "I have an idea,"

she said. She walked across the room to her nursing bag, rummaged around a bit, and pulled out a small pouch that held a small Saint Christopher medal. She slipped it onto the chain.

"Brilliant!" Elena beamed. She rummaged in her box for her own little brass medal and followed suit. "I remember when Mama gave us these." She got very still, her eyes and mind full with the memory.

Then she was off to the baby's room again.

"And I got a kit to make bottles, with a funnel and spoon and everything. Carmen! Let's fill the bottles! C'mon, you can show me how!" Elena headed toward the kitchen.

Elena chattered eagerly as Carmen showed her how to sterilize the bottles and add just the right amount of sugar to cow's milk. For a few moments, they were laughing and giggling, just like a couple of girls.

"Though you should be nursing the baby," Carmen said. "It's—"

"We talked about this already," Elena said,

putting her hand up, "Francisco doesn't want me to ruin my figure. So it's cow's milk or evaporated milk, period."

Francisco again. Carmen would have liked to forget he existed.

"About Francisco—" Carmen said.

"Enough, Carmen. You don't understand, so I will tell you. It's not just the sex. Oh, sure, the sex is unbelievable. But you just don't understand. He's bad. I know he's bad to the bone. He's mean, but not to me. He does what he wants. But he's mine," Elena said.

"Were you with anybody else? Is that Francisco's baby?" Carmen had to ask. She couldn't stop herself.

"There's nobody else. Why would there be anybody else? I don't want anyone else." Elena put her chin up, angry at being questioned. "Of course it is his baby!"

Carmen had hoped the baby had been from some other man, but she knew her sister. Knew when she was telling the truth. The baby was Francisco's. Her niece or nephew was going to be a devil child.

Elena put her palms on either side of Carmen's face. "You don't understand. You're good. But me?" Elena gave a stark smile, as sad a smile as Carmen had ever seen. "I must be as bad as he is. I love him. I don't care what he does as long as I'm part of it."

Carmen bit back her words, and put the hot, sterile bottles on the counter. It was crazy. It had to be the pregnancy talking. How could her sweet, innocent Elena be saying such things? There wasn't a bad bone in her body. She didn't know what to think. The only thing she did know was that confronting Elena about Francisco while she was in the middle of labor was still the wrong time to do it. She'd just bite her tongue and put off the talk until another day.

"The bottles need to cool before they go in the refrigerator."

"Let's walk some more," Elena said, panting. "Let's get Manuela up. Make her suffer too."

"I thought Francisco chased everyone out of here."

"She doesn't count. She lives here."

"You stay, I'll get her," Carmen said. "Unless you want to walk back with me to the maid's quarters. It's still in the same place it was when her mother was housekeeper here, right?"

Elena changed her mind. "No, wait, I forgot, she sat up this week with her mama, at the hospital in town. When she got back, she went straight to bed. Let her sleep. Let's keep walking."

They went into the courtyard and strolled around the garden. The heavens had broken loose, but they kept under the awnings. Elena squeezed into a straight-backed rocker on a little porch across from the house.

"Sit in the other one," Elena insisted.

Carmen finally sat. Rain pounded on the tin roof over their heads.

"Sometimes I sit in my room over there," Elena pointed to her brightly lit bedroom, "and I picture you living here."

"In your utility shed?" Carmen gasped in mock horror. She tilted her head and looked critically behind her. "It does look like the de-formed stepchild of Mami and Papi's house. "

"If only you were that close..." Elena sighed.

"No, thank you. I see quite enough of your worse half every day at work."

"It's just so far from town. And I don't get out as much as I used to. But that will all change once the baby is here, once I have my fig-ure back."

Carmen wasn't so certain. "It does kind of remind me of home. Maybe I should put in a porch with a tin roof." They both laughed, and rocked, knowing Carmen would not make any changes to the old homestead.

"I wonder if this is what Seattle is like."

The rain slowed and they made their way inside to check to see if the bottles were cool enough to put in the refrigerator.

Carmen, who had been following the timing of the contractions, saw that Elena seemed a bit pale. Hours were passing quickly. "Let's get you in bed, and I can see if you've dilated."

Elena agreed, but insisted on bringing a bottle with them, for luck, she said. They had to stop twice in the hall for her contractions. Carmen took the bottle away and put it on Elena's dresser before she arranged the pile of pillows. She made Elena wait in a chair for a few moments as she arranged a rubber cloth and folded some extra sheets across the lower two-thirds of the bed, for easy clean up later.

"I remember Mama doing that," Elena said. "I never pictured you doing it for me. I miss her so, sometimes."

"She's here with us, you know that." Carmen touched the tiny gold St. Christopher medal on the new chain.

Elena reached to the one around her own neck.

"I remember when she gave them to us." Then another contraction hit, and she ended the sentence in a screech.

Carmen helped her into bed.

"If it's a boy, he will be named Mario. If it's a girl, she'll be Maria."

"Maria," Carmen repeated softly. "For Mami."

"That one really hurt bad," Elena said as a new contraction struck. Carmen checked again.

"You've made a lot of progress," Carmen told her. "You just might have that baby before sunrise after all." She gathered a stack of clean towels for the baby and piled them beside the size-zero newborn outfit Elena had already chosen for her baby to wear on arrival.

Elena patted the bed beside her. "Come, sit."

Carmen bustled about, gathering items she would be using. Washcloths, a tray of ice to cool the washcloth for Elena's forehead, a sterilized needle and thread should Elena need it, iodine, sterile twine to tie off the cord, a bulb siphon for the baby. Elena patted the bed again.

"Come on, I insist."

Carmen relented. She settled beside Elena and took her hand.

"You're the best of sisters," Elena said.

"I'm your only sister," Carmen reminded

her, and rolled her eyes.

"Quit playing around—I mean it," Elena said. "You've always been there for me. I just wish you could have been as happy as I have been this year with Francisco. And I wish...I wish..." Elena panted through a pain, as Carmen wiped her face with the wet cloth. "That feels so good," Elena whispered. She should have looked worn from the strain, the sweat, but her face glowed with loveliness. "If something happens to me—"

"Nothing is going to happen to you. I won't let it," Carmen said. "All laboring mothers think something is going to happen. But nothing will—"

"If something happens, take care of the baby for me."

"I said—"

"Please! Just say it to make me feel better," Elena said.

Carmen was not superstitious, but she felt the icy feet of a ghost course down her spine, and wished Elena had said nothing.

"I promise! Now, stop thinking bad

things, and concentrate on having this baby. I want to hold her in my arms!"

Francisco's car drove up the driveway, and Carmen heard the door slam. Elena's expression eased with his return. Carmen could not help marveling at how much Elena really did love Francisco. For Elena's sake, and for the sake of the baby, she resolved to try to get along with her brother-in-law.

Carmen moved the baby bottle on the dresser close by, even though she knew the baby would not need it yet.

"Thank you for not arguing—I know you don't want me to use the bottle, but he doesn't want me to ruin my figure."

For once in her life, Carmen held her tongue. She was planning to argue the issue, but not now, while Elena was in labor.

As for the baby, it wouldn't be much longer.

Mario was delivered at four a.m.

Carmen cleaned him up and put him in Elena's arms. It took only seconds to roll back the messy sheets and toss them to the floor at the foot of the bed.

Elena looked down at the baby in her arms. From Carmen's vantage point, kneeling by the sheets, the mother and child seemed a holy sight. What she saw caused a catch in her throat and made her eyes fill with tears.

"He is so beautiful. He sees me. Carmen, he sees me. He knows me."

"It is true," Carmen agreed softly, not wanting to break the moment.

No Madonna and child painting was ever so lovely. Elena was glowing with love, and the baby gazed into her eyes with an expression of pure wonder, their faces inches apart. All the times Carmen had been told that infants could not focus at that age, that their smiles were simply gas—it was not true. The vision was caught like a snapshot in her head, a lifetime of love trapped forever in that instant of recognition cut short.

The door to the hall burst open and Francisco staggered in, woozy from drink, an empty Jalisco tequila bottle clutched in his fist. Not the trumped-up kind they'd recently begun bottling in the US, with a worm added for good measure to impress the gringos. None of that for Francisco. His bottle came from one of several cases that had been shipped from the city of Tequila, not far from Guadalajara.

Ignoring Francisco, Carmen knelt at the foot of the bed and bundled the dirty sheets.

The proud father waltzed around the room, staggering a bit. First he kissed his wife's mouth and thanked her. Then he looked down from Elena to the baby.

The baby's complexion was pale, paler even than Elena's. And he had green eyes.

His whole demeanor changed. The demon was back. Francisco's face twisted darkly as he screamed out, "That is not my child! You betrayed me! You're a *puta*!"

Elena had no time to react. Exhausted, still sweaty from labor, she looked over in his direction, not really comprehending.

"This baby is a *güero*," Francisco cried out. "You are a *puta*! You betrayed me. You've been whoring around! This baby is not mine!"

It was like a nightmare. This could not be happening. Before either of the sisters could react, before Elena could utter a response or Carmen a defense, he opened a drawer in the nightstand, took out his Banker's Special, cocked it, and shot Elena at close range. She jerked from the impact and was still. The baby screamed. Elena's arm dropped against the pillow and the baby rolled face-down, his screams muffled by the best fabric money could buy.

Francisco was standing with the Colt still out, still pointed. He was slobbering drunk, disbelieving what he had just done. He hadn't moved, but was frozen, staring at the hole in his Elena left by the bullet.

"Elena?" he said. "You can stop that now. I forgive you, even if you are a *puta*. Elena? We can try again, make another baby..."

Carmen could never remember exactly how it happened, only that her bastard brother-in-law had lost his mind. Part of her was waiting to wake up, because this had to be a nightmare.

Still on her knees from gathering up the linens, she dropped the sheets. Stood. Like a doe in the woods, but reversing the roles—the prey stalking the hunter. One step. Two. On the third step, she was around the other side of the bed, beside Francisco. He seemed to have forgotten she was there. She didn't even have to wrest the gun away from his slack, disbelieving fingers. She just reached over and took it from him. As if he were paralyzed, he stood in place, staring and gibbering at Elena, ignoring the muffled screams of the hysterical infant. Carmen didn't care if his condition was from the liquor, shock, or disbelief.

She turned the gun in her hand, stared at it. She'd never held one before, but she'd just seen him use it, not four feet away from her. She walked away from him, crossed to the other side of the bed so the infant was between them. She pointed the barrel at Francisco and mimicked him. Cocked and fired and shot—or tried to. The first squeeze, she hadn't quite cocked it. Nothing happened. Her first actual shot went wild and knocked her into the door. He didn't even look up. Carmen righted herself and squeezed the trigger again, glad the baby wasn't behind her target, in case she missed again. She didn't mean to shut her eyes, but it happened by reflex as her eye muscles anticipated the recoil. This time, the shot actually hit him, but badly—the bullet caught him sideways through his paunch. She staggered without falling. That made him notice her. He looked down at his punctured beer belly as if it weren't a part of him, turned to face her with the expression of a dumb animal, and pointed to Elena.

"Fix her," he said.

"I can't fix her, *desgraciado*. You broke her, you killed her, you bastard! But I'll fix you."

That time she aimed vaguely for his midsection, his widest part, and fired again and again until all the gun did was click, and click. Some time after she had stopped clicking the gun, he was still standing, looking at her, but finally he slumped to the floor like a marionette whose strings had been cut.

Chapter Fourteen

"Elena," Carmen said. "Come on, let's go, he's gone. We gotta go." She bent over Elena, wanting to help her, hoping in spite of the blind, staring eyes that her little sister was still there. She pulled her close into a hug and rocked with her for who knew how long. Too late. Then she realized she was still holding the *pistola*.

Carmen threw down the empty gun, then picked it up and laced Francisco's fingers through it. She had to get out of there. She'd just killed a man. He deserved it, but Nogales might not be too happy about her shooting the biggest employer in the whole of Santa Cruz County. And that was just counting the American side. She had no idea how far his reach extended into Mexico. She couldn't think. Her mind was numb, her hands shaking. What to do? What to do? She saw blood on her hands, and raced to the bathroom.

She looked at herself in the mirror at the stranger staring back at her. Blood on her face, spatter like oil from frying tortillas. Nothing much on her clothes. She'd been bent down when he'd fired, but bore a splotch where she'd hugged Elena. She ran water, took a washcloth, wiped off her face and arms, scrubbed at her hair, but didn't touch the red stain on her blouse. A sound penetrated her crazily racing thoughts. The baby!

Elena was a shock. Still there. Still bloody. Still dead. Even as Carmen saw the evidence, her mind veered from the impossible truth of her sister's death. The baby was here. Dimly she realized he was crying, startled from the blasts of the gun or from his awkward position. Frozen in a position for a good ten seconds, her hands outstretched to either side as if she were going to dribble balls to her left and right, she couldn't think of what to do next. She made a grab for an armful of Elena's maternity shirts, wadded them into the nursing kit, and kicked it down the hallway toward the door to the garage. What was that noise? She turned to face the sound, then ran to it. To him.

Mario.

She picked him up. His face was scarlet from anger, gasping for air. She rocked him to a hiccuppy silence. What a way to enter the world. Mechanically she diapered, dressed and comforted him, and swaddled him in a baby blanket. He was a big baby, straining the size zero infant-wear to its max. When he turned his face toward her breast, nuzzling, she realized he must be hungry. The bottle was where she'd left it on Elena's dresser. She didn't heat it, but Mario didn't seem to care. He had no trouble taking the first meal of his life, and was soon burped and asleep beside his mother, a sheet away from her life's blood, oblivious to the drama of his entrance into the world.

Carmen stepped into his nursery, the room Elena had gone to such lengths decorating. It had only been a month ago that she and Elena had picked out the crib. It was the sight of that crib that unhinged her. She felt the wall at her back and collapsed, crying.

But she had no time for hysteria. Elena was dead. Francisco had murdered Elena, and Carmen had murdered Francisco. She had to get Mario out of there or he'd end up in an orphanage, raised to become another monster Sanchez, or killed by some criminal for his inheritance. Maybe she could get safely to family in Mexico City. Her father had gotten a postcard from a cousin there, years ago. Once Mario was safe, it wouldn't matter what happened to her.

Carmen went into the kitchen where a set of hooks held the keys to a dozen cars and farming vehicles, and grabbed one. She wasted several minutes trying the key on car after car parked in the hacienda's massive garage and, when that failed, on the cars parallel parked in the driveway. The rain was a roar in her ears as it poured in icy sheets, drenching her as she went down the line, car to car. Every step was a thundering crunch of crushed shells and sand. Every cold drop of rain washed a bit more blood away. Finally able to open a door of a brand new 1948 black Super

Estate wagon, she pulled the big Buick into the garage where she could load it up out of the rain. Back in the house, Carmen filled all the baby bags she could with clothes, stuffing them in haphazardly, barely comprehending what she was doing. She squeezed the stroller bed into the back seat, jammed beside luggage, baby bags filled with diapers, powder, and the bottles she'd fixed so hopefully. It seemed like another life, but it had only been that morning that she'd mixed the formula. She managed to cram the rolling part of the wheeled perambulator into the trunk. Her teeth were chattering, but she didn't stop to dry off when she was back inside. Back in the nightmare in the bedroom.

The awful vision of her sister froze her in her steps, stilling everything but her clacking teeth. She was transfixed for a long, horrible moment, maybe even a little mad, until she saw Mario. Mario sleeping.

Elena was the past. Mario was the future.

She could see Elena in his face. She could carry on, *had* to carry on, for Elena's sake.

Elena's son had to survive.

Carmen avoided looking at Francisco's face as she rifled his wallet and found a bundle of hundreds. One by one, she went through his drawers and found more stashed bundles of cash. She'd never held so much money. She picked up Elena's jewelry box, the one that was exquisitely hand-carved from a block of Mexican cocobolo and had costume jewelry in it, and clutched it to her chest.

Elena had said he'd just come back from one of his money-collecting trips to Tucson or Phoenix or somewhere in Mexico. He wouldn't miss the money now, but she could sure use it. How else would she survive to take care of her little nephew in an uncertain future in Mexico? Would this be enough to keep them and, more importantly, hide them from Francisco's cronies? She had no idea what it cost to survive outside of Nogales where she'd never had to pay rent, and had always had a job, repugnant as it was.

He must have a safe in the house. She looked down the dark hall to the only room where light was shining through an open door.

His office. She'd been to the house a hundred times since Elena had married him, but had never been in that room, not that she'd ever wanted to go in. She'd kept her equilibrium over Elena's crazy marriage by pretending Francisco didn't exist. Now, she grabbed Elena's jewelry box and made her way through the dark hall that seemed to have gotten miles longer.

No big surprises behind the door. The room contained a wall of familiar cardboard boxes on one side, a table bearing an opened case of tequila, an empty bottle tipped on its side, and another bottle that had been open, and was half gone. A shot glass. She poured herself a shot, took a hesitant sip and spat it out with a shudder.

She slammed down the glass and bent in half, coughing. After a moment to recover her breath, she picked it up again, and rubbed it off with the hem of her shirt. A glance revealed the boxes were dated and labeled Baja, Chihuahua, Coahulla, Nuevo Leon, Tamaulipas. It did not miss her attention that these were the Mexican states bordering the US. A great many were labeled Sonora, dated with a number of years, and that one box was standing open. She stepped closer and glanced inside, finding, as she'd expected, bookkeeping balances from the tool and die factory that she herself had totaled earlier that week, but labeled in Spanish as for some company she'd never heard of. There were also dozens of folders labeled with the names of individuals. The first one was open enough to reveal a man's profile and history, with a list of arrests circled in red ink. Without removing anything, she ran her finger over the folders, revealing more such histories. Trust Francisco to hire spies and keep blackmail records on everyone. She wondered how many of the records were true.

     It was only when she turned to leave that she saw by the door a wall of filing cabinets and two huge safes. The safe labeled SONORA was closed. Francisco's coat hung over the edge of the one labeled ARIZONA, blocking the lock from being able to engage. She caught the tail end of the coat and tugged. The big iron door swung ajar. It was open. It had to be a sign from God.

Her jaw dropped. So did Elena's cocobolo jewelry box.

The thing was packed to the ceiling full of money. Shelf after shelf jammed full of neatly wrapped packages of bills. Bills in stacks. Surely to make everyone in Nogales rich. Enough to make everyone in Arizona rich. Without even stopping to think, Carmen put one bundle in her pocket and then almost shut the door, leaving the coat still blocking it.

She stopped. Reached into her pocket, and pulled out the stack of hundreds. What was she thinking? She had forever to face an uncertain world, a baby to raise. The child of the man whose money this was.

Her feet started running, almost by themselves, back to the horror scene. She stared at the suitcases, at that one standing open with Francisco's belongings still in it.

Perfect.

She stepped over Francisco's body. Opened a drawer. Dumped his clothes into it.

Her hands shook, but she straightened the stacks of pants and shirts so nothing looked much out of place. Grabbed the suitcase. Dashed back into the office, and dropped the open suitcase on the floor.

There was still no stopping to think. She reached to the bottom shelf; it was deep, and she found herself leaning in up to her shoulder as she swept everything out. The stacks, most of them, fell neatly inside, piling high. But when she looked back at the safe, something was wrong. That whole shelf empty; the rest of the safe jam-packed. It looked wrong. She ought to just leave it, but there was plenty around she could shove in there.

The filing cabinets. She jerked open one, then another, thumbing through and grabbing whole sections marked "Confidential." In short order, she'd snatched stacks of folders from Francisco's desk and cabinets, and slid them in, one by one, filling the empty shelf. But it still didn't fit perfectly; there was a gap. Her foot nudged the jewelry box. She looked from the box—really, just a wooden box, not painted or anything. Sure, it was carved, but it had been a gift from Francisco, which sullied its value in her eyes. She picked it up and looked at the safe, at the space still left.

Didn't it make sense that Francisco would keep his wife's jewels in a safe? Of course he did; Elena had said they were usually in the safe. She turned the box on its side and wedged it in. And that's when she noticed the tip of a folder sticking out of another shelf. Curiously, she tugged at it, and a manila packet slid out, not unlike those she used at work. She dumped its contents on the table. There were receipts, typed pages, and IOUs. She swept everything into the suitcase. She'd look at it all later.

She looked at her handiwork on the shelf. It wasn't perfect, but it was full enough not to draw attention. She lifted the sleeve of the jacket, pulling it out of the way, and the safe clicked shut. Then she saw the tip of an envelope sticking up through the side of the safe, and tried to open it again to fix it. However, it was not just a metal cabinet full of money—it was a safe that was now firmly shut. And she was no safecracker. Nothing else she could do about it.

And the suitcase wouldn't shut. She had to stop and breathe. Knelt. Tried making order out of chaos. Fitted in the little book, put the bills in neat stacks, grabbing what had not made it inside the suitcase and somehow making it work, even though she had to sit on it to get it to close.

"I knew you could do it," she told the suitcase. Her heart was still racing. She remembered Elena again and wanted to throw up. Her knees gave out and she slumped to the ground. She shook with hysteria, but there was no time now to stop. She lurched upward.

Carmen looked at her still-bulging pockets and at the floor, where she'd missed a pile of cash beside the suitcase. What had she been thinking? She almost ran out of the house. Was it crazier to take it, or leave it? Hard to say. She only knew one thing. She would have to take care of Mario. She'd need another carry-all. Damn Francisco for being so rich, and herself for being so careless.

She dashed down the hall and grabbed the green bag with the embroidered sheep, which seemed to glare at her balefully as if it knew what she'd been up to. It was the one Elena had tossed her, laughing, earlier that night. Earlier, it hadn't looked so malevolent. She dashed back to the office with it, stacked the money from the floor into it, dumped in everything in her pockets, and stuffed the diapers, pins, and powder in on top.

At the door, she stopped and turned around.

"Courage," she said in a shaky voice, looking toward the case of liquor.

She looked past the open tequila and grabbed an unopened bottle out of the case to jam into the bag. It might be good for something.

She thought she heard the squeak of a door, as if someone were inside the house. She didn't see anyone, but the noise still put a scare in her. She tore down the hall as if the devil were on her heels, the bag and suitcase swinging madly, the tequila sloshing, and dumped everything at the end of the hall by the garage entry into the house.

She had to hide. Had to get away. How could she do both at the same time? Guards must be here, there were always guards somewhere. They'd be at the property gates. One of them might not be drunk, not out whoring around. She'd never make it out of the rancho, much less to Nogales, with Francisco's thugs around.

Carmen backtracked and ducked through French doors in one of the bedrooms that opened to the courtyard. She checked that the courtyard gate was locked, but it was ornamental, after all. The key was in the lock. She turned the deadbolt and put the key in her pocket, hoping to block one way into the house. There was another entry through an outbuilding that looked like a little Mexican *casa*. That door, partly hidden behind the chairs that she and Elena had rocked in earlier, was padlocked. She checked it to be certain and made sure the courtyard entries were locked down as tight as they could be before returning to the garage.

Carmen got the Buick's door open and made a final trip, into the house for the baby's car bed and to load up the rest of the bags and money. She stood back to see her handiwork. Piles of stuff wedged the baby's bed in place. Mario was packed for the duration. She tugged on the bed to be certain of its stability before she ran back in to get Mario. Getting the baby settled into the bed felt like another miracle.

She turned the key. The car roared to life.

"Shhh," she whispered, not that it made the car quieter. No one came out. She shouldn't have been surprised, though—it wasn't as if anyone wanted to be around Francisco, or stand out in the rain on his behalf.

She had already decided on Mexico as a destination. Papi had family in Mexico, not that she'd ever met them. She'd have to stop at a gas station for a map.

She inched toward the gates. Should she drive like mad straight through them, honk for someone to let her out as she usually did, or turn around and cut through the field? But the car would never make it through the rugged Arizona terrain, so it wouldn't do to panic. If a guard tried to stop her, then she'd rush the gates. She didn't want to run over any guards. One dead Francisco was one too many deaths on her soul already. But oh, Elena. She started crying again, or maybe she'd never stopped.

Looking through the rain was like peering through Flemish glass, but she could tell there were lights on in the bunkhouse. She stared at the lights.

She honked the horn.

No one appeared. All that slinking around and careful quietness, and now this. She slammed the base of her palm on the car horn and it bleated again. Then she just sat at the gate, the car running, the baby sleeping, the tears pouring down her face, the rain pouring on everything else, the dead bodies back in the house. She took a breath.

She honked again.

Someone came out of the gatehouse, his face hidden under a yellow mackintosh draped over him like a blanket. She saw pajama bottoms slosh through puddles as he ran to the gate, unlocked it, and dragged it open. He was huddled against the rain and could care less about who might be driving one of the boss's new cars.

But that was too good to be true. She was pulling up when a *chupacabra* jumped out at her. She shrieked and jerked back. Maybe not a *chupacabra*. Maybe something big and black, like a bear. She used her arm to brush the condensation from the inside of the car window and saw Blasio's face leering at her from outside. She jerked back. He wore a big black overcoat of some kind, dripping with water.

"I'm supposed to take you back," he growled. "I've been waiting up here for hours."

"Nothing's happening for a long time yet," Carmen manufactured. "There's really plenty of time. Really. I gotta go get some supplies. You might as well go back to bed. I guess you can pick up this car tomorrow. I'll leave it parked by my house. I wouldn't bother them if I were you. He's in a mood."

"Yeah? I heard them breaking things. So what else is new. Hey, *chica*, want to go to the movies later? I mean, tomorrow?" He gave her a look he probably thought was seductive. It was a change from their usual relationship, which was Carmen pretending he did not exist. His come-on would have been funny in another situation, from another man. But Blasio was never funny, at least not by intent.

She knew Blasio watched when he could. He was a voyeur and she didn't want to think about what else.

She put on a big smile while, behind her back, she fumbled around in a bag, desperately groping. Her hand finally closed around the long cool neck of a glass bottle. She pulled out the tequila, ignoring his invitation. He never noticed there was a baby among the mass of junk she'd stuffed in the back seat. The night, the rain, the hour, Blasio's hormones, and especially the tequila all helped.

"He said to give this to you."

Blasio's face lit up like a sunrise in Tequila.

"The good stuff," he said with delight, dropping all mention of interest in Carmen. He didn't bother to wait, but uncorked the wired top, fumbling a bit as he tilted the bottle. Carmen rolled up the window and inched the car closer to the gate.

Blasio yelled something about coming to get the car, but the torrent washed the words away. She kept going, but slowly. She was afraid she'd run into the gate. Streams of water ran over the pajama-clad guard who stood hunched against the rain, easing it closed almost before she was clear of it. Carmen crouched low in the seat as she drove on, wondering what he could see. He seemed more interested in getting out of the rain than in detaining her. He and Blasio got into some kind of shouting match, but she left it behind without a second thought and drove on into the pouring rain toward a new future for herself and her infant nephew.

Chapter Fifteen

Trigger Oliver had been roused from a cozy bed by a call from Cain down at the station, giving him the address of a crime scene on the outskirts of Nogales. He'd have preferred to stay in bed, listening to rain on the roof instead of Cain's curt summary of the ambulance driver's description of a female victim on the bed, and male victim on the floor. He wasn't exactly thrilled at the prospect of driving through the deluge instead. Fueled by a thermos of black coffee, he'd managed to arrive before sunrise, well ahead of the rest of the investigative team, but long after the ambulance had carted away the gunshot victims. He'd gone to bed grouchy and had woken up no less so, not that he would allow his mood make his investigation any less professional. Rarely was there drama such as this in Nogales, and that was the very reason he'd recently relocated here from Tucson. He still hadn't unpacked the boxes piled in the crummy room he'd rented close to the station. Nogales was supposed to be such a sleepy little old-world town. Somebody lied. Maybe he should have stayed in the bigger city. But no, he had left behind his small, wood-frame house where his ex-wife and her new husband were living now. They were like a splinter he couldn't reach, just enough to make him miserable whenever he got close to getting over it. He had supposed leaving Tucson would help, but it hadn't yet.

Driving out past the outskirts of Nogales in the rain, he'd imagined the call was to some country house, a farm house, a little bungalow. It was a good hour's drive, and he took his time. When he'd seen the ramshackle wood-framed farmer's bunkhouse from the road, he was busy patting himself on the back over his own cleverness, and taken by surprise when the victim's actual residence had loomed into view—his guess could not have been more wrong. It was some kind of Mexican palace, complete with a medieval fiefdom—a full complement of field hands, protecting their downed arch lord like some kind of reverse "The king is dead, long-live-the-king" ritual, although, judging by the comments, the king must have been a real son of a bitch. A bunch of vaqueros straight out of the history books opened the gate for him, although there were among them, a couple of young hot heads who looked like they were playing dress-up mobsters straight out of Chicago.

"You the detective?" one of them asked, looking as grizzled and out of time as a frontiersman from the 1800s.

He nodded in affirmation.

Chapter Sixteen

Carmen turned the car around and headed south. The rain was coming from every direction, in torrents, reminding her of pictures of Juanacatlán Falls. Occasionally, she glanced into the back seat where Mario was safely nestled.

Suddenly everything changed. Maybe she'd glanced away from the road one time too many. One minute she was on the road, driving like a normal person; the next, the car felt as if it had rammed a rubber wall. She heard the distinctive smack of water impact. The headlights revealed two sky borne streams of water arcing from twin collisions with the tires. The pavement was submerged, then gone. The car was caught up like a skiff in the advance guard of a flash flood of muddy water. She was still steering as if the pavement would reappear, as if she could see where they were going as they spun around in the dark.

"Oh, come on," Carmen said, looking up at the sky. "Who the hell builds a road in the middle of a ditch, anyway?"

They were caught in the current of storm water that overflowed the ditch that ran by the side of the road. Only heaven knew now where the road actually was. She was still steering, though nothing she was doing with the steering wheel was of any use. She could have benefitted from a rudder, sails, and oars.

Mario was quiet in the back seat. Maybe he didn't mind being flung around by the current, but Carmen was terrified. The car spun and rocked like a floating battering ram, moving faster and faster, slamming into trees and who knows what else was out there. Her own car would never have survived the impact. She released her pointless death grip on the wheel. She'd have to get the baby and get out of the car before they sank or worse. Making her way over the seat was like trying to climb a running horse. Thank goodness Papi had made sure she could swim. She would be swimming in a moment, whether she liked it or not.

But Mario! How could she save the baby? Just born, to die like this. She had to act.

She thought of those moments with her sister showing off all her baby gifts and an image flashed in her mind. The infant carrier. She tore frantically through the baby bags until she came to a band of cloth. It was a tourist item, wrapped and labeled for those on the Sonora side of Nogales, with an illustration of how to wrap it, but not one that said how to keep from losing an infant while you were swimming. No problem. Before she was ten, her mother had her training new moms how to wrap babies in a sling. She tore off her jacket and shirt. December bit into her wet skin. Wearing only her bra, she held up the carrier, looking at buckles and straps that made no sense to her. She ripped open a seam and wrapped it the way she knew, like a double hammock, in a way that made a seat facing her for the baby. She wrapped it around herself and tied off the knot. She picked up the sleeping baby, who awakened and fussed at being disturbed and at her awkwardness in fitting him in securely. The fabric engulfed him. Her clammy skin made him wail, but soon there was heat between them. She found and tugged on one of Elena's maternity shirts, mostly buttoned it, and did the same to her jacket as far as it would go. She knew under the clothes was the wrong way to wear this, but if she ended up in the water, she didn't want a single chance that Mario would be washed away.

He nuzzled angrily. She'd first intended to place him crosswise against her, but instead, his feet hung down and his head pillowed naturally against her breast. In spite of the day's crazy cascade of events and her roiling emotions, there was room in her to feel something else. An ache of tenderness grew somewhere in the region of her heart. She wadded up the sling instructions and jammed them into her pocket. She'd study them later to see if there were benefits to wearing it another way, assuming there would be a later.

"Auntie can't feed you, little one. At least I can keep you warm."

Carmen pulled the cloth secure, adjusted

the buttons on the shirt and jacket, and hoped she would not have to swim. If she did, at least her hands would be free.

She almost opened the door, but then wondered if the vehicle were afloat or the charging tide of water was shallower than it seemed. Then there was a crash that nearly knocked her out, and a grinding noise. The choice was made for her. They stopped moving or at least stopped progressing in a direction. The left front end seemed to be wedged into something, though the car was still bouncing and flailing in the current, bucking like a horse with an unwanted rider. She couldn't see what was holding it in place, but at that moment, the rain stopped. The car was caught in a slow inexorable river of water and mud.

She braced herself against the bucking car and opened the passenger door. Beyond the water's edge, she could see what looked like solid ground rushing past. It would just mean a little leap to safety. Wait…she was forgetting the baby's stuff. First she must get that out. She groped for and found the green bag. She started tossing whatever she could reach to the bank, the nursing bag, followed by the suitcase, the bag with Mario's bottles. Some things fell directly into the flow and were washed away. While her attention was tuned inside, the car was buffeted from without by a hard, massive impact that knocked her to the floor. A tree trunk? Another car? Beyond knowing it was big and heavy, Carmen was unable to discern. It slammed into the car, knocking them into a pivot. The car surfed a half-dozen feet downstream, sweeping the open door and ripping it away. The car tipped and rocked, grinding. It threw her from side to side, slamming her sides and back against the seat and roof.

Hinged by something that caught the bumper, the car swung in a half-circle. Now, instead of dry land, water rushed past the doorless opening, an invisible and deadly flood of death. The bank was now beside the other door. Carmen got splashed as water rushed at her; she moved as far from the opening as she could get—the driver's side seemed to be perched at a higher tilt.

Metal creaked, horribly. The car shifted. They could be washed away at any second. She slipped the last bag she saw over her shoulder, but it unbalanced her. The door nearest the ground would not open. She tried it, rattling the handle. Jammed. She wanted to cry. It was too much. The last straw.

The window rolled down easily enough. She shoved out the bag that had been throwing her off balance. Cradling the baby with one arm, she crawled awkwardly through, water and wind battering her from head to toe, launching a stream of cold water down her back. She perched on her bottom in the window and took a breath.

"So far, so good," she told the baby.

The narrow edge of the door beneath her hurt, but felt almost stable until the car groaned and shifted. She braced her feet against the door, and one hand against the top of the open window. Beneath her, the car shuddered.

She took a flying leap—maybe more like a falling leap.

Carmen landed on one hand, her knees

and face in sandy muck, one arm wrapped securely around the baby. She was all in motion scrambling forward, and a good thing, too, even though she was pile-driving her own face into the mud. It got her out of the way as some lethal projectile on the car brushed harmlessly above her back. Mario wasn't thrilled with the change in logistics, but he was uninjured.

From the hips down, Carmen dripped cold water, magnifying winter's chill to a fine point. The temperature and texture of the mud made her realize she'd been drying off from her earlier dousing and now was wet all over, all over again. The mud made a clinging, sucking noise as she stood. Backing another six feet from the water's edge, she wiped great chunks of muck off her face. She was cold, wet, and filthy, and Mario was screaming but alive.

She didn't see any of the bags she'd tossed. It was time to start beating the bushes. Once she was upright, Mario was completely unconcerned.

Carmen wiped her palms on the driest part of her skirt and looked behind her. The car was gone. Nothing remained but a contortion of twisted metal wrenched from the Buick's front end. The rest had washed downstream. She made her way along the bank to gather what she could.

Chapter Seventeen

Trigger pulled out a cigarette and started smoking. He'd been meaning to quit, but waiting for some drunken vaquero to lead him to the scene of a bloody homicide was not the time. The grizzled Bronco Billy type who'd taken charge of the milling herd of cowboys and street toughs let out a cackle, then hollered, "Eber!"

Eber turned out to be an insubordinate brown-suited puppy, neither vaquero nor street tough, but a kid on the cusp of becoming one or the other, dressed in a raincoat and what looked like soaked pajama bottoms. He was indignant about being elected as the detective's escort and wanted to get back inside. The rest of the crew got back to whatever they were doing before he'd arrived—milling around in the rain, joining forces with a truck full of cowboys to repel some internal faction that was arriving. On the basis of his prior experience with family squabbles in general, he guessed that maybe the target was the boss's relatives—a plump married couple looking extremely out of place. The crew barred the new arrivals from invading the gatehouse.

Typical mob family dynamics. Trigger yelled in their direction, but he was out-yelled by a crack of thunder.

Three of the crew passed him coming back from the main house, carrying a couple of broken tiles that had been blown off the roof. He could hear them grousing amongst themselves. They were workmen and dressed as such, a marked contrast to the blue-jeaned cowboys and wanna-be mobsters.

"Damn roof."

"Every time it rains."

"You know he found a picture of this house in a magazine. Had to have it. Hired an architect from Tucson to come down here and change it to look like..." he gestured loosely toward the house.

"Yeah, well, I ain't complaining. If he didn't have to have his digs just like they is, maybe he wouldn't need no tile roofers on staff year-round. I ain't complainin' long as I got a job."

One of them turned back toward the house.

"Where you goin'?"

"To get the ladder."

"Nah. I got it tied down good. Leave it. We'll have to go put more tarp on the roof later anyway. Heck, ain't hardly no reason to even dry off, not till this storm is done, cause we gonna be in it all night."

Across the yard, tension was brewing.

Trigger volunteered some advice. "Take a powder, people. The poor guy's being raced to the hospital on the cusp of death. He's not gonna sweat it over the roof." He wasn't sure anyone was listening, but one of the cowboys aimed a thumbs-up in his direction.

"Poor guy?" someone said, "He don't know the boss."

"Good thing he didn't hear you say that."

One of the workmen stopped. "Work's gotta be done right away. You don't gaff off Francisco's standing orders. Not if you like breathing."

Trigger nodded, and yelled into the crowd, "Then interpret it this way. It's a crime scene. No one allowed in."

Another thumbs-up.

Some of the cowboy wannabes fired handguns into the air. Shootout at the Nogales corral. He could have flashed his badge and taken them all in, but he was just here to investigate the murder. He wasn't about to get himself embroiled in some domestic matter that meant a lot of paperwork. The sight and sound of guns had taken the heat out of the relatives though, one of whom reminded him of his ex-mother-in-law.

Tucson was starting to look pretty damn normal by comparison. When he'd gotten to Nogales, he hadn't expected the whole department to be crooked, but it was. The hell of it was that it all seemed to be under the thumb of one guy Trigger hadn't been around long enough to meet. He'd heard the name, though. Sanchez. Same family as this guy here, maybe even the same guy.

As his business was in the hacienda, he

ignored the pending riot—or hanging—and silently bore the chilling shower that showed no sign of ever stopping. Eber led him up a gravel path, ignoring the front entrance, and headed for a side gate to the courtyard, taking the long way around.

"Not the front door?"

"Taking you to the crime scene, right? Straight to it."

Eber looked at him sideways with a scornful expression curling his lip and continued down the path toward a stand of trees. The water didn't seem to deter him. He didn't even seem aware of being soaked as he shook a massive iron gate that clanged and did not open. He fumbled in his pocket and pulled out a massive, old-fashioned gate key.

"Shit."

"So Eber, tell me about the relatives."

"I don't know shit. All I do is work the gate."

"I'm sure you know more than you think you do."

"Okay, well, they turned up. They live close by in Sonora. Said they were first cousins. They weren't that close relationship-wise. I man that gate every day, and I never seen 'em before. If they was close, I'd have seen 'em."

"Yeah, I get what you mean. Go on."

"The whole town came to the boss's wedding a while back, but those two weren't there." He gestured to the woman, now out of sight. "Her I'd have remembered."

Her hair was bleached an improbable blondee, cut short in painfully rigid ringlets and topped a tiny pillbox hat with bedraggled feathers. Her jacket had shoulders puffed to her ears. She was old enough to know better.

"Yeah, she'd be hard to forget," Trigger agreed.

Chapter Eighteen

For a good hour, maybe two, Carmen paced the bank of the arroyo, looking for what she'd tossed out. She'd found the bag with Mario's bottles and the suitcase and bag with the money. There were some baby clothes scattered around. Her purse was gone, along with her identification. And, of course, the Buick. She had no choice but to trudge back to Nogales to get her car. On foot. In the rain. Lugging a baby and assorted bags over some forty miles in terrible weather, it might take her days to get home.

"Well, *mijo*, it looks like we're going for a walk."

Mario didn't answer.

She knew from experience that it took an hour, with Blasio's lead foot on the gas, to drive to town from the rancho. With the baby and everything she had to carry, it was going to feel like it was taking forever, especially if she stayed off the roads.

There was no one around, so she adjusted her buttons to give Mario more air. As he gazed up at her solemnly with his baby-green Elena eyes, she knew she would do anything to keep him safe.

She shouldered the bags and set out. Dawn had broken along with her life, but all she could see were storm clouds ahead.

Chapter Nineteen

The rain bothered Trigger Oliver, whose sodden trench coat slapped at his legs with each step. He stepped off the path into what amounted to an ankle-deep stream where, under the trees, the rain seemed to have abated a bit. A massive wrought iron gate came into view. In the distance, the single gate appeared to be no larger than an ordinary door to a house, but it was curved, fitted into a curved stucco arch, and composed of a lacy pattern of interwoven curlicues.

The gate was set into a wall adjoining the house. On either side, twin streams of water gushed from gutters and pipes into overflowing wooden barrels. The rush of water on either side gave Trigger the momentary sensation of walking through a waterfall. He angled his head down, not that it actually helped him dodge the sheets of rain, not lifting his face until, after several

clumsy tries, Eber managed to successfully maneuver the key. The gate creaked.

The gate swung open to reveal the kind
of courtyard he'd only seen in history books. Trigger Oliver felt as if he had stepped back in time
to an earlier century and a different country. He
stood with his mouth hanging open, dumb-
founded. The courtyard was surrounded on all
four sides by a porch that ringed the interior of
the hacienda, punctuated by dozens of doors protected by eaves. Bedrooms, and maybe other
rooms, faced the cobbled center with its wrought
iron benches and tables, plethora of potted plants,
outdoor fireplaces, and statuary. More than a
dozen French doors leading into the house stared
back, shining like obsidian in this light, reflecting
back the beam of his flashlight without revealing
what was inside. It looked more like an elegant,
deserted hotel from eighteenth-century Spain
than an American residence on the brink of 1949.

His guide turned the knob on one of
those doors.

"Hold it," Trigger said. "What is it you

do here again?"

"I'm a guard. I told ya." He swallowed, and when he did, his Adam's apple rolled in his throat not unlike a yoyo.

"Been here long?"

"A while. Since before the boss got hitched."

"So you should have seen something, if you're a guard."

"Not that kind of guard. I just open the gate and..."

"And?"

"...close the gate." His nervousness was palpable. "Look, I didn't see nothing. If I seen something, I'd sing like Ethel Merman. Honest."

Trigger pointed at the garden gate they'd come through.

"Was that open when the crime occurred?"

"I don't think so, but you'd have to ask Manuela. The housekeeper. She's who unlocked the house so we could let in the cops." He shoved the door. It slid few inches, caught short by the sheers. "She found them, came screaming down the driveway into the gatehouse."

"And where is she?"

"She rode in the ambulance with the boss."

"Don't move," the detective said sharply, tugging Eber backwards and out of the way. "I don't want more footprints disrupting the crime scene."

His command elicited a shrug from Eber, whose glance at the carpet telegraphed an urge to jump around on the floor, disrupting footprints.

The detective took off his sopping shoes and left them outside on a wooden table under the overhang. He stepped over the threshold into the master bedroom in his stocking feet, into the scene of the crime. The sensation of carpet was warm and plush, a welcome relief against his clammy socks. He left Eber pacing the cobblestones outside, his path clinging close to the wall and its protective overhang. The wind played at the drapery and moaned like a wounded woman as the storm wound down.

Any number of people had been in this room since the crime had occurred late in the night or early in the morning. Trigger avoided the chaos of bloody footprints in the vacuumed carpet. They led down the hall. He could make out the path where two men had put the bodies on stretchers and walked them to the ambulance. The maid had not walked through blood, but her smaller tracks disturbed the lay of the carpet. She'd been here to discover and report the body in a hysterical call to the police station. That made at least three people here to disrupt the evidence.

He was drawn to the dark stains that had soaked into the depths of the fawn wool carpet—a multiplicity of stains from a multiplicity of wounds, all apparently from one body.

The mark of the other victim was across the room, where brighter red stood out against the white sheets of the bed, spreading from the headboard halfway down, its path vaguely outlining the half-shape of a woman. A startling quantity of blood soaked as far as the middle of the mattress and stopped abruptly, visually a shock on this beautiful bed—something out of a magazine, except for the gore, of course. Egyptian cotton, embroidery, lace, satin. A blanket across the midrange of the mattress must have been removed. The bullet that had exited the female victim's head was embedded in the wall, marking where she had been before her body had been carted off. There was no sign of another bullet around her.

The detective stared at the stains silently for an interminable time, gave his head a mournful shake. He glanced back at his young guide, whose shadow had stopped moving as he stood under a ledge that protected him from the driving rain.

Detective Trigger Oliver was good at his job. Twenty years the detective's junior, he summed up Eber practically at a glance. He could see the boy was impatient to be elsewhere. Like most of the rancho's crew, Eber was probably from town, where there were few jobs available, so he probably counted himself lucky to have a wage for doing whatever it was that he did at the rancho. Oliver's imagination filled in the blanks based on what little interaction he'd seen. As low man on the totem pole, Eber would frequently get the shit jobs no one else wanted to deal with, like this one—taking the big dick to the big house. No doubt, he would have preferred being in his bed at this early hour and in this lousy weather. With the crowd facing off outside, bedtime for Eber wasn't happening any time soon.

Trigger snapped photos from every angle and distance.

The French door he'd entered through swung back and forth in the wind. Oliver caught it and opened it to ask his drenched escort, "So, what happened here?"

"It's obvious, ain't it?"

"What's obvious?"

"He shot her, and then himself."

"You got it all figured out."

The detective crouched to examine the bloody footprints, took another picture, and stood. He paced around the bedroom, walked around the bed a few times, and jotted a reminder in his notebook to have someone pull the shell from its location low in the wall behind the bed.

An airy bit of translucent drapery fabric fluttered in the breeze from the open doors to the patio. A cool, wet morning, but warm for December. The sky was brightening. Not dawn yet, but it would be soon.

His eye caught a photo, presumably of the couple. The husband was old enough to be her father, a cliché, but nevertheless true—an older man with a brutish look about him. The wife was young, delicate, and more than pretty. Even caught in the frame, she was vivacious, sparkling.

Trigger turned back to Eber. "Do you have another key?"

Eber lifted the key ring, showing some smaller keys dwarfed beside the wrought iron monstrosity of a gate key.

"Go open the garage door to the house, and meet me down the hall."

Eber frowned at the rain. "But..."

Oliver slammed the door and turned the bolt. He made his way carefully around the edge of the master bedroom, then down the hall. Some scratches in the wood floor trailed from the nearest door which he opened. It smelled of paint, the windows hung with white curtains across which a rainbow of bright ponies danced. The floor was scuffed with furniture drag marks, but the room was empty. He wondered when the scratches had been made in the otherwise perfectly polished wooden floor. The ponies on the curtains seemed to indicate a child's room but without the wear and tear one might expect. He knelt to drag his thumb across a scuff, and the mark disappeared. He shut that door and moved on to the next, continued opening the closed doors and peering inside at impersonal, hotel-like bedrooms, none of which were empty of furnishings. Bloody footprints led into one of the last rooms—an office, by the look of it. He checked every door along the way. He glanced into a shabby apartment that could only be maid's quarters, snapped a photo of the unmade bed, but did not go in.

Trigger was perusing Francisco's office by the time Eber made his way back inside. In the office, he found stacks of papers. An empty liquor bottle lay on its side on the big desk, beside a single small glass turned face-down. Someone had been drinking alone and had spilled some liquor on the floor.

"Hey, you're supposed to wait for me," Eber complained. "You're supposed to be following me, not going off half-cocked."

"Hah," Oliver said. "You made a joke."

"A joke?" A blank look crossed Eber's face. He was obviously unaware of the detective's name. Trigger let it pass.

"Forget it."

Eber didn't like being dismissed and made a weak attempt to take back his presumed authority. "You shouldn't be in Señor Sanchez's office. No one is allowed in his office."

"No one?"

"Hardly ever, and never without Señor Sanchez."

"Perhaps we should make an exception since I'm here to investigate your Señor Sanchez's shooting. Which brings me to a point... Do you know why anyone would want to shoot him?" Judging by the wealth on display elsewhere, this was no doubt the same Sanchez who owned the police department. There were probably hundreds of people who would like to see Señor Sanchez dead.

Eber paled. "I can't even imagine—"

"Then don't. I'm only interested in facts, not what comes out of your imagination. I'm done here, but I'll be back. No one is to touch anything. Is there a garage? In that direction, I suppose?"

"Yeah."

"Let's go see if any vehicles are missing."

Then he'd have to go lean on this Manuela to hear what she had to say.

Chapter Twenty

Carmen didn't want to be seen trudging through the city looking like something an alley cat wouldn't touch with a ten-foot claw. Her hair had already been soaked and dried twice, and now it cascaded in frizzy ringlets, frosted with mud. With the baby in her shirt, she looked like she had grown a nine month pregnancy overnight. Someone would notice. It was hours before she'd get to town, though.

Some time during the day across endless desert and fields, it had begun storming again. She'd stopped in a utility shed full of corn to wait it out. She might have dozed off. She fed Mario, relieved that she had plenty of full eight-ounce bottles. He was barely drinking two ounces at a time. Because of the weather, she slacked on changing his diapers. How was she going to wash them? She'd have to figure it out as she went. The only good thing about it being December was that the milk wasn't going bad, and there was enough to last a while.

It had been dark, and now it was light again. All she knew for certain was that her arms were killing her and, if this had been a normal day, she would have been at work already. That she wasn't behind her desk was going to get the gossip mill rolling—until someone found Elena. Maybe the police had already been to the hacienda. She couldn't let herself think about that or she'd be crying again.

The suitcase full of money seemed to weigh as much as a car. The baby bag full of absorbent cotton diapers had more than done their job and were carrying an impressive amount of flood water. She had squeezed them out and hung them for a while in the shed, and though she hadn't stayed as long as needed for them to actually dry, they were pounds lighter when she set off toward Nogales again.

Eventually, she made her way back into town. She took her time, walking through brush, and fields, backyards and alleys, skirting neighborhoods where she was known. Now that she was close, she thought about making her way home through the tunnels. It would be safer, but the twisting route was anything but a shortcut. A good portion of it would be at a crawl through narrow burrows more suited to animals than humans. It would be hard to negotiate that with a newborn tucked into her shirt. Just the thought made her claustrophobic. She really did not like tight places, but it might be necessary.

Before she got to the tunnel entrance, it started raining again. At least it washed off the mud.

She had to cross the street to reach the entrance behind the feed shop. Her luck had run out again. Ambrose had parked his police cruiser where he had a full view of the street. It looked as if he were waiting for something, and that something might be her, since sometimes she walked this way while going to work. She had no idea if his interest in her was still social, or he was planning on her being his next collar. Were they looking for her? She had no idea and didn't want to find out.

Just as Carmen was about to give up, luck seemed to be with her. Ambrose had dozed off, his head tilted back, his snores echoing all the way to the narrow alley where she hid. After walking right past him and braving the opening of the rear door of the feed store, which led not to the store but to a basement that opened to a corridor... her luck changed yet again. Looking down into the black basement gave her chills, and she could see in far enough to tell it was flooded. The whole tunnel must be submerged.

Damn, damn and damn.

Taking the back alley, she half-ran, half-walked toward the corner bodega, turning away when the early delivery trucks rolled past her. It was all uphill and she was out of breath, but almost there. But Blasio was parked at the foot of the path to her front door. If he was waiting to pick up the Buick, he'd have a long wait. She scanned up and down the sidewalk, wondering where she might be able to hide until he went away.

What was he still doing there? Wasn't he drowning in that bottle of tequila she'd given him? But no. That was at least 24 hours ago, maybe longer. It felt a lifetime ago, but she'd bet money Blasio was still working off the hangover.

She had spent every minute since the baby's birth and Elena's death just trying to stay alive, something that was getting increasingly hard to do. She yawned hugely. Had Mario been born last night or the night before? She'd walked a day and a night, at least. She squatted in the alley, leaning against the brick wall with her eyes shut, and forced down another yawn. She'd dozed in that shed, but the nap hadn't been all that long.

"I'm losing it," she said to Mario. "I need to find a newspaper just to see what day it is."

Since Mario's birth, she had survived her sister's murder, murdered her brother-in-law, stolen a fortune in dirty money and a baby, swiped a car, surfed the car through wild whitewater hurtling over a formerly dry creek bed, lost the car but saved the baby, survived a monsoon (at least, a monsoon for Nogales), acquired a mouth to feed, and was on the run for her life. How many felonies was that? She thought perhaps she could be forgiven for losing track of time.

Okay. Blasio was out there. He was parked, but he didn't look conscious. His head seemed to be slumped over the steering wheel. Why wasn't he still at the rancho? She had no clue why he would be waiting at her doorstep. He was the kind to go on a tequila binge until he was sent for. Maybe someone at the rancho had called for the drowned car. Not Francisco, since he was still dead. Okay: Mario had been born at least 24 hours ago, maybe a day and a half, since it was morning again. Maybe the police were investigating the deaths at the rancho by now. But if that was the case, why weren't police at her door? Maybe the police had asked questions, and that was why Blasio was nosing around. It didn't matter who was looking for her now. Eventually, when they realized she was missing, the police would be on her trail. She needed to disappear, and fast.

But Blasio was sitting out there, blocking her way like the Rock of Gibraltar. His presence prevented her from reaching her own vehicle. He was still expecting to fetch Francisco's car. Good luck with that.

Carmen leaned against the brick wall of the alley, letting her eyes fall shut again. She was so tired. If she just had her keys, she would drive away, Blasio be damned, but she didn't know how to hotwire her car. She should look on the bright side. If her keys had been in her purse, they would be lost with her wallet and ID, probably in Sonora by now, or maybe in the Gulf of California. At least the keys were hanging inside her house.

Maybe there was a set of stairways she could sit under until Blasio went away. It was a good thing she hadn't taken Francisco's gun. If she had it, maybe the stranger who had taken over her body would shoot Blasio, too. Or else she would wake up and this whole nightmare would be a dream. That would be good. If she could shut her eyes, maybe she would wake up to a normal day, lying on her clean sheets in her own bed.

Someone tapped her on her shoulder.

Carmen jumped. She had all but dozed off, and now sprang awake. Dropped the bags and put her hands up. Turned. Found herself face to face with the ancient owner of the bodega. At the sight of Papi Pasquel, warm relief poured through her, melting the icy chill of terror. She wanted to hug him. She wanted to cry on his shoulder and be seven years old again. She stood tall and put her hands down. She picked up the bags.

"Mr. Pasquel. Good morning."

The old man looked her over, a veil of sadness and anger shuttering his eyes.

"This has something to do with Francisco," he said softly, looking from her swelling shirt to her soaking shoes. "I know that look." He should know. He'd been a father seven times over and a grandparent many times more than that. He knew what a baby in a sling looked like.

"Elena's?" he asked softly.

"Don't ask."

He would have done anything for her. She was pretty sure that every time he saw her, he also saw the face of his little granddaughter, bound like all the girls to be Francisco's future victim. And maybe he saw the face of her grandmother, whom it was rumored he'd once been sweet on.

"I've got to get out of here," she said. "But my keys are hanging in the kitchen, and I need my car."

He turned his head toward her house, saw Blasio waiting.

"Vulture." He spat on the ground and crossed himself before giving Carmen a pat on her shoulder and leading her into the dark clutter in the back of the bodega, with its homey ambiance. Moments later, one of his Pasquel grandsons went to her house carrying a cardboard box of groceries, as he so frequently did on other occasions when she was off at work. Only this time, the box was empty, and he went into her kitchen, and snatched her car keys.

Another Pasquel grandson everyone

called Junior had been sent to distract Blasio during the daring caper, but he came back almost immediately and announced that caution was unnecessary. Blasio was drunk on his ass, and it would have taken a mariachi band to wake him. He and another guy were passed out in the front seat of his car with a bottle of tequila between them. Junior also came back with a tale to tell.

"So I found Blasio and some other bum, dead drunk in a car full of tequila bottles, and barely made it into the bushes—"

Two in the car. Carmen realized that Blasio would have needed someone else to pick up the sedan had it been where it was supposed to be. She considered herself twice lucky to have evaded them. She hoped that maybe the police weren't involved yet, but she had finely honed instincts, and knew from the Pasquels' shared looks that they knew something more. Papi Pasquel verified it when he confided, "We've all been looking for you."

"But that's not all," Junior continued. "A plainclothes cop came beating on your door. I dived for the bushes."

"What makes you think he was a cop?" his brother asked. "You got x-ray vision and can see his cop underpants?"

"Funny." Junior smirked. "I knew on account of how after he quit knocking, he looked in at Blasio's car, and then went up to Guzman's car, and kicked him awake; and tore a blue streak over him sleeping on a stake out. Then Guzman got pissed off, pulled out a pad and wrote a ticket and put it on Blasio's car. Didn't wake them up, though."

The Pasquel brothers were a mischievous pair, with a prankish history that made them well-acquainted with the whole police force. They never confronted authority directly but had a long history of doing things that made the corrupt boss of the police department scratch his head.

After Guzman and the new cop had left, the brothers cooked up the scheme of pushing Blasio's car out of the way and coasting Carmen's car down the hill where she could start it out of Blasio's earshot. In its place, they put a rusted-out Ford jalopy, a model that had a decade or two on Carmen's well-kept car. It had been through a dozen owners and was currently the nighttime resting place of a homeless drunken refugee from Utah, and looked it.

As she got in her car and drove away, she wondered what Blasio would think when he woke up. Likely he'd be too drunk to figure out what had happened and when.

Back on the road in the car, Mario was cozy in an old wicker bassinet. Carmen had been down to her last bottle, but Mr. Pasquel had given her a tin of sugar and cans of evaporated milk, and she'd prepared a dozen bottles while hiding behind the counter. He had refused payment, but when he'd been distracted, she'd stuck a whole packet of hundred-dollar bills in the register. It might be more money than had passed through the register since the store's inception as a trading post.

She thought about returning to the arroyo to try to gather more of Mario's stuff, but the arroyo actually was the road to the rancho, and if it weren't still under ten feet of rushing water, there would probably be someone driving on it who would recognize her in her car. She settled for stopping at a strange gas station where no one knew her to pick up a map of Mexico. Once she crossed the border, she'd find her way. From the way the cashier looked at her, though, she realized she had to change her clothes; the dark pants and shirt she wore were stained, damp, and muddy. Her hair was a filthy mess. She thought about home, her closet of clean clothes, her bathroom with its bars of hard soap and clean towels. Then it struck her. She couldn't go back now. She'd never be able to go back.

It hurt. The road home was still warm with her footprint, but she could never return. She wished she'd had the Pasquels grab Papi's guitar and the lace mantilla Mama had sometimes worn to church. She'd miss home.

And Elena, Elena, Elena.

Her heart bled. She looked at Mario. Her back straightened. They'd manage, somehow.

She reached the exit to the south road,

but before she took the turn, she saw a bunch of Francisco's cronies. It didn't matter if they were after her already or if this was a bunch out to drink and whore around at their usual bar. She couldn't let them see her. She took an evasive route and went east.

That's when the police car began following her. She slowed, but didn't stop until it flashed its lights. The slower she went, the faster her heart raced.

Carmen pulled over and sat with the car in neutral as the officer approached. She glanced in the mirror to check the backseat and, without changing her stance, made an effort to be stealthy—tugged a wispy blanket till it draped over the wicker basket the Pasquels had given her. If one didn't look too closely, it might pass as a pile of laundry, as long as the laundry didn't start screaming. Her purse and wallet were somewhere in the arroyo. All she had was a suitcase full of wet money and Elena's wallet. Either one would be a genius thing to pull out, and send her straight to jail. But she hadn't been speeding. Then why had he stopped her? They must know already. She wondered how terrible it would be in jail.

Some criminal she was turning out to be. Her heart raced a mile a minute, but her brain was in reverse.

Tap. Tap.

The policeman, at her window.

Her heart leapt in her throat.

She was seconds away from being hand-cuffed, jailed, her baby nephew taken away and given to strangers, or worse, a bunch of Sanchez demons.

She put her foot lightly on the gas. Foot on the clutch. Hand on the gear.

Looked left.

Straight into the worried eyes of Ambrose.

Her racing heart eased. It was just Ambrose, again. She could have kissed him. Well. It was Ambrose. Maybe not.

She rolled down the window.

"Hi there, Señorita Garcia," Ambrose said. "I guess you're just coming from delivering a baby in another county. Looks like this was a tough one." He smiled, but there was a strained look on his face.

He seemed troubled about something. His speech was hesitant, and as he looked back at his patrol car, he seemed almost nervous. She focused directly on him, wishing she could read minds or something. Earlier in the day, his car had been parked on the route from her house to work. Had he been waiting for her? But if he knew she was on the run, wouldn't he have his cuffs out by now?

"It's funny how they always come at night." She smiled at him but it felt like her face was going to crack.

She held that smile.

Just as he always did, he asked her out.

"Aren't you dating that new hairdresser in town?"

He looked surprised. "Well, I..."

"It's ok," Carmen said. "It's not like either of us is married."

"We went out a couple of times," he admitted, but then looked at her earnestly. "But she's not you."

He asked her for a date to the next church dance. Then he wanted to chat. His sister was having a baby, and she couldn't decide if she needed a midwife or wanted to go to the hospital in Tucson. Maybe Carmen could chat her up, give her some advice.

"I'm so sorry, Ambrose. I'm going to my cousin Chad's in Puerto Vallarta. His wife is due in a month with her first, and is having a hard time."

His face fell.

Of course, there was no Cousin Chad in Puerto Vallarta. Not that she had anyone in Puerto Vallarta, much less a Cousin Chad. Puerto Vallarta had just popped into her head after looking at the road atlas while trying to figure out a route. Let Ambrose try and find her there. She made a mental note to herself to never go there, not even to visit. Not even to look at it on a map.

"Maybe when you get back, we can go out to the movies. You know I been strong for you for an age."

She heard the basket creak. The baby was awake. She had to get moving before he tuned up.

"That sounds good, Ambrose. When I come back in town, sure, if you haven't made plans with the hairdresser," she agreed, beaming back at him, with a smile that showed every tooth in her head. She was never, ever coming back.

Ambrose tipped his hat back.

"I wish we'd had a chance before this to talk. I'll be taking you up on that movie, Carmen."

"Good," she said. One word, and she felt like she was babbling nonsense.

He took his hand off the ledge of the open window, reached in and with both of his, took her hand, a gesture that startled Carmen. His hands engulfed hers. He felt big, and warm and strong, and made her realize how chilled and alone she was. She'd never given him a chance. How could she have done so, with Francisco in the picture? If she looked at his face again, she was going to cry. He didn't even know he would never see her again.

"Goodbye Carmen," he said softly. "Whatever happens, I will always be here waiting for you."

Chapter Twenty-One

As Carmen circled back toward the border, she watched Ambrose in her mirror. After a while, his lights curved around, and Ambrose drove off.

She was nearly gleeful with relief until she realized he would be boasting about their future date and telling people how he had run into her on the way to Mexico. Damn and damn again. If she hadn't been so nervous, she wouldn't have outed her own escape plans. She was also uneasy about the way he'd said goodbye with such finality to it, in spite of the "date" they'd made.

She turned north. The first sign she saw said "Tucson, 70 Miles." Tucson it was, then.

There was an airport in Tucson. She'd never been on a plane. Carmen had Elena's passport and money enough to build a rocket to the moon, if there were such a thing. But would they be able to find her through the passport? She didn't know. Maybe she would have to stay in the country until she found a criminal she could ask. Where did you find knowledgeable criminals who gave advice? It's not as if they were in the Yellow Pages.

All the way there, her sense of paranoia expanded. Would they look for her in Mexico? Would they follow her to Tucson? It was the nearest big city. They'd find her too easily if she went straight to Tucson and stayed, or went somewhere else straight from Tucson.

But what choice was there? She committed herself to going to Tucson and playing it by ear. Let chance tell her where to go. Surely her fingers had been doing the law's work when she pulled the trigger. Or maybe she had lost her mind, and was deluding herself.

Carmen waffled all through the hour's drive north to Tucson, changing her mind a hundred and thirty-seven times.

She found herself standing in tears in front of a Salvation Army store that had a half-broken baby crib in the window. It was a sad little crib, but it reminded her of the lovely room Elena had put together for Mario, a room he would never know. The agony of grief hit her again. A passing woman with a kind face asked her if she was okay.

Carmen looked at the stranger, and realized that, as she was now a fugitive, standing out here in the open on a sidewalk as if her feet had turned to concrete, making a spectacle of herself was probably not the smartest move of her life.

She barely felt the light weight of the sleeping newborn. The kind-faced woman complimented her on the baby. Said how much he looked like her. The words prompted a wave of tears. Her little nephew didn't feel like the devil-child she'd anticipated. He was like a little piece of Elena, an angel. More people stopped what they were doing to stare at the crying woman holding a baby.

Another well-meaning stranger patted her on her shoulder.

"Don't worry about it, honey, the baby

weight will come off before you know it."

She thought she might laugh hysterically in her face, but instead blindly shoved her way through the crowd forming around her, and into the first door she saw, the secondhand store. She grabbed a stroller, threw some clothes over the back of it, and a garish blonde wig that had seen better days. No one had followed her inside. As long as she was here, she might as well look around; she'd need a change of clothes, wouldn't she? She assembled a small wardrobe for herself. It was still early, and there were no other customers, so the shop girls gathered around, ooed and aahhed over the baby, didn't ask intrusive questions, and threw in so many free clothes for Mario that she didn't know where she would put them.

"It will be okay," they said. "All new mothers are overwhelmed."

She was so overwhelmed in fact that she let them take care of her, disarmed by their kindness. They assumed she had been dumped, and tried to talk her out of the wig and red streetwalker heels. A dark-blonde woman patted her on the back and confided to her that men were all dogs.

"You don't need him, honey. Better to find out now, 'stead of in twenty years when your good years is gone."

One of them mistook her for a woman called Inez who lived in the alley in a packing crate. Another tried to talk her out of walking the streets, and gave her directions to a church where God could find her. In the alley behind the Salvation Army, instead of God, she found Inez, and showed her the title to the car Elena had given her. The Salvation Army shop girl was right. Inez could have been a third sister to Elena and Carmen. It was almost like looking into a mirror, which might be more a statement of her current disarray than any actual likeness. Inez gave her the glimmerings of an idea. If someone she did not know followed her this far, Inez's looks might confuse them.

Inez was more interested in money than conversation, but Carmen asked, "Can you drive?"

"If I haven't forgotten how."

"I don't need my car anymore," Carmen told her. "You can have it. I'm leaving it at the airport. It's full of gas. I'll tie a big white bow on the steering wheel."

Inez smiled and then frowned with the expression of a wounded dog that had been offered treats but got kicked instead—a hundred times.

"Why?"

"It's not like I can take my car on the plane to Mexico," Carmen said. "Since I'm not coming back, I might as well give it to somebody who reminds me so much of my own sister."

She launched into a description of the car. Said Inez could pick it up at the airport in a day or two. She babbled some more imaginary details about her mythical cousin Chad, now in Mexico City. For a guy who didn't exist, Chad sure got around.

At the airport, it seemed like everyone was dressed up. She thought she must look like a refugee from an asylum. But no, according to her reflection in the windows she passed, she looked impossibly normal, if very sad and dirty. She hadn't had a chance to change. Her clothes still needed a wash and looked like she'd been struck by a wrinkle bomb. Behind her reflection, a policeman inside the terminal gave her a hard stare. Something about her had snagged his mental radar. In no way did she look ready for a plane ride. People on planes looked like they were dressed for a party. She looked like she'd been living in a garbage truck, then run over by it, twice. At least it was a problem that was easily solved.

Carmen was tired of hauling everything around, but didn't want to go near the car because it was sure to be found in the airport parking lot. City buses were anonymous—cabs less so. Maybe she could use that to her advantage. She found the address of the city bus stations in the yellow pages.

She left the stroller and suitcases in a locker at the Greyhound bus terminal and used their restroom to get herself partly presentable. With Mario in her arms, she left Greyhound, boarded a Tucson city bus and got off at the first fancy department store she saw, one she'd never been to in her life, though Elena might have been here with Francisco. She purchased and changed into a flashy, tight, short red dress that flaunted cleavage that had never before seen the light of day, long legs no man who knew her (except maybe Ambrose and Francisco) had ever realized she had, and a huge hat. She put on the ridiculously high heels of the kind Elena would call "Fuck Me" shoes—the red ones she'd gotten secondhand, which the good clerks had failed to dissuade her from buying for the princely sum of twenty-five cents. They hurt her feet but frugal Carmen was glad she'd not had to buy them new, since she was intent on wearing them only this once. She bought makeup and let the demonstrator put on so much she could have passed for Mae West or Betty Hutton, not that she actually looked anything like Mae West or Betty Hutton. She was more of a Myrna Loy, but the blonde wig and make-up worked magic. Underneath bleached blonde curls, gobs of makeup, and a floppy hat, she could have been anyone. It was a perfect disguise. She hoped they would lose her trail.

At the airport, she passed the formerly suspicious policeman without anything but her legs catching his eye. She found herself under siege from the long looks of men. Mario was sleeping happily and invisibly in a barrel-shaped carry-on bag. Carmen prayed silently that he would stay quiet, although there was enough noise in the airport to cover any noise he'd make.

In her best Betty Hutton voice (she'd seen "Perils of Pauline" twelve times when Elena had been ushering), Carmen energetically tried to purchase a couple of tickets to Puerto Vallarta. While her imitation wasn't at all like Betty Hutton, she was pretty sure no one in Tucson had seen anything like her, nor were they likely to forget. She complained about the length of the line, asked about where she could eat in the terminal. She argued with the ticket agent who tried to tell her there was no plane directly to the tiny port of Puerto Vallarta; she'd have to fly to Los Angeles and catch a flight there to Balbuena Military Airport in Mexico City, and from there take a bus or a small local plane to the state of Jalisco where Puerto Vallarta was located. When she crossed her arms on the counter and leaned forward, she withdrew from her cleavage a pair of slanted sunglasses. Her breasts rose from her décolleté like double scoops of French vanilla, like melons, like cream before the cat-green eyes of the ticket agent. His eyes widened. Like metal shavings stuck to a magnet, his eyes fixated a foot below her face. He forgot completely what he was talking about, dumbly agreeing with whatever she said. She quietly accepted a handful of tickets and pretended to listen to his babbled instructions.

Maybe he wouldn't remember her face.

To the irritation of the women accompanying them, men stopped to watch her walk past, all of them reminding her eerily of Francisco. Between the counter and the bathroom, at least four passengers and two pilots tried to look down her décolletage, and offered to buy her a drink. She pretended not to hear.

As soon as she reached the bathroom, she wanted to lock the door, but had to wait for the slowest woman on earth to leave.

"I'm going to Mexico," Carmen announced baldly, in her almost-Betty Hutton voice.

"I just got here from Phoenix," the woman said. She was washing her hands, and stopped to get under every nail. She scrubbed up a big head of soap, and foamed her arms.

"What are you, a nurse?" Carmen asked.

"No, why do you ask?"

Carmen shrugged. "Do you not have a bathroom where you live?"

"Certainly I do."

The woman kept washing. She started on her neck, working her way up, and patted her face dry with a paper towel. Carmen thought she was going to stop, but then she pulled some lotion from a giant handbag and started rubbing it on her face.

"That cheap stuff will give you blemishes," Carmen said, and pulled out the cream she'd gotten at the department store.

"Thank you," the woman exclaimed, reaching for the soap.

Carmen knew she'd made a mistake when the woman turned on the water to wash the cheap lotion off her face. She cracked the door open and tossed out the woman's big purse. It was not at all subtle, but the woman wasn't paying attention to anything but her face full of lather. Carmen cleared her throat, but couldn't get her attention.

"Oh, no. Your handbag." Carmen pointed out the door as if it had walked out under its own steam.

"Oh, dear!" Slow Woman abandoned the soap and bent over in the doorway. A blob of froth flopped onto the floor, dissolving.

Carmen might have even given her a little push on the ass so she could lock the door. The woman thumped to get back in.

"Hey! I'm not done!"

At last she was able to unzip the bag. Mario was still sleeping. She knew that was what babies did, but she was glad to get him out into the air and see for herself. In a stall, she kicked off her shoes and quick changed into a dark uniform with a housekeeper's apron. Unlike Slow Woman, it only took a moment to scrub away the heavy makeup, and work her feet into her old loafers. Glad to see her own face and hair, she pulled down the tightly braided bun and fingered the strands into long, loose curls. The thumping stopped.

There was just enough room on the small counter to balance Mario with one hand. With the other, it took but a moment to jam the heels and clothes in the barrel bag, then shove it into a paper grocery bag. As for Mario, she picked him up, and carried him in her arms. She might have come in as Mae West, but she was leaving as a female Charlie Chaplin, complete with orphan.

She unlocked the door and walked out carrying Mario and the paper grocery bag.

Slow Woman was coming back in her direction, dragging a security guard down the hall. She breezed right past Carmen. People see what they expect to see. The security guard tried the door and found it open.

"Problem solved," he said, trying to leave.

Slow Woman, still unaccountably upset she'd been locked out, ran up to Carmen.

"Did you see a blonde come out of there? There was a woman in there, and she locked me out and threw my purse in the hall."

"*¿Qué?*"

Carmen suddenly lost her recall of English. The woman was hanging onto her arm, jostling it. The corner of the red dress poked up out of the barrel bag stuffed into the grocery bag. She wanted to fix it, but didn't have a free hand to do it with. She adjusted her hold on Mario. He woke up and started crying, a confused, new-born-infant kind of cry.

"Now look what you did," the security guard said, in the voice of a man who had children of his own. "You woke her baby. There's certainly no blonde in there now. Maybe she boarded a flight."

"Surely someone saw her. Where did she go? She locked me out! Why did she throw my purse down? Maybe she took something." She turned from the guard back to Carmen accusingly. "Did you see a woman in a red dress? She didn't just disappear. Woman. Red. Dress." She spoke slowly and loudly as if Carmen were deaf.

"*¿Qué?*" Carmen repeated. She was losing her grip on the paper bag. Any minute, it was going to fall to the floor and the dress was going to fall out in front of everyone. What a stupid way to get caught. Carmen again realized how unsuited she was for her new life of crime.

The security guard noticed the paper bag slipping out of Carmen's grasp. He grabbed the lumpy bundle, and helpfully rolled it into a more compressed package. Carmen's heart just about stopped.

He unscrewed the woman's vise-like grip on Carmen's arm.

"Pardon," he said to Carmen, shoving her bag under her free arm. "You have a happy New

Year, ma'am."

Turning to Slow Woman, "You should apologize," he said. He wagged his finger at the woman, who was getting more frantic as he grasped her arm.

"It's not the end of the world. Locking a bathroom door is not a crime," he pointed out. "Lady, if you don't mind my saying so, you're paranoid and neurotic."

"I do mind. And what do you know anyway, you're not a real policeman. And you're sure not a psychiatrist." She snarled, offended. "I know when something is up, and something was up."

He sighed, rolled his eyes at Carmen, and waved her off, indicating that he had it covered, in a casual the-customer-is-always-right gesture between two working people aligned against an upset customer out of her cotton-picking mind. He navigated her away from the scene of the alleged purse-tossing and vaguely toward the Standard Airlines counter. Carmen headed in the opposite direction, but heard him say wearily, "Let's check on her flight now."

As casually as she could manage it, Carmen hot-footed her way toward an exit. Her eyes met those of the policeman looking in her general direction. Now he was outside managing traffic, but he seemed to be looking at her again through the glass. Stopped what he was doing. Definitely looked right at her. She turned her back toward him and feigned intense interest in a map of the terminal in a glass frame. She might as well have been looking at a map for the stairway to heaven or hell. She wished for the anonymity of the blonde wig. She put her finger on the YOU ARE HERE mark, and started tracing the path, her face about a quarter inch from the glass. Just to look busy.

"Are you in trouble?" A voice whispered in her ear in Spanish.

"Why would you say that?"

"I don't know any housekeepers or cleaners in this country who bring their babies to work."

The speaker was another Hispanic woman, probably in her forties, wearing a gray uniform that looked like she might be part of the staff of a kitchen somewhere inside the airport. "I thought maybe you don't have your green card, the way you turned away from that *poli* over there."

"Si," Carmen lied. She felt vaguely startled when the woman leaned in to look closely at the glass, and brought her finger right next to Carmen's at the YOU ARE HERE x. She didn't take her eyes off the map, though she registered the woman's air of stress, the creases ironed into her forehead, and a strong scent of fried food.

"There's another way out, if you work here. Follow me."

She stepped toward a door, casually beckoning with a jerk of her head.

Carmen followed the Good Samaritan through an Employees Only door, around a corner, through a break room with a time clock. Inside was a cluster of women, all in gray uniforms, waiting as the time clock ticked out seconds. For a moment, it was eerily like the factory back in Nogales, with Francisco looking over their shoulders as his girls clocked in. Then the ghost of a moment was gone, and Carmen was swept along in the group of chattering women.

Carmen emerged into the sunshine, in the center of the cluster of women all chattering in Spanish. Remarkably, they had a whole hour for lunch. (An hour! Francisco would roll over in his grave, or wherever he was now.) At last, she was outside. She felt free, as if she might really get to safety, wherever that might be.

Cushioned in the group of women as they crossed the parking lot, she couldn't resist glancing toward the policeman. He was talking to a burly-looking dark-haired guy and pointing in the direction where he'd last seen her. She saw the other person—well, just the reflection of his profile—for an instant, and would have sworn it was Blasio. When she looked again, he was gone. Had she imagined it? She couldn't risk another look.

Her heart was racing when she found her car still sitting in the airport parking lot, not yet picked up by Inez the street woman. Carmen had asked her to wait, and luckily she hadn't jumped the gun. She shoved the fancy clothes, some bills, and the plane tickets she'd purchased through an open window.

If it really had been Blasio, Carmen had to get out of the neighborhood fast. She hopped on the first city bus she saw. Rode to the city station and got directions to Greyhound. Retrieved her suitcases. Paid for a ticket on the next bus out.

With nothing but the clothes on her back, a suitcase full of Salvation Army seconds, luggage stuffed with cash, and little Mario in her arms, Carmen found herself on the Greyhound to El Paso run on one of those new GM Silverside air-conditioned buses.

She wondered if the homeless woman would claim her car or use the tickets and clothes in Puerto Vallarta, maybe find a guy named Chad there, or lead whoever was following her in some random direction. She wasn't betting on it, but hoped Inez would lead her pursuers on a wild goose chase.

Carmen fed Mario one of his lingering supply of bottles and changed his diaper in the empty seat next to her. He got fussy, but she wrapped him in the carrier again, and he went to sleep instantly. Someone on the bus had a radio, and she dozed off listening to Vince Monroe crooning something deep and mellow; she dreamed of being in a strange place where everyone had left her alone in the dark. She woke in tears to Nat King Cole.

In El Paso, Carmen stopped off at the Post House for a meal but the food looked disgusting. She'd gotten good at making bottles at restaurant tables from evaporated milk with hot water delivered by waitresses. They had soft spots for babies. Canned milk was portable and found everywhere; whenever she saw it, she bought enough small tins to fill several bottles for Mario.

Eventually, Carmen braved her first plane ride, gaining confidence after the first of several short flights that eventually zigzagged to New York. During the layovers, when she could have gone to a hotel, she never left the airports. Mario never left her arms, and she never shut her eyes.

She was dazed with exhaustion but frightened of sleep. When she could resist no more, she was pursued by dreams of evil, crazy monster Francisco, killing her sister minutes after she'd given him his perfect son. Or Ambrose following her across a dozen states in his police car. Or Blasio, talking to everyone who had talked to her. Or that burly gray stranger. And then, back to Francisco, rising from the dead to take his son.

No, not his son, never his. He was all Elena's.

Chapter Twenty-Two
Downtown Nogales

In an office at the police station, Oliver conferred with two other detectives. He had been part of the department long enough to see that his co-workers functioned like Abbott and Costello—without the humor. Everything was a pissing match. He figured he'd have to spend most of his time biting his tongue and doing for himself whatever he wanted to get done. The two other detectives—Will Cain and Abelard Abel—didn't get along any better than their names implied. They'd managed a ten-year working relationship by splitting jobs and spending as little time together as possible. Oliver had found that, unless he planned otherwise, most of his hours on the clock were spent mediating between the two other detectives.

Cain had spent the day at the Sanchez

hacienda, looking through garbage and talking to people. Abelard had spent the day digging up dirt on Sanchez and his business dealings without coming up with much more than a stack of car registrations.

"Damn, Sanchez owns a lot of cars," Cain swore. "I'd like to have a couple of these babies. We went down there today and checked out the ones on the grounds in addition to the ten in the garage. Maybe a dozen more were outside on the driveway and scattered around the farm."

"What about the Buick Super Estate Wagon?" Oliver asked. "Did you see that? I didn't see one when I was there, but here's the registration."

"That baby would be hard to miss." Cain handed over a stack of photos that had come from the lab. He stapled the registration records to each one, leaving only two registrations left over: an old Ford and the new black wagon.

"The one that puzzles me is the junker," Oliver said. "The old Ford. I did see it parked by the Garcia house when I knocked on the door the day after, but it was gone later."

"That's not a junker," Abelard disagreed.

Cain had to put his ten cents in. "A ten-year-old Ford? Why would a millionaire with a yard full of showroom jalopies be driving a ten-year-old Ford?"

"That's a perfectly good car. I drive one myself." Abelard pushed away from the desk and sat straight in his chair. "Nothing wrong with it, just because it isn't straight out of the showroom. Most people would be happy to drive that car."

Oliver spread his hands expansively, as if laying hands over vast acreage. "Maybe they just use it on the farm." From his investigations so far, he'd determined already that the car was provided for Francisco's sister-in-law.

He'd already called his old department in Tucson to put out an APB on the car.

"Shows what you know," Cain said, confirming what Oliver had heard. "The housekeeper told us Sanchez got the car as an insult. Bought it to give his wife to give to her sister but the sister was too proud to use it. Only maybe she did use it, because it's gone."

"Talk to the sister-in-law yet?" Abel asked.

Cain shook his head. "Not yet. She lives a couple of blocks from one of Sanchez's garment factories. She's his bookkeeper. But a patrolman with a hard-on for the older sister said she's gone off to visit some relative in Mexico."

Abel laughed. "Guzman. Nothing if not persistent."

Oliver had already checked Guzman's schedule, finding he had regular morning traffic duty at Sacred Heart Catholic Church on N. Rodriguez. His conversation with Manuela had yielded nothing, but Cain and Abel were having a go at her.

He penciled in his calendar to "accidentally" drop in to see the officer on the morning of Monday, January 3. By then, Elena Garcia Sanchez would have been dead a little more than half a week.

* * *

Oliver waited across the street, finishing

off two cigarettes as he casually watched Officer Ambrose Guzman handling traffic on a four-way stop near Sacred Heart. He wasn't the only smoker, but the others were grabbing a last smoke before services. They stomped out their butts and joined a migration toward the church. The early Mass foot traffic on this Monday morning was more than he'd have expected, but then perhaps that was because the memory of Christmas was still fresh. He wasn't much of an attendee himself, though he at times called himself a lapsed Catholic. Sometimes he was a lapsed Baptist, Protestant, or Methodist, depending on which denomination was most convenient.

Oliver waited until the stragglers were gone to approach Guzman. He would have about thirty minutes with the patrolman before the service let out.

"Officer Guzman? Nice to see you awake."

Guzman tipped his hat, appearing to take no offense. He was a round-faced man in his mid-thirties, a little on the husky side. He had dark hair and eyes, and an affable expression. Nothing in Guzman's record stood out as exceptional one way or another, but he had been caught asleep on a stake out a few times. If he was in Sanchez's pocket, there was no departmental notation of it—but then, there wouldn't be.

"Detective Oliver," Guzman said, extending his hand. "What can I do for you today?"

"Just a couple questions, if you have a second." Oliver accepted the hand and they shook.

"I gotta apologize for the circumstances of our first meeting. But Nogales is a small pond, and we're more relaxed here than Tucson. I hear you have an impressive record. I served overseas, too, in—"

"I'm following up on the Sanchez murder," Oliver interrupted, refusing to get sidetracked. "Elena Garcia Sanchez. I'm told you're acquainted with her sister Carmen. You have heard, perhaps, that she is missing."

"She's not missing," Guzman said, frowning. "I already told a detective she's gone to Mexico."

"That's unlikely. She was scheduled to work, but didn't come in Friday or Saturday."

"Shame the hours that factory keeps. It's strictly for the birds. Scheduling them in on New Year's Day. Maybe she got off on account of being the sister-in-law. But knowing Sanchez, that's not too likely, is it? Seems like, with the boss in a coma, somebody would let them have some time off." Guzman shook his head. "No, she was definitely headed to Mexico. She told me it was a family visit, but it was urgent. You know she's a midwife, right? She's always going off someplace to deliver babies. Her car was packed up like she was off to deliver the Dionne quints. She was already beat, too." His brow furled. "I think she was coming from a hard birth in Pima or Cochise County, but I don't remember exactly."

"Any details would help the investigation," Oliver said, drily. "There's also a missing car."

"We're going to the movies when she gets back," Ambrose said slowly. "I'll let you know when I hear from her."

"You two are dating?"

"I wish. I been trying to get her to smile on me since high school. With no luck."

"Do you think it is possible she witnessed something and is now on the run?"

"Carmen Garcia?" Guzman thought for a few seconds. Oliver could practically see the rusty wheels turn. It was painful to watch. "No way. I can't see Carmen backing down for anything. Especially if Elena was involved. She was real protective of Elena. That Elena was a humdinger. Hell, both them girls were humdingers, only Carmen didn't realize it, and Elena realized it too much. So, who you got in the hot seat for this? You think Sanchez offed her, and tried to off himself? I wouldn't bet the farm that he's got that much conscience. Sanchez got his start in running hooch, you know. I wouldn't put much past him." Guzman looked embarrassed, or maybe something more than embarrassed. "You won't tell anyone I said that, right? I don't want to piss off Sanchez, or whoever Sanchez pissed off. Them folks play dirty."

"Your secret's safe with me," Oliver said. "Besides, he's in a coma."

"Coma or not, in these parts, any man says anything about Sanchez, he gotta have rocks in his head. The walls have ears, and they all belong to Sanchez."

The whole conversation impressed on Oliver that Carmen wasn't exactly infatuated with Ambrose Guzman. Before the service was over, Oliver wasn't either. Carmen Garcia rose another notch in his estimation. He hoped that Guzman, one of Sanchez's boys, or Sanchez's enemies hadn't killed her, too. Her murder was becoming a distinct possibility.

* * *

Days had passed since the murder, but there were a few more things that Oliver had already verified to his satisfaction. He'd had a feeling the housekeeper, Manuela, knew more then she let on. As a result he'd gotten a lot closer to her than he'd intended, but she'd never let a word slip that helped the investigation.

Francisco Sanchez was indeed a slave

driver at his factories, and he had indeed been the Sanchez currently pulling the strings of the Nogales Police Department. It wasn't as if someone had told him this, but Oliver figured it out after the investigation became a comedy of errors, with the murder weapon, bullets, and hard evidence disappearing at the station house; witness's stories changing; and blank looks from the supposed first responders. Why was it that the victim's body had been cremated before there was an autopsy? Where were the bloody sheets from the crime scene? The housekeeper denied that sheets had disappeared, but, on the basis of his discovery of a scrap of burned fabric, Oliver believed they'd found their way into a bonfire set by the cowboys a few days after the murder, when there was wood dry enough to burn. It was scant evidence and next to useless. There were dozens of barrels around the property that the hands regularly filled with wood and trash and burned to keep warm on winter nights when work kept them from their beds. And why would the sheets have been burned? What secrets could they have taken with them? It seemed far fetched.

Evaporating evidence was why he had tried to check out the factory on his own rather than sending in someone else, but he had been unsuccessful in getting past the company gate-keepers.

Cain had joined him. The jury was still out on Cain—Oliver wasn't yet certain on which side of Sanchez Cain stood, but it took the two of them to get Oliver in to examine the ratty office that the victim had shared with her sister. He looked through the files and papers, and stared at a crumbling subfloor, through which the hum of sewing machines could be heard. Two desks, one bare except for a dead plant; the other stacked high with ledgers. No ceiling. A sparrow loose in the rafters. Paint chips flaking off the old walls. He wasn't sure what struck him more—the wretched excuse for an office starkly lit by a single bare bulb hanging from a very long cord nailed into a rafter, or the solid door that had originally locked him out that took an hour to bring the company's inept maintenance man to throw his hands up in defeat and cut a new entry directly through the wall with his circular saw, bypassing the door entirely, so Oliver could be admitted.

The bare desk belonged to Mrs. Sanchez, though she had long since stopped coming in to work. The other desk belonged to the sister, Carmen, who had been missing at least as long as Elena had been dead.

Oliver suspected Francisco had killed his sister-in-law and dumped her body in his new Buick. Ambrose Guzman could not recall for certain if she'd left the area in the old Ford or the new wagon.

The factory's front doors were bare slats that could have been disassembled by a two-year-old with a spoon, but Oliver had expected to find something valuable in this room. There was nothing special, though, except maybe the women who used to work behind that door. He found himself wondering if the floor was strong enough to support his own weight. No way anyone had ever put in a safe, much less dragged one out. So why the sturdy lock on the door?

"Get the ledgers," he told Cain, who snapped some photos of the office before going off to find a box big enough to put the record books in.

The mousy woman who had escorted Oliver up here was still standing, waiting for him. She had not been introduced, but one of the thuggish workers downstairs had jerked a thumb in the woman's direction, and she'd been quick to push away from her sewing machine. He looked at her speculatively. Maybe she wasn't quite as mousy as he'd thought, but she had a beaten-down look, in spite of bright-red lipstick and a white dress decorated with a festive-looking red rose pattern.

"Did you know them?"

She looked at her feet. Anyone so eager to avoid eye contact had something to hide.

"Do you have a name?" he asked in a softer voice. She glanced up, and down again.

She whispered something. He stuck his finger in his ear as if he were cleaning it out, and cupped his hand to his ear. "Eh?"

"Delores." Barely louder.

"Delores, I know no one introduced us downstairs." He reached over and took her hand, shaking it gently. "I am Detective Oliver, and I've been assigned to this case. You know that your boss Francisco and his wife were shot, that his wife is dead, and that Carmen Garcia is missing."

She didn't nod, didn't move a muscle in the hand he was holding, didn't turn her eyes up to his, but he sensed she was listening.

"You knew Miss Garcia, didn't you?"

He walked up to the new entrance that had been cut in the wall and ran his hand over the rough edges, his attention straying again to the door. Peculiar.

Cain shoved past him with a box.

"The drawers, too. Everything that might be of interest."

"You do your business, Oliver. I don't need instructions." Cain glared at him with all the resentment of an employee who had been passed over for promotion while some jerk from Tucson got the coveted position. Oliver turned back to Delores, maneuvering her to walk beside him.

"Things weren't too rosy here, I presume."

She flashed him a startled look. He glimpsed alarm, and something else in her face. Confirmation. He dug a little deeper.

"Why the impregnable door?"

Delores looked at her feet again. He moved her down the steps, talking as they went.

"I'm guessing the boss didn't hold his sister-in-law in the greatest esteem. His office is just a few doors down. A fortune in furniture—cherry and mahogany paneling. Someone went to the trouble of putting up a ceiling, a window, decorating his office. The floor's not about to fall through like it is in there. And he's got sister-in-law Carmen and his own wife working in a garret not fit for rats. Even that sweatshop you're in downstairs is a cakewalk next to the cracker-box Carmen was working in. Hell, I wouldn't even put my ex-mother-in-law in a dump that bad. So why the disparity? What was the deal?"

She didn't answer. They arrived at the

foot of the stairs, and still Oliver hadn't weaseled past her guard. He turned toward the exit.

"Do you know Carmen's house?"

"Everyone knows. She walked here every day."

"Care to show me?"

"I have to get back to my sewing machine," Delores said. "Besides, you know where she lives. You've got her address on file, I'm sure."

"I need to see how she got here every day. For all I know, she's locked herself in her house." It was a lie. The day after the murder, he'd sat on the empty house for hours before setting Guzman to stake it out. "It would help to have someone she knows, if she's barricaded herself in. She could be there, traumatized—."

"Berto would never agree."

"Berto?"

"The shop head." Delores pointed toward the nervous-looking man circulating among the seamstresses. Berto must have had antennae because he looked up just in time to see Delores's finger aiming at him.

"Oh, shit." Delores's hand dropped like a brick.

Oliver broke away from her and went straight to Berto, introducing himself and demanding Delores's time.

Berto, as ever, was only concerned about quotas.

"She finished her quota already, boss," someone said. "Let's count them."

Oliver had to restrain himself to keep from laughing at two of the seamstresses who "helped" Berto count that quota; they were as good as any Marx Brothers routine of sleight of hand and distraction he'd ever seen, as a stack of perhaps twenty garments passed for a hundred. When he hauled Delores out, they were still counting.

He walked Delores across the street and down a few blocks. Delores was close to how he pictured Carmen. The cheap dress, the bright lips, the shy demeanor, the worn down aspect. It was hard to picture powerless girls in circumstances such as these as not running away at the first sign of trouble.

Oliver's expectation was that Carmen had witnessed a shooting, got caught running away, and had been killed by whatever thug had committed the crime. Maybe it was just her luck that Sanchez had not inspired any great loyalty among the culture of his vast organization. There were lots of underlings, but no one that Oliver could see as being groomed for greater things.

As they passed an old bodega, he noticed Delores had stopped to stare into the glass. A police car was stopped in front, and a young officer he did not recognize was inside, obviously manhandling an elderly man.

"Excuse me," he told Delores. "Please wait out here. I have to make a purchase."

He went inside, selected a bottle of milk from the small refrigerated case, and took it to the counter. At his entry, the police officer dropped his hands from the ironed butcher's apron the old proprietor wore, but the material bore creases from the young man's grip. Oliver read the cop's nametag aloud.

"Hello, Officer Gomez. Good to meet you. I'm Detective Oliver, new to Nogales. We haven't yet had the pleasure."

Gomez tipped his hat, glared threateningly at the shopkeeper, and left abruptly.

"I hope everything is all right here," Oliver said as he watched Delores duck into an alley out of view, avoiding Gomez, who got in his police cruiser and drove away. The shakedown was just one of a hundred things Oliver had recently made note of that needed investigation. He paid for his milk, and drank it as he and Delores walked into a neighborhood of crumbling properties.

Delores pointed out Carmen's house, and he acted surprised. He knocked. The Ford was still gone, and there was no plainclothes surveillance on the house.

He thumped the door again.

"You're not breaking down the door?"

"It's not a police state," he said. "My gut tells me the woman who worked behind that door in the factory needs her home doors intact."

Delores, who had hardly said a word the whole way there, looked up at him with enigmatic eyes. "You're right about that. If you find her, what will you do?"

"I will follow the letter of the law, Delores."

"There's no way that Carmen Garcia would ever do anything that was unjustified. She's the nearest we got to a guardian angel, even if she worked for the devil himself," Delores said. She looked thoughtful. "You took up for Señor Pasquel."

Oliver nodded. "No shakedowns on my watch. I got Gomez's badge number," he said.

"You're the only one then," she said. "Wait here. I will be back in ten minutes."

It was the second time Carmen Garcia's house took him by surprise. The vine-covered cottage was straight out of a childhood fairy tale. The adobe was shedding its whitewash but in a charming way, and vines thick as arms crawled over the sides of the house. Herb gardens nested in niches on both sides of the door, in pots and in every bit of ground. The place reeked of charm—instead of the poverty surrounding it. He half expected the Bear-Prince or the Gypsy Queen to respond to his knock, although he wasn't too surprised that no one did.

But then, abruptly, Delores floored him by opening the door from the inside.

"There's no one here," she said. "I was hoping Carmen would be here."

Oliver didn't ask how she'd gotten in. He assumed there was a key stashed somewhere, or an open window that people close to the family knew about. He glanced at the miniature rustic kitchen to his left, with its tiny tiled table, and then the pair of unassuming bedrooms straight ahead and a trim, homey den to his right, centered around a massive fireplace deep in cold ash. The bathroom was an afterthought, tacked on at the end of the hall. The place was a perfect anachronism, with gas lights and no electricity that he could find. He had no idea when the fire had gone out. In spite of its charm, and a surfeit of lovely quilts and throws that someone must have spent decades knitting and sewing, the place was as cold as death.

"Now you've seen it. We should go." Delores tried to get him to leave, but a medieval-looking chair in one of the bedrooms caught his eye.

"Good Lord." He stared at the contraption.

Delores crossed her arms.

"Carmen was our midwife," Delores said defensively.

"That thing is for childbirth?" He looked at the chair, then looked away. "Looks uncomfortable. Damn uncomfortable."

"Rumor was Elena was pregnant. She didn't come round any more, after she married Francisco," Delores said. "It's a shame that Carmen didn't get a chance to deliver her niece or nephew."

He didn't recall anyone mentioning a pregnancy. No one had mentioned a baby. He thought of the empty room in the hacienda, the one with ponies on the curtains. They hadn't even gotten around to furnishing the kid's room. She must not have been far along. He wished, not for the first time, that he'd seen Elena Garcia Sanchez's body before it had been cremated.

Delores faced him, her quiet features twisted in pain. "If our Elena would have had her baby, Carmen would have delivered it. Instead, Elena is dead, and Carmen has disappeared. What kind of monster shoots his pregnant wife? If you ask me, the boss did away with them both. But if you quote me, I'll deny it. I don't want to end up dead in a river, too. So now you got my opinion. You can't tell nobody. If you don't keep it to yourself, I'm dead too. And I got a kid to take care of." She looked out the window and saw something that spooked her. One of the company goons was walking past the house.

"Look, mister, I'm going out the back. You may mean well, but I gotta survive. Don't never talk to me again."

With that, she left. Trigger Oliver took the opportunity to look around, finding the place full of little gadgets, including what seemed to be a trap door he couldn't figure out how to open. In one of the bedrooms, he found a photo of the sisters. He picked it up and gazed at it for a long time, before slipping it out of the frame and into his pocket, though he had already picked up a couple from an album at the crime scene. There was something about these women that intrigued him, especially Carmen. The more he heard about her, the more he hoped the crime boss hadn't gotten rid of her, too.

* * *

As a man with no social life, Oliver made it his habit to visit the hospital occasionally to check on the coma patient, until he found they had moved the insensate body of Francisco Sanchez from the city hospital to a nursing home providing coma patient care. Since the nursing home was convenient to the detective's house, the change was such an improvement in convenience for Oliver that he started dropping by every day on the way home from work.

The decision to relocate had been made by someone in Francisco's organization rather than by a family member. With no progeny or close relatives, guardianship would have normally been delegated to the state, as Elena, the deceased wife, had been the next of kin and, being dead, was no longer available. However, Sanchez's organization had its fist in the legal process, muddying the works with an entourage of lawyers and crooked judges long ago bought and paid for with Sanchez graft.

First, against the organization's wishes, the Nogales courts had gone back through the records and appointed a Sanchez cousin as guardian. The ink was no sooner dry than that cousin (son of the deceased Captain Rico, who had formerly served on the police force), had been caught at the hospital with a pillow over the patient's face. Rico Manuel Sanchez was now domiciled in a federal lock-up, being detained for attempted murder. Rico claimed his father had been murdered years ago by Francisco. True or not, those charges had been tried and the case lost, years ago. Rico's trip to incarceration was being held up as an example to anyone on the take (which was essentially the entire force, as best the detective could tell) that even unconscious, Francisco Sanchez was still in charge of his organization.

One of Francisco's lawyers had provided the courts with records of his prior will, listing one Miguel Trujillo as executor. Oliver had seen Trujillo in person in court once—a small man who relished going in for the kill, but otherwise came across as a nonentity. He kept out of the detective's way like a slippery forest animal seen only out of the corner of his eye. Only Oliver's access to court records had provided the name.

Everywhere else—at the factory, at the ranch, and in mob circles—the man was addressed as Segundo. He was a lawyer whose most distinguishing feature seemed to be unerring loyalty to Francisco. Loyalty—or maybe he was just a man who knew which side of his bread was buttered on. He lived modestly, but had a big bank account, and spent a lot of time flying when Francisco was in residence and at the factory when Francisco was flying.

Segundo had made the arrangements for the nursing home, for Francisco to have his own room, not that he was aware of it, and for the couple of "guards" standing watch over the patient round the clock. These guards were straight off the rancho. They had come to know the detective from his regular visits, which were generally fruitful for the investigation. He'd met doctors, who had explained in a vague way that there was spinal damage from one of the bullets that had nicked a vertebrae. There had also been significant blood loss, but no internal organs were damaged—the bullets passed right through. He was expected to wake up eventually, as he had already gained consciousness briefly, now and again.

Late one night after the move, Oliver had come to check on Francisco, and found the guards seated some distance away from the door. He recognized Eber. The other guard was a heavyset stranger, new to the guard rotation. Oliver stopped at a vending machine, feeding it coins.

"What's up?" He sauntered in their direction, handing them two coffees and keeping one for himself. He sipped the bitter brew.

"He's in there," Eber said.

"Who? Sanchez? I knew that."

"Segundo."

"What's he doing? Suffocating your boss, like the other guy?"

"Nah, he always sends us over here. He doesn't want us to listen in on the meeting. He calls it a meeting." The two guards looked at each other, and lowered their voices.

"It's kind of creepy, I think."

"Like Frankenstein."

"Yeah, he reads off his shit like the old guy is listening."

"He ain't waking up."

"What do I care? It pays the bills, it's dry, and there are chairs."

Oliver took a step toward the room and stopped, looking back at the guards for affirmation.

"You care if I—?"

The new guy straightened up and tried to look important. "Better not," he said.

"Don't get caught," Eber contradicted. "If you get caught with your ear to the wall, we gotta deal with too much shit."

Oliver gave a thumbs-up and sidled up to the window. Meanwhile, they continued arguing between themselves, quietly hushing and poking each other with elbows and thumbs.

He peeked into Francisco's room and saw Segundo standing there with a clipboard, reading off notes to his unconscious boss. He backed out of view, and listened to the recital clearly audible through the door.

Segundo was talking about factory business, apparently.

"...the number of garments sewn is up. The US factories aren't keeping up with the two in Sonora. Carmen's been out, but I been going over the numbers. We gotta get a temporary bookkeeper until she turns up. Also, I got more product in Sonora, supposed to be coming in by train. And speaking of product, your favorite, that Johnny Pinto from LA, is calling every day like clockwork, wanting money for his goods. Holding off since he's two-bit, and I know how you feel about him. Blasio thinks Pinto's the one who stole Carmen's shitty car, but Blasio's still an idiot. My money's on Blackstone for that favor you did Mando Armas. By the way, Blackstone was getting in the way of business, so I sent him on a wild goose chase. I told him on no account to harm the goose. But I know you want her limping back, broke and chastened and ready to work."

Oliver backed off from the wall with his hands in his pockets and sauntered back.

"Does he always come by here like that?"

"Every day, different times. Except when he's out of town, which ain't been too much, with the boss laid low," Eber said.

"You talk too much, kid," the other guard said.

"You gonna rat on me? My own brother-in-law?"

Oliver said, "Tomorrow. Doughnuts or biscuits?"

"Doughnuts. We get here at five."

"At least you two agree about something."

Oliver made a mental note to get a bug in the room. He'd want to run the names Johnny Pinto, Blackstone, and Mando Armas. They'd have to commandeer the room next door but that would be easy enough to manage.

Chapter Twenty-Three
On the road

The miles sped by, whisking them farther and farther away from everything familiar. Away from home. Away from Elena.

Carmen swore she would spare the baby the knowledge of his monstrous father. Poor little Mario was innocent in all this. She would teach him all about his mother. The baby would be all Elena. Francisco would never be part of his son's life.

She hardly slept, but when she did, every instant was packed with nightmares. If her eyes drifted closed for a second, she saw Francisco, big as life, murdering her sister. The vision snapped her awake and filled her with such rage, she wanted to kill him all over again. Her sleeping self seemed to think she could do it, and that it could bring her sister back. Under the boring lull of transportation, exhaustion kept tipping her over the edge of consciousness, dropping her into the night of Francisco killing Elena. She woke from the sleeping nightmare into the real life version, cycling between burning rage at Francisco, terror that she was being followed, and grief for the loss of her beautiful, innocent Elena.

* * *

New York was a lost place for Carmen, a jumble of people, monstrous buildings, rushing traffic, and bitter cold. She felt like the little girl left on the merry-go-round when everyone else went home. It was all spinning, the whole world—mad circles racing that made no sense, a nightmare of lost time she'd been sucked into, and yet, here she was, traipsing up the stairway of another tenement building.

"This is about the best deal you can find in Spanish Harlem," the landlady claimed, on the verge of unlocking the door to the second floor walk-up.

Dubious praise. If that meant cheapest, then maybe it fit the bill. The landlady's wide load scarcely had clearance to fit up the narrow gray-brown flight of steps, and the climb had given her conversation a strange, panting rhythm as she had introduced herself as Mrs. Beulah Beebe. The last name had been her husband's, she had explained, entirely invented by his grandparents, who had been tired of explaining an unpronounceable last name. Her hair—except where threads of gray snaked through it—and eyes were the exact hue of her tawny skin. To Carmen, Beulah appeared an indecipherable mixture of Mexican, Chicano, black, white European, and Eurasian; Carmen couldn't tell which she was most of, which struck her as just one more symptom of being a stranger in a land of strangers. Back in Nogales, even if she hadn't known a body's origins, she'd have known which side of the border was home as soon as she opened her mouth. The only thing in this woman's voice was Brooklyn.

As Beulah sorted through a massive key ring until one worked, Carmen tried to see past her. The communal hall was as narrow as the stairway, faced with thickly painted doors gouged and scored from years of use. The ceiling was as low as the residents' expectations. Instead of looking at the dismal surroundings, Carmen turned to the back of the landlady's head. The sharp line of her ear-length bob with its rigid pin curls and upturned rolled bangs belonged on the head of a much younger woman.

The carpeting might have had color once, but now was a dingy gray, with a diamond-patterned border, badly cut with diamond on one side, half-diamond on the other. Beaded plank paneling went halfway up the wall, dark and heavily scratched, the hallway so narrow that Carmen could stand in the middle, raise her elbows, and touch both sides; not that she really wanted her elbows to contact the walls that looked more heavily coated by vermin tracks than paint, wood, or paper. Mrs. Beebe's bottom was still vibrating with her effort to manhandle the lock, so Carmen looked up instead of straight ahead at the quivering flesh. Heavily watermarked rose wallpaper covered the ceiling and showed its age, curling away at the edges, browning in places, and giving off a heavy odor of cigarette smoke, stale beer, and sweat.

The lock clicked.

"Watch yourself with that door, it'll knock you into next Christmas," the landlady said, without turning to face her, her concern presumably cued by Carmen's sharply drawn breath when the door had smacked into her shoulder, slamming her into the door jamb. She might thank the saints it had hit her shoulder and not the baby, but it had been no accident. She'd already grown an instinct to protect his frailty. The force nearly bowled her over. Mario, asleep in his *rebozo*-style carrier against her skin, wasn't fazed. Most of his week on earth had been spent in that carrier, being jostled, bounced, and carried some twenty-five hundred miles.

As Beulah nattered on about the room's dubious assets, Carmen turned to the door. She slammed her fist against it. It felt like solid steel. She examined the lock: a latch-key mechanism. No deadbolt. This was the fourth apartment building she'd seen this morning in East Harlem, and she'd come to the conclusion that none of the walk-ups would have been secure enough to please Turcios, if he'd been around. This was the first door that would have found his approval and it felt like some kind of message from heaven. She almost blurted out she'd take it, but Mrs. Beebe was a type of woman Carmen recognized. She'd only get respect if she dickered. She had not forgotten Tomas's lesson, and was already the proud owner of a new and expensive deadbolt lock just waiting for a place to secure. She'd picked it up at the hardware shop by the bus station, along with the awl and screwdriver necessary to install it.

Her would-be landlady had noticed her attention to the door.

"That door will knock you off your sensible shoes. You'll hurt your hand, hitting it like that."

"How come this door is different from the rest of these apartments we passed going up?"

"This apartment was used as the front office for the warehouse downstairs before the truck driver rented the space. He stays in the warehouse when he's around, don't need no office. Keeps his truck down there. The stairway out your back door goes down into the warehouse." If sharp-eyed Beulah knew anything, it was when a tenant was interested in something. She pointed out the other, similar, door.

"Them doors, that's as solid as they come."

She reached under Carmen's arm and thumped the door to prove her point. Then she caught sight of Mario shielded under Carmen's big coat, and did a double-take.

"Huh. I just thought you was fat, didn't see the kid. This place for just you and the kid, or you, the kid, and the baby's father?"

Carmen could practically see the price of the unit going up. She had all that money. She could buy the building if she wanted. But she was here to hide.

"That would be difficult. His father is dead." That was the truth, anyway. Carmen put her chin up and her hand in her pocket to hide the absence of a wedding ring. She needn't have worried. Beulah cared more about the cash in her pocket than respectability, baby or not.

She shrugged and went on with her explanation. "That stairway to the warehouse vestibule downstairs is private. It's why the doors is different from the—"

"Who's renting the warehouse? You mentioned a truck driver?" Carmen interrupted. She didn't like the idea of a business below having access. She walked over to the back door and turned its unkeyed deadbolt. She gave a massive shove, and the door budged a few inches, enough for her to see it opened into complete darkness. The only thing she could make out was the wire-mesh platform, then she realized it was a fire escape built inside the building. She let go, and backed out of the way as it slammed shut.

"Stairway? That's just a fire escape."

"It's got stairs, don't it? The truck driver what rents it lives down there sometimes, but mostly he's on the road. He lives in New Orleans,

New Mexico, New-vada, New Port...one of them New states, but when he's here, he stores his truck. He sublets the storage space. You got extra stuff, you can put it down there. If you want to move this stuff out, it's twenty dollars."

"I have stuff coming. Furniture, so yeah, move it out." It was a lie, but she had all that money to spend. It had been years since the sofa had seen better days, its pattern faded but not threadbare. The cushions were square, and the edge of one corner had been chewed off, baring the welt cord. The mattress creaked when she tested it with her hand, and she could clearly make out the marks of each coil pressing up against a mattress stained with decades of sweat, blood, and detritus. Carmen wanted to wash the sofa crud off her hands. She went to the kitchen sink and turned on the water. It groaned, the pipes shuddered and vibrated for all they were worth. Winter-cold rusty water came out of the hot tap.

"Still, the furniture comes with. It's extra to move it."

The accent was still a shock to her ears, but not so much as the apartment was to her eyes.

"So you said. Twenty."

Except for a toilet hidden in a tiny enclosure, everything was in the one room. A kitchen sink and stove were on either side of a counter that rested atop a bathtub. The "come with" furniture was a kitchen table that had seen better days, three mismatched wooden chairs with missing slats, and the low, square sofa with the chewed edge. A couple of cockroaches warmed themselves by the radiator. At least it was working.

Beulah pointed out a second couch that lay flat to make a bed. The bed's bare mattress looked like it was a hundred and six years old and had come from a bordello. Carmen's skin crawled at the thought of touching it. She recalled her lovely hand-carved bed, and the lovingly stitched comforters she'd left behind. She hardened her resolve. She could afford linens, too. She thought about that suitcase full of cash. Why not put it to good use in this place?

The window had been covered over with paint that might have been white once and was gray now, but Carmen didn't mind. It was cold. It was January. There was snow outside. The grayish color let in the light. There was no way Carmen would open that window until spring arrived and, with any luck, by spring, she'd be somewhere other than Spanish Harlem.

The apartment was shabby and filthy, but no worse than any of the others she'd seen that day. At least it was only one flight up and, because it was on the end, it had an extra window, even if that only looked into the brick of the next building. What more did she need than a door with a lock, a refrigerator, and room for a crib? After she bleached everything that wasn't nailed down, it would be livable. Okay, she'd better bleach the stuff that was nailed down, too.

"Seven a month per room."

"So that's seven dollars then?" Carmen opened the bathroom door. "You can hardly call the bathroom a room."

"It has a door, don't it? That makes it two

rooms and fourteen a month. And I need a month in advance."

"I don't know. I haven't looked at that building across the street yet." Carmen lied, and turned to leave. She'd spent an hour at the tenement across the way. The rooms had been a little cheaper, but even drearier, if that was even possible, with kitchens that were hot plates and iceboxes. Plus she had to qualify through the New York City Housing Authority and that would take time she didn't have, and too much disclosure.

"Okay, seven a month," Beulah agreed, eyes narrowing on Carmen's hand as she dug around a deep pocket in her coat.

"Here's twenty-one," Carmen said. "Three months in advance for the one room, and I'm replacing the lock." She handed over the extra twenty. "Do what you want with the furniture. When I go, you can keep the new lock I'm putting in the door. Please send somebody for the furniture now."

There was a moment while the landlady

hesitated, realizing she could have gotten more, but the extra twenty Carmen gave her kept her from carping about the furniture.

She accepted the money. She withdrew a wadded paper from her pocket that turned out to be the contract. Carmen signed it on the rickety table. When it collapsed under the pressure, she didn't bother straightening it up, but kicked the disengaged leg toward the door. Before Beulah had made it out of the hall, Carmen had already started unscrewing the old lock. Fortunately, the new lock was a standard size and fit the holes already in the metal door.

Carmen walked over to the couch and pushed the lever that made it into a bed. The furniture shuddered and groaned, and the back and sides collapsed flat, spewing out a dust cloud. She leaned her back against the couch and pushed. It took some maneuvering but she managed to shove it far enough to jam the door open. The exertions woke up Mario. She took off her coat to lay Mario on it in the corner, and rolled up her sleeves to shove all the furniture she could move into the hallway. The janitor and his son, who came up eventually, were surprisingly pleased at the logjam in the hallway. As they examined it, Carmen could hear them through the open door taking credit for the work involved in getting it that far.

Chapter Twenty-Four

Carmen had installed the lock, bought sheets at the dollar store, and fetched luggage from the locker at the station, all before noon. To her way of thinking, she still hadn't cleaned up the place enough to warrant letting a molecule of that apartment touch Mario's skin. The only good thing she could come up with was that there were more shops in walking distance than there were in all of Nogales, and that was including the tourist section on the Sonora side.

After all of her worldly goods were stowed away, Carmen went out to the nearby corner market. Dusty cans, dusty bins, even the produce was covered in the dust of the city. The bodega could not have been more different from Pasquel's back home. In Nogales, there was almost always a Pasquel sweeping sand out of the store. Here, it looked as if no one had ever wiped off a package. The film of dust on the cans was black from settled coal soot. But it was handy, and stuff she needed.

She got fresh milk for Mario and some cleaning supplies, and counted herself lucky that the electric icebox needed no ice to keep cold. She had more than enough to carry up the flight of stairs without also having to lug a block of ice.

"Back again?" A name tag pinned at the clerk's collar said "Tina." Her black hair was cut short and lacquered heavily to maintain a stylish curl far more elaborate than necessary for working behind a grocery counter. She looked around seventeen and had the same resentful look as the herd of young Pasquels back home who had also been compelled to earn their movie money by sweating at the family business. Carmen didn't bet, but she'd have bet the paycheck she didn't have that, like the teens back at Pasquel's bodega, the girl was related to the owner.

"Looks like it, Tina. You on school vacation?"

"Graduated last year."

"Congratulations. You're probably the same age as my sister." Carmen's words suddenly stuck in her throat.

"Yeah? Your sister's in school?" The girl looked her over resentfully.

"No. She died," Carmen said abruptly, tearing up. She stared blankly at Tina's gold cross on a chain, and fought for control over her pinched throat when hot tears filled her eyes. Impulsively, she tugged the necklace from inside her collar. "She had something exactly like this." She waited as the girl expressed some enthusiasm over the jewelry, then quickly keyed through the merchandise.

Carmen took her change in stoic silence.

"Listen, I'm sorry about your sister." Tina reached up and tugged at the cross around her neck, twisting it nervously.

The quick change of attitude reminded Carmen of Elena's volatile emotions. She looked at the girl's cross, and ignored the tears that ran down her own face. "Is there a church around here? Catholic church, I mean."

"There's the Church of the Holy Rosary at 444 East 119th, Monsignor Arcese, he's Italian. I'd confess to an Italian, but I hear he speaks Spanish, too, so what's the point?" She smacked at a wad of gum at her own cleverness and stuffed Carmen's few items slowly in a bag. She looked over Carmen's shoulder at a blonde in a polka-dot dress with a skinny leather belt who had just walked up that instant and was already tapping her foot impatiently.

"Bet that one's not from this neighborhood."

The cashier smiled at the blonde and said, "*Tu madre es una puta fea.*"

The blonde smiled back. She had a lot of nice, very white teeth. Maybe her father was a dentist.

Carmen waited for a reaction, but the blonde didn't have one. "I guess not," Carmen said, and responded in Spanish, "I doubt her mother is an ugly whore, since her daughter is quite pretty." It was true. She was pretty in a cosmopolitan, fashionable sort of way. "That wasn't a nice thing to say." The chastisement was out of Carmen's mouth before she could stop it. "I shouldn't have corrected you, but you just reminded me of my little sister."

For an instant, Tina looked disconcerted. She patted Carmen's hand, but otherwise ignored the rebuke and the apology. "There's also St. Cecilia's Parish on 106th Street, with Father Jeremiah J. Scannell. That's where my family goes. There are some Italians, but mostly it's Irish and Puerto Ricans, if you don't care about that."

Carmen put the bag of groceries in the big stroller she was pushing. Mario was awake, and solemnly looking up at her.

Belatedly, Tina noticed the stroller, and came out from behind the counter to gape at the baby, and touch his hand.

"Oh, what a beauty! Look at those eyes. She looks just like that little girl in that Christmas movie."

The blonde in line said, in the distinctly American Spanish of the daughter of immigrants, "That's clearly a boy," then hastily, to Carmen, "but still beautiful. His eyes remind me of some-one. Natalie Wood?"

"That's it! 'Miracle on 34th Street,'" Tina agreed. "You have to let me babysit when you go out. He's such a dear! And so tiny. What is he, a week old?"

"Close to that," Carmen said, evasively.

"By the way, Tina, *y tu mama tambien,*" the blonde said. "And your mama also."

"Tina, you know perfectly well my mom is a bitch and a half, but ugly she's not." She turned and shook Carmen's hand. "I'm Marilyn Cordes. I go to St. Cecilia's, too. We grew up in an old fashioned Roman Catholic Puerto-Rican Italian-Irish Jewish apartment in the barrio. Next door to her." She chucked Mario under his chin. He gave a perfect week-old baby grin, the kind some people (not Carmen) called gas.

"Not her—call me if you need a babysit-ter," Marilyn said, arching a look at Tina and sticking out her tongue.

"It just so happens that I have a meeting later. A whole bunch of meetings. They'll probably take all day," Carmen said. "Let's talk. You can both watch him."

* * *

It was going to take a lot to make the place livable, but the first thing she did was fix up a hiding spot in the corner under some loose floorboards. Even though it was undetectable from all possible angles, she shoved a trash bin over the spot. Even better.

The bookkeeper in her made her finally sit down to take stock. She'd secreted the money from Francisco's wallet everywhere: in all the pockets of all of her clothes, loose in her purse, and in various pockets of Mario's baby bags, even rolled up in diapers. She made a pile and started counting. Even after what she'd spent so far, she was only halfway through the pile and had already gotten up to $2,000 when someone knocked.

It wasn't as if Carmen really knew anyone in the city except for Mrs. Beebe. Her heart beat so hard her hands shook as if she was running an invisible jackhammer. She rolled the counted bills into a coil and shoved it in her only pocket. The remainder of the pile she wadded into her purse.

She was almost too afraid to answer the door. A clatter sounded outside. Someone squealed, and screamed "Ouch!"

"Who is it?" Her voice shook. She swallowed and repeated herself, a little louder. She pressed her ear against the panel, but didn't hear anything.

"We were wondering if we could come babysit," a girl said. "There's a ton of furniture out here. I don't know if we can get to the door." Carmen thought that was Tina. Something fell, clattering and bouncing. It sounded like pieces of the chairs.

"Never mind." That was Marilyn.

The girls from the bodega. Both of them. Carmen opened the door. Tina had climbed over the upended sofa. Marilyn was halfway over and looked like she might be stuck.

"Babysitting. You know. Like you said at the shop. And we already talked about it. We can do like Solomon and split it. I mean, we'll do it together, and split what you pay, not the baby."

Carmen had had second thoughts about leaving Mario, but she had things she had to accomplish in the city, like getting work and setting up the household with nicer furnishings.

"Sounds like a plan," she said. "I hope you don't mind the place being empty. But I have furniture coming."

* * *

She worked out the details with the girls. On the street, she caught a ride with a talkative Brooklynese cabbie who drove for a serpentine hour before finding a furniture store where she bought everything she needed, and arranged for delivery. When a second cab took four minutes to get her home, she realized the first guy had taken her for a ride. She'd have to be more careful.

By the time she was back, the old furniture had been rearranged in single file down the hall. Passing through was still a tight squeeze in the narrow hall. The girls said the janitor had been coming by every so often to pick up another chair, or cushion, but he and his son were already too drunk to manage the stairs. The big stuff was wedged in the third-floor landing, and they had decided to come back when they were sober. They hoped Mrs. Beebe would not wake up and notice. The gossip was that she went on a bender every night, so they might get lucky.

Mario was asleep on blankets on the floor. Both the girls were happy to split their dollar. They declined Carmen's offer of a meal, and headed to the corner for a burger and shake.

The gas cooktop in the apartment didn't work. She threw out milk she'd bought that had already gone bad. She took the produce from the refrigerator, which apparently warmed rather than chilled, and set it on the window sill farthest from the radiator. Then she used the downstairs pay phone to make arrangements for a new refrigerator and cooktop to be delivered with everything else.

Carmen had bought piles of quilts to serve as her bed until her new furniture could be delivered. The delivery guys visited her daily, knocking on her door every morning to let her

know they'd checked that day to see if the hall
had been cleared. She spent the nights watching
dust motes and dirt waft in the cold air coming
in through the gaps in the window. It reminded
her of Francisco's factory.

Beulah got into a shouting match with
the janitor, and finally got them to haul everything to an empty apartment on the fourth floor,
including the nonworking stove and refrigerator.

Carmen had never bought furniture before, so when it was delivered, it barely fit.

But the girls were impressed.

"You didn't argue over how much we
wanted to be paid," Tina said, "plus look at all
this stuff." She brushed her hand down the side
of the new couch and shoved her nose in it, in-
haling deeply, but mostly inhaled the tang of dust
that had been disturbed when the old furniture
was hauled away. Tina coughed for five minutes,
but managed to choke out, "You must be really
rich."

It was on the tip of her tongue to tell
Tina that no one with more than two dollars to

rub together would live in this building, but caught herself. "Not really."

It was a lame response. Carmen realized she'd need to control the impulse spending. She had left a trail of bus and plane tickets to New York. It was a maze, but if anyone knew how to follow it, the trail was behind her like a flashing sign saying "FIND ME!" Buying sprees were out. If she was halfway careful, it would not take much to fade into this community, especially because no one she had met in New York was actually from New York, but spending sprees would be noticed.

"I came into some money, but look at this place. I spent it all," Carmen lied.

Carmen was getting better at deception. She still had pockets full of cash, and that didn't include the untouched full suitcase stashed under the floorboards. "And now I have to find a job."

Chapter Twenty-Five

The New York winter was getting the better of her. The carriage's top protected the baby, but sleet pelted her. She'd had no luck in finding a midwife to help her get a birth certificate for Mario. No men of the cloth here she'd seen had led her to a midwife who worked with immigrants. Back in Nogales, the clergy had been a steady source of women in need of midwives. In her New York search, all the priests she'd met so far were the kind who promised hell instead of help. She didn't know if that was because she was a stranger here, or because she was unmarried with a baby, or if the culture was just that different.

She wasn't looking for Florence Nightingale, just a warm body who was at least sober and literate enough to fill out the forms. The classified ads she'd chased down turned out to be false leads.

Her neighbors were exactly the type who would sometimes require the kind of semi-legitimate midwife she needed, but she hadn't had a chance to ask any of them anything yet.

She had found a flyer tacked to a lamp-post a block from her building, promoting a women's hospital that seemed promising because it was geared to immigrants. One thing she knew about immigrants was that sometimes their poverty forced them to shave the edges of what one would call legal. She called the number from the pay phone in the vestibule of the apartment building.

* * *

"I'm looking for a midwife," Carmen whispered for the hundredth time. Whispering because there were always people walking through or standing within earshot. She'd gone through the script so many times, she could have repeated it in her sleep.

"You're calling the right place," a woman replied.

"I'd like to meet and…"

"You can come to the hospital and check out the facilities at—"

"I want to meet you. Not at the hospital. You are the midwife, right?" She didn't want to go to a hospital looking for a midwife when she was clearly not full term, especially when she was going to so obviously be out and about with a full-term baby right away. After a bit more back and forth, the voice on the phone gave her directions to a place to meet. It wasn't a church, as she had expected, but a night spot.

As soon as she stepped into the Green Parrot Bar and Grill, her eyes were drawn to a bigger-than-life perch and parrot playground taking up a generous corner of the restaurant. The green parrot himself, he who famously pointed out the killer of his beloved Max Geller, still reigned there, well-known and beloved by long-time patrons. At this moment of the day, he was sitting on his perch, preening himself in front of an adoring crowd. In the library's stash of newspapers, she had read articles about the mystery of the restaurant owner's death on July 12, 1942, the date that Geller was shot by Robert Butler. The killer had been named by the parrot and sentenced by the state of New York. A frequent topic of conversation in the bar was whether or not the bird had been sworn in at the trial.

Carmen allowed herself to be seated in a booth well away from the parrot watchers and ordered coffee. She was wearing a *rebozo* she had bought from Valeria Zayas, who lived across the hall. Valeria was fresh from Puerto Rico, on her last dime, and hopeful of shedding anything that marked her as new to New York. She'd been happy to also sell Carmen some beaten-up looking huaraches that Carmen's mother would have tossed to the coyotes.

"I'm expecting someone to join me. If a lady comes in and asks for a Miss Elena, that's me."

The waitress looked her over from head to foot, as if second-guessing whether she would be able to afford the restaurant, but assured her she'd keep an eye out. She left Carmen to pretend to browse through the menu while she was actually scrutinizing every woman who entered alone.

This was the fourth day in her *partera* search. She had begun her quest following an ad to one bar, and then another in a rough area of Spanish Harlem, where she'd gotten a dozen names of midwives from exactly the type of shady characters who might deal with Francisco in his illegal enterprises, though they were mostly from Puerto Rico rather than Sonora. Sometimes she called herself Elena, and sometimes Delores. Under her borrowed *rebozo*, she had sewn in a fringe of bright red hair and topped it all off with sunglasses. Dressed like this, she'd then gone to two little bars on Lexington, asking around for a midwife. Dressing up had served its purpose in keeping her identity secret. It just remained to be seen if any of the backroom abortionists so far recommended to her turned out to be actual midwives. She had almost gone to these hardcore places in her normal dress, but after she'd met neighbors all working toward citizenship and prosperity, she realized she wanted to stay respectable in their eyes. Without her family history to buoy her, she found her reputation to be a fragile thing. One rumor and she was sunk, and, along with it, Mario's opportunities. Hence the disguise. And she realized if she looked like an immigrant, maybe she'd get some empathy leverage with the midwife.

The Green Parrot Grill, in spite of its notorious history, was a respectable tavern and restaurant, so it didn't feel like a risky environment to be herself, or almost herself. She didn't watch the parrot, or even the odd group of people looking at the bird. Her interest hung on the door, as several women appeared to be alone, but turned out to be in couples or family groups. Like a watched pot never boiling, the door she observed never did anything for her. It wasn't until she became absorbed in the menu that the waitress led up the potential midwife, the one who had put out the flyer and who had sounded so normal on the phone.

Carmen could tell immediately that this one was above the run of the mill. She was in her mid-thirties. More than the pearls in her ears and around her neck, and the prim little collar on her shirtwaist, more than the fashionable cut of her dress, there was something about her posture that radiated elegance. It made Carmen want to stuff the *rebozo* and the fake hair under the table. Instead, she tucked it more firmly around her head and hoped she wasn't jiggling the wig loose from where it was basted in.

"Miss Elena? I am Linda Villanueva."

"Have a seat, Mrs. Villanueva."

This applicant took control of the conversation even before she sat down. "Please call me Linda. I understand from your phone call that you have need of a midwife."

"That is correct." Carmen took off her sunglasses. "The situation is somewhat delicate."

"Are you planning a home birth?"

"Eventually," Carmen said.

"I don't do abortions," Linda said.

"Neither do I," Carmen said. "Um. I mean, I don't want one."

Linda looked at her oddly. "I should ask you if there's a history of birthing problems."

"Good question. No birthing problems. At least, none firsthand."

Linda hesitated, trying to look Carmen over without seeming to. "When are you due?"

"First, before we talk about my situation, I was sort of interested in becoming a midwife myself," Carmen said. "How do you go about getting certified here?"

"There's a program that can fast-track you in. There's a nurse-midwife program—I can get you in if you qualify," Linda said. "But I thought you were here about a pregnancy?"

"You are not the first midwife I've seen about my situation," Carmen confessed. "You're actually midwife number four. The first legitimate one turned out to be a nun who was out to save the souls of wayward girls. She offered me sanctuary for my baby in a church-run orphanage. I think she was campaigning against abortionists."

"Was this possibly the oldest woman who ever lived?"

"Yes, she was."

"I know who she was. Sister Mary Unibraugh."

"Exactly right," Carmen said. "I thought assisting at an actual birth might be too much for her."

"There was once a time when she was the best midwife around, but that was a number of years ago."

"At least a century ago, from the looks of it."

"The truth is that Sister Mary is really..." Linda's voice faded to a conspiratorial whisper.

"Is what?"

"She's really twenty-three. But being a midwife in New York is so demanding she aged prematurely."

Carmen laughed out loud.

"Sister Mary is living in another century. She means well, but I can certainly understand why you would not want her to deliver your baby."

"All the obstetricians are men, and what do they know."

"Indeed."

Carmen evaded the reference to delivering her baby. "And then I ran into a couple of doulas, one who joked about hangers and blood, and another who brought a grisly toolkit. They were clearly unsuitable. They masqueraded as midwives but they were abortionists with no medical training, and certainly no certification," Carmen said. "I hope you don't mind, but the truth is that you look too fashionable to be serious about your work."

"I don't need to prove myself," Linda said. "I have no reason to wear a nursing uniform everywhere I go. I've been at it for more than ten years now and rely mostly on word of mouth."

"Reasonable," Carmen said. There was something about the way Linda had said that she didn't need to prove herself. "That's what I always...that's what I heard to do."

The waitress returned. Carmen asked for two of the daily specials.

"That's okay," Linda said, "I—"

"No. It's on me. Really."

"I wasn't expecting that," Linda said. "Many, if not all, of my expectant mommies are from out of the country or poor. You don't seem to be either. I don't care how you're dressed. You lost your accent along the way. There's no way you're not American-born. At first guess, I'd say Texas. And if you're pregnant, you're either carrying the baby very well, or it's the early days."

Carmen neither confirmed nor denied Linda's speculation.

"What I need may be a little unusual," Carmen said.

"Go ahead."

"Actually, my baby is already born. I just need a birth certificate."

"You know a midwife can only officiate if she delivers the baby."

Carmen skirted the actual story, just said the baby had come when she was on the road, and wouldn't elaborate more than that. Afterward, they walked out on the sidewalk together.

"I've had immigrant mothers who had the baby on their own with no witnesses. I'm not saying I'll agree, but I'll take a look at the baby."

"All right. But not yet. I'm just moving in. Give me your number and I'll let you know when."

Chapter Twenty-Six

Carmen was in love. After days of hand-washing diapers in the rusty water of the kitchen sink, she'd discovered her building's basement washing machines. She walked down two flights of steps every day to wash the baby's diapers. After a week of dealing with diapers on buses, planes, and trains, and in the apartment, the machines were a miracle. Coin-operated washing machines hadn't hit Nogales yet, but they'd been in New York already for a year, and she was delighted.

In her apartment, she'd pried up loose boards, and with cleverness that would have rivaled her father's, made a better hiding place, a cunning spring-loaded hiding spot for Mario's money. It was convenient; it was safe; it was invisible. The stash of cash was Mario's, not hers, and she vowed she would break into it only if he needed something she couldn't pay for. Nothing about the hiding place indicated it was there.

She was already well on her way to getting to know the girls, who had been tag-teaming to watch Mario as Carmen made her daily sally into the city. Marilyn the blonde, who lived next door to Tina, was actually Mary Lynn. They'd grown up neighbors and there was a good chance they were going to end up marrying each other's brothers. The girls had watched Mario when Carmen was at the Green Parrot securing the midwife's signature on the birth certificate. Sometimes they worked together, and sometimes Carmen alternated the girls' babysitting shifts to keep everybody happy.

* * *

There had been something about Linda that Carmen trusted. It wasn't her manner as much as their mutual passion for midwifery and scorn for male obstetricians. On the way home from the Green Parrot days before, she'd spent thirty minutes in a shared cab as Linda filled her head with passionate stories about being a midwife. By the time they arrived, Carmen was not only ready to enlist in Linda's program, she regretted being unable to tell hundreds of birthing stories of her own, all of which were even more dramatic and more interesting. None of them had happened in a nice, polite hospital, but against the backdrop of a harsher reality. But she had resisted the urge to call. She'd waved goodbye from outside the building and walked away, feeling Linda's eyes on her back.

If Carmen missed a profession, it was not bookkeeping. Midwifery was in her blood. Women of Nogales had been relying on the women of Carmen's mother's line in their time of need for centuries. Carmen might be the first to be medically sanctioned in the world of men, but the commitment was unchanged. Regardless of their shared passion, Carmen worried that it was risky to bring Linda to the baby. It may have been, but she was learning to take chances. Eventually she called. Eventually, in the *rebozo* and wig, she met Linda downstairs in her building.

"It's a bit dark in here, isn't it? I don't mean to complain," Linda said.

"Better hang onto the railing. The stairs are a bit steep."

Linda was behind her, but she glanced back and saw Linda's reluctance to touch the railing, a feeling she shared herself.

"Don't tell anyone, but I bleach it twice a week. I promise you can touch it without contracting impetigo. But maybe don't go up to the third floor."

Once inside, she could sense Linda judging the apartment. Tina was in the new wooden rocking chair—not that there was room to rock it without moving some other piece of furniture—and reading a new volume, number 22, of "Amazing Stories." Tina's jaw dropped at the sight of Carmen wearing the wig.

Carmen excused herself to go behind a folding screen. One could hardly say it separated the bedroom area in these crowded conditions.

Linda was politely speechless, enough for Carmen to be embarrassed at the cruddy apartment, and how crowded it was with big new furniture. She saw Linda looking over at the cradle she'd gotten for Mario. It was about the only thing that was not still wrapped in brown paper. All the furniture was still covered in it, though the girls had tried to get Carmen to take it off.

Carmen emerged from the screen without the wig and *rebozo*. Tina looked relieved; Linda froze at Carmen's changed appearance. Although she was too prudent to comment, she made her way to the *rebozo* and checked out how the wig was sewed in.

Tina silently accepted a dollar as she slipped out. The expression on her face demanded an explanation. Carmen knew she was going to be the subject or object of Tina's next gossip sessions.

Linda saw Mario, who was lying awake in his crib wearing only a diaper. She picked him up, checked him over, and dressed him in a sleeper that was draped over the back of the chair. He didn't fuss, not even when she set him down, but that might have been because she started the cradle rocking. When she was done, she walked back to Carmen, standing rigidly by the door.

"Two weeks old," Linda said. "He still has the stump of his umbilical cord. And he couldn't look any more like you. He's your spitting image."

"A bit younger than that," Carmen admitted. "He was too big for newborn clothes when he was born."

"Daddy was big?"

Carmen's heart raced unpleasantly at the thought of Francisco.

"Yes." Carmen looked away. This midwife was altogether too perceptive.

"Not too fond of Daddy. I don't care if you don't have a ring," Linda said. "Was he there for the birth? Were there witnesses?"

Carmen hesitated. "Just me."

After a keen look, Linda said, "If the lack of a ring bothers you, you can always say he's your nephew."

"So...the birth certificate," Carmen choked out. "How much?"

"Not so fast," Linda said.

Carmen's heart raced, wondering if Linda

was going to demand something, like maybe to look over Carmen. That examination would prove Mario was not her son.

Linda continued, "Do you want to get into the midwife program? Did you graduate from high school? Are you under 35? I think you'd be perfect, and I have one open slot, even though the program's officially closed."

Carmen's mouth turned dry. Without hesitating to think about it, she answered.

"Yes, yes, and yes."

"Okay, let's talk."

In the end, nothing else was said about Mario's parentage. Linda filled out the birth certificate form with no exchange of cash and also accepted Carmen's signature on the nursing program application. After she left, Carmen felt like she'd been given some kind of blessing. Maybe the fates were looking kindly on her at last.

Chapter Twenty-Seven

With Linda Villanueva's assistance, Carmen enrolled in the United States Cadet Nurse Corps's nursing program. A student nurse who joined the Cadet Nurse Corps got a government subsidy that paid for her tuition, books, and uniforms. As Elena, she was accepted (in spite of Elena's math grades). The only standards were that she be between the ages of seventeen and thirty-five, healthy, and have graduated from high school. Carmen had not graduated from high school, but she was good at math, ready to believe in the science she was taught, and willing to take on both the classes in the mornings and the hospital shifts that were also a part of the program. The girls were happy to babysit. Life developed a routine.

She'd started doing laundry in the afternoons between school and work, when the laundry room was least crowded, as most people in the building worked during the day. While her daily load of baby diapers cycled in soap from Tina's father's store, she read whatever reading material had been left behind.

Along one wall of the basement, metal folding chairs in varying condition were empty except for a stack of newspaper and magazines. A line of naked incandescent bulbs burned from the low-slung ceiling. The basement smelled strongly of chlorine and mildew, but not overwhelmingly so. The black-and-white tile floor was slick in places, with traces of soapy water pooling under one of the washers. After dropping her laundry into a coin-operated machine, pouring in the shaved soap flakes, and making certain the machine was closed, she would back the sturdiest-looking folding chair up against a wall to wait for the load to finish and dig through the abandoned reading material.

One day, she scavenged a ragged section of the *New York Times* from January 11 while the machines were running. Pushing his stroller a few feet further from the noisy machines, she noticed Mario was awake and staring with great interest at the ceiling. She turned the stroller away from the bare bulbs to protect his vision. His eyes then fixed on a tattered theater poster taped to the painted concrete-block wall. "Make Mine Manhattan," a play, had apparently ended a run of 429 performances at the Broadhurst Theater on January 8, 1949.

"Sorry, Mario, we missed that one," she told him. He didn't look too upset over it.

"Are you interested in the news?"

Mario cooed and kicked his feet, but his eyes seemed to be on the poster, so she turned a page and read silently until a couple of her neighbors, two Hispanic women, walked in chattering in Puerto Rican accents. Their animated voices reminded her of home. They were more interesting than day-old news, so she hid behind the paper and listened.

They were griping about the inequity—that the Americans in the building only paid seven dollars per room, but most of the tenants were Puerto Rican, and the landlord charged Puerto Ricans and Cubans eight dollars a room. Carmen slouched behind her paper, surprised that her Arizona-born English had qualified her for a discount—something not to tell her immigrant neighbors, if they asked. The day before, she'd heard other tenants discussing sermons, Mass, and the new school that a Father Scannell was going to open in the next year. She needed to finagle a meeting with this Father Scannell. The only way she knew how to fit in was as a midwife, and the only way she knew how to do that was to be a pillar of the community. That meant church, and church here meant Father Scannell.

The two women looked not much older than high school girls, one of them with dark hair, the other's dyed an unlikely shade of blonde. They started arguing about the landlady's parentage, starting off with her bastardy and adding more colorful forebears to her pedigree with every volley. Carmen lost track of the lineage, but somewhere after the bastardy came the mating of a goat and a jackass, pretty much the whole farm-yard plus some zoo animals and cats and dogs, and Carmen had to stifle a laugh. This, unfortunately or not, made them notice her. She held the newspaper up higher, but the younger of them, the well-endowed blonde with red lipstick and a tight sweater, aggressively shoved down the not-too-absorbing article on weather that was nearest Carmen's face.

"Anything interesting in that newspaper?" she asked in Spanish.

"It snowed in Los Angeles," Carmen said in kind. "For the first time, ever. Cats and dogs." The reference to animals first made the girls exchange embarrassed looks, then hoot with laughter for three minutes straight. "No relation to Mrs. Beebe," Carmen added, which set them off into giggleland again.

The tough attitude evaporated. They introduced themselves as Olinda and Orquida Oropeza, sisters who worked as waitresses at one of the neighborhood greasy spoons. Orquida exclaimed over Mario's tiny hands and feet, which brought him to Olinda's attention, and they both made faces at him while they talked. As he was still under a month old, Mario didn't really respond; pretty much all he was good at was messing diapers and sleeping, but at both of those things, he could not be outdone.

The girls shared an apartment on the fourth floor, next door to the one their parents lived in with five of their siblings, all brothers. The boys were *piragua* and pushed *piragüero* carts, except in weather like this, when no one bought the pyramids of flavored shaved ice. In winter, they sold tamales. The whole family was saving together to start a restaurant, but there weren't enough savings in the world enough for the sisters to move back into that two bedroom apartment with five of their brothers.

Chapter Twenty-Eight

Braving the pellets of sleet that made the streets so slick she had to lean against buildings to stay upright, Carmen had pushed the stroller several times past the outside of St. Cecilia's. She hadn't gone in, intimidated by the grand red building that had been built sometime in the 1800s. She felt the burn of guilt each time she came close to the church, because she didn't think God would forgive her for killing her brother-in-law, even if he was a bastard straight from hell who had killed Elena in hot blood.

She decided to ride the train home but missed the stop. She always rode the train back and forth to the nursing program, which was both school and work. It felt familiar.

The wooden trains had open-ended platforms. A conductor manually operated the gates between cars and pulled a cord to tell the engineer when the gates were closed. She had every intention of getting off and riding back, but Mario, who had been grouchy, had been lulled to sleep and she didn't want to wake him. She found herself riding the whole circuit, and she spent it gazing out the window. The city flashed by, sometimes dragged by as the train slowed for traffic.

In her first days in New York, if she wasn't talking to midwives, when one or the other of the girls arrived, she pretended to go to a job and rode the trains all day, just like some of the city's homeless, who slept on the train and rode until they were kicked off. The newness of riding the train soon palled, but it helped her learn the city. Carmen tended to study her companions. The homeless ones were easy to spot because they wore the same clothes, shoes, and dirt from day to day. Carmen's attention was particularly captured by a woman who was always there with two unusually sedate children, thin and pale. Their clothes fit badly, the knees and elbows were frayed and heavily patched, and never changed. If they were rousted by the conductor, they always exited at "their stop" near a particular overpass in the Bowery. An older girl, Virgie, always held hands with her little sister, who Carmen learned from eavesdropping they called Little Peg. Peg never failed to greet her with a smile in her big eyes that only emphasized her hollow cheeks and sickly pallor. The pair of them reminded her painfully of the hole in her life left by the loss of Elena.

When they did not appear for several days, Carmen got off at their stop, in a part of the city where she'd never set foot. Asking around did no good, but she had the idea of following some people who struck her as being homeless. After returning a few days in a row and following first one and then another, she found where they were staying—a warren of packing crates, cardboard boxes, and makeshift detritus-built dwellings hidden under the bridges. She walked through the cringing horde till she found the children. Their mother was noticeably absent.

Carmen squatted down beside them until the older girl noticed her and said hello.

"I haven't seen you lately," Carmen said.

"Little Peg caught a chill."

Carmen peeked into the shaky wall of discarded packing materials leaning against a wall and saw the little girl, bundled up, sleeping, with bright color in her usually pale cheeks.

"Where's your mother?"

"You ain't a social worker, are ya?"

"Do I look like a social worker?" Carmen asked.

Virgie didn't answer.

"Well, I'm not."

"Mama's got work cleaning houses," Virgie confessed. Her stomach growled, loud enough for Carmen to hear.

"Is there a food cart nearby?" Carmen asked.

"Sure. There's a guy what sells sweet potatoes, and another who sells drinks. There's tamales and hot dogs, a whole lot of stuff if you know where to look." She looked at her foot and scuffed it in the dirt, which there was a lot of. "But we ain't got no more money, and Mama's off cleaning houses to pay for medicine."

"Can I tell you a secret?" Carmen whispered.

The girl brightened. "Sure. I like secrets."

"I'm not from around here."

"I can tell. You talk funny."

She lowered her voice. "I got lucky, see. I got some money in my pocket, but I don't know where to get sweet potatoes and tamales and hot dogs."

"Since you're not from around here."

Carmen pulled out a dollar bill. "I got all this to spend, and I don't know where to go. And I'm so hungry."

Virgie's eyes grew big. A hot dog was five cents. A dollar would keep them in food for days. Sometimes her mother worked a week and came home with a dollar.

"Gosh, I can tell you where to go. Just go left by the corner, and go across the street, there's a short cut between them two buildings, then—"

"I'd never remember all that," Carmen

said.

Virgie stared at the dollar bill.

"I know where-all to go, but I can't leave Little Peg."

"I'll wait here till you get back."

Virgie didn't take much convincing. Carmen pulled out a second dollar. "Look, I found another one." She pressed the bills into the little girl's hand. "Make sure you get everything you want, and whatever your sister and mama like," Carmen said.

No argument there, either.

As soon as Virgie disappeared into the light at the end of the alley, Carmen turned to where Peg lay sleeping. There were two pallets beside her. It was like in Goldilocks and The Three Bears—easy to see whose pallets were whose. Carmen took all the bills from her wallet except train fare and used a diaper pin to stick the money onto the mother's pillow. She took out an eyebrow pencil and then wrote on the backside of the pillow, "Spend it well. A friend."

Virgie was back in no time, laden down

with hot dogs and tamales, sweet potatoes, baked apples, and a moist handful of change.

"What a good job," Carmen said, setting down her newsprint-wrapped hot dog and bun beside the still-sleeping Peg. She accepted the change Virgie gave her, but dropped it into the blankets. "I have to go to my own work now."

"What do you do?" Virgie asked, her mouth full.

"My best job is that I help mamas have babies," Carmen said, standing up. Her legs ached from squatting so long, but it was worth it. She stretched her legs. "Sometimes I'm a bookkeeper, and sometimes I sew things for people, but just by hand. I'm no good on machines."

Virgie was about to launch into another stream of questions. Carmen hastily told her goodbye, and left at a run to catch the next train.

The next day, she rode the train again, got off at the stop, and checked the underpass. The girls were gone. Another family had taken their spot. She hoped the best for them, and felt better about herself than she had in a while.

Maybe she could give away more of Francisco's money and feel even better. Still, she wanted to go to Mass. Not to pray, it was too late for that. But she wanted to meet people, make a place in the world for herself and for Mario. The first weeks she spent riding the train pretending to work—before she'd gotten into nursing school—had not been wasted. They had taught her a lot about New York, and had given her a chance to see some of the worst of the city, places not visited by tourists. And there were the headlines. She had spent a lot of time reading abandoned newspapers left on the train. Every day, there were mob shootings, missing persons. She'd look at the articles and think of Francisco's cronies and underlings. She still wondered if they would come after her, but there was no way to know. She thought she was safe, but what if the police were looking for her?

She got her hair bobbed. Short, her hair turned surprisingly curly. She looked like a different person.

This was not Nogales, where her day job

had demanded anti-Francisco diligence, but the world outside was still a place where she was pursued. Every time she left the apartment, she could feel someone out there, looking for her. The back of her neck would prickle, and she'd look around but see no one. Home was that place behind a door with a good lock. The apartment was still a refuge from New York, but she questioned if it could keep out the whole world.

It was worst at night, waiting for the darkness to end in a city that never slept. The clamor of the city was always just outside the glass of her window. The roar of traffic. Planes, trains, spinning tires, sirens, horns. Who were these people, and where were they always going, always moving, alive in the night when they should be in their beds? The city was packed with people. The brick-and-plaster building façade might keep out the cold, but it trapped inside the voices of the unknown. On her side of her solid door, through the thin walls, the drifting voices of strangers, their laughter, tears, fighting, visited Carmen. Arguments and reconciliations, whispers and yells.

In her building, even in the buildings sandwiched on three sides, the vents and thin walls brought strange acoustics into play. Like the tunnels in Nogales, sometimes voices were clear, sometimes whole conversations could be heard, sometimes only indistinct sounds, but all of them intrusions in this unfamiliar place, marked her the outlander, the refugee.

Nothing bothered Mario, contentedly asleep in the dresser drawer she'd made up into a bed for him.

Night after night, she lay awake, staring at a spot on the ceiling, wondering if it was a shadow cast from the outside or if she needed to paint. Neighbors across the way would stand in the hall, talking in loud voices with two or three others for what seemed like hours before finally slamming their door. A good baby, Mario slept through it—she checked frequently to make sure.

Carmen had hardly slept since Mario had been born, an irony since she kept being advised by strangers that, as a new mother, she could forget sleeping until the baby turned eighteen. Since his birth, they had been on the road. Now, even with this place of her own, she still felt far from safe. She was like a tree without roots, feeling she could topple at any time.

She'd pushed herself till she was beyond exhaustion, to the point where she'd been so tired tonight, she'd barely been able to access her strange bath. It was hidden under the kitchen counter, the unwieldy spawn of a compact urban mind that cared nothing for beauty. Her father would have scorned it, and would have made some elegant solution, but this building's architect lacked her father's graceful mind. She wrestled the counter out of the way, against the wall. It was only the promise of a hot bath that had egged her on.

The water came out tinted a strange color and smelled of rust, but it was reasonably hot, and she hadn't had to heat it on the stove. She'd even drifted off for an instant until the persistent specter of Francisco walked behind her eyes. She jerked awake before the steam had even stopped rising from the water.

Even the new flannel gown, the mattress she'd had delivered, and crisp new cotton sheets failed to induce her to sleep. She dwelled in darkness, flickering between muted city lights tracking across the ceiling until the shadows grew and engulfed her. She wondered what she was going to do. Most of all, she wondered when any of the Sanchez family would catch up with her. How was she going to evade them? But she had to. There was Mario to protect.

A distant door slammed. For some reason, this one woke Mario. He cried out.

Carmen got up. "Hello, little one. Can I cry, too?" She looked up, past the flickering patterns on her ceiling, straight up to the heavens, and asked, "God? What next? Maybe you can find someone else to pick on? No, I'm sorry, I didn't mean that. Just forget everything I complained about, and give my love to Elena in heaven. Tell her I'm doing my best."

There was no answer from above, but about eight inches under her left ear, Mario yelled again in that puny, baby voice, demanding and inconsolable.

"I know what you want."

Carmen held up a diaper. He batted his hands and feet, orchestrating his baby-demands like the conductor of an invisible orchestra.

"Hang on, maestro. There's a magic solution to your problem."

She changed his diaper, continuing the one-sided conversation. She hadn't turned on a light but there was enough already to see he watched her intently.

"Shame on him, that bad neighbor of ours, slamming that door and waking you up. Are you hungry, little one? This is what it is like to be in one place, with your own kitchen, your own bottles, your own diapers in your own room. No more buses, no more planes. Do you notice what it's like to wake up in the same place where you went to sleep? Not that you've ever complained. Maybe you miss the traveling, eh? We're so far from home. Maybe we can stay here. You can grow roots and turn into a New Yorker." If he understood her, the prospect did not seem to make him happy. Some neighbor didn't like the sound of baby screams, and thumped a wall, yelling for quiet.

"You want quiet, you quit slamming your doors!" she yelled back. "Serves them right," she whispered to Mario.

She'd been trying to be positive, and had nearly talked herself to tears. No more of that.

As a bottle heated, she walked about with the baby in her arms, singing "Rice Pudding," a lullaby from her childhood. She could recall seeing her mother doing the same thing with Elena when Carmen had been so little she could only hold the baby when she was sitting down, with the baby resting on a pillow in her lap. She fought to close her mind to the memories that washed her in sorrow. She returned to her couch bed, fed him his bottle, and kept singing. She'd made him so comfortable, he was asleep in moments. He had already stretched out another inch or more in length, and was nearly sleeping through the night. Reluctantly, she put him back in his bed, put the milk back in the icebox, and returned to her couch to stare at the phantom shadow dance across her ceiling.

Then she heard a note. And another.

Night music.

At first she thought it was her imagination. But no, after only a few notes, she realized she must have disturbed another neighbor with her singing. She could feel her face heating in embarrassment as she clearly made out the strains of a guitar. Someone in the building was playing "*Arroz Con Leche,*" a complex interpretation, the silly lullaby rendered silvery by Spanish guitar, interlaced with a cascade of chords and notes.

The embarrassment did not continue. The notes were sweet, like music playing directly to her hungry soul. It was like listening to her father. She knew it was some neighbor with a guitar, but still, she pictured Papi in heaven playing the rice pudding song. She closed her eyes, and saw him playing. His quick, clever fingers. His dark eyes, shining with mischief and love. For the first time since the endless weeks of her new life, she fell into a deep and healing sleep.

Chapter Twenty-Nine

Carmen ran into the sisters again on her daily laundry trek.

"Why do you come down here?" Carmen asked. "You never do laundry."

"Our mother does our laundry."

"Orquida is stalking the guitarist who lives on the third floor," Olinda ratted on her sister. "She heard from Jenova in 302 that Mister bumped into Mr. Rios in the hall outside her door and asked to borrow some detergent, so he must be about to do his wash. His name is Ramon."

The musician. Of course they heard him, too. Carmen felt a little deflated at that. Ever since she'd heard him play, she had been thinking of him as all hers. Of course they heard him. Probably everyone below the sixth floor heard him.

Orquida was apparently not a very good stalker. Her informants had made a mistake. Ramon the guitarist did not come down after all, though the sisters were still waiting after Carmen's laundry was done. Carmen was glad she didn't see him. As long as the guitarist was unknown, in her mind, it was still her father who played sweet music from heaven every night.

She trudged up the steps, hauling the stroller packed with clean diapers and little Mario wedged in, but she wasn't paying attention to the dark, narrow stairwell. She was thinking about the night music. In her mind, she'd known it wasn't her father playing from behind the pearly gates, but her heart was not so sure.

After she turned out the lights and the baby was sleeping, well after midnight, the soft strains of the guitarist continued to slip through the lonely night and touch her. Touch her not like the stranger he was, but in the most personal way, as if it were a secret whispered between common spirits. There was a lonesome quality to his songs, as if the musician, too, were adrift in a friendless world, and privately sharing his music with Carmen, the only thing in the entire city that had spoken to her.

* * *

She was frozen at the entrance of St. Cecilia's. Literally, she felt as if she could not move, that maybe God had chosen to turn her into a pillar of salt for murdering a man. Then Tina, who stood behind her, gave her a hard shove. Carmen took a staggering step through the church doors without turning into salt or catching on fire, being dragged straight down into hell, or any of a dozen horrible consequences of murder that had crossed her fertile imagination, but Mass was no comfort. It merely gave her time to think that God knew she'd dallied for weeks, twiddling her thumbs outside, watching the parishioners stream in without joining them. He knew she'd never have come inside if Tina hadn't seen her standing apart and practically dragged her in.

Not that Tina was devout; she'd only commandeered Carmen to have someone to whisper to during the lulls. She promised to introduce her to Father Scannell after Mass. Mario had chosen his time well, and halfway through the service, started squalling his lungs out. Carmen took him out, and she got him quiet. Too embarrassed to go back in, she waited till it was over, and found Tina in the foyer.

As promised, Tina performed the introductions, but it had been a hasty thing, done in a line as they were shaking hands after exiting into the endless grey winter of New York. She wore no ring and had a baby, and found herself shunted out of the group. Tina didn't notice, not then, and not when Carmen never returned.

A cold wind blew straight through Carmen's Salvation Army coat, the coarse fake camelhair that had been worn gently for one Tucson season, after which the owner had judged it heavier than necessary. What was too warm for Tucson was too breezy for New York. She was paying now for her lack of foresight. Beneath it, Carmen was insulated with so many layers of sweaters, shirts, and hose that when she moved, she felt as clumsy as Orson Welles' Macbeth—a whale on land. The chill would have sent her back home if not for a bad case of cabin fever.

The deceitful day had dawned a sunny blue and misled her, or she'd not have braved the weather, cabin fever or not. Now that she was out, it had grayed into a winter storm in the time it had taken her to cross a narrow side street. The white clouds that floated so benignly moments ago were now gray and threatening, heavy with snow. Her desert-bred soul was aghast as sleet began to fall, a sudden blast of pellets that struck with the impact of coins, bouncing up when they hit the salted sidewalk and laying another sheet across the already ice-glazed pavements.

All that could be seen of Mario in the stroller were rosy cheeks and bright eyes. He wasn't complaining, even though he, like Carmen, was wrapped to the edge of paralysis in clothes, Mario topped with an extra layer of blankets. He wore even more layers than she; with his growth spurt, few of them fit. It was impossible to tell if his color was from the icy air or his trapped body heat. She checked to make sure he was secured by the rolled blankets on either of his sides, as she stood observing a herd of pedestrian working stiffs waiting for the light to change.

Back in her apartment, she'd taken to watching a rush hour phenomenon, something she'd never have imagined in Nogales. Clumps of crowds gathered at the corners to rush across when the lights changed. From the pinprick peephole scratched into her white-painted window, it had looked like some kind of orchestrated game, but from here on the ground, it was a deadly earnest, desperate race as pedestrians made tracks to avoid being mowed down by iron-footed, clock-hounded drivers fuming to race to or from work. She tried to stick to smaller streets and had done a pretty good job up to now of avoiding the herds of pedestrians navigating major thoroughfares.

She finally approached the corner, thinking she was at a safe distance and ready to participate in the mad dash. She was close enough to see and admire the detail of a gentleman's well-made tie, a woman's beautiful coat with an over-sized collar and bell skirts, a leopard-print clutch. Beneath a full-length fur that had been carelessly left unbuttoned, she glimpsed an ornate beaded twinset. Even on the street, common fashion was a world away from Nogales. She was actually cran-ing to see some beadwork when someone knocked the carriage out of her grasp.

She lunged forward to stop it and was swept into the crowd bounding to beat the light. Locked in the throng, she was tall enough to see above other heads, where traffic waited to cross the lines of pedestrians, foaming like angry bulls, scuffing the dirt about to race the matador. The waiting cars glared their headlights and steamed with impatience. Before her, the crowd dragged; behind her, they pushed. There was no leeway, and less breathing room. A boy wearing *tenis* stopped abruptly to tie his shoe with his foot up on the curb. Carmen had reached the handle and swerved Mario's stroller to avoid barreling into him, and the crowd behind her knocked her down and marched straight over her. Not a march exactly, but a quick storm of feet, most avoiding her, but several stepped squarely, possibly even deliberately, on her: hand, leg, hip. One kick nailed her in the side of her face.

She pushed halfway up from the pavement on ripped mittens—but couldn't get her footing, and crawled the last few feet, just in front of a yellow cab turning right, impatient for the green light, the driver's face glaring at her from behind the wheel as if she'd spent all week making plans to fall on his personal green light today, just to delay him—of all people in this outrageously huge city. He narrowly missed her, didn't even wait till she'd made it to the sidewalk. His cab had its revenge, deliberately or not, when it smartly clipped the stroller's handlebar, shooting it careening up the icy slope and straight up the building at the corner, where it stopped, sitting up like a begging dog, propped up on its handlebar. Mario, rolled up like a little sausage, turned end over end, flopping out the carriage like a rolling football, and wobbled across sidewalk and curb into traffic.

Carmen saw this almost in slow motion and shrieked. She had no footing, but scrambled forward like a football player on ice, her shoe caught in her hem. She heard the fabric of her skirt rip, and skidded on her hands and knees, bypassing the curb and making a beeline for Mario.

Meanwhile, a dapper young businessman about to take his last step over the curb picked up the baby an instant before he would have rolled past the grating into the icy depths of the sewer. Carmen, without enough traction to get upright, managed to launch herself directly into him. He was tall, slim, and athletic, and easily caught her under her armpit with Mario nestled in the curve of his other arm. With remarkable balance, he was upright as Carmen's forward rush carried them both several yards across the ice, without a wobble. Mario, who by all rights should have been knocked senseless, was giggling.

"Problems?"

"That taxi driver could have killed me!" Carmen's face grew hot.

"Did you lose something?"

She snatched Mario from the stranger's grasp and stole a quick glance behind her.

Carmen gathered what remained of her dignity and left the stranger behind as she approached the buggy. It had come to rest with all four tires in square contact with the red brick wall as if their next casual stroll was going to be straight up the side of the brownstone. She bent down and tugged at the handlebar. When the stroller bounced down on its buoyant bicycle tires, it was more of a parallelogram than a rectangle, in dubious condition. When she pushed it, it moved like a horse with legs of four different lengths—each wheel now had its own oval. It struggled to roll in four different directions.

Flakes of snow floated down, in rapidly increasing number. She pushed. The stroller didn't really cooperate. She dragged it a few feet, and stared blankly at a pink poodle skirt in a window before stepping into the shop on the corner. The sign on the door said SIMINIS. The shop was tiny, with shelving all along one wall that had scraps of fabric and a number of fashion books. A clutch of dressmakers' dummies was frozen in various stages of completion, not posed but shoved in front of the window in the least attractive positions, but set to take up the least amount of space. A naked one awaited the garment currently being worked on by the tailor. He knelt at the hemline of a woman standing on a stool, fitting her in an inside-out wedding dress poked with pins and slashed by chalk marks.

"With you in a moment," the tailor mumbled, over a mouthful of pins.

"No rush," Carmen said. Her body still felt frozen, but her lungs caught a full draught of the store's manufactured heat. The shop was stifling and smelled like burning dust, like the old furnace in Francisco's factory that never kept the place warm, but made it stink of burnt lint.

Carmen tested the inside of the carriage with her fist. It seemed sturdy enough, so she put Mario down inside and began the business of unswaddling and unwrapping him so he wouldn't overheat in the sweltering store. A waft of cold outdoor air rushed over her as someone entered, but she didn't look up. She took off her coat and a sweater, adding it to a mound of garments hanging over the handlebars.

"Any more undressing and the carriage is going to collapse," a man observed.

Carmen looked up to see the guy who had rescued Mario.

"Thank you for helping," she said decisively and turned her back, wishing he hadn't followed her. "Good day." Every stranger had the face of Francisco, as far as she was concerned.

The inside-out bride stepped off the stool and disappeared into a dressing room. The tailor rushed over to a little glass counter and began writing furiously in a little book, stopping only to settle the date of the bride's next fitting.

He took off his glasses and stuck them in his shirt pocket next to his scissors and measuring tape. Deep patches of sweat marred the armpits of his well-fitted shirt. He glanced at Carmen, and the man behind her, and she could see his eyes registering them as a couple. He looked harried, even tired, as he cast an exhausted glance at Mario. He took a step, then another, then bent over, looking closely at the baby.

"What beautiful embroidery," he exclaimed. "Where did you get it done?" he stopped as if trying to remember her name, which of course he could not do as they had never met. He started over. "It's always nice to meet a potential customer—you are...?"

"Carmen Garcia." She could have bit off her tongue in chagrin when she realized she'd used her own name, but it was too late. Next time, she could just save everyone the time, and announce to the next stranger, "Hi, I shot a murderer in Arizona."

"Jim Smith," the man behind Carmen said.

He put his palm possessively on Carmen's shoulder. She flinched, instantly reminded of Francisco. Smith took his hand off Carmen's shoulder and reached out to shake the tailor's hand.

The tailor shook Smith's hand. "I am Simini. I assume you will be getting married? I have some wedding books over here." He gestured toward a shelf, but his eyes roved down Carmen's body until they registered surprise somewhere around her middle.

"Highly unlikely," Carmen told the tailor. "I don't even know his name."

"Jim Smith," the man behind Carmen repeated.

Carmen followed the direction of the tailor's eye, looking down to see her own naked leg—naked but for black winter hose and garters, and the bottom of the lacy scarlet teddy she'd worn beneath her disguise at the Tucson airport—bared by a rip that snaked through her pencil skirt from hem to waist. At that point, the only one not looking at Carmen's leg was Mario. She'd also caught the attention of a few men outside. She grabbed the edges of the skirt and tried to pull it closed, then opted for her coat, which Smith held out for her.

"I think I have a dress situation," she said. "I had an introduction to the pavement outside.

Maybe I could borrow a needle and some thread?"

As soon as the little Italian disappeared into his workroom to search for the right thread, Smith murmured, "A shame to cover that up."

"Look, Mr. Smith—"

"Call me Jim," he said.

"Look, Jim, thank you for saving my nephew, but—"

Smith ran the side of his thumb down her torn garment.

Carmen shivered and stepped back.

"No," she said distinctly.

Smith gave a little bow and dropped his hand to his side.

Carmen felt a little surprised. It's not as if she were accustomed to a man who noticed— and listened to—a woman saying no.

"No offense meant," he said. "You're a beautiful lady."

Carmen gave him a skeptical look.

"I could buy you...and your lovely leg... some dinner and maybe some wine." He inclined his head toward Mario. "Junior here is invited, if you want to bring him. I would stick around now to become better acquainted, but I was on the way to a meeting."

She made the date, knowing she would never show up.

"Let me send a car to pick you up."

Carmen pointed out a random building through the window, down the street a few blocks over in the wrong direction. "That's my place," she lied.

Moments after Smith had left, the tailor came out carrying a beautiful silk kimono, as well as a needle and thread.

"You can put this on if you want. The dressing room is in back. But you don't need to do it yourself; if you give it to me, I can have it done in a minute. I have an electric machine out back."

"Seriously," Carmen said, "I can do this."

"I bet you can," he sighed. "If you're the one who did that dragon on the baby's shirt, you're one hell of a seamstress."

Carmen shrugged. "Just a satin stitch,

some straight stitch, split stitch, stem stitch. I'm not a real seamstress, just an accountant who can mend a tear. I can't operate a machine without wrecking the material. Believe me, I know. Everyone I know can sew circles around me on a machine."

She took off her skirt, slipped on the kimono and sat on a tall stool behind a curtain, mending the rip in her dress.

"Machines," the little tailor spat. Carmen wondered what he'd do if he knew she'd learned to sew by suturing immigrants.

Carmen watched his feet in the gap under the curtain. Time and again, he walked toward the baby. She wished she'd brought him in, but really, there was no room for the stroller. She wasn't alarmed; the tailor was back to studying the needlework of the dragon again. He kept exclaiming over the stitching, and she relaxed a little. "Such perfect handwork. Think you could embroider a poodle? I could pay pretty well for some poodle appliqués, all you can sew, actually. And I'll give you ten dollars for that shirt."

Carmen bit off the end of the thread and put her skirt on. Ten dollars was more than a month's rent. She looked at the mending. It would look better if she had ironed it, but she was nearly satisfied with the result. It was close to invisible.

"Spectacular!" Simini bubbled when she came out. He was even gaping at the mending.

"Fifteen dollars for the baby's shirt. I can use it as an appliqué for this—" He gestured with a jerk of his head toward one of his dressmaker dummies wearing a brick red confection cut on oriental lines.

Carmen was less than bowled over by his enthusiasm. Piecework was too much like Francisco's. She might as well be back in Nogales. But it would be a cold day in hell before Francisco would have paid fifteen dollars for a dozen embroidered dragons much less one.

The tailor told her he would pay 80 cents an hour or a dollar per appliqué—whichever turned out to be more. He showed her what he wanted—the designs were simple, much less complicated than Mario's shirt. And he would provide the materials.

That was twice the minimum wage that Francisco paid. Four years earlier, in 1945, minimum wage had gone up to 40 cents an hour. It had taken Francisco a couple of years to comply, and his seamstresses were still making less than that.

"Now, what was that you were saying about piecework? What exactly are you looking for?"

He pulled out some samples.

In the end, Carmen refused to part with Mario's shirt until he outgrew it, but she made a promise to make another sequined dragon that would look perfect on the red dress, and then she'd undertake some "poodles."

Chapter Thirty

A beautiful hazy day. Carmen was relaxed on a field of green, a red plaid picnic cloth stretched out on lovely spring grass with none of the painful cockleburs she remembered from Nogales turf. Yet she knew she and Mario were in Nogales from the quality of the sun and the lay of the land. The picnic basket was full of goodies. Mario wore only a diaper, and he was lying in a nest of blankets, kicking his feet and cooing. Carmen was waiting for someone, but wasn't sure who, or even how she had gotten to this lovely spot. There was no car, no pavement, no matted path where feet had turned down the tender blades of grass—just this idyllic spot, and no one else.

Far on the horizon, the sky was an impossible blue, intersecting land of an impossible green. That's where the distant trace of movement caught her eye. At first it was imperceptible, a red and white speck, but as it drew closer, the figure of a woman appeared, grew larger, achieved the size of a grain of rice. Closer, the bright red of an embroidered skirt and crisp white embroidery edging an off-the-shoulder white shirt became clear, her face shaded by a flat-top wide-brimmed hat, black as death. Carmen felt a sense of welcome for her guest, but she was drowsy on the picnic blanket, transfixed. Mario was more interested in his feet, even when the woman was close enough to pick him up.

"How is my little man?"

It was Elena.

"I have missed you," Carmen said. "Where have you been?"

"Here and there. Mostly keeping an eye on you. Who knew you'd be having such an interesting life?"

She held up the baby, who cooed and tried to play with her face.

"He knows you," Carmen said.

"Of course he knows me. We visit all the

time."

A great rumbling commenced. The vibration came from nowhere and everywhere. The grass waved and quivered, and the sound rolled like the purring of a massive cat, emanating from below. The earth quaked. Carmen's visitor seemed to have more to say, but the field dissolved along with the brilliant sky. Carmen found herself in bed in the cold and dark of her Harlem apartment.

The color was gone, and with it the warm ambiance of summer. Elena had faded into the mist of a dream, and Mario was screaming at the top of his lungs. Carmen felt like joining him.

So why was the room still vibrating? She was in her bedroom, safely in the dark bedroom in Harlem, in the middle of the night. But the room trembled and the blast of sound still echoed in her ears.

Carmen swung her feet over the edge of the bed, sliding into her slippers. She touched the wall and the floor. The mattress made a crisp sound, as did the couch as she brushed against it.

She'd never removed the brown paper covering. On her knees, she felt a vibration coming from the floor through her palms.

She dragged open her back door and propped it open with a block of wood. A blast of frigid air struck her. It was dark, but she could see the bay doors standing open, and the rumbling seemed to be coming from the opening. A silhouette of a figure was hunched over the back of a tractor-trailer. That shadow stood, and stepped outside the bay doors. A moment later, the semi's cab backed in, the driver holding the door open, and looking behind him as he backed in beside the parked trailer. The vehicle rumbled, rocked, huffed, and roared, partnered with a duet of a string of muttered curses and grinding gears, and finally thumped to a stop with a long belching sigh, like an old man after a case of beer, belching in relief. The cab door creaked open. The driver jumped out and kicked a tire, yelling, "Take that, you sonofabitch!"

"You're the sonofabitch," Carmen screamed back. "What the hell did you do that for? It's the middle of the night!"

"Fuck," the driver said, leaping back from the truck and eyeing it in alarm. "Fuck, fuck."

He glanced around but saw no one, reached out gingerly and touched the cab, and jumped back. "I should have turned down that last round."

"Who are you anyway, king of the world that you can come in here at three a.m. shaking the building down? Seems like you could have some consideration for the rest of the world who are asleep in their beds where they should be. I should call the police and tell them you were disturbing the peace."

Carmen's voice echoed strangely against the garage-style acoustics of the downstairs.

The driver turned away from the truck.

"Who's there? Is somebody there? Shit, I thought my truck was talking back."

"Sure, I'm your fucking talking truck."

He walked to the foot of the fire escape and looked up.

"Who the hell are you? Mrs. Beebe providing women in my room now? Tell her I'm grateful, but I'd like some notice if she's sending me roommates."

"I'm the upstairs neighbor you blasted out of bed with your damn horn."

"I was just pulling in from a long haul. I hit the horn by accident when I got out." He craned his neck to see who he was talking to, then gave in to his curiosity and vaulted to the lower stairs to climb up the fire escape. He got a good look at her, and a long slow whistle came out of his mouth like a mountaineer who'd seen Angel's Landing in Utah for the very first time.

"They call me Moonie," he said, manhandling the fire escape, already halfway to Carmen. "I take that back. Tell Mrs. Beebe it's okay. I owe her a bonus."

"You can hold it right there," she said. "That's close enough. I see the art on your trailer, Moon." She looked at the moon painted on the truck and back at him, but he had stopped just beyond the scope of the light of a single bulb from downstairs. Carmen couldn't determine much except that there seemed to be a lot of him. The trucker seemed to keep back in the shadow.

"Moonie," he corrected.

"You always keep this place so dim?" Carmen asked. "You scared of light?"

"I just pulled in," he said, "but yeah. I got nothing worth looking at. I was going to turn in, anyway. Bed. Pillow. What else do I need?"

Carmen didn't see a bed anywhere. Her anger was gone, replaced by curiosity. It was not her imagination that he seemed to draw away from the light. "You got something wrong with you that you live in a garage?"

"You could say that," he said. "Mostly I live in the truck."

"Come on then, show yourself. I won't call the police."

He complied, not pointing out that she had burst into his unit. He leaned forward into the light. It was dim, but enough for Carmen to make out a scar on the left side of his face. He must have been caught in a fire, but otherwise, his face was untouched. He was, if not handsome, at least built along strong lines. Certainly no Phantom of the Opera. A big man. Tall. The physique of someone who worked. He must load his truck himself. Even just driving the truck might fall under the category of physical labor, if the sound of those grinding gears was any example.

"Not too scary," she said. "You're no Frankenstein monster. Good thing for you. If you roared in with a pretty face, I might have blown you away. You were in the war?"

Carmen lifted her hand, revealing the unloaded Smith & Wesson Victory model handgun she'd bought from one of the Oropeza brothers.

He nodded. "Don't think that little peashooter would dissuade me if I was inclined not to be a gentleman," he said. "I used to have two pop guns just like it, and I can't tell you how many Nazis I put down with them. These days I like something warmer in my hands." He jerked his head toward his rig. "Unless I can find me a beautiful woman... Speaking of which—what are you doing in my place? Not that I object. I'd sure as hell rather have you screeching at me than my sonofabitching haunted-ass truck. I'll fix up a cup of motor oil, if you're interested in some caffeine."

"No, I'm in the middle of a good night's sleep—or supposed to be. You blasted me out of bed with that Zeppelin of yours." Carmen waved around the gun for emphasis.

He looked offended.

"Peterbilt," he corrected. He listened to the unearthly wailing, and looked around with a perplexed expression. "It's not you. So who is still screeching?" He glanced suspiciously toward his truck.

Carmen stopped, realizing that the baby was awake.

"Mario!" Carmen dashed into her apartment, Moonie at her heels.

Chapter Thirty-One

Carmen barely made it into the cadet program, where admissions ended in 1948 with the war. The program accelerated her with thirty months of training instead of the traditional thirty-six. She had no shortage of babysitters to take care of Mario when she was in classes at Bellevue Hospital Training School for Nurses. Living expenses were slight. She sewed appliqués every spare minute and carefully stretched her stipends, and the stolen money grew a layer of dust. The at–least seven dollars a week she made sewing while riding the train was more than some families lived on in Nogales.

There were only so many times she could come home from the sterilized hospital and all of its lectures on cleanliness to the grunginess of her apartment. One weekend, she left the baby with the girls and spent a session sweeping, wiping, scrubbing, scraping, sanding, painting, and bleaching. She left no trace of floor, wall, or ceiling untouched. She painted everything white, and finally, after it was all dry, took the brown paper off the new furniture. It felt like things were beginning to change for the better.

* * *

Carmen clambered onto the Harlem Line to the teaching hospital, not paying much attention, and didn't grab a seat fast enough. There was a reel in her head playing the names of the bones of the hand, so she barely noticed that the seats were full of commuters reading their papers. She braced herself, holding onto the pole, oblivious to the rumble and breeze of the subway. As far as she was concerned, the sign inside the bus said "carpal, metacarpal, proximal phalanx, distal phalanx" instead of "Spitting on the platforms or other parts of this car is unlawful. Offenders are liable to arrest by order of the Board of Health." If she had gotten a seat, she'd have pulled out a study sheet, but she could wait until the next stop and hope someone got off. A man seated under the sign was reading a novel, something called *The Second Confession*.

"Ma'am," he said. She realized he'd been repeating himself.

He stood up, a little brown man, somewhat wizened, with glasses riding low over his nose. He looked at her over the tops of his glasses. She realized that her lips had been moving. She must have looked a little crazy, but in New York, who would notice that?

"Please take my seat." He leaned over, indicating the empty bench.

"No, I couldn't."

A kid tried to slip past to capture the seat, and the older man stepped on his foot. It seemed accidental, except that it wasn't.

"I insist," he told Carmen. "You look preoccupied. I respect your profession. And I know you're on your feet all day."

Carmen looked down and tugged her coat closer over her cadet uniform.

"I'm not really in the service—just the nursing program. I'll be spending most of today sitting, not in the wards. I was just thinking aloud. I have a quiz today. I was trying to remember—" She visualized the picture of the bones of the hand, and tried again—silently this time—to list them all.

"You're in school?"

The kid, who was still trying to sneak into the empty seat, appeared to have recovered from his foot injury. He seemed to find Carmen being in school positively hilarious.

"Go to the head of the class, Junior, before I step on your other foot," the little brown man said, quickly flashing a badge. "Want to make something of it? Do I need to take you in? Didn't your momma teach you to give your seat up to the ladies?"

The boy backed into the crowd of open newspapers.

"That wasn't necessary," Carmen said, finally sitting at his insistence. "You put that badge up pretty quick."

"Yes, ma'am," the man said. "Since I didn't want him to see I ain't no cop. I'm security down at the Maternity Center. I recognize your duds. We been riding in to the same shift all this week. Sorry about the kid. Kids these days have rocks in their heads." The guard, who introduced himself as Waldo, was one of half a dozen people who shared the subway into the late shift. They clocked in at different places, but all got off at the same stop.

"You're coming in earlier than usual," Waldo said. "I usually take the next run, but I got an early start."

"I have to make a stop at the post office today before I go in."

The detour to the post office today was driven by insatiable curiosity. She had called the newspaper in Nogales and ordered back copies of all newspapers from the week of Elena's death to the current date to be delivered to a post office box in the name of T. Turcios. The newspaper had cashed her cashier's check weeks ago but was taking its own sweet time to deliver. She'd gotten the post office box and had checked it a dozen times already. Maybe today would be the lucky day. She took out her study sheet and became engrossed in phalanges. She'd have missed the stop if Waldo hadn't tapped her shoulder and pointed out the post office.

This time it was a jackpot. Her box was full of Nogales newspapers from December 1948 and January 1949, packed into a big box.

When she got back on the subway, Carmen had newspapers of her own to read. They had been delivered in a big box, which she placed on the unoccupied seat beside her, and opened while in the subway.

She glanced at a headline and saw that Commander Antonio Martinez of the local firefighters had died, and that Miguel Noriega was elected as their new first commander. Carmen didn't recognize the new guy, but she was sad to hear Commander Martinez had died. She thumbed through several more pages without unfolding the papers and put the top back on the box.

Later, at home, she found the issues dated the week after the flood and put those on top.

She read those first, and found that she was among those presumed dead in the arroyo washout that had drowned Francisco's car, several small farms, and a number of roads. There were no details about Elena's death, just the date of her funeral and a sketchy obituary that a stranger had written. Odd there was no mention of Francisco, but maybe that was because of Segundo. He wouldn't like anyone saying anything bad about his boss and without bad stuff, what else was there to say about him?

Before she let the post office box lapse, she ordered her own and Elena's birth and death certificates, in case she'd ever need them.

Chapter Thirty-Two
Nogales

Trigger Oliver had gone on a couple of dates with a divorcée named Pam who worked in the classified department with the newspaper. It was a pretty small newspaper, and she handled most of the cash transactions that came in over the phone. They had no chemistry whatsoever, and Pam's little boy Mikey had hated him on sight. After the first dinner or two, the dates had come to nothing. But she still called whenever something happened she thought was interesting.

"Funny thing," Pam told him over the phone. "You investigated the death of Carmen Garcia, right?"

"I did," Trigger told her. "You know the story, right?"

"What story?"

"We got a call from the Texas highway

patrol that Carmen wrecked her Ford driving drunk near the border."

"Carmen driving drunk? I don't believe it. She'd never do that," Pam said. "Though I heard she went to stay with a cousin someplace in Mexico."

"I'm just telling you what the highway patrol told me. Smashed the car all to hell. It was definitely her car. I drove down there and took custody of someone who was supposed to be Carmen, and brought her back. Only she didn't look right. A couple of years older, and gaunt, like beef jerky."

"Carmen wasn't gaunt."

"That's what I'm saying," Trigger continued. "I have a picture of her. This looked like an older cousin or aunt, but not exactly Carmen. We got her here, and she turned out to be some drunk named Inez. She swore some woman in Tucson gave her the car, but she'd lost the bill of sale. Judge threw the book at her."

"So you think Carmen's alive?"

"I don't know what I think, but I know

Inez was masquerading as her down in Texas. I just don't know if there's a connection to the shootings."

"Don't get it in your head that I'm crazy, but I thought she called."

"She who? Inez?"

"Hell, no, I never heard of Inez. Carmen. I thought I recognized Carmen's voice over the phone. She delivered Mikey, you know. But it turned out to be someone else, a Mrs. Turcios."

Oliver had interviewed Tomás Turcios, whose name was on a list of people fired by Francisco shortly before the shooting, as people who might potentially hold a grudge.

"Kind of unexpected to get a call from a dead woman. Who was it?"

"This Mrs. Turcios said she was some secretary in New York, a company that was ordering a few months of issues of newspapers, everything from 1949 on. We sent them to a post office box. It wasn't a library, either. Once the library in Tucson ordered a whole year's worth of newspaper for its circulation department. But this place, they just ordered—"

"Hey, if you still have the address and phone for that order, set it aside for me. I'd like to know what they wanted those papers for."

"Yeah? They paid with a money order," Pam said. "Not a check. But they mailed it in, so we got the stamped envelope."

Which is why Oliver spent that next weekend up in New York, tracking down the post office box and return phone number.

The call had been made from a hotel lobby pay phone, and the post office box had lapsed by the time he got there. It was a complete dead end, but Oliver had the feeling he was on the right track. Especially when he got back home, and there was a message from Vital Records that someone had requested that Carmen and Elena's birth and death certificates be mailed to the same post office box.

Chapter Thirty-Three
New York

At this moment of my induction into the United States Cadet Nurse Corps of the United States Public Health Service, I am solemnly aware of the obligations I assume toward my country and toward my chosen profession; I will follow faithfully the teachings of my instructors and the guidance of the physicians with whom I work; I will hold in trust the finest traditions of nursing and the spirit of the Corps; I will keep my body strong, my mind alert, and my heart steadfast; I will be kind, tolerant, and understanding; Above all, I will dedicate myself now and forever to the triumph of life over death; As a Cadet nurse, I pledge to my country my service in essential nursing for the duration of the war.

Thirty months earlier, Carmen had pledged, and now she followed the rest of her class in procession off the podium, receiving a diploma in her gloved hand, carefully aware of the crisply ironed creases in her Cadet Nurse Corps uniform. Although she never admitted it to herself, in the back of her mind, an evil imp was waiting for someone in the auditorium's folding chairs to leap up and yell, "Hey, your name isn't Elena! It's not your name on that certificate." She felt like someone was watching her. Not the whole auditorium, but someone.

Nothing so dramatic happened. She shook the hands of a lot of strangers, her teachers and classmates, and a few people from the Woman's Pavilion and the new Pediatrics Building, both parts of Harlem Hospital on Lenox between 136th and 137th, where she served while learning.

Some of the strangers noticed that she wore not one but two graduation pins.

"This is the Bellevue School of Nursing pin," Linda Villanueva explained to a small group of husbands and parents. "And the one with the mother and baby is the Nurse Midwife pin."

Linda was there in honor of Carmen's

graduation, and of a number of other fledgling midwives she'd recruited. The crowd around her just got bigger, trapping Carmen with all of the hand-shakers and back-patters straining to reach the administrator. Carmen had graduated with honors, easily, with so many years of practical experience informing the textbook theory, and her expertise had helped many of her classmates. It was not where she would have placed herself if she'd been thinking on her feet, but she made the best of it.

Carmen nodded politely and accepted congratulations from parents and family of her classmates. She didn't go into detail about her simultaneous six months interning in the small twelve-room hospital at 223 East 26th, which had earned her the graduation pin from Bellevue Training School for midwives. She didn't talk about how she'd had to persistently refuse accommodations in the training dorm. Refusing accommodations had been most irregular, according to the school administrators, but she'd gotten through that crisis, thanks to Villenueva's official signature. It was ironic that getting her into nursing school had become such a big deal, when her original goal had only been snagging Villenueva's signature as Mario's official birthing midwife. But now, two and a half years later, she had a folio stuffed with official papers declaring herself, as Elena, a midwife.

Eventually, she managed to back out of the small group around Linda.

The hair on the back of her neck prickled—it was getting to be a familiar feeling. She could feel someone watching. In the course of work and school, she had gotten to know many people, but everyone belonged in their own little knots. She scanned the room, her eyes moving over the clusters, but she didn't see anyone with a particular interest in her. Still, the feeling that she was being watched persisted.

From behind her, a big hug. Olinda and Orquida, Ramon from the apartment. Tina and Mary Lynn, with Mario swinging between them. He pulled free of them and put his hands out, reaching for her, squealing "Mama!" Her whole apartment family had shown up, and brought the baby with them. Not a baby any longer really— at two and a half, he was a handful, determined to explore the world on his own feet and on his own terms. For the occasion, someone had found him a clever little coat and tails, but Mario spoiled the effect by staggering at her, like that dancing boy Joel Grey on the Colgate Comedy Hour, with a cup of grasshoppers poured in his britches.

Carmen swept him up, and her friends embraced her.

"You look so important," Olinda said, on the arm of one of her brothers.

Orquida oohed and aahed over the uniform. "Are you acquainted with any military men?"

"Not really," Carmen said.

"Doctors?" Orquida persisted.

"None you'd be interested in."

"I have a few friends stopping by the basement," Ramon said, "if you want to get away from this dull crowd." The crowd of families, academics, doctors, and nurses were treating this happy occasion with all the joviality of a funeral.

"That's not a bad idea," Carmen said, and before she knew it, her friends were all cheering and dragging her out of the formal graduation dinner, leaving behind a wake of silence and disbelief.

It was so quiet that Carmen heard one of the parents ask Linda, "Are they entertainers?"

Carmen's apartment family had arranged a blow-out in the Laundromat in the basement of her building, which had been decorated with streamers, the funnies section out of the *New York Times*, and coolers of beer in honor of her graduation. Even Mrs. Beebe was there, sitting in the corner, glassy eyed, draining a limp paper cup of some clear liquid. One of the Oropeza brothers kept refilling the cup with something that smelled like turpentine.

The trucker who rented the first floor to store his truck, he who was nicknamed Mr. Moon for the big white moon on a blue background painted on his trailer, sailed in just as things got rolling. He had parked his rig after the party had started, and it was not at all a surprise to see him as his arrival always vibrated the entire building, especially when he blew his horn. He'd been trying to date Carmen for two years, but was cursed with being "a good friend." To his great delight, tonight he was the only one tall enough for Carmen to look up to, and that night he danced with her at least ten times. For a little while, she lost the feeling that someone was watching her.

Mr. Rios had brought his guitar. Carmen had long since discovered he was not at all like Papi. Small and dark with a New York accent, barely twenty-one, he was well on his way to making his fortune playing music in East Harlem clubs. The five Oropeza brothers came down with their instruments—two violins, two trumpets, and a vihuela. As musicians, they were great makers of *piragüero*. They had, in fact, brought spiked syrups, ice, and ice shavers, so the drunker everyone got, the better the "band" sounded, especially after the brothers stopped attempting to follow Rio's talented lead, and fell into a simple melody even their drinking fingers could manage. Olinda and Orquida were persuaded not to sing, but could not be talked down from dancing on top of the washing machines. Eventually Orquida fell off, but by then, she was too drunk to notice. She landed on the man from 4B, Juan Manuel Hermosillo, who was quite large and rather soft. Juan was rewarded for breaking Orquida's fall by the honor of the next dance. After he helped her up, they danced the last few sets before they snuck upstairs, where Orquida got a guided tour of all the benefits to be had in 4B. Mary Lynn and Tina alternated half-hour shifts of babysitting Mario. At thirty months, he was out like a light the instant it was dark, and up at dawn, so he slept through their stealthy exits and entrances even when they were too tipsy to be quiet.

Carmen thanked everyone and excused herself, going upstairs and relieving Tina, who tiptoed downstairs where the party continued without its honoree.

She took off the cadet uniform, something that had cost her a full week's worth of appliqués. The sore fingers had been well worth it, even if she would probably never need it again, since her duty station was a civilian women's hospital. She hung it up. There wasn't a real closet, but it fit behind her two nursing uniforms where they hung on a hook on the bathroom door. She looked critically at the uniform on top—just a standard white nurse's dress with buttons, pockets, and a pin with the name CARMEN on it. No one at the school or hospital had batted an eye over the name on her paperwork being Elena, and the pin saying Carmen. There were so many girls named Mary that many of them went by nicknames like Cookie, or by middle names.

Carmen dismantled her kitchen and took a hot bath, till someone knocked. The light tap made a metal "ting" not unlike a tuning fork.

She wrapped herself in a towel and cracked the door to peek out.

"Who's there?"

"Piscola!"

Her late-night guest was Moonie from downstairs, bearing gifts. Or rather, bearing munchies swiped from the party buffet downstairs.

"When are you going to open that door without a towel?" he whispered.

"Behave yourself," she whispered back, "or I'll shut the door in your face."

"I'll be good, I promise," he said. "You can't see my fingers are crossed, can you?"

"Quit the comedian act. Give me two minutes and come in. No peeking." She grabbed her pajamas and stepped behind the screen that protected the corner that served as her study nook. While she quick-changed into her thick flannel pajamas and a thicker housecoat, Moonie stood behind the door, counting off the seconds. Then she disposed of her bath and put her kitchen back together. He had one just like it downstairs in the warehouse.

A fully covered Carmen checked on Mario, who was still asleep, before she and Moonie walked out on the back steps. She let the door close.

"Where do you get this sexy lingerie?" he asked her, rolling his gaze over the sedate red polka-dot flannel that covered her from high-buttoned collar to her red-painted toenails.

"Macy's. In Manhattan."

The indoor staircase gave a scenic view of the interior of Moonie's unit. The warehouse took up the building's entire first floor, except for the part partitioned off for the apartment building's narrow entry. Perhaps at one point it had been intended as a garage, but instead it had been rented out. Great pillars to the third floor interrupted the space, and Moonie used them to demarcate areas of different function, as if there had been walls. Much of what once had been a shop was now taken up by his parked trailer, painted with his trademark white moon on a blue sky. A makeshift kitchen not like Carmen's had been assembled from items discarded from up-stairs apartments. His "bedroom" could not be viewed from this angle, as Moonie had put it in a nook directly below the fire escape, where he had placed a twin bed on top of a bit of carpet he'd found somewhere. The lights were off, but street-lamps cast beams of light that the window glass splintered and fragmented, making the deep shadows of the warehouse flicker with what seemed like stretching, moving lights.

Moonie had installed a thick rubber mat on the landing and had boxed it in so, if toddler Mario ever made it past the back door, it would be safer than a play pen. The baby never had ventured so far, thanks to a back door that needed a forklift to open it.

This was not the first midnight picnic Moonie and Carmen had shared. In fact, after discovering the shifts they worked often made them the only ones—except for Mr. Rios—awake during the wee hours, these nighttime forays had become a regular thing. They often shared takeout picnic dinners after long shifts with no chance to eat.

Moonie handed Carmen the bottle of champagne. He'd already set down a plate three inches deep in finger sandwiches.

"Need a glass?"

Carmen shook her head, took a careful sip, and sneezed. She laughed.

"That wasn't nothin'. Take a gulp, like this." He poured champagne in his mouth and coughed as bubbles came out of his nose. He coughed again and selected a sandwich, ridiculously small in his big hand.

"Maybe not like that. I'll try your way."

She laughed harder, took another sip, handed him a napkin, and sneezed again.

"I guess I'm allergic to bubbles."

"That's the fun of champagne." He held up the bottle and squinted, trying to read the label. "I think I carried a truck full of this from Chicago last year. They were labeled from France, but I'm thinking somebody's got a still or two left over from Prohibition." He burped and smacked his lips. "Definitely Chicago. Austere and velvety with a hint of smoke. Cosmopolitan with just a dollop of ..."—he belched and smacked his lips again as if tasting—"...stockyard."

"Moonie, why do you live in this cavern? You don't have to live in a warehouse. Why don't you get a regular apartment?"

"Why would I want one when I can have

this?" He reached toward Carmen until a glitter of light curled around his fingers like a bright glove. "Every night that I'm not on the road, I can shut off the lights and live in the stars."

"There is that," Carmen said.

"And I know you're right there, floating above my head."

His glittery hand was too close to her face, and she nipped the finger sandwich he waved around.

"Mmm. Needs peppers."

"Hey, you, that was mine."

"Hey, you, might I remind you that was stolen from my party."

He leaned toward her, and she backed away.

"I wish you weren't so...reluctant. I'd like to kiss you."

Carmen shrugged. "You can try."

Moonie leaned closer, backing Carmen up against the wall.

"Then I could kiss you now." But when his lips touched her forehead, he drew back sharply. "I could if I didn't scare you to death. You're vibrating like a 1948 Peterbilt with six square tires. Honey, what's wrong?"

"Guess I haven't had the best experiences with men." She looked away. She could feel his eyes on her, fluctuating between curiosity and concern. She didn't want to remember, but she could never be close to a man without picturing the monster who had stolen her youth and her sister.

"Mario's father? Tell me his name and I'll break his face," Moonie said.

"I think you really would."

"Damn straight I would."

"Thanks for the thought. But I think it's a little late for that."

"Even if I can't kiss you, I can toast your accomplishments. Best nurse in the five boroughs. Best midwife in the five boroughs. Best student in the five boroughs. I bet you're the best kisser in the five...okay, okay, I drink...I drink to your eyes."

He tilted his glass toward hers and they

clinked.

They sank down to the floor, both of them woozy and propped up against the wall. Moonie's hand had slipped inside her shirt, not doing anything, just sitting there, like a chick under a roosting hen. He sighed, then she sighed.

"It's been a long time since I trusted anybody," Carmen said. "Maybe I never did. There's never been anybody but me, not since my parents died, and that was a long time ago. My mother was a midwife, too, but not the kind with a government certificate. She learned at her mother's knee. And hers before that, going back a long ways. She'd be proud of me today, would my Mami. She always had a respect for the past. Papi preferred the kind of learning that comes from books."

Moonie's weight lay heavily against her. She pushed back to see his face, and heard from his breathing that he'd fallen asleep.

"You'd better go downstairs. I can't leave you asleep on the fire escape," she told him. "You'll fall on your head."

He was a light sleeper, and up on his feet in seconds.

"I've got a delivery that will take me up in New England tomorrow," he told her, barely opening his eyes a slit, "but I'll be back in time for dinner, if you and the boy want to go out. Anyplace in town."

She pulled at the door, which barely budged; he pulled it the rest of the way. She went inside, where Mario was still sleeping. After she'd gone in, Moonie went through his shop, got some tools, and installed a lever to make it open easier, and a hook in the wall so it could be propped open.

Chapter Thirty-Four

It was a weekend shopping day, and they were approaching the street market where every vendor in Harlem hawked their wares. The crowd couldn't have been any more different from the farmer's market in Nogales, but still the bustle of it reminded her of home. The night before had been close to freezing, but the day's temperature was in the mid-sixties and felt like spring. Mario, who had halfway graduated from his stroller, was too grown up to actually sit in it—or at least that was his response when he was awake and fresh. He liked having it along, but only to push along the sidewalk, impressing everyone with his maturity. Carmen brought it mostly to carry groceries as they shopped at the street market.

It was a Saturday like any other, now that her classes were done and she hadn't found a good nursing position yet. The sun was shining, the fumes of the traffic hanging heavy, and kids were out playing marbles and hopscotch on the sidewalks, enjoying a break from the winter weather. It hardly seemed possible it was the same sun that burned so hot in Nogales—maybe a lesser, drabber cousin.

Carmen held a mackerel up horizontally by the head, and its body drooped. Its eyes were glazed over. She dropped it back on the pile. It had been the best-looking one of the bunch, but it still wasn't fresh. She moved on. The booths were full of fresh produce, South American fruit from the docks, early greens, fish freshly caught. A man at the fish booth was the only one around cursing the sun as he dumped precious ice on top of his day-old mackerel.

"That fish needs more than ice," Carmen said.

He shook his fist and flung a withered lemon at her head. She caught it.

"Thanks," she called back. "Maybe the lemon will kill the stink of bad fish on my fingers."

He cursed some more. A couple of shoppers took a wide berth around him, and some of the other sellers laughed and teased him.

Carmen kept change in her pocket for purchases. Mario pushed his stroller along importantly at a constant rate, never waiting as she paused to shop or haggle on the run, tossing tonight's dinner and tomorrow's breakfast in the stroller's seat. It started out a merry little expedition, marked by Mario's earnest and adult deportment as he navigated the sidewalk crowded with buyers and sellers. Carmen haggled with the best of them, but had a strong tendency to overpay the sellers she liked regardless of the price agreed upon; and she kept her ear to the ground, following the rumors of who in the farmer's market might be having trouble keeping their bills paid.

Barely able to see over the seat as he pushed, Mario could not observe how the path cleared as he plowed through when shoppers saw him coming, and he certainly never noticed the smiles that followed in his wake.

Carmen was checking out some fresh-

caught cod, making a running decision on possi-
bilities for dinner, when the feeling that someone
was watching struck again. She dropped the cod.
Without a word to Mario about her concerns,
she pressed close. She made no more purchases,
and shushed his angry protests when she dumped
him in the stroller seat with their items. She de-
toured without making their usual stop in the
park— by the time they got there, she was nearly
at a run. Mario's protests turned to encourage-
ment. He squealed and yelled for her to go faster.
As they turned the corner with the stroller on
two wheels, she caught herself looking in a shop
window, trying to make out the familiar face of a
trench-coated man who seemed to be following
them, but the reflection was at a crazy angle, and
when she turned to verify her suspicions, he was
not there. Of all people, the last she'd have expected to see was Ambrose. It must have just been
a stranger.

Carmen went in the back way, as she always did when she used the stroller, since she
stored it at Moonie's place so she didn't have to

lug it up and down the front stairs or the back fire escape.

Outside the building, the fire escape had rusted, and was falling apart. Inside, safe from the elements, the section running up the inside wall of Moonie's place to Carmen's back door was better than new now that Moonie had taken some care with it. He'd installed some bolts the size of her stovetop percolator to keep the cantilever from pulling it up. It was anchored like a real stairway. Sort of. It was never her first choice with Mario, mostly because the gaps between the stairs made it look insubstantial and she could picture too easily how he could fall through. She'd used it few times before Moonie shored it down and made her landing into a play yard for Mario; she'd never forget how she'd been boosted off the first time she'd tried to go down it, when she didn't know where (or what) the counterbalance was. Like a live wild thing, it had bucked her off, as if she were a wet-behind-the ears bronco buster.

It was a measure of her fear that she chose to use the fire escape now as an evasive maneuver, just in case someone who was following her might know where her front door was.

She put Mario down, and he scrambled up like a little lemur. Carmen followed. The lemon she had been tossed fell out of the bag, bounced down some stairs, and rolled through a gap to the floor below. She shivered. Once inside, she locked and double locked the doors, and even double checked the floorboard stash of money.

Carmen was putting groceries away when there was a knock at the front door. She froze. Most everybody in the building hollered instead of knocking. Her solid door was a local challenge.

Mario had no interest in putting away groceries and was in the corner trying to stack blocks against the wall. The wall wasn't flush or even straight up and down, so his stack kept listing over along the incline of the paneling.

Mario toddled over and asked in his lisping voice, "Who dere?" When there was no answer, he wriggled his shoulders and told Carmen, "Nobody home."

He went back to his blocks without a

qualm. Carmen was not so complacent.

A current of alarm ran through her when the knock came again, simultaneous with the roar of Moonie's truck pulling in, an event that made her apartment tremble as if in an earthquake.

Moments later, with the back door open, she heard Moonie roar, "Here I am!"

He thundered upward with a bottle given him by Mr. Boneroti, to whom Moonie had delivered a load of wine from the docks. His long hauls were regular contracts, but many of his city deliveries were spontaneous, word of mouth from friends. Beneath his substantial weight storming up, the fire escape rattled as if it would come to pieces. As soon as he reached the top, Carmen flung herself in his arms. Not her typical behavior. Carmen was a handle-things-herself kind of gal, when there wasn't some mysterious stranger banging at her door not saying who they were.

"I wasn't sure if you heard me," he said. "Look, another Chianti from Mr. Boneroti!"

He held her away from him to ask, "What's wrong?"

"Nothing," she said. His expression told her he knew she was lying, but he didn't call her on it. He told her with a funny story about a salesman he'd met, and Carmen told him about how the women's school had asked her to stay on as a midwife in their clinic to mentor the next class of nurses. It was good news, but Carmen was still on edge.

That night, when Mario was asleep, Carmen and Moonie shared more of Mr. Boneroti's largesse while sitting on the front stoop of the building. Wine in paper cups, with the whole un-sleeping city walking past. Everyone had somewhere to go, even in the middle of the night.

"Some seasons of the year, at certain times after sunset, the third step down is the best place in New York," Moonie observed.

"I know," Carmen agreed. "There's no better squat for moon-gazing." She slanted her eyes in his direction, but he was looking at her, and not even pretending to look up.

"I thought you came out here to see the moon," Carmen teased him, but she felt her cheeks warming in embarrassment.

"I am the moon," he said. "I am the moon, and every night I come out looking for you. I cannot rest until I've seen you. In moonlight, of course." He filled her cup and his own. "I drink to your eyes, Miss Carmen Elena."

* * *

Another nightmare. This time someone was chasing her. The dream fell away, leaving her safe in bed, but she was left with the impression of switching from planes to trains to cars to trails, winding footpaths, and back to city buses, no memory of the journey itself but boarding and exiting with Mario. Sometimes she misplaced him, but when she looked, he was always right beside her after the panic subsided. The last place she'd gone was to Moonie's cab.

"Where have you been?" he asked. "I've been waiting. I've got your reservation."

She remembered then—that's where she was supposed to go. It didn't seem strange that the door to his truck opened to the twin of the sumptuous hotel suite at the Waldorf that was posted on a Times Square bulletin board. No wonder he didn't want an apartment! With that in his truck, why would he ever go anywhere else? In the dream, she got into Moonie's cab, climbed into the fluffy dream of a Waldorf bed, pulled the silk sheets over herself and Mario, and went right to sleep, but then cruelly, going to sleep in the dream woke her up. For a moment, she wondered where the fine sheets went, then she saw herself, saw the apartment gleaming white where the night light reflected on the walls.

Once she was back in the real world, the first thing she checked was Mario. Snug in his bed, wrapped in blankets, he slept the sleep of the innocent. She adjusted the blanket around him, the softest finished fabric she could find, like a quilt that was in its heart of being, a pillow only pretending to be a cover. It was handmade, feather stuffed, and the color of happy dreams— not like the nightmares she had.

She pushed open her back door and peered into the darkness of Moonie's place. His truck was there; that meant he was there. His bed was in a nook beneath the fire escape. They had become better than friends. He came up and she cooked for him; she came down and he cooked (or reheated) for her. In his unhooked cab, sometimes he drove her the few blocks to work, his truck vibrating with horsepower, looking far down at the lowly cars from the height of the Peterbilt, blaring his horn and waking up the streets of Spanish Harlem at odd hours, and laughing about it, but not unkindly.

Carmen found her way to him, propping open the door so Mario could be heard if he stirred; she crept down the creaky fire escape, cringing as the earsplittingly shrill grinding of metal scraped out her eardrums. Her bare footfalls were silent across the chill concrete floor to the scrap of plush wool carpet in the nook he had designated as his room. She walked through a maze of moving lights and shadows from headlights traveling the streets of Spanish Harlem, shining through the high transom windows.

She surprised him, found him in the dark, in the bed barely big enough for him, certainly not long enough. His bare feet hung off the edge, looking cold and forlorn. She almost giggled at them, but then tugged the blanket down to cover them. That's what woke him up. Surprise...

He woke like a man accustomed to cat-naps. Seeing her, his eyes grew big as those of a man presented a gift from a genie's lamp. He scooted as far as he could—not that there was room—and patted his twin bed as naturally as if she'd only left it a moment before, not visiting it for the first time.

She sat beside him and put her palm against his bare chest.

All the warmth in the world beat beneath her hand, his flesh solid. The dream had made a change, turned a corner in her head. She'd always stood her ground until she had to run. But she'd never had somewhere to run to. It was too soon to know if he was an illusion, but her dream was telling her she could run to him. Were dreams something she could trust?

"Are you real?" she asked, her voice a whisper.

"I hope so," he whispered back. "If I was going to conjure myself up, I'd sure do a better job than a dumb old truck driver with an ugly face." He pinched his own arm. "Feels real. Ouch." He slid his finger down her neck, and dropped his hand to the bed. "You, on the other hand, feel too good to be real. I must still be dreaming. I hope I never wake up."

"I had a bad dream, but you made it better," she said, simply. Without moving her palm, she curled up beside him. He adjusted the blanket, and rested his hand over hers.

"Here is where all bad dreams are banished," he said.

Chapter Thirty-Five

Outside, Waldo the security guard walked his rounds, rousting a drunk and giving him directions to the mission. The nightly traffic continued on the streets, oblivious to the drama inside the twelve-room Bellevue Hospital Training School. Inside, wails echoed down the hall, not an unfamiliar sound, but still some of the students looked at each other in newly educated alarm. It could be a normal delivery—or a complicated one.

From the hall, easily audible through the curtains, the conversation made little sense.

"I don't want to friggin' lie down."

"But you should, here, lie down and you—"

"If the mama wants to sit up, let her. The gravity helps."

Three different voices: the mother, the

student, and Carmen.

"Ma'am, that's not in the books."

Elsie was in her first hands-on delivery, and wasting her efforts trying to persuade Mary, the young mother, to lie flat. Carmen, in defiance of the school texts, had decided to climb on the bed to help the laboring woman into a sitting position. To Carmen, her role as a teacher meant interjecting some of her practical experience, much of which ran counter to what was written.

"Then those books were written by men." Carmen turned to Mary. "Here, let me help." She called to an intern to come in, and directed him to sit at the foot of the bed to counterbalance her. She felt the mother's shape and figured the baby's angle.

"Ma'am, what are you doing?" Elsie's voice got shrill with alarm as she watched Carmen clamber onto the cot and spoon behind the young woman, bracing her to give her something to push against. Mary lay back against Carmen and the cot tilted up, emitting creaks as it protested.

"Elsie, use your head! Put your weight

on the mattress so we don't tip over," Carmen shouted. Elsie parked herself next to the intern, who looked like he wanted to be anywhere but there.

"Ooooh, that's so much better!" The patient's wails turned into words. Mary leaned back, her knees bent, feet braced squarely on the mattress. With the angle adjusted, the contractions did their work. Carmen wondered whether there would be a lecture coming from the head nurse about teaching the girls things that conflicted with what was being taught in the classroom.

"Well done!"

"I see the head. Just another push, you're doing fine."

At least Elsie didn't need to be told which way to face, and what she should be doing.

"Don't feel like fine!" The words dissolved into a yell.

"Try to keep your breathing, it's the newest thing," Elsie directed, panting along with her. "Yes, here's the head, good job, baby's out. She's perfect."

After they made Mary comfortable and the baby was cleaned up and squared away, Elsie whispered, "I hope we get to the sinks before next shift swans in and takes over."

They made good time through the pre-dawn hall, where there were fewer students around than the usual number requiring Carmen's attention. Other than snores from a couple of exhausted patients, the only sound was from the sticky rubber soles of their shoes on linoleum.

Luckily, no one was hogging the locker room sink. There was much competition for the location, as it was by the nurses' showers and had better water pressure than the rest of the taps. Carmen washed the Betadine from her hands a shoulder away from Elsie, who was also working sudsy lather up to her elbows. Every time Carmen did this, which was several times a day, she remembered the Tucson airport.

Carmen said, as casually as she was able, "I'm available if you want me to answer any questions."

"You know I have questions. What was

that about?"

"The tradition in history has been getting the mother to an angle where gravity helps—you've seen birthing chairs. There's a reason they put the mother at that angle."

"Didn't look that easy—but I know what you mean. But that's not what the books say—"

"It's controversial. Let's just consider it supplemental learning. Like that lecture you were telling me by Marjorie Karmel."

"It was all about that doctor she assisted. He delivered babies in Russia and taught mothers classes in how to have a baby," Elsie said. "It's not as dramatic as standing on a bed, though. But what you say makes sense. About the angle, I mean."

"They're liable to burn me as a witch just for telling you about it," Carmen said.

Elsie looked a little frightened. "Mum's the word."

"Okay, maybe not actually burn me. Maybe that was an exaggeration. They'll just give me a 'talking to.' But it's worth it. I just like to think that when the time comes when you're on your own, without teachers to advise you, then you will have a couple of extra tools to work with, especially when some woman comes to you wanting to have a baby the way her foremothers did—"

"Once, I had a mother say—" Elsie's mouth clamped closed when a gaggle of first-years rushed in as one, dispersing like cream in coffee, with half streaming to the lockers to change into their uniforms and others heading for soap and water. Carmen and Elsie dunked their hands, quickly rinsing to get out of the way of the herd.

One of the first-years asked, "Is one of you called Elena?"

"That would be me," Carmen said.

"So why does your name tag say—"

"That's her middle name," Elsie volunteered. "Is your name really...," She read the nurse's tag. "Bootsie?"

The first-year shrugged. "One of the fathers is at the front desk asking about you. His name was Toliver. Something like that. He's got questions." She rolled her eyes.

"Thanks," Carmen replied in the general direction. She didn't remember a father named Toliver.

"I love the questions," one of the new girls said. "Especially the ones that the fathers ask when the mothers aren't around. Men are so stupid!" All the girls started talking at once.

"I know, right? If his wife puts her hands over her head, will it strangle the baby?"

"Will eating watermelons make the baby's head big?"

"Will her using a vibrator make the baby stutter?"

"Will eating strawberries give the baby a strawberry mark?"

"Will it have birthmarks if the mother puts stuff in her pockets?"

"Will going outside during an eclipse give the baby a cleft palate?"

Carmen stopped at the door and added one of her own.

"The one I've heard is whether having sex would poke the baby and cause an injury."

"Wait," Elsie said, "that's not true?"

The first-years stopped dead and looked at each other.

Elsie managed to stifle her snicker until she stepped out.

"That was mean," Carmen said.

Elsie giggled.

"You know Dr. Brown has that as a true/false on his final?" She yawned hugely and headed to her room in the small house behind the hospital.

Carmen headed for the errant husband who had asked for her.

Chapter Thirty-Six

His clothes marked him as being new to New York. The man, presumably Mr. Toliver, was wrongly dressed for the season in a damp trench coat over layers of sweaters unlikely to keep him comfortable. He wore heavy boots that left a wet trail on the pristine floor. He was going to sweat in all that gear, and end up chilled. New York's knee-high spring snow had led Carmen and the rest of the staff who commuted to buy heavy long pants and thick knit socks to wear over their store-bought stockings and thick overshoes that they could stuff their flimsy shoes into. But after enduring several New England springs, Carmen had acclimated.

He was in his mid-forties with dark hair and eyes. He might have been married to one of her patients, but Carmen didn't recognize him. The quality of the clothes he wore was somewhat better than those of most of the fathers she'd chatted with in the examining rooms; the midwives' teaching hospital tended to draw poor refugees and recent immigrants, exactly the kind of patient Carmen knew most intimately, though in New York, they weren't all from Mexico. He wore glasses and a low-brimmed hat that had seen better days. Though wrongly dressed for the weather, he did not wear the clothes of a working man. The knot of his tie showed, barely visible under a collection of ugly sweaters. The bundle of clothing did nothing to disguise the beginning of a spare tire around his belly. Not that she was studying him by intent—all was observed in a blur as the desk nurse, Nancy, greeted her. Carmen signed off the roster, put a clipboard in an overflowing in-basket on the reception desk, and was about to introduce herself when Nancy beat her to it.

"Mr. Oliver wants to speak to you. Is the coast clear?" As she asked, Nancy craned in both directions in case one of the sterner hospital officials was lurking, put down her pen, and pulled out a tube of bright red lipstick and applied it to her mouth, barely glancing at the reflection in her open compact. She blotted her lips, and beamed at Mr. Oliver. "He says this is not a complaint about one of the girls, so it must be about his pregnant wife."

The first-year must have gotten the man's name wrong, Carmen thought. He looked at her, took out a cigarette, and stuck it in his mouth unlit.

"Hope this doesn't bother you," he said. "I'm trying to quit. I can keep from lighting up, as long as I can taste it." He drew on it as if it were lit, and sighed.

He didn't glance twice at Nancy or her red lips. "I reckon you're the nurse called Carmen Elena Garcia Sanchez. That name is quite a mouthful, young lady." He put his hand up in a friendly fashion, and she shook it mechanically. "I have a few questions—"

Carmen studied his face and the hand that had not yet let go. He was a complete stranger, and she told him so. "I'm sorry, I don't recall you or your wife. I'm sure we can address all of your concerns, but I am past the end of my shift. I can introduce you to—"

"I'm certain I'd be more comfortable with you," he said firmly. "Go ahead and finish whatever you need to do. Might I get us a cup of coffee? Is there an all-night diner close? I'm in no hurry."

It was an irregular request. Nancy, who had been known to have dalliances with anxious fathers-to-be and assorted waiting room strangers, made her own assumptions.

Carmen flexed the arm Mr. Oliver was still hanging onto as she glanced at her watch. Plenty of time to get home. It was several hours before sunrise. Tina was babysitting and wouldn't be bringing Mario home until eight a.m. Where Mario slept depended on what Mary Lynn and Tina were doing. Sometimes they handed off the baton in the middle of Carmen's shift, like marathon runners. Both girls were dependable and still lived with their parents within a block of her building. Carmen had learned to be flexible.

"Sure." Carmen didn't want to agree, but he was still hanging onto her hand.

"My car is outside," he said.

"Not yet," Nancy interrupted. "You got work." She handed a bundle of shift-change paperwork to Carmen.

"The paperwork is never-ending."

"I can relate," he said. Something about the way he drawled the "I" made her look up. It took her a second to register the lack of a New York accent. He sounded like home. Maybe New Mexico or California, but she'd wager her last paycheck he was from Arizona. She took a step back and gave him another once-over. Her arm was now extended as far as it would reach, and he was acting like he'd taken ownership of her hand.

He had signs of a fading tan. He didn't sound like an immigrant. He wasn't wearing a wedding ring. She put the facts together and came up with a conclusion of her own.

"You're not here about your wife's pregnancy, are you?"

"No." His eyes flickered with some emotion, maybe pain. His voice was sardonic. "The wife traded me in for a more expensive model." His expression cleared, then he met her eyes aggressively. "You look like your sister. We should talk."

The tug of war for her hand escalated. Maybe he read the intent in her face at the mention of her sister, because he suggested in a low voice, "Don't run." He pulled her closer, and pivoted. It was practically a dance move, but it put her with him to her left, and his right hand on the small of her back, as if they were casually side by side, walking out. His face came closer to her ear.

"Don't run. I'm not here after you. I'm just going to clear things up. Get the facts straight. Let's visit a diner."

"No need for a diner," Nancy volunteered, revealing a stunning capacity for misunderstood eavesdropping. "There's a classroom downstairs that will be unoccupied at this hour. You can have all the privacy you want till the sun comes up." She blew them a kiss and pantomimed zipping and buttoning her lip.

Carmen protested, "I need to finish this up." She indicated the papers Nancy had given her, which were trapped between her arm and Mr. Oliver's trench coat.

"Live a little." Nancy waved her hand. "Turn in the forms tomorrow, I won't tattle."

"Fine with me," Mr. Oliver agreed.

Carmen was trapped. She felt much as she had in Francisco's clutches, but he was no Francisco, and, what was more important, there was no Elena to give him leverage. Behind her, interns trickled down the hallway. Now that Nancy had engineered the "tryst," she was suddenly so intent on the stack of pages in front of her, Carmen might as well have been in Brazil.

"Let go of me," Carmen said, hoping he didn't notice the quaver of fear in her voice.

He nodded, but failed to release her. They must have looked like a cozy couple as they continued to the empty classroom. Preoccupied by the dawning sensation of her own terror, Carmen didn't notice Nancy's amused glance. She was only aware of the buzzing in her ears, the return of that horrible feeling of being trapped. The pounding of her heart. Her limbs shaking. Without conscious thought, she navigated down the stairs and into the unlocked room. He let go of her and flicked on the lights.

"Have a seat," he said, straddling a chair with the door bracing his back. Waving his hand, he indicated the thirty or so wooden tables arranged in neat rows.

As soon as he let go, Carmen put several desks between them and, her old instincts kicking in, declined to sit down.

"Mr. Oliver, what do you need?"

"Miss Garcia-Sanchez," Oliver said, "it is not Mister, but Detective. I'd like you to describe the events that happened on the evening of Wednesday, December 29, 1948, when your sister shot her husband four times, and he shot her back."

Carmen heard the date, heard the name, but didn't register what else came out of his mouth. Her knees buckled and she slithered in slow motion to the floor. It wasn't exactly a faint, but it was close. Oliver was out of his perch and helping her into a chair before she could focus on his face.

"I am a detective, Miss Garcia, with the Nogales Police. I have a pretty good idea of who Francisco is, and why you would run, even if he is your brother-in-law and your employer. So you don't need to worry about this any longer."

She knew he was there to arrest her. He knew what she had done. He knew she'd killed Francisco. He had gone to all this trouble to track her all the way to New York. So his words weren't making much sense. She stood in a wobbly fashion, put her wrists in front of her, ready for the cuffs. Her hands trembled.

Oliver put his hand on her shoulder, pushed her back into the chair. Put his hand over her quivering wrists and pushed them down to the desktop, covering them with his big hand, in as soothing a fashion as he could muster, with no force but as if coaxing a frightened bird.

Carmen's throat was so dry she could barely speak.

"Detective out of where did you say?"

"I'm working out of Nogales, Miss Garcia." He let that sink in.

"*Dios*." Carmen wilted on the desk like a stalk of last week's celery.

"Knowing the caliber of your brother-in-law's nasty friends, I can see why you left."

Carmen stood. The man was a detective with the Nogalas Police, which Francisco had owned. "I guess you're going to take me in."

"Sit down, Miss Garcia." He put his hand on her shoulder and pushed down again. "I've been working in Nogales going on three years now. I know what goes on. I'm still an outsider, and have personally run into the iron wall of protection that circles your boss. I know the kind of men you're hiding from. Sit and tell me what happened." He studied her, came to some kind of conclusion, and said softly, "It was staged to look as if they shot each other, but we never had anything close to an eyewitness account. No confession from either of the victims. Tell me what happened."

"I don't know," Carmen said. Her voice shook, barely audible.

"You heard shots. Did you hear shots?"

"I don't know."

"You were in the house. How many shots? Who did you see fire the gun?"

"I don't know. I don't know what you want me to say."

Carmen looked at Detective Oliver in desperation.

"I want the truth. I know you saw one of Francisco's so-called business partners shoot them. I know you're afraid to rat on him. But we can protect you."

"What?" Carmen could not believe her ears. She babbled something, but wasn't sure of what she said. It was neither agreement nor denial. She wasn't making much sense, but then neither was he. She tried to sound like she was agreeing with Oliver. Tried to make what he was saying fit into her recall of that day.

"Miss Garcia, I understand why you ran. Your boss has a long history as a criminal, a fucked-up businessman, a lousy boss, and a shitty human being. I saw the door to your office, your house, and the door to your apartment. I've seen that baby of yours. I think Sanchez raped you and fathered your bastard child. But of all that, I think what mattered most to you was that he was a piss-poor husband to your sister."

Her face froze into a mask as she tried to make sense of the words.

He believed her innocent? He thought Mario was hers? He believed Francisco and Elena had actually killed each other? He wasn't here to take her to prison? But there was evidence, wasn't there? What had happened to the pile of sheets from Mario's birth? Francisco had made sure Elena barely left the rancho after she conceived, but it hadn't exactly been a secret she'd been pregnant.

"In running, I think you have found the best solution to keeping yourself alive. The proof is that you are still alive. Staying in Nogales, for you, would be suicide," Oliver said. "It's not the police department you need to worry about. You worked for your brother-in-law. Kept his books. I may not know exactly why, but some of the people Francisco did business with are bad guys, and they are looking for you. Maybe you know something you shouldn't."

Carmen, beyond words, shook her head violently.

"I talked to Father Villalobos. He had only good things to say of you. Not that he said much. But the old man, Pasquel—hell, the whole brood of Pasquels, their lips weren't even close to buttoned. According to that whole town, you're practically Saint Carmen of Nogales." He paused to let that sink in.

"We found the wagon half buried in mud. That's why you've been declared dead. But I'm not too sure those drug running buddies of your brother-in-law read the news. The last one I locked up said he was going to look for your body till hell freezes over. Not to my face, of course. To my face, he swore his innocence. I only heard because I listened in on another detective's inter-rogation. To be honest, I wasn't too sure who was interrogating who. But I've learned this much: these crooks are looking for you. They've got a hell of a bounty out for your head. I don't know why, not yet, but give me time. I'll ferret out all Francisco's secrets. I'm good at my job."

Carmen turned away from the detective and bent over a desk. "*Dios*," she whispered, look-ing toward the windows, which were dark, the night beyond as invisible as the future. Was he telling the truth, or did he know about the money she'd taken? She'd bet the secrets the detective was looking for were already circulating the fac-tory. The seamstresses knew everything, thanks to Francisco's famous temper. But now that he was dead, who would know there was money missing?

Detective Oliver shed his coat, and re-moved two sweaters. Underneath, he wore a plain white button-down shirt, and a black tie. Some-thing about his bearing telegraphed to Carmen a military history.

"I didn't join the Tucson police force twenty years ago to get rich," he said, "I joined it because once, when I was a kid, a police detective was a good guy and helped me. I know a victim when I see one because I've been there. And then there's you. I knew I'd have to get a look at you in person to know. You've got a spark most victims don't have. But every instinct I have tells me you're a victim."

Carmen turned around and thumped down into the seat.

"Ready to listen now?" He lit the cigarette in his mouth, and started talking. Smoke swirled around his head, making him look faintly devilish.

She looked at the cigarette, and looked away.

He must have remembered he'd quit. He swore softly, pinched off the flame with his bare fingers, sucked once on the defunct stub, then told her in detail how he tracked her through school records, announcements, poring through newspapers. He told her about a deposition he'd typed up for her and then had torn up, deciding that he didn't want her signature proving she was alive. But then he pulled out a form and shoved it in front of her.

Oliver said. "You can start writing what you witnessed. In Tucson, I know a notary who'll take my word that you wrote this. I can take you in, and you can write your statement in front of him, or you can do it here and now." He snatched up the pages and made a motion to tear it up.

"No, I'll write." She grabbed the pen, and looked blankly at him.

"It's not like Nogales is the big leagues," the detective said. "It's a one-horse town, and the police department runs on pennies and nickels. I paid my own dime, and came here on my own time." He leaned in so close to Carmen she could smell the coffee on his breath, "You might wonder why. I'm close to being able to throw the book at a couple of these..." he hesitated, "coworkers of your brother-in-law. I'm so close I can taste it. I want to bring down this gang. I want it bad."

He saw she wasn't writing.

"You have to bear down to make it through all the carbons," he suggested.

She hesitated.

His eyes narrowed. "I figured," he said slowly, "you were somewhere in the house. Your sister and her husband were in their bedroom. You made regular visits to see your sister—"

"I didn't drive myself there," Carmen said. "You know I'm a midwife. Blasio picked me up. I was her midwife."

He nodded his head toward the desk, and she wrote down what she'd just said aloud.

"We knew your sister was expecting. The housekeeper, Manuela was it? Told us Elena wasn't very far along. I never saw autopsy results; she was cremated quickly. Miss Garcia. Carmen," he cleared his throat. "I'm sorry about your sister and her baby."

Carmen's eyes filled with tears at the mention of Elena.

"Thank you," she said. "To just hear her name spoken..." She sighed, and put down the pen.

He continued, "You were waiting for her in the den?"

"In the rocker on the back patio," she improvised.

"—heard the gunshots and fled. You got scared, right? And ran out the back door, grabbed some keys and drove off."

"I had to go in the kitchen for the keys. They were hanging up," Carmen said. But for the most part, she scribbled down what he was saying. She added a detail or two about the darkness, mentioned the rain, mentioned seeing Blasio at the gate.

"They know when I left. I didn't look at a watch," she said, "they keep a log at the gate. I don't know what time it was, but it was dark. They let me out."

"Write it down," he said. "Did you see who did the shooting?"

She stopped writing, and looked at his face.

"Did you see any of his, er, business associates?"

She shook her head.

"Keep going."

She scribbled some more, and glanced dubiously at his badge as she signed it. The badge *looked* real, but the whole string of events had an aura of unreality, like a dream. Oliver gave her a carbon copy and folded the other pages for his pocket. "This will be a powerful instrument to flush the killer out of the woodwork," he said. "I'll leak that there's a deposition here and there. I'm after the gators. You're a guppy. Your former boss worked with some hoods." Then he changed the subject. "The post office box helped, but your nursing license was a dead give away. I've seen thousands of Carmens and Elenas and Garcias and Sanchezes, but none all squeezed into one name, and a midwife to boot. That was five red flags all in one. I'm a little surprised you didn't change your name to hide your tracks."

Then he congratulated her. "I'm sure your mother would be proud. Not about the name appropriation. Not too sure she'd know which daughter has that license. I'm pretty sure your mother is sitting in heaven with a smile on her face, but you're aware that slippery identity of yours might not sit too well with the state of New York, even if you graduated with top honors."

Carmen's heart raced.

"I'm willing to let it slide," he said. "Like I said, I'm after the big fish."

The alarm must have transferred to her face, or maybe it was her shaking hands. It took a lot to make her speechless. She squeezed out the words.

"Is this a threat?"

"No, if I threatened you, you'd know it. I figure you can always change your name to fit the license. And don't worry. It's not like a single soul in the parish of San Filipe de Jesus got and read the *New York Times* from cover to cover on the very day of your graduation announcement. Everyone at home thinks you died in the flood. At least all the normal people. Not too sure about the sociopaths. As far as I know, everyone in the police department is happy to wrap up the investigation of your disappearance with you being declared dead. And if there were any relatives, they'd prefer you dead too, since even Francisco's illegitimate kid would be a legit heir." He took a long draw from his unlit cigarette, and exhaled. "When I first came in from Tucson, I was so green, I tried pinning a cold case on Sanchez."

"Not in Nogales," Carmen said. "That would never have happened."

"Can't argue with that. It's Francisco's so-called friends and business associates I'm worried about, the ones who have waited for years for his organization to show weakness. Now they'll be ready to come in for the kill. I'd really like to catch them. Under the circumstances, I could take you in. Put you in protective custody."

"No."

"I agree. Not sure how safe you'd be in a cage."

"With Francisco down, his partner will take up the slack."

"Partner?"

"Segundo. His lawyer. His real name is Miguel Trujillo. Birds of a feather."

"I've come across him."

The detective put on his discarded sweaters and folded the trench coat over his arm. Now that he had her signature in his pocket, he seemed less driven, but anxious to be on his way. She was anxious for him to be on his way too.

"Thanks for answering my questions," he said, although she hadn't really answered them. She'd just agreed with all his lies. He stood there for a few moments, looking toward her. He pulled a picture out of his pocket. "Pretty girl," he said. "Smart, too." He stared at her for so long she began to feel self-conscious. "I was so wrong when I thought Inez resembled you."

"Inez?"

"The one with your car. She was picked up for drunk and disorderly, and leaving the scene of an accident. Did some time in Texas. She's out now."

"Oh." She didn't pretend not to know who Oliver was referring to.

"We need to keep in touch," he said as he crossed the room and took a couple of cards from one pocket, with his name and office information. He wrote something on the back of one card. "My home number," he said. "I'm not there much." He stood with his hand out. The cards looked small in his big palm. Carmen just sat there. He gently put them on the desk along with the photo from his pocket, which he placed face-down.

He tipped his hat, the gentlemanly gesture reminding her unexpectedly of Tomás Turcios. He paused in the portal for a moment, again staring at her.

"We will see each other again," he promised. "Don't let them shoot you." He turned off the light. Carmen heard his hard-soled shoes on the linoleum in the hall, tapping, falling off in the distance. The creak of a door, the bang as it slammed, to her frayed nerves sounded as harsh as a gunshot.

She sat alone in the dark, her heart racing.

I answered his questions, she told herself. He won't be back. The past is the past. The past lives in Nogales and it won't follow me to New York. She looked down at the back of the photo. He'd had a picture of her beautiful sister. She turned it over, but it was just a picture of herself. She flushed. She knew better; he'd just been playing her. But there was a big sense of relief to know he was the man who had been following her. Sure, he'd been taller and leaner than she'd thought, with a kink in his gait. Now there would be no more silly fears, no more jumping at shadows.

As she was leaving, Waldo the watchman stepped out of the dark, tipping his hat to her.

Carmen nodded back, then stopped. She sometimes brought Waldo a hot coffee when the nights got cold. He was a little, dark man of indeterminate age with skin the color of weathered wood, and he always wore a pair of gold-rimmed glasses low on his nose, though he only needed them for reading. He had a way of looking over his glasses that made him look more like a disgruntled librarian than of a security guard. A tattered paperback sticking out of his coat pocket contributed to that effect.

Carmen stared at him, wanting to ask how he did his job. Hundreds of people came into the hospital every day. How did he know when one of them didn't belong? Every day, he dealt with kids intent on graffiti, drunks, vagrants, ordinary people wound up in violent emotions coming to see babies new to their families—how did he even recognize the ones who had to be kept out?

"Don't worry, ma'am," he said, "you're safe. Do you need an escort?"

Chapter Thirty-Seven

It was that time of day that was, for night workers, both late and early. She was exhausted when she walked into the building's foyer, but she couldn't help remembering the detective's words about the rat hole. It only took a glance around to prove him correct. How could she have become so blind to it? Cigarette butts and beer cans; crumbs and a broken plate with someone's dinner quietly rotting away; a crust of dried leaves up against the battered baseboards; a crop of cobwebs hanging from the ceiling, particularly the corners, like ephemeral stalactites of grimy gray silk with a dirt patina. Behind the peeling wallpaper, there were traces of yellowed paint that had once been a distinguishable color. The peppering of roach droppings over all conformed to no recognizable pattern.

She stormed up the stairs and came down

with the broom. Swept her way down like a whirlwind, accumulating at least a bushel's worth of detritus coming down the stairs, and was attacking the cobwebs on the ceiling as people started drifting in and out from and to work. The whole time she mumbled to herself about nosy detectives, ratty tenements, and just exactly what she'd like to do to a certain bunch of hoodlums who didn't have the sense to stay down in Mexico out of her way. She goaded neighbors as they trickled down the stairway, strong-arming them to "just help for a moment," and shortly, the pile was nestled in trash bins, revealing in the brume-cloaked dawn the ragged foyer in all its exhausted glory.

It was no wonder the spontaneous custodial flurry drained her, after a double shift and the shock of encountering the detective. Run ragged, sucked dry, all pooped out—she flopped down in her bed fully dressed, not even waking when Tina carried Mario in, put him in his high chair, and fed him scrambled eggs and tortillas to the accompaniment of merrily jingling baby ware.

A good rest and a new day brought Carmen a complete change of heart. The detective had found her, but he had decades of experience at his job. The kind of people who ran with Francisco were good at strong-arming, bullying, threats, and violence, but they weren't good at looking up records, nor were they guilty of thinking too much. There was no way they could duplicate Detective Oliver's methods. That meant she was free. Free of Francisco. Free of Nogales. Free of fear.

With a new, bolder step, she set out with the latest stack of poodles she'd embroidered during her lunch hours at the nursing school. They were wrapped in cotton batting at the bottom of her purse. She was headed to the tailor's shop. She only did special requests for the tailor now—fine embroidery to order, nothing generic. Mario was safely at Mary Lynn's. Later, Tina would take him home and put him to bed so he could sleep through the night in his own bed.

As she unfolded the batting to the music of Simini's "Oooh"s and "Ahhh"s, Carmen felt gratified. She didn't know what Simini charged for them, but for each one, now he paid her what would have been a week's wage in Francisco's factory. She decided on the spot to give the extra income to Mrs. Beebe for a few more months' rent.

As always, Waldo tipped his hat as she arrived at the hospital for her shift, where the time flew by until she spent at least an hour dressing down some girls at the nurses' station for laughing and comporting themselves as if they were at a party while there were patients around who needed attention and support.

Something about her was different, but it wasn't until she was walking home that she realized what it was. It was a sense of freedom. In all of Nogales, only Detective Oliver knew her whereabouts, and he was on her side. The two-and-a-half–year weight of terror and guilt she hadn't realized she was bearing had all but disappeared.

She turned the first corner feeling no fear as she walked past a knot of police in a huddle. It seemed as if they were everywhere tonight. She passed two police cars beside an accident, and saw two police officers sitting at a corner table in the all-night diner. There was a policeman in the bakery where she stopped to pick up a couple of sweet rolls to take home.

She passed a couple more policemen on the sidewalk, walking the beat, talking to each other. One was large and round, the other lean with the face of a movie star.

The handsome one tipped his hat to her.

She walked past with a smile on her face, but turned and walked backward for a moment to say hello to him. She even flirted a little. He flirted back.

The whole episode of terror was over. The city seemed a different place now that she had friends, and work, and the threat was gone. She even stopped at the church to give thanks to the powers that be that had led Detective Oliver to find her.

It seemed possible that maybe she could return to Nogales if she wanted to, but she didn't think she would. She'd made a life here. It was impossible that her life had changed in moments, but now that the detective had her back, the sky was the limit. He'd even told her how to straighten out the discrepancy in her nursing records; once she did that, everything would be as close to perfect as it could be.

It was approaching dawn. The sidewalks near her building already buzzed with men going off to work. The day dawned gray to a smoggy dullness that shaded the sunrise, almost like a surreal black-and-white photo. She was about to open the door to the building, planning to stop in the foyer to check her brass mailbox for mail, but through the glass, she saw that someone had left something on the floor she had swept clean only days ago. She shoved open the door. To get to the mailboxes, she had to step high over a big lumpy coat someone had left on the floor, lying at the foot of the last stair. Too high. She straddled the coat and wrestled the door to her mailbox open. The key had never fit very well. As she got it open, she realized there was something under the coat. Something solid. Carmen bent to pick it up and found Mrs. Beebe lying under it, staring straight up, sightlessly.

Carmen jumped back in shock. Her mail erupted everywhere.

"Mrs. B!"

Carmen repeated the name a few times and pushed at the landlady's shoulder. Mrs. B. was cold and rigid. She didn't breathe or scream, and neither did Carmen. They were both as silent as death.

Carmen looked up the staircase. Mrs. B was lying as if she'd fallen down the stairs, but what were the odds? True, she was a big woman who had always struggled with the stairs. But having fallen, she wouldn't have covered herself up. On the other hand, there were plenty of tenants in the building who could have innocently been going to work, who would have covered her up and then moved on, and never would have called the police. The police were frequently not too friendly to the low-income residents of this building, and the owners of the building did not like residents who needed police interventions.

Carmen backed out. She realized she was holding her breath, and filled her lungs with the bitter, fume-filled morning air. Her heart raced as she backtracked. In a blur, she ran down blocks, braving standing-still traffic across streets all the way to the corner where she found the policeman she'd flirted with only a block away from where she'd left him. She was so out of breath she could hardly form the words.

"Emergency, please." She tugged his arm.

He and his partner followed her to the building. She didn't explain, just pointed to the door.

The rotund cop stood in the open door and called it in. Mr. Handsome had a nametag and she noticed it as he bent over the body—Beasley.

"She wasn't like that when I got here," Carmen volunteered, from where she stood on the sidewalk. She peered around the belly of the fat cop who held the door open patiently, waiting for her to go in. She stayed on the sidewalk, unsure she'd ever set foot in the building again. "I stepped over her. She was covered up. I was reaching for my mail and...pulled back the coat. She was just like that, staring up. *Dios*, the look on her face—"

"Show me." Beasley stepped back from the corpse.

Carmen didn't want to go back inside the foyer, but the second cop gave her an encouraging shove.

She stumbled in, not wanting to step over poor Mrs. B's body, but at last she did. She pantomimed opening her mailbox. It wasn't difficult, as her keys were still stuck in the lock. She retrieved them, dropped them in her pocket, then showed how she'd bent over and pulled back the coat.

Beasley gathered the mail and glanced at the name.

"Mrs. Garcia Sanchez?"

Carmen nodded uncertainly.

"I presume these are yours."

He handed her the letters, all bills and

circulars. No one she actually knew was aware of her address.

"What's her name?"

"Everyone knows her," Carmen said. "It's Mrs. Beebe. Everyone called her Mrs. B. She rents out the apartments." She had stepped away and was leaning against the wall at the foot of the stairs as if for strength. "She lives up there." Carmen pointed up the steps. "On two. On the same floor as me."

"Which is her apartment?"

Carmen pointed up the stairs again, and he shook his head.

"What's there?" he asked pointing to the doorway to the basement.

"The basement. I mean, the laundry. There are machines down there."

He pulled his gun, and disappeared through the door, his footsteps echoing on the concrete steps. Carmen heard the click of the light turning on and then off. After a quick check, he returned to the foot of the stairs where she was waiting. His gun was holstered. She wasn't sure she could move her feet.

He put his hand on his holster. "Show me her apartment. Don't go in, just point it out."

Carmen led him to the first landing and pointed up to Mrs. B's, which was the first door on the right. Carmen's was the last one on the right, at the hall's opposite end. There was a cardboard rectangle, the remains of a shipping box, tacked on Mrs. B's door with the handwritten words:

"Any nuisance at this address that requires police intervention will result in a doubling of the rent. The management."

Above a small hole in the wall where a buzzer used to be, there was a rusty tin sign that said "DO NOT RING." A grimy contract was taped to the wall, with several areas circled in red, mostly details of late fees, administrative fees, cleanup fees, move-in fees, move-out fees, and the like.

Beasley waved her to stand aside. Carmen backed into the corner. The door was ajar and creaked when he touched it and swung it in.

He drew his gun and disappeared inside. Carmen caught a glimpse of the mess. The apartment had been ransacked.

"Is it always like this?"

"No. Not this bad."

The heavyset cop motioned for her to come down the stairs and repeated the same questions Beasley had asked. He had a little yellow pad out and scribbled in it as she responded.

"Did you witness anything?"

"No, I just found her here." Carmen repeated the whole thing again. "I already told the other guy."

"Her hand is broken," he said. "Was it already broken or did it break in the fall?"

"She was fine when I saw her a couple of days ago. But she usually has her keys on a ring everywhere she goes. Where are her keys? Her keys are missing," Carmen said. "*Dios*, someone has her keys, no one is safe."

No one was safe, she realized. No one but she. She'd never given Mrs. B a copy of her key. She didn't mention that to the cop.

Residents had come down, some to go to work, some curious about the police cars parked outside their front door. News traveled fast in the tenement. The fat cop wouldn't let anyone leave, but made them stand in line while he took names and interviewed them. Plenty of them were grousing about being late for work.

"Anyone who objects is free to ride to the precinct. Might be a good idea. You guys might be safer in jail. Seems like last night was a big night in the murder business. Not that there's any connection, but some antique of a security guard outside the Women's Hospital was shot."

Carmen thought: *Waldo*. She did not volunteer that she worked at the Woman's Hospital.

Her throat choked up. Poor sweet Waldo, who had never failed to compliment her, to open the door for her, to tip his hat. Waldo, who might have died trying to keep her safe.

She wasn't safe after all. She didn't need it in writing. She knew these deaths happened because they were after her. She should never have let her guard down.

Beasley came down and whispered low-voiced to his partner that the landlady's apartment had been gone through with a forklift and a fine-toothed comb. A new batch of police cars had arrived. Beasley sent her to lean on the building to wait for him. She did so without argument, imitating Tina's frequent air of boredom, with her arms crossed and an air of dull exasperation, meanwhile inching away from the entrance. Another cop caught sight of her and, thinking she had breached the crime scene, shuffled her off into the crowd. Beasley yelled for her, but in the confusion, Carmen was able to slip away into a bunch of rubberneckers. She went the back way through Moonie's place to her apartment. The police were apparently not aware of that entrance to the building, or just hadn't had the forethought to have a look-see. She felt a frantic urge to check on Mario.

Up the fire escape. So far, so good. Carmen heaved her back door open and stepped in. Devastation slapped her in the face. Every drawer had been dumped out, the wardrobe tossed, the mattresses pulled from the beds and couch and shredded. The rocking chair was missing. Mario's bed was smashed, and all their clothes were strewn everywhere.

The solid-steel doors were intact. How had anyone gotten in? She checked the locks. They were fine, good as new. In fact, they were about the only thing in her place that was intact.

She stared, disbelieving at the mess. This soon after the detective had traced her to New York, it could not be a coincidence. But Mrs. Beebe had no key to let anyone in. She took a few steps in and looked behind her dressing screen, and saw her next-to-worst nightmare.

Blasio stood there, not in his chauffeur's suit, but some natty double-breasted plaid suit straight out of a Kuppenheimer ad. Mary Lynn, who was not even supposed to be there, was taped to the rocker, and there was no sign of Mario. Mary Lynn's blonde hair was askew, her face flushed, and she stared at Carmen in terror over her taped mouth. The sweater of her twin set was unbuttoned and the shirt beneath was askew. Knowing Blasio, Carmen was pretty sure Mary Lynn had been mauled.

"So nice to see you, C...C...Carmen."

"I wish I could say the same, Blasio," Carmen said. "Why are you here?"

"A little thing about some m...m...missing money," he said. "There's a nice little reward for your....h...head. Attached to your neck. Go sit over th...there."

With the pistol, he gestured toward the wrecked couch. Carmen ignored him, and started unwrapping the tape from Mary Lynn's mouth.

Blasio frowned at being ignored, but as Carmen expected, did nothing.

"Get out of my house. Go down the front steps. There's a whole troop of cops out there, waiting for you," she said, steadily, her back to Blasio. She apologized to Mary Lynn under her breath as she pulled the tape from her mouth, then started on getting Mary Lynn's hands free.

"Cops? I don't believe you."

"Look out the window if you don't believe me."

His eyes flickered in that direction, but he saw the glass was painted white.

"You're shitting me," he said.

"Go ahead, scrape off some paint and take a look. I'm not lying."

She left Mary Lynn's side and shoved past Blasio.

"Whoa," Blasio said. "C...can't you see? I'm p...packing heat. Wh...w...where are you going? I'll shoot you." He indicated his gun, as if she could have failed to see him waving it around like a tambourine.

"I need my scissors to cut her free. There's no need for you to scare her."

Disgusted at failing to terrify Carmen, Blasio turned his back on her. Heartened to feel he was at least scaring somebody, he waved his gun at Mary Lynn, who was still mostly taped to the chair. She worked her arms against the tape.

"You better stay put!"

Mary Lynn stilled and nodded furiously. She couldn't have moved if she wanted to. Her eyes got big. She bit her lip to keep from saying anything.

Blasio, thoroughly impressed with himself, took another menacing step in her direction. He never heard the clang of Carmen's cast-iron skillet against the back of his head. He fell like a rock. Carmen stepped over him and cut Mary Lynn free.

"Carmen," Mary Lynn squeaked out, "you're so brave!"

"He's nobody," Carmen said. "Always was nobody. Always will be. Where's Mario? How did that *bastardo* get in here?"

"It's my fault!" Mary Lynn wailed. It was rare she came out of her house not looking like a pin-up, but she'd cried off most of her makeup and her hair was a frazzled mop. Her arms trembled as she straightened her clothes. "Mario was asleep, so Tina decided to stay over at my house with him. I used my key to get in. I was coming here to get his blankie, and there was a knock at the door. When I opened it, there were these two guys. They came in and went friggin' nuts."

Carmen got very still. "Two guys? This one wasn't alone?"

"The other guy went off someplace," Mary Lynn said, looking down at Blasio. She grabbed the tape he had used on her and taped his hands together. She added two more layers for good measure. "Take that, bastard."

Carmen wondered if the detective had been two-faced. Had he been the second guy?

"What did he look like? Was he fortyish, dark hair and eyes? Wearing a trench coat?"

"No. Younger than that," Mary said, looking at her handiwork. Blasio had arms like a gorilla. No way would he be getting out of that without losing a lot of body hair. She wrapped some extra tape around his upper arms just for spite. "I thought at first he was a poli." She pointed at Blasio. "Should I tape his feet, too?" She didn't wait for an answer, taping his ankles together anyway.

Carmen shook her head. If the second guy wasn't Detective Oliver, who was it? She wished she'd gotten some answers from Blasio before she bonked him on the head, but she'd been more frightened than she'd let on, and had acted on instinct.

"Listen, I'm not kidding, there's a ton of cops downstairs. Someone broke Mrs. B.'s hand and shoved her down the stairs."

Mary Lynn looked as if she was about to faint. "Who did it?"

Carmen shrugged. Who, indeed. "It was probably Blasio here, and his buddy, what's-his-name. Go downstairs and tell them what happened. I'm going to get Mario. He's at your house?"

The instant Mary Lynn was out the door, Carmen slid aside the braided rug, tripped the switch that locked the boards in place, pulled up the floorboards, and lifted out the suitcase with the money. After she laid the boards back, moved the rug over them, and put the rocking chair in its usual location on the rug, she stood back for half a second, squinting to make sure it looked as it always did. As if it mattered when the rest of the place was a shambles. It was too straight. She leaned the rocking chair on its side.

     There was no time to pack. She was suddenly back in running mode. Gone was the sense of freedom; pursuit was real again. She scooted out her back door, dashed down the fire escape. She heard something creak.

     "Moonie?" she called out. No one answered. The noise must have been the fire escape, which frequently creaked on its own without any assistance from feet. Moonie's bed was empty. He had probably walked to the diner for breakfast. She grabbed a pair of his pants and slid them on. They were huge on her, but the right length. She found a belt, which she pulled tight. It wouldn't do for the pants to fall off. She tossed her skirt in the trash and put on one of Moonie's bulky jackets over her blouse. Tucked her shortened hair under the souvenir New York Yankees baseball cap Moonie had bought when they'd gone to a game, which now felt like a million years ago. She shoved the case with the money under the passenger seat of Moonie's semi-tractor and then headed to the babysitter.

* * *

Tina was outdoors on the screened-in porch, rolling a ball back and forth to the baby. Mario saw her first and squealed, "Mami!"

Carmen opened the wire-mesh door and held out her hands, and he ran at her full force. She gathered him up in a hug.

Tina's jaw gaped at Carmen's get-up.

"Not your best look, Carmen," Tina said.

"Agreed. Moonie said something about going on a...picnic."

"It sounds like quite an adventure." An excited look washed over Tina's face. "There's plenty enough adventure as it is. Did you hear? Mrs. B. is in the hospital."

Carmen, who had been rolling faster and faster, came to a dead stop. The last she'd seen, Mrs. B. had been dead.

"What happened?" she asked carefully.

"They found her on the first floor laid out like a ham for Christmas dinner. She fell on the stairs. They're going to do an autopsy."

"Autopsy?"

"She's dead, didn't I say? Cops tore up her apartment. I got it from the Oropeza brothers. There's a convention of cops in your building like they're giving away free doughnuts. The guys got caught sneaking out the laundry room emergency door, and had to do some fast talking to keep from getting thrown in the poky. Poor Mrs. Beebe. I wonder if she had family."

"Listen, Tina, I wanted to thank you for taking such great care of Mario."

"Oh, he's a sweetheart. He's much nicer than my own brother."

Carmen pulled out all the money she had in her wallet—much more than she usually paid the girls, but then, she wasn't expecting to ever see them again.

"Take this. Half to Mary Lynn."

Tina saw the money and whistled. "What did we do right?"

"I gotta go." Carmen looked at her watch.

"Better go the back way," Tina said. "The Oropezas said there were cops out the kazoo on the stoop."

"Sure thing."

"Catch you later." Tina waved, stashing the money in her pocket, already planning how to spend her half.

Chapter Thirty-Eight

Carmen let herself into Moonie's place. "Moonie?" Still no answer. She didn't check his bed this time.

She went to his cab and opened the passenger door, looking under the seat where she'd stuffed the case. Mario was asleep, and Carmen lay him down on the passenger seat to free up her hands to search better.

"I know I put it in there," she mumbled to herself, sticking her arm underneath as far as it could reach. She was awkwardly positioned in just the kind of way Francisco had liked to take advantage of. When Moonie came up behind her quietly, her hackles rose, although he did nothing. Her instinctual awareness of that approach was still finely tuned, and she whipped around.

"Looking for this?"

It took a second for Carmen to extricate

her arm from beneath the seat, but she untangled herself and fully faced him. Much to her distress, Moonie held up the case.

"Now, where'd you get all this money?" he asked.

"I can explain..."

Moonie stared. "Go ahead."

She hesitated.

"What's going on?"

"It's a long story."

"I have all the time in the world," he said.

"I don't."

She reached for Mario. With his longer reach, Moonie plucked him up off the passenger seat. He cradled the boy, the little body dwarfed against his big shoulder.

"Not so fast. I want answers. Does this have anything to do with the crowd of cops outside? Does this explain why you're always as jumpy as a ring-tailed cat in a room full of rocking chairs?"

"Can't tell you."

"Hon, don't you know by now you can

tell me anything?"

"It would put you in danger."

Moonie laughed. Somehow it looked to Carmen as if he grew a full foot taller, even though he hadn't moved an inch. Mario grinned in his sleep, and coiled his hand in Moonie's hair.

"Tell me," he coaxed.

"Go take a look at my apartment."

"I've already been up there. Checked it out first thing after I found this shitload of money in my truck. See, I was on my back working on the transmission of the old Roadster when I heard you open the cab. You were gone by the time I got out from under."

"There's someone after me."

"I figured out that much on my own. Are they after you or the money?"

"I don't know."

"Trust me."

"I am not telling you any more. This is ridiculous. Give me my baby and let me go. You're wasting time. I gotta get away from here."

"Get away? What took you so long to

ask? Get in the cab. I'm making a run."

"Where to?"

"Los Angeles. Did I ever tell you I got a little house there? Picket fence and all that shit. I haven't been back there since you moved in here. Bet the yard has gone all to hell."

"Okay, big guy," Carmen agreed, "I'm game."

Chapter Thirty-Nine
Two years later in LA

Mario Luna was master of all he surveyed. And what he surveyed was a yard with a fence. He used to hide behind doors with his pop gun, jumping out and taking Papi and Auntie Carmen by surprise, till they scolded, said he was no Roy Rogers or Gary Cooper and took his holster set away. His favorite part of his kingdom had been a huge pile of tiny stones he had played with until the grown-ups spread them to cover deep grooves left by the tires of Papi Moon's big truck. He had been warned not to play in the driveway after Papi nearly ran over him. Auntie Carmen told him to leave the gravel alone, or else. And he didn't want to find out what "or else" meant.

But he was a clever boy. They couldn't accuse him of being in the rocks when he was on the roof. No one had told him yet to stay on the ground, though he figured it would be coming soon. Climbing up the pipe wasn't that easy, but it was the kind of challenge he liked. He was pretty good at the physical stuff.

He might as well enjoy his time up here while he had it. His pockets were stuffed with pebbles if he needed them. He hoped not so full they would impair his flying. They were good for so much, like stacking and road building and throwing. Even better, he'd gotten the red-and-blue striped pillow case from the laundry line, and used a couple of clothespins to fix his new "cape" to his T-shirt so he would be able to fly off the roof like Superman did on TV. He was just waiting for Papi to come out of the back of the house to see how he could fly. He was patient, because up here, there was plenty of stuff to see and do. As long as he was standing on the garage roof, he could look over the fence and see the street, and into the Ortiz's yard next door where Mrs. Ortiz's little poodle Fifi yipped madly at nothing, as he frequently did. If Mario had his pop gun now, he could use the little poodle for target practice, but he'd never do that. Fifi would always run off with the cork bullets and eat them. What a stupid name for a boy dog.

Mario continued entertaining himself by counting cars passing on the street. The problem was that, at four years old, he could only count with any degree of certainty to ten. He'd figured out a solution. Every time he got to ten, he put a rock down. He'd been standing here for ages. So far, he had already put down twelve rocks and his pockets were still full. He got so caught up in car-counting that he almost forgot his plan when Papi finally came out of the house to call him in for dinner.

"Mario!" Papi yelled, looking in the wrong direction, toward the fence. He didn't see Mario, who was practically right over his head.

"You better be in this yard, boy! Dinner-time!"

Mario didn't want to miss dinner.

"Look, Papi!" he yelled, "Get a load of this! I'm Superman!" He launched himself off the roof.

He didn't stay up as long as he planned. Papi snatched him right out of the air.

"Boy, are you out of your mind?" Papi asked. "You nearly had a smash-up."

"Did you see me fly like Superman?"

"You better never do that again! Carmen will beat the daylights out of you if you so much as scratch a fingernail falling off the roof, Mario." Papi tossed him high and caught him, something he hadn't done since Mario was very little, but Papi was strong enough to do things like that, even though Mario was a big boy at four.

"I din't fall off! I flew! See my cape?"

"Party's over, little man. You better keep this little escapade to yourself." Papi jerked at Mario's "cape." The clothespins snapped sharply and flew off. Papi gathered them from the grass and clipped the cape back on the clothesline.

"Better keep your hands off Aunt Carmen's good sheets," Papi suggested mildly. "We better keep this to ourselves, okay? No more flying off the roof, Superman. This is just one of those boy-type things ladies aren't impressed with."

"Like making roads in the gravel? She din't like that."

Papi nodded. "Just like that."

Mario thought of how upset Auntie Carmin was the last time Papi had been backing the truck in and stopped an inch from Mario's backside. He'd been so engrossed in driving his toy car up the rock mountain that he hadn't once thought to get out of the way. He'd just been happy Papi was home so he could come down on the dirt and make roads with him. Papi was right. Oh, she'd never hurt him, but Auntie Carmen would make a fuss, and cry and say "or else," and make him go to confession and waste the whole weekend in church.

"Deal?"

"Okay, Papi, it's a deal." They shook on it and went in to dinner.

Chapter Forty

On the way to California, when Moonie stopped to pick up a load in Taos, New Mexico, Carmen had sent a telegram to Linda Villanueva, telling her she had a family emergency and had to leave New York.

In Los Angeles, they finally had eluded rogue Nogales gun punks or whoever had been after her. Carmen may have spent the first few months looking over her shoulder, but after a year and a half, she felt safe again and no longer suffered neck strain from turning to look behind her; no longer hid at corners peeking out to see who might be out there; no longer felt like she was suffering a heart attack every time she heard a car horn, or a train go by, or a backfire.

The lifestyle in Los Angeles was a far cry from Nogales, and just as far from the tenements of Spanish Harlem in New York City. Life had a whole different pace on the edge of the Pacific. Her last name was legally Luna. She had moved in Moonie's house. Her identity problems were shelved.

On the long cross-country drive, she'd told Moonie the whole truth of what had happened the night Mario was born. That night was enough of a shocker that she was entirely comfortable leaving out what Francisco had done to her, and what her job had been like. In fact, she skipped telling him anything about her life from the death of her parents on. Some things even Moonie didn't need to know. Honesty might be the best policy, but some things were best left asleep in the dark, along with Francisco in his coffin, six feet underground.

They were living what felt to Carmen like a fairy tale life in Moonie's California bungalow, which really did have a white picket fence. He was still driving for a living and parked his Peterbilt in their big backyard.

Carmen didn't know how Linda Villanueva had smoothed over her emergency exit from the cadet program, but behind the scenes, she had helped Carmen with the paperwork to change the name on her nursing license to Carmen Luna. As soon as she was settled in and the red tape cut through, the cadet nursing program had been happy to assign her to the old and crowded Mount Sinai Home for the Incurables on Bonnie Beach Place in her new town. It had lots of nursing positions open because it was expanding into a new building on Beverly Boulevard, but that place wasn't finished yet.

Transit in LA wasn't as convenient as it was in Spanish Harlem, but even with LA's special brand of smog, it was cleaner than coal-warmed Harlem.

Carmen had decided to be modern about the whole thing and approach her vocation the same way Linda Villanueva did. She had health department-style flyers printed up in Spanish and handed them out to the local churches. Most people were having their babies in hospitals these days, but she made it known that Nurse Luna was available for home births. She was meticulous in her paperwork, so there was nothing in her flyers to connect her to Carmen Garcia or Elena Sanchez.

Through her employment in the cadet nursing program, Carmen had gotten to know a couple of young Hispanic obstetricians who were flexible enough to recommend her sometimes and to whom she could direct her own patients when there were complications.

All in all, life in California was pretty good, but that was about to change. In Carmen's world, trouble never stopped, and all good things came to an end. Usually a bad end.

She was in the ward of the Mount Sinai Home for the Incurables when she saw him, just as she had two years before, at the nurses' desk. Detective Oliver. This time she knew him. Their first meeting could have been a week ago. He wore the same trench coat, but not the sweaters underneath.

It was the end of her shift. She saw him and didn't run, but she grabbed her purse and headed for the exit, knowing he would fall in beside her.

"You look well, Miss Garcia," he said. "Or do I call you Mrs. Luna now?"

"Detective Oliver," she said, walking briskly without turning her head to face him. "You need to go away. Two years ago Blasio followed you to New York, and for all I know, someone has followed you here. I am not going to let you ruin the life I have built here."

"Ah. Blasio. He was briefly incarcerated in New York for assault on the Cordes girl. That girl's story never made much sense. I never could understand how she managed to defend herself while she was taped to a chair. I always assumed you had a hand in his concussion. You swing a mean saucepan."

"I seem to recall a cast-iron skillet," she said. "Thanks. Now you can go away. Lead whoever is following you someplace else. Go hang out in Tucson. Go to Hawaii. Go to Mexico. I highly recommend a visit with my imaginary cousin Chad in Puerto Vallarta. Go anywhere else and pretend I'm there."

"I came here to warn you. Maybe to offer some protection. We had word that Francisco sent some of his people..."

Carmen stopped walking so abruptly that the detective took several steps and left her behind. He turned sharply and the Santa Ana wind caught at his jacket, blowing it open. Carmen glimpsed the police-issued holster strapped over his shoulder, and wondered randomly if he'd ever shot himself in the armpit while drawing the gun it held. Right now, in her current mood, she hoped he had. It looked to be an inconvenient place compared to where cowboys in westerns wore their guns, but who was she to say? Other than his tracking skills, Detective Oliver had never impressed her with his acuity. It took a few seconds for her to recall and register the full impact of his words.

"Francisco? What do you mean Francisco sent some of his people? Where'd he send them from? Hell?"

The daylight in Los Angeles just changed in quality, suddenly darker, grimmer, the smog sucking away all color. Carmen found she had trouble catching her breath.

"I came to warn you. Francisco sent some people here to find you."

"But Francisco is dead."

"Where did you get that idea?"

"You said so, didn't you? You were in New York to arrest me for his murder, but..." Carmen thought back on that night Detective Oliver showed up at the hospital. Had he accused her of murder, or had she just assumed? She didn't recall his exact language. Her heart started racing so madly that her hands trembled. Francisco was alive? How could that be?

"I was in New York investigating your sister's murder. Maybe Francisco had more bullets in him than a hog has buckshot, and it was a month of Sundays before he was talking at all, but he wasn't the talking dead. He was and is alive. He was in a coma for a while, but once he came to, he swore up and down he didn't remember what happened that night. You—or one of his enemies, or one of his own goon squad—emptied a gun into him. Probably for good reason. He's not what he was, but he still sits on top of a big crime mob with fingers from California to Arizona, all along the border, and deep into Mexico. I don't know how he feels about you personally, being his sister-in-law, but he's got some associates who are convinced you've had four years of living high on the hog on their drug money. But I saw for myself where you were staying. I've seen cockroaches with better addresses."

She was reeling from the news that Francisco was alive or she'd never have let the next words slip.

"I never spent a dime of that money that I didn't put back. It's all for Mario. It was always all for Mario. Circumstances have changed. Moonie and me, we don't need it."

The detective's eyes narrowed. "I see. I was still hoping you were an innocent victim in all of this. But if you did take that money... You know, you've got a smoldering look about you, but you downplay it so much I never figured you for the type."

"What type? What are you talking about?" Carmen swung around and faced him. "Do you want the money? Take it. It's been nothing but trouble," she said. "Do whatever you want with it, if it will get you, and Francisco, and his hoodlums––off my back."

"Sister, you think I'm going to hand it over for you and tell them to make nice? You've got another think coming. They're the 'shoot first, ask questions later' squad. If you think handing over the cash will get them off your back, do it. Only don't come crying to me when they blow your pretty little head off."

She took a few more steps toward the bus stop where she usually caught a ride home. Then she recalled the last time she'd seen the detective, and what she'd found at home a day or two afterward. A familiar horrible sinking feeling grew in her chest. At least Mario was still safe at nursery school. She hoped.

She grabbed Oliver by his lapel. He looked startled.

"I've got to get straight home. Do you

have a car? I sure as hell hope you do, and that it's fast enough to outrun whatever trouble is following you this time."

Oliver did, in fact, have a rental. He did not seem surprised at Carmen's assumption, but led her to the vehicle, even opened the door for her and brushed off the seat. A glance at the pile of clothes, bags, knee-high trash, and a half-eaten, melted chocolate bar showed her that the front passenger side was out of the question. Carmen opened the back door herself and climbed in. The detective shrugged.

Once he had the car started up, Oliver could not drive fast enough to suit her.

"I know where you live," he volunteered.

"Then hurry," she said, tersely.

She leaned forward, watching traffic as if she were driving, as if it would help him go faster, when she noticed a holster slung across the back of the seat, the gun in it swinging back and forth with the motion of the car. She didn't think about it. It was as if her hand had a mind of its own when she grabbed the gun, and stuck it in her purse. Oliver didn't notice.

The last time she'd had a firearm in her hand, she'd shot Francisco with it.

What did it matter? Carmen thought. He was wearing a holster. Why would he need two? She felt no need to mention to Detective Oliver the hours of drills Moonie had put her through at the gun range. Moonie had not been satisfied with her explanations of her past. He knew there was more than she said, and he wanted her able to defend herself.

She had the door open and was out of the vehicle before it had rolled to a stop in front of her house.

Refusing to listen to Detective Oliver's orders to wait behind him, she burst through her front door and ran willy-nilly from room to room. Moonie should have been somewhere. His truck was visible in the backyard. It was about time to pick Mario up from the nursery school that was a mere block away, housed in a steel-framed house built by a young architect named Koenig—his first house. Moonie had pointed out the odd-looking building at Carmen's first sight of the neighborhood; he was certain that Koenig's steel shoebox of a house would never catch on.

As she glanced at her watch, she realized that's probably where Moonie was—at Mrs. Trennor's kindergarten and nursery, picking up Mario.

She could hear Detective Oliver clomping along in her wake. He followed her into the master bedroom. She ran to her closet and grabbed her biggest, ugliest handbag from the farthest corner. It was a spectacularly homely receptacle she'd gotten from a "secret Santa" at work the previous Christmas, the kind of thing a tourist would buy as a gift for someone they didn't like very much, and something Carmen would never actually use. She jerked it down from the top corner of her closet and chucked it in the general direction of the detective, who missed the catch.

"Here," she said without stopping, but pointing to the lumpy, overfilled bag where it had landed in the corner, looming like the over-stuffed ghost of a very bad vacation. "It's the money, all of it. Every dime. Every cent I spent getting to

New York, I put back as soon as I had work. You want it, you take it, you give it to them, get them off my back. Now I have to go pick up my boy."

She ran past Oliver and made it to the school on foot in record time. It was just a couple of houses down and around the corner in the formerly six-bedroom, now six-classroom steel residence-turned-school. On the approach, Carmen could hear Moonie shouting from two houses away. He was easy to find, standing in the office screaming at the principal.

"Where is my son?"

"I told you twice already, your brother-in-law picked him up."

Carmen wasted no time. She elbowed her way through the eavesdropping parents and teachers, and shoved open the door. Moonie had the principal backed up against the wall and was holding him pressed there, his feet dangling about three inches off the ground.

"What's that you were saying?" Carmen said, low-voiced, to the principal.

"Mrs. Luna," the principal rasped, with

great relief. "Please explain to your husband that your brother picked up little Mario."

"Mr. Meeks," Carmen said, still softly, "I don't have a brother. Can you please describe the man?"

All they got from Meeks was something about the gray pinstriped suit the so-called brother had been wearing. With impressive self-control, Moonie let him down, and Meeks lived up to his name by promptly falling into a useless faint. His secretary contributed that the man in question had been Hispanic, attractive, and spoke with what she thought was a Texas accent, though her New Jersey drawl rendered that opinion on the questionable side.

Carmen and Moonie dashed from the office and shoved back through the growing crowd of teachers and parents who had come to pick up their kids and stayed to listen to the ruckus in their normally quiet neighborhood. Carmen and Mooney looked frantically for the man in the pinstriped suit and their boy, but without luck. Mario's whole class—indeed, all six classes of nursery schoolers, kindergarteners, and their teachers—was among those milling about. But no Mario. And no pinstriped suit.

Mario was nowhere to be found.

They were leaving when Detective Oliver made it into the school building.

Out of breath, he wheezed, "Where is the boy?"

Moonie took a look at Carmen's pallor, and at the burgeoning group of parents and children burning with curiosity and concern, and said, "Let's go home and regroup."

They returned to the house on foot in, again, record time, leaving Oliver in the dust.

As they walked up, Moonie asked Carmen, "Whose car?"

"His." Carmen gestured back toward Oliver, who had just rounded the corner a block behind them. "He's a detective from Nogales."

Moonie looked back to Oliver, who had given up the effort to keep up. He focused his attention on the street. "Who's parked in the Ortiz's driveway next door? Those are Arizona plates."

Slowly Carmen shook her head. "They're not friends. They weren't there ten minutes ago."

"Ortiz is gonna be pissed," Moonie said. "You know how he is about that driveway being blocked."

Carmen looked from the house to Moonie.

"You were just here, right? Did you leave the door unlocked?" Moonie asked.

It was not just unlocked. The front door was standing wide open. Moonie saw the open door and stepped back, bumping into Carmen.

"Get down, woman. Get back and down, behind the fence. I gotta think." He sank into a crouch and peered through the slats in the white picket fence. Everything looked normal, except for the open door and two strange cars, but Mario was missing.

Oliver arrived, finally, at a staggering walk. He leaned over, coughing, resting his hands on his thighs.

"I gotta give up cigarettes."

He straightened painfully and looked

with surprise at Carmen's house. "Someone busted out your screen door."

"Back in New York, two years ago, I thought you said you were quitting," Carmen said.

"Two years ago?" Moonie asked, his eyes narrowed. "Good thing I'm not a jealous man." He looked more than a little jealous.

"Whoa, big guy," the detective said.

"A year and a half." Carmen shrugged. "We met at the hospital just before Mrs. B fell down the stairs."

"At the time, I thought I was. Quitting smoking."

"You left the door open?" Carmen accused the detective, turning to Moonie. "I hope it was he who left the door open. He brought me home from work. He was behind me when I went to the school."

Oliver shook his head and drew his gun. "I didn't lock it, but I pulled the door to. Looks like someone did a job on your screen door. That wasn't me. It's whoever's inside."

Moonie said, "Mario got to that screen door long before you got here. He likes scissors. But who left that door standing wide open?"

"It's whoever belongs to that car with the Arizona plates," Carmen said. "Do you know who that is, Detective Oliver?"

"Detective?"

"Nogales's finest," Oliver grabbed Moonie's hand and shook it. "Pleased to meet you."

Moonie's response was unintelligible, and he didn't look pleased.

"The car," Carmen repeated.

"It's some pretty bad guys," Oliver said. "Not sure exactly which ones. But definitely gun punks who did business with your brother-in-law."

The screen door fell shut with a bang, not that it was much of a barrier. The previous week, Mario had cut shapes from the mesh and now it was pretty much a bedraggled mess. It had been on Moonie's agenda to replace the screen after he'd given Mario a talking to that he kept putting off.

"What is wrong with you guys?" Carmen hissed. "Get my baby out of there." She shoved hard, but Moonie was planted like the red column at the Angels Flight rail station, not moving unless he wanted to. She was wedged behind Moonie, who wouldn't let her pass, as if Oliver's solid grip on her forearm weren't also holding her back.

"I gotta get in there. There's some *pendejo* in there with my baby." But she couldn't wrangle her way past two stubborn grown men with well-defined hero complexes.

"You stay here," Moonie said. "I'll get him, or die trying."

"No," Carmen said, fearing his words, "not you. I know what they want." She bit her lip, wanting to call back the words lest they stir Moonie's curiosity or move him to greater hero-ism.

She cut her eyes at the detective, hoping he'd keep his mouth shut about the stolen money. Moonie, concentrating on their house, didn't ask what she was talking about. He wasn't in observation mode; he was in hero mode, determined to rescue Mario, who must be inside, since the lunchbox he'd taken to school that morning sat on the steps.

They both had too much testosterone to hear a word. Both men were in concert, as if they were long time compatriots instead of strangers who'd met a minute before, as if there were something in male DNA that clicked in as a result of the emergency situation. Both had been "over there" and military training had kicked in, however rusty or absurd in the LA setting.

"Seek-Strike-Destroy," Moonie said. "774th Tank Destroyer Battalion."

"*In omnia paratus*. In all things prepared," Oliver replied. "179th Infantry regiment. Trigger Oliver at your service."

Carmen thought about reciting her nursing oath, but it was too long. "Hey," she interrupted.

"Wait here."

"You. Stay."

As if they were following some script she

wasn't privy to, both men insisted she cower behind the fence like a little girl. She wasn't buying it. No one in her life had ever fought Carmen's battles for her. As much as she loved Moonie for his big heart, she had no great respect for his wit; and so far, nothing Detective Oliver had done had proved his mettle to her. As far as she could see, his only accomplishment had been to lead the bad guys to her doorstep—twice, after she had twice managed to evade them. She'd have to handle this herself.

The men crept along the picket fence toward the side of the house and, out of eyeshot of the front door, vaulted over the fence. They made their way against the garage perimeter, working around bit by bit, until Moonie was peering through the open door and the mangled screen, He made an obscure signal to Oliver, who flattened himself against the house, behind Moonie, gun drawn.

"I think the guy with the gun should be first," Carmen hissed, but they ignored her.

"Idiots," she said softly.

She thought she heard Mario squeal from inside and clenched her fists. She'd have to do something soon or burst.

Chapter Forty-One

Moonie and Oliver made it through the screen door without a creak, slam, or whisper, but Carmen had had all the inaction she could tolerate. She waited until the men were inside and couldn't see her or get in her way, but neither did as she had been told, nor did she follow their elusive path over the fence. She took a third course of action, which was going straight up to the front walk, near where her neighbor, whose driveway had been commandeered by the strange car, stood watching the goings on.

"You got guests?" Frenchy Ortiz asked.

"Unwanted ones."

Frenchy was slapping her keys against her flowered housecoat and carrying a Snyder's drugstore bag, out of which a tin of hair spray stuck out. Her hair was done up in pin curls and curlers, with a pink hairnet tied on top. Her harlequin glasses were decorated with rhinestones that glinted in the sunlight and a drop of water from her still-damp hair shimmered on one of her lenses. She walked in a cloud of Aqua-net. "I was gonna ask about the car."

"Go back inside, Frenchy," Carmen said, not taking her eyes off her porch. "And call the police. Tell them there's some guy there who broke in the house. Tell them Moonie went in there after him, so they don't shoot my husband by mistake."

"Oh my," Frenchy's hand flew up to her mouth. "Maybe I should pull my car in the drive so he can't get away."

"Good idea. But whatever you do, it better be fast. I'm going in."

"Carmen, should you? You better wait for the cops."

"No. Mario's in there."

Carmen shook off Frenchy and headed up the walk to her house. The path from the sidewalk to the steps was made of random-shaped slabs of gray rhyolite cut from a Sonora quarry, inlaid with brown gravel. Not since the day the past summer when Moonie had put in the path had it ever seemed so long. Up the steps, through the doors. Inside, she hesitated. Outside, Frenchy's car started and stopped. Someone honked. Seconds later, Frenchy's red wooden door shut with a bang. Carmen jumped at the sound and took another step, her heart slamming in her chest. Who was in her house, and where were they? Where were Moonie and the detective? And where was Mario?

"Hold it right there, missy." Carmen heard a strange voice. She felt something hard and cold poke against the back of her head. She didn't need to be a brain surgeon to know what it was. Heard a click.

"You ain't going nowhere, doll."

She turned to look at the guy with the gun.

"I'd appreciate you putting that thing away," Carmen said, fighting to sound normal. She wanted to scream, to rant, but not in Mario's hearing. "This is a residence, not the OK Corral, and you sure as hell aren't Gary Cooper or Roy Rogers. Who are you and what are you doing here? This is my house, and we don't play with guns here."

"Name's Jughead," he said.

The stranger looked her over rudely, whistled out of the side of his mouth, and used the barrel of the gun to tilt up his old fashioned fedora. He was a youngish man, but no one could have called him attractive. His nose had been punched to one side of his face and healed that way, like a clay pot that had been dropped before it was fired. His suit was black, not pinstriped. Unless he'd just changed clothes, someone else had Mario.

"What does the other guy want with my son?"

"Guess you can ask him yourself. Hey, Blackstone, we're coming in." Jughead poked her in the back with his gun about the time she heard glass shatter and what sounded like firecrackers going off in her bedroom.

Carmen ran toward the noise, ignoring

Jughead and his weapon, and nearly tripped over the detective, who was laid out cold in her hallway, a hole in the shoulder of his trench coat leaking blood onto her freshly scrubbed floor. While she'd been fending off Jughead, Trigger Oliver had been shot. She reached into her laundry hamper and quickly twisted one of her laundered nylons around his arm, tying it off in a tourniquet. As she wadded a towel and held it hard against the wound, he started to come around. She put Oliver's hand over the towel, pressing hard to stop the blood. He followed her lead. The detective's face was marked, too. She'd spent enough time in emergency rooms to guess he'd been kicked by Blackstone's cowboy boots. Needless to say, Blackstone was in a pinstriped suit. He was the last person on Earth Carmen wanted to see holding Mario in the crook of his arm like a football. Unlike a football, Mario was kicking and fighting to get loose.

"Quit it, kid, or I'll plug your Ma."

Mario caught sight of Carmen and redoubled his efforts, twisting and squirming, unable to break free from Blackstone, but clearly nowhere near giving up. Moonie took a few steps to the left, putting himself between Carmen and Blackstone's gun.

"Put down the boy," Moonie said. "We're here. Deal with us."

Blackstone turned his attention and his firearm from Carmen to Moonie. His concentration was split just enough for Mario to squirm free, leaving behind his wooly sweater. He ran out of the room like a greyhound out the gate. Carmen heard the back door slam and felt a rush of relief. Mario's safety was all that mattered to her.

"Just tell us what you want, mister," Moonie said. "Leave our boy out of this. We'll do whatever you want." He looked toward Carmen, and she read in his eyes: Let me handle this.

No way. He didn't know anything about punks like these, but she'd been dealing with them all her life.

"She's got something what don't belong to her. She knows why we're here. You know what, don't you, doll? Get me that package and I'll forget about the kid."

Carmen, not resigned to handing over Mario's future, said, "The package is mine. It's a family inheritance."

"Who gives a shit? That Segundo said you're a sly one. I don't want no funny business. I ain't saying what you got is ours, or if it ain't. You got away with a bundle, you ain't got no protection, you can't go to the cops about it, and word is out that whoever gets it, keeps it. So pony up."

Moonie looked at her with a perplexed expression as purses and shoeboxes rained down on her.

"Wait," she said, remembering the detective, "I gave it to him."

Carmen launched out of her closet, raced back out to the hallway, and fell to her knees over the detective. She didn't know if he was down from blood loss or the boot print on his face. She put her hands on his shoulders and shook him fiercely. He groaned.

"What did you do with it? Come on!

Tell me!" She glanced out the window surreptitiously, trying to see where Mario had gone, but he had disappeared somewhere in the backyard. She prayed to herself that he'd gotten out, maybe gone to a neighbor's house. She shook the detective again. His head lolled back in unconsciousness.

"I gave it to him, just an hour ago. It must be near here somewhere."

"I hope for the kid's sake you got it," Blackstone said. "You want the kid back, you give us the cash."

"If you think you're taking that boy, you're wrong," Moonie said. "Blackstone, if that's your name, you can take him over my dead body." Moonie charged forward one step.

"Deal," Blackstone said. "I can do that."

The gun barked fire, and Moonie went down.

Carmen screamed his name and lurched to his side. Blackstone got a grip on her forearm and jerked her away.

Carmen set her stance, but she might

have been made of popcorn and feathers for all
the success she had. He kept on dragging her
through her hall, out the kitchen door, into the
backyard.

"I told you, I gave it to the detective."

"Yeah? So what did he do with it?"

"I don't know! Let go of me and let me
look for it. It's got to be close by." Carmen looked
frantically around as if the money would magically appear in the yard.

"I ain't lettin' you loose, sister, not till I
have the kid or the loot. Call the kid."

"You don't need Mario."

"Let's call him insurance. I like a little
insurance."

He pointed the gun point-blank at her
face. His face twisted into what might have been
a smile. He pulled back and aimed it skyward as
he contemplated his options, then laid them out
for her.

"I got a better idea. What do you need
more? Arm or leg? Call the kid." He waved the
barrel vaguely toward her hand and her calf. Car-

men strained hard, leaning away from him, but there wasn't much traction in the gravel.

"Run, Mario!" She had no idea where he was, but Carmen screamed at the top of her lungs.

From out of nowhere, a lump of something fabric-covered came flying through the air, colliding with Blackstone with a meaty sound and slamming him into the dirt. Carmen fell back, landing on her backside. It took a few seconds for Carmen to realize the burly hand was gone and she was free. She crab walked backward a stride or two and clambered to her feet, recognizing the still form under what turned out to be her crumpled pillowcase. It was Mario! She rolled him over to find that his beautiful eyes were open as wide as they could be, and he was gasping.

"Mario, baby, talk to me!"

It seemed to take him forever for him to get his breath back, but he wheezed out proudly, "I got him!"

"What did Moonie say about you getting up on that roof?" Carmen's voice cracked.

"But I flewed. Just like Superman!"

Carmen got to her feet, Mario hanging on her neck.

"We have to get you someplace safe."

"I'll protect you," Mario said proudly.

She moved toward the house, but a burly hand suddenly grabbed her ankle. She tried to step on it and failing that, tried to shake it loose.

"You ain't goin' no place, sister. Not you, not the kid. Not till you hand over the cash." Blackstone was like an anvil on her leg. He still had the gun in his other hand.

"I don't want it! You can have it!" Carmen screamed at him, stomping at his hand. "Let me find it! I swear you can have it."

"You ain't got it. So you and the kid are gonna be my leverage with your boss. He's got the dough, ten times over."

Carmen's back was to her door, Mario hanging onto her neck for dear life. She staggered, struggling to get out of the implacable grip on her ankle. She stomped again and ground her heel. Something cracked underfoot. She watched Blackstone's face fill simultaneously with pain and triumph, knowing he had her in spite of her actions. Nothing mattered but getting free, getting Mario safe.

That moment, the direction of Blackstone's eyes changed, his expression stolid, looking over Carmen's shoulder. He raised the gun with his uninjured hand and it went off twice. Something heavy fell against her back, wordlessly knocking her flat. Mario lost his grip and fell beside her.

She heard Mario scream "Papi!"

Carmen felt something hot and liquid dripping down her face, pushed at the dead weight; the weight had a terrible motionlessness. She could smell the bitter, metallic tang of it, felt a presentiment of horror, knew it was blood. The weight was too heavy to be real. She saw him, Moonie, expressionless, eyes blank.

"It can't be," she cried out. "We were safe. We were happy. Get up, Moonie, damnit. No, stay there, be still, I'll fix it, I'll fix you."

She ripped his shirt and wadded the pieces, pressing them against the wounds, trying to stem the bleeding with pressure. Her mind had gone a hundred eighty degrees out of focus. It was impossible, but the face she saw was Elena's. This time, she would do it right. This time she would save Elena.

A door slammed. She realized Blackstone was gone, and with him, Mario. Everything shifted. It was Moonie who had been shot.

Moonie was already gone.

She could not lose Mario.

Mario in danger was the only thing in the world that could have pulled her away from Moonie. She ran out of the house and heard the sound of crunching metal. She tried the gate, but it was padlocked.

Carmen bounded up the steps, raced back inside, and dashed through the front room in time to see through the window as the brown heap with Arizona plates backed for a second or maybe a third time into Frenchy's car, shoving it backward into the street. Beneath her feet, the rag rug she'd gotten from a vendor at Gilmore's Farmer's market skidded like a sled on ice across her polished floor. She didn't stop running, but catapulted through her front door at a record pace.

Blackstone drove forward and then lurched back over the Ortiz's cactus garden, struck the Ortiz's car again for a third or fourth time, and bounced over the curb. Carmen had made it close enough for her nails to graze the car's fender. She lunged with all she had in her, but Blackstone's car went squealing down the street. Carmen's heart stopped. Everything in the world stopped. All the world had been reduced to the size of a pinprick, and in the center of it, the only thing she could see, the only thing that existed for her, was Mario's face pressed against the car's rear window. His mouth moved. The distance might as well have been miles instead of feet, for all the good it did her. Carmen read the words, rather than heard them: "Auntie! Auntie," he was calling, over and over. She could feel Mario's voice cut its way into her heart.

"Mario!" Carmen screamed. Jughead came out of nowhere and grabbed hold of her arm, the second time that day he had tried to control her.

"Son of a bitch."

Carmen thought he was talking to her, but realized that he was swearing at his companion, who was already out of sight.

She jammed her elbow in his face.

"Peeling out and leaving me! How am I supposed to get out of here? Son of a bitch. And I hear sirens already. Come on, we're taking that car." He dragged her back inside. "Where the hell are the car keys?"

"It's not my car. How am I supposed to know?" she hissed. She turned in a fury and slammed him with the first thing in her reach— a brass lamp Moonie had gotten from Deardon's department store. Carmen dropped what was left of her favorite lamp and ran back outside, as if somehow Mario would magically appear. Jughead staggered after her, grabbing the metal stem of the lamp that she'd just dropped and shaking off the blood pouring from a cut on his head.

Carmen ran down the steps and out into

the street, but the car with Mario in it was gone. Frenchy's car sat in the middle of the street, with a massive dent in one side and the bumper half disengaged and lying in the ditch. Frenchy peered out, white faced, through her dotted Swiss curtains. Carmen stood, feet planted in the middle of the street, shocked, not moving until an old car came up behind her, honking.

"Take a picture, why don't ya?" some kid yelled from behind the wheel of his fifth-hand jalopy as he slammed his horn. Dimly, she stumbled out of his way and he squealed out, just missing Frenchy's car, and jamming out one last bleat for good measure.

She was still looking toward the car that had taken off with Mario when Carmen felt a blow from behind. She didn't see it coming. Jughead had hit her from behind with the lamp. His aim was bad, but it still knocked her off her feet.

"You're coming with me, sister," he said. "You're gonna cough up that money for my boss. My ride left me, but we'll be right behind him."

He shoved her up against Detective

Oliver's car.

"We're taking a little trip," he said. "Going back to your old stomping ground."

"You're mistaken," Carmen said. "You tell me where he took Mario. I'm not going anywhere with you."

"I gotta bring you or the money, or both," he said. "So come on."

"No."

Light exploded in her face. He'd dropped the lamp and used his fist. She felt the pain after, but it seemed inconsequential. His face was red and blotchy, lips drawn back in rage, his teeth bared like a rabid dog. He drew his arm back to hit her for a third time, but instead of landing another blow, he staggered into her with some force as a loud bang came from behind them; he collapsed where he stood. Behind him, inside the house, Carmen saw a hole in her window and a battered-looking Detective Oliver carefully putting his gun back into his shoulder holster before he too fell out of sight. He must have made the shot, even though it didn't seem possible, given his condition and location.

Then everything became chaos. Police cars pulled up. Ambulances screamed into the street. Neighbors rushed out, standing in knots while they watched and gossiped among themselves. Policemen surrounded her. She tried to answer their questions through the fog in her head. Who were these men? Did she have a photo of Mario? Did they leave a ransom message? A paramedic in horn-rimmed glasses drew her away to an ambulance. He gave her a cloth to clean the blood from her hands and started working on her battered face as other medics took Moonie away in another ambulance and brought the detective in on a gurney.

Trigger Oliver was lying still, with his eyes closed, and the only obvious sign of life was how he winced when the medic worked to stem the bleeding.

"Damn good job with the tourniquet," said the medic. "Even the sling over it is perfect, in fact. Tight enough to stem the bleed, loose enough that your arm isn't strangled. Who did that?"

"She did. Made me hold a pad on it," the detective said when Carmen didn't volunteer. "She's an obstetrics nurse. And a midwife." He coughed, and blood dripped from a cut on his lip. "A bruja, son."

"Lie still," the medic said. "What happened in there? You go a round with Rocky Marciano?"

"Maybe Rocky Marciano's boot," Detective Oliver said, then ignored him to talk to Carmen. "We gotta talk in private."

"I'm not going anywhere," the medic said, "and neither are you."

"Where's Moonie?" Trigger said, trying to raise up, and failing. Trying again. "Where's Mario?"

Carmen ignored the question. "Where's my handbag?" she asked, "The one with..." She looked at the medic, unwilling to mention the money in front of anyone. "You know the one I mean."

"Where do you think?"

Detective Oliver moved his hip, which jostled his coat pocket, rattling his keys. It also jarred his injury, eliciting a grimace.

"Thanks," Carmen said. "I don't know why I didn't think about your trunk." She slipped her hand in his coat pocket and found his keys.

"There goes my shot at some of that dough," the detective said, reaching out and grabbing Carmen with one hand.

She could have shaken him off, but didn't. "I can't tell if you're kidding."

"Neither can I."

The medic pulled a bandage tight. Trigger groaned and shut his eyes, "Where's Moonie? He got the kid?"

"They took Mario."

"Give me a minute. Coming with ya. Beard the lion in his den."

The medic frowned at Carmen and shook his head.

Carmen didn't respond. The only thing on her mind was getting Mario back. She took the keys and shook them so the detective could hear.

"Don't get any big ideas about going after the kid without me," he said. "Soon as they plug up this hole, we can go."

"Hold still," the paramedic interrupted. "This is going to hurt."

The paramedic was telling the truth. Pain or unconsciousness cut the detective short. The wince on his face disappeared. He went slack.

"Can't wait for you," Carmen told him, although she was fairly certain he was beyond hearing. He looked unconscious. "You stay here and clot. I'm going to get my baby back."

Chapter Forty-Two

True to her word, Carmen didn't wait for Detective Oliver to be mended. She ran into the house and found the purse where she'd hidden one of Oliver's guns and barely managed to wait for the ambulances to leave before she was in Oliver's rented car headed southeast. Off again, running without a safety net, but for the first time in her life, she was the one in pursuit, not running away.

She hadn't packed, hadn't done one bit of preparation, but the one thing she had done was pull up behind a Mobil station. A freshly painted white pillar with the red flying horse hid the car from traffic and prying eyes. Imagine if she got face to face with Blackstone and didn't have anything to bargain with? Fortunately, when she opened the trunk, it was there. From the stolen money, she took out a single hundred-dollar bill—a bill she'd borrowed and replaced dozens of times. If she had anything to say about it, she'd never touch it again. She had cursed the bag a thousand times, damning the day she'd brought it with her as the stupidest act of her life. She checked to make sure Detective Oliver hadn't gotten sticky fingers (he hadn't), then stashed the bag inside the spare tire, just to be sure it stayed hidden. She pulled out from behind the sign and let the Mobil service station attendants flock around the car, fill it up, and check the oil, as she waited.

"Nice Mercury," the attendant said, tipping his hat. "Eight cylinders, right? Touch-O-Matic overdrive?" Unlike the service station crews in Mobil's television ads, in their spiffy, spotless uniforms, these guys wore plenty of grease and had black-rimmed nails.

"I don't know. It's a rental."

Gas had gone up to twenty cents a gallon. Filling up the nineteen-gallon tank took almost four dollars.

Thankfully, in the trash pile on the passenger side, the detective had accumulated a collection of state maps, with the route marked all the way to Nogales highlighted in yellow. The trip was routed through highways and back roads. Carmen stopped at a country bait shop and picked up a couple of shotguns and all the ammunition she could carry.

Chapter Forty-Three

In the four years she'd been gone, Nogales hadn't changed. Same old faces, same old jobs. She hadn't worn a disguise, but the short hair and changes Los Angeles had wrought on her appearance —plus sunglasses—were enough. She stopped at a café outside of town to wait until it got dark.

It had been a long drive. To keep from thinking about what had happened, she tried to second-guess the kidnappers. Where would they go but to Francisco's? Carmen was still shaken by the idea he was alive. Still alive, still running things. Her sweet, naïve Elena was still dead. Apparently only evil came back from the dead. It wasn't fair, but little about life was fair. She'd learned that much.

Carmen had the detective's handgun and her two new shotguns. Maybe she'd even the odds. She thought about it. Her subconscious kept reviving the old images of Elena in death, and the fresh, raw image of Moonie. But vengeance would be Carmen's. Her mind's eye kept refocusing the camera, transposing Francisco's face on Elena, on Moonie. If a kidnapper so much as harmed a hair on Mario's head, Carmen would gut and fillet him, and Francisco and every one of them as well, and serve them on toast.

She made good time. She pulled off the highway near the arroyo where Francisco's car had been washed away so long ago. If she were lucky, the household would be asleep. In the dark she could slip in, and slip out just as easily. She wasn't going down the driveway, though. She cut across the fields. No roads, no witnesses. That was the plan, anyway. She loaded the shotguns, wound her belt around them, and looped the excess over her shoulder as she'd seen Moonie do at the shooting range.

She'd do whatever she had to do to get Mario. She put on the shoulder holster, tugging it tight, and retrieved the bag with the money in it. Maybe it was stupid to carry it into the lion's den, but maybe she could stash it somewhere along the way. She hid the car keys under the seat.

On the drive there, Carmen had thought about the punks who had stolen Mario. They were Francisco's type, even if she didn't recognize them personally from her life before. Just the kind of brutal, stupid men he'd hire or do business with. Bottom-feeders who skirted the law. They were just the kind of lowlifes who'd show up at the factory after hours and talk among themselves in secretive voices about things Carmen didn't want to know.

The ground was as hard and dry as if there had never been a flood in that exact spot that washed the car she had been in into the drainage ditch with her in it. She'd spent four years running from memories, running from this place, running from nightmares, running from a life that had dissolved into horror and that now seemed unreal. The area that bordered Francisco's land was familiar, a step back in time to a life she once knew and loved.

Carmen approached a slight valley, where there was easy entry through the formidable barbed wire fence—seven feet tall, seven rows high, twisted with sharp wire.

There was a trick to getting through. Carmen recalled how Elena used to widen the gap between the two loosest rows by bracing it open with a y-shaped branch—really a small log. Carmen got to her knees and rooted with her hands for so long that she thought perhaps she had parked her car by the wrong section, but then she found the limb directly beneath the bottom wire, exactly where Elena had left it nearly five years ago. Finding it was confirmation that she was in the right place, but also showed how much time had passed. She pulled it from its hiding place, but it crumbled in her grasp. Dry rot.

Under other circumstances, Carmen might have gone looking for a substitute prop, but not now. She tossed the bag through and followed, or tried to, picking an area about waist high, right beside a fence post she could grab for balance. Goaded by the knowledge that Mario was so close, she poked her head through, bending at the waist and lifting her leg to step over, testing the tension, tentatively, just to see if it was loose enough to keep her from being gored by prongs. She stopped for a second, smoothed her short hair, then started again. So far, so good. Her backside butted up against a post. The straight edge of the top wire glided along her back, caught in fabric and skin. She felt barbs here and there, leaned down trying to avoid them, and then they snagged her from beneath. She adjusted her angle, her grip on the lines. That changed the tension and she was able to move her back, but then a barb bit into her palm and another barb got a solid grip on her shirt at another spot. Prongs tore at the skirt, at her face and arms, and grazed her skin.

> She shoved away from the fence.
> Into the field.
> Into the dirt.
> Falling.
> The sound of ripping material hardly gave

her pause. That wasn't going to stop her, even though she was taken aback at how much material was left hanging on the wire, like a Raggedy Ann's laundry line. Her skin stung in a dozen places, but that didn't matter. She was in. She jerked the patches of material off the fence and shoved them in what was left of a pocket, lest anyone see a scrap and get curious enough to nose around. She brushed herself off, picked up the bag with the cash, and plodded on.

The route to the house zigzagged through the field. In the dark, the rocky creek bed with sharp valleys and pits made an unforgiving trail. In daylight, she'd walked the grounds with Elena often enough, after Francisco had forbidden Elena to leave. The sharp pang of the memory cut like a knife.

In the darkness, the field was hard going. Planted furrows were obstacles in themselves, roughening the terrain, although it was surprising how light the night seemed once her eyes had adjusted. Carmen turned, trying to get her bearings, and tripped, skinning her knee. When she rose, her hem was underfoot. Her skirt ripped again, not made for lurking, fence-hopping, hiking, digging, dirt-crawling, or sneaking around. She tied the blouse together as best she could, and ripped away part of the disintegrating hem. More clothes were gone than remained. She'd have to do something about covering up if the opportunity presented itself.

There was no electric light cutting through the night sky, except in one place—her destination. From a distance, the air around the hacienda was surrounded by a bright haze visible to her long before she was close enough to see the outer walls of the courtyard, or make out specifics in the long lane of parked cars belonging to the rancho's crew and visitors. Even though it was close to midnight, the rancho blazed with light. She took advantage of the brightness to detour to where she could check the driveway for the rattletrap that had been driven by Mario's kidnapper.

She had to walk down a row and duck behind cars to stay out of sight, but she found it.

They were there, but it was scarcely a relief to know she was on the right track. It was not a good sign that the lights were on, and that the building rang with angry voices. There were too many people milling about for this hour. They seemed to be mostly ranch hands.

A man's angry voice yelled, "Hey, kid!" over and over.

She prayed that Mario was okay.

A number of field hands passed so close she had to duck behind parked cars again. She backtracked to an outbuilding near one of the bunkhouses, coming along laundry lines with lots of clothing there for the taking. She grabbed an armful of pants and shirts that she hoped might be wearable, and continued toward the hacienda.

The voices grew louder as Carmen came closer to the house. She moved behind one shed that held farming supplies, then another that held gardening tools for the house.

The gardening outbuilding breeched the courtyard walls; it was built into the wall, extending on both sides, about the size of a small apartment bedroom. Carmen recalled when it had been put up. Once there had been a plain aluminum shack, ugly but functional, holding the tools for the courtyard gardens. Francisco had demanded that it be pulled down because it destroyed Elena's view. The picturesque miniature adobe house had been built in its place. She remembered that its wooden porch extended into the courtyard and housed a couple of rugged rocking chairs in front of a set of charming farmhouse doors, and how the night Mario had been born, she and Elena had rocked in those very chairs. A big log door that was wide enough to admit a small tractor was set in the back, away from view of the house. The padlock she remembered was no longer there, so Carmen was able to step inside the log door and avoid the lackadaisical meandering of ranch hands coming and going. They might have been on sentry duty, or going out to get drunk, whore around and gamble. It was hard to tell with that bunch.

This building had been Carmen's planned entrance through the courtyard. She was glad it was still here. It was a perfect opportunity to change into the stolen clothes. Carmen unbuckled the holster and felt around in the dark for a protrusion where she could hang it. She stripped down to her underwear, feeling horribly vulnerable. At least she'd worn loafers, although they were much the worse for wear from her struggle through the fields. She slipped them off. Groping among the clothes she had grabbed, she dug out an undershirt that would do and, as soon as it was on, strapped on the gun. She found a big flannel shirt and put that on top—the fit wasn't great, but the shirt helped hide the gun.

Then she heard the voices. More of the ranch hands.

"Where the hell are we supposed to look for the kid?"

"I don't know, don't care. Going to the joint in town..."

"But what about..."

She heard the drunken voices approach and held still. They came close to the shed. One stopped, noticing the door ajar. He opened it.

Carmen smiled at him.

He smiled back, looking her up and down, appreciating her naked legs.

"Well hello," he said. "Having a tryst with one of the boys? Have you seen a little kid running around?"

Carmen whacked him in the head with a shovel. He fell like a brick, backwards.

She pulled the door shut. The other sentry noticed the loss of his companion and returned.

"Hey." He nudged him with his foot. "You could'a told me you had a head start. You can sleep it off right here. I'm still going to town to tie one on as soon as this shift's over, whether or not we find the kid."

He disappeared into the darkness as an argument continued raging inside the house.

Carmen had to try on several pair of dungarees until she found one that was okay, if a bit short and tight. She couldn't find her shoes. Voices from inside the house got louder.

Not Francisco's usual rant. It struck her

as strange for someone else to be yelling in the bad man's house, but it definitely *was* someone else. She thought she might have heard the sound of a slap. A man whose voice she did not recognize was yelling, and another voice was keening, whining back in response. The second voice struck Carmen as someone familiar, but it was off-key, like a song she didn't remember, a song with the wrong words. Try as she might, she could not put a face to the voice. Male and hoarse, but whiney. The only thing she knew for certain was that it was not Mario.

Carmen finished dressing in her laundry-line clothes while listening to the rise and fall of the argument in the house. She could feel a chill, her feet bare against the crud on the unswept adobe brick floor. Her soles were awash in dirt and who knew what else. She couldn't tell and lifted up her feet to brush them off.

Inside the shed, it was pitch-black. Changing in the dark had disoriented her a little. Light would help. She thought she recalled seeing the shutters standing open once or twice, but wasn't certain. She fumbled carefully in the dark, making her way, bruising her shins on farm equipment, stubbing her toe against immobile objects, groping along the inside of the walls until she found the wooden shutters set in the farmhouse door that led to the courtyard.

The louvers were designed to move in parallel by adjusting a slat down the spine. Carmen nudged the slat until the louvers opened their widest, letting in enough light from the illuminated courtyard for her to make out the shapes of farm equipment. There were shovels, post-hole diggers, augers, rakes, hoes, and an assortment of hand tools hanging from wall hooks. Buckets. Pruners and bars, and something that looked like it might be a javelin. Sacks of seed and fertilizer. A crate full of empty feed sacks. She shoved the rags of her clothes underneath and dropped the laundry she hadn't worn in a pile on top of them. She was able to see where she'd dropped the money bag inside the shed. She retrieved it, and dropped it through the shed's window into the courtyard to a pile of ferns below.

At last she saw the loafers. She brushed off her feet again, and slipped on her shoes.

There were men dressed like city slickers walking the path in pairs. She reasoned they must be part of the entourage who'd schemed to get Mario. Carmen positioned herself on the path and swung the rifle like a baseball bat when they rounded the corner. Once. Twice. They dropped like flies. She dragged them into the bushes. On one of their hard heads, she'd broken a rifle. She left it where it lay in pieces.

The easiest way into the courtyard was through the shed, so she went back inside. Through the slats, the courtyard seemed very bright, but maybe that was just her eyes adjusting. All the lights in the house still seemed to be on. The voices inside continued, loud, but muffled. She tried to make out the words.

"So where is he?"

"How the hell should I know? And why should I care?"

She heard phrases:

"...missing woman...Los Angeles."

Something about the money and then, "...come for the kid."

Her heart raced. There was only one kid. Mario must have gotten away. That seemed to be what the hands were doing—looking for a scared little boy. That wouldn't do. She had to let him know she was here. She had to do something to distract his pursuers.

When she pushed at the doors on the courtyard side, they swung wide with a screech that could have waked the residents of the City of Nogales cemetery. The sound made Carmen's heart beat so hard she thought someone else could have heard it if they'd been within a dozen feet of her. She waited for what felt like hours. When no one ran to investigate, she ventured inch by inch out onto the wooden porch, wincing as the door creaked shut. Still no one came out, probably because something had escalated inside. She heard glass breaking. She dropped the moneybag behind a bush and inched off the porch.

Then a voice—what she thought of as Francisco's voice—as harsh and horrible as she remembered:

"You find the kid!"

And the whining voice came back with, "What can I do about it? Look at me!"

There was a harsh laugh.

"Yeah, I am."

The sound of a slap.

Was Francisco having someone beaten? He'd done it before, Carmen knew, but never in her earshot. She edged up to the window of the den, but no one was in there. She checked a bedroom, and another, and the room that would have been Mario's. The lights were on, but the rooms were empty of people except for Elena's bedroom, where she could see someone moving around behind the sheers, although the shape was formless, undistinguishable.

Her heart was in her throat when she reached to the bedroom door. The design had been adapted, and a small incline added. Carmen guessed Francisco had wanted the changes to dim the memory of Elena. She hoped that did him no good. This whole rancho had been rebuilt for her. She hoped it was all one big bleeding memory in his head, one that wrenched his heart every day, every hour, every minute—if he had a heart.

She touched the door. It slid open easily, an inch or two, in complete silence. The voices were loud here. The whiney guy was now sobbing openly.

"You've got all the fucking money," the voice said. "You got everything. Every penny is here, so get the hell out. What more can I give you?"

"You can give me what's missing, you son of a bitch. There's more. You welched on that deal in '48, you know when I'm talking about. If you can't come up with it, we'll take it out of your hide. You better hope that woman shows up, cash in hand."

Another slap. Derisive laughter.

"Man, you're pathetic. To think we used ta be scared of you. When we get the dough. I say we get rid of you."

She heard several more slaps, more laughter. The whining voice had ceased to make complaint. Hr was just crying now, not making anything that sounded like words. Nothing was more pathetic than the sound of a man crying.

Carmen's heart twisted with hatred of Francisco. He was the worst man on earth, and deserved what she was about to do to him.

"If you don't like it, do something about it."

Carmen thought, *If he's killing someone in there, I'll shoot him. I don't care if I go to jail, I'll shoot him. I owe him, for killing Elena. I'm going to step inside and shoot him in the face.*

She pulled the gun out and held it straight out in front. Her hands shook. She took a breath to steel herself. She put the gun back in the holster and pulled the shirt closed. Maybe she could get by without the gun. She shoved the door open wider and stepped through it. The sheers parted. Her mind did not immediately register what she saw.

She yelled at the top of her lungs, hoping that, if Mario was around, he'd hear her and know she was around as well.

"If anybody's going to do any killing, it's going to be me. So, where's my boy?" Then for good measure, "If you're out there, Mario, stay where you are! Do not come in here. If you're out there, you stay out there, keep quiet, not a sound! If you hear me, you better not make a peep!"

Her brain almost caught up with her body. She tried to make sense of what she was seeing. She'd stepped into Elena's old bedroom. Or what she thought had been Elena's old room. The fine bed and lovely furniture was gone. The room was empty except for a hospital bed and a wheelchair collapsed against a wall. In the bed was a withered, shrunken, ancient man and beside him, Blackstone. Blackstone with his back to her, turning.

"Did you bring the money, bitch?" Blackstone asked, his teeth drawn back in the rictus of a grin.

"You get it when I get Mario. If you don't hand him over, you'll never get so much as a thin dime."

"Elena? You wanted to name our son Mario. But you're not my Elena. Carmen..." the voice whimpered. Carmen looked at him in disbelief, finally registering the shattered husk that was all that was left of Francisco. The last four years had not been kind to him. She could not believe how much he'd aged. There was nothing but confusion in his face.

"Shut up," Blackstone hissed, slapping him again.

The slap smashed the invalid flat on his back. Blackstone grabbed the collar of Francisco's nightshirt and propped the practically boneless body back up against the pillows.

"Stop it!" Carmen said, stepping forward. "Enough. Give me my boy."

"He ran away—the boy ran away," Francisco cackled. "He's yours? I should have guessed. He was smart enough to get away from this yellow-bellied skunk. From this...You called him Mario." A dim sort of knowledge crossed his face. "His name is Mario?" Shock, knowledge, and real fear showed in his eyes. "Get out of here, Mario!

Run!"

Blackstone made a fist. "You talk too much, old man."

The fear left his face. Francisco cackled. "You'll never get him. He's Elena's boy. Mario." He looked at Carmen with knowledge in his expression.

Blackstone swore, "You're a nutcase, old man. Elena's baby is long dead. She was dead before the baby was even born, remember?"

Francisco's arms, withered and useless, flew up to guard himself from Blackstone's next blow. It didn't come.

"I said stop it," Carmen said.

"What are you going to do about it? You care about this old man?" Blackstone shoved past Francisco's defenses and gripped him by the throat, cutting off his breath. He leaned down, pressing him backward against the pillows.

"How much do you care?"

Carmen said, "I just want my Mario back. I don't care about the man who killed my sister."

But that was another man. This Francisco

was something else entirely. Weak and helpless, gasping for air, flailing at the hand at his throat, too feeble to pry himself free.

"Let him go," Carmen said. Almost against her will, she leaned forward over the bed and pried at Blackstone's fingers wrapped round Francisco's windpipe. She and Blackstone, both leaned over the hospital bed, Francisco between them, choking, turning blue. She poked Blackstone in the eye.

He swore at her.

"I'll let go when you bring me the money."

"I'll bring you the money when you let go. And when you show me that Mario is unharmed."

"No deal," Blackstone said. He turned his attention to Francisco. "This one's going to die."

Carmen saw Francisco, minutes, probably seconds from death. She pulled out the revolver. Blackstone saw the gun, but it didn't frighten him. It made him laugh.

"You can't pull the trigger. I saw you in

Los Angeles. You're the nurse, the one who tried to keep those guys alive. You ain't no killer." His grip eased up on Francisco as he talked.

"That was Detective Oliver you shot. And my...and Moonie."

"So what?" He taunted. "What are you going to do about it?"

"Moonie was a good man. He didn't deserve—."

"So what, sister? Cry me a river. I ain't scared of you." He waved his gun around.

"So *this*." Carmen pulled Oliver's gun and fired. The bullet caught him in the left shoulder. His gun arm fell limp. His pistol fell on the floor.

"Fuck," Blackstone said, looking down at himself, at his bloody hand, in disbelief. He wiped his hand across his shoulder "You shot me. You can't shoot me! You ain't got no balls."

"I don't need balls. I got this gun. Who do you think put him in that wheelchair? I only came back to finish it. And to get my boy." Carmen squinted at his shoulder. She knew her anatomy. "I don't know much about killing, but

I know the circulatory system. You're already dead, Mister. You've got some pretty big blood vessels in your left shoulder. You better say your prayers."

"No way. I feel fine." He wavered on his feet.

Francisco's quivering hands rubbed his neck. "She can be a hell of a bitch sometimes." His eyes turned toward her, but they were admiring. "A hell of a bitch."

Blackstone went down.

Carmen walked around the side of the bed, still holding the gun. Blackstone's eyes were open but vacant. Carmen stared at him in disbelief, hardly believing here, in the same room, she'd done it again. She bent down and picked up Blackstone's weapon.

"Carmen," Francisco—or what was the ghost of Francisco—rasped, "Give me the gun."

She had never pictured Francisco as this crippled shell of his former self. As personal hell went, it was perfect.

"I came here to kill you," Carmen said,

"and to get Mario back. To trade Mario for the money."

"Fuck the money," Francisco said. "You raised my son. I saw him. He looks good. He's smart. He's tough. He's brave. He looks like you... He looks like my beautiful Elena. But he's my boy. I can see it in his face." He swallowed. A glass of water sat on the table beside the bed, but blood floated in it.

"Take my son and get the fuck out of here, and if you know what's good for you, never come back."

"I came here to kill you," Carmen said again, dully. She picked up Blackstone's gun, and pointed both guns at him. "You shot Elena. You killed her. You have to die. I thought you were dead already. All this time." Carmen's finger was on the triggers, both barrels against Francisco's temples. "This time, I do it right."

But something made her hesitate. A noise behind her. The door creaked. A sheer whisper of someone walking through. Light footsteps. A little voice.

"I heard a gun," Mario's voice piped up. "I heard a shot."

The something was Mario.

Carmen turned toward Mario, holding the guns behind her back, then dropping them behind her on the bed. "I told you not to come in here," Carmen said, her voice cracking in relief to see him safe. "I told you to stay out there and wait till I found you."

"I heard you. Are you okay? Please be okay. Don't be mad 'cause I went and hid on the roof."

"I'm not mad. You did good." Carmen dropped to her knees, checking Mario over and finding him unhurt. "I'm not mad, I'm just... here."

"He listens about as well as you and your sister." Francisco cackled again. "My boy. God-damn it—my boy." He cackled again. Carmen had dropped the guns on the sheet within his reach. Francisco's shaky hand snaked out and strained to grab one of them.

Carmen whispered something in Mario's

ear, and pointed outside.

He nodded gravely and went out.

"I got the guns now," Francisco laughed, waving one wildly. "Go lift up that dead son-of-a-bitch Blackstone and drape him over the bed so it looks like I did him. Come on, woman. I'd do it myself, but you put half of me in the grave four years ago. Son of a bitch works for some shithead outside of Denver. I'm going to call in some favors for tonight. They're gonna pay. Heads will roll. Blood will spill. That little shit Johnny Pinto is gonna be Johnny Headless."

"I'm not touching him," Carmen said.

"It don't matter," Francisco said with macabre joy. "You splattered him like a tomato."

Mario returned, carrying the ugly souvenir bag Carmen had told him to retrieve from the bushes.

"I have something of yours," Carmen said.

Francisco looked at Mario and said proudly, "I know."

"Not him," Carmen said. She ignored the waving gun, opened the bag, and dumped the cash out all over Francisco's bloodied sheets—most of the money still in stacks wrapped by Francisco's own fingers some four or five years before.

"I used a little of it at first, but put it back. I don't want it."

"Keep it," Francisco said, gleefully. "I'll get more, now you rubbed out Blackstone. He's been a real pest."

Carmen heard a thud against the wall. Her heart leapt.

"I don't recall you being so jumpy," Francisco said in his broken voice, "but maybe you could let Delores out of the closet. Shithead Blackstone stuffed her in there. You remember Delores. The dumpy one with the brats. I hired her to take care of me, but they put her in there. Glad he didn't shoot her in the head. She ain't no nurse, but she minds a hell of a lot better than you ever did. You were a hell of a fuck, though."

"Shut your mouth," Carmen said, and opened the door while Francisco was still talking.

Delores was sitting in a chair wrapped

with enough rope to immobilize a dozen steers. Tape was fixed over her mouth. Her eyes were wild as she looked over the tape at Carmen, who couldn't get the ropes off fast enough.

Delores stood, groaning, and gave Carmen a hug.

"I been hogtied for hours," she said, "I gotta go pee."

She waddled quickly out of the room.

"Who's that, Mami?"

"An old friend," Carmen said. "At least, I think she's a friend." She turned to Francisco. "And you should give me that gun back. I gotta give it back to the detective who owns it."

Her immediate problem taken care of, Delores promptly returned, stepping over Blackstone's body. She went straight for the phone on Francisco's end table. Almost.

"If neither of you wants it, I'm getting some of this money. And I gotta report a murder."

Delores dialed. Neither Carmen nor Francisco did anything to stop her.

She said into the mouthpiece. "Yeah, a murder. No, I don't know what happened. I was locked in the closet. No, this is not a joke. I mean it. You come out to the Sanchez rancho, pronto."

"Give me the phone," Francisco commanded, still waving the gun. The effort exhausted him, and he dropped his hand on the covers. Carmen reached for it.

"Unh unh," Francisco warned Carmen.

Delores handed him the phone. Carmen glared at her.

"He's still my boss. And he's got a gun." Delores whispered so the police wouldn't hear. "Hey, you look good. The short hair, I mean. Like Doris Day. What the hell are you wearing?"

"I borrowed the clothes. Mine were torn up."

"Some guy came here and tried to rob me, and I shot him," Francisco said on the phone. "Yes, I'm still a damn cripple. You gotta send somebody here to get the body. He bled all over my floor and my payroll. And I need a doctor before I croak—the bastard tried to choke me."

He gave the receiver to Delores. "Hang it up, and get me a clean glass and some water without his blood in it."

Delores left with the glass.

"So. You should get out before the cops get here," Francisco said. "You can take the dough, I don't give a shit." Francisco looked at Mario, who was watching him with big eyes. "I mean, I don't care. Take the money."

"I don't want the money. But I could use a ride to my car."

"Tell Delores to ring the chauffeur."

"No." Just the thought of Francisco's chauffeur was enough to turn her stomach.

"It's not Blasio," Francisco said. "Blasio's doing a job for me in Mexico. I should'a been smart enough not to send Segundo and my body-guards with him, or this shit wouldn't have happened, but he can't tie his shoes without screwing up. Are you gonna stay in town? I been keeping your place up," Francisco said, "in case you came back."

"Thanks, but I...we...won't be back."

"That's best," Francisco said, his eyes on the boy who was now leaning against Carmen's leg, with one hand in hers. The boy's eyes were shut, and maybe he was snoring a little.

"I still got enemies. Is that boy asleep on his feet?"

"Almost. It's past his bedtime," Carmen said, picking Mario up and bracing him on her hip. His head tipped forward to rest on her shoulder, and his arms coiled around her neck.

"I would have shot you," Carmen said. "I was planning to, but when I walked in, he was slapping you. And you..."

Francisco's eyes were fixed on Mario. On Carmen holding Mario. His eyes were moist.

"Don't say that. With the kid, you look like a fucking Norman Rockwell magazine cover for the fucking *Saturday Evening Post*."

"I would have shot you," Carmen repeated.

"But you didn't. And before...what happened before, I can't remember clear. Were you here?"

"When? What are you talking about?"

"I know you were here. Blasio brought you here to deliver..." he glanced at Mario again, "...the baby. But that night...it's a blur—I remember drinking. I remember leaving. I remember seeing you standing there with a gun."

She realized his mind had drifted to the night when he had shot her sister. He didn't remember? How could he not?

A frantic look crossed Francisco's face. He reached out and grabbed Carmen's other hand. He had invalid hands, weak from long illness, soft like a woman's, not a callous in sight. His fingers felt as if they were built on rubber instead of bone. Carmen could have easily pulled away.

"I gotta know...did I...I don't remember that night, the night she...my beautiful Elena. How did she die?"

It was on the tip of her tongue to answer him. She hesitated, just as Delores returned with the water.

Francisco dropped the gun on his chest

and cupped the glass with both of his hands. It wasn't a frivolous motion. It took all the strength in both hands for him to hold the glass, and still his hands quivered with weakness. She looked again at the wheelchair that was folded and propped against the wall. The significance of it registered in her brain. She saw the way Delores tugged at his hips, how easily she adjusted his body upright against the pillows. His lower half had atrophied.

He was a paraplegic.

"Drink," Delores said. "You sound like shit. All that yelling fried your voice."

"You're lucky Blackstone didn't break your hyoid bone," Carmen said. "You're lucky to be talking and breathing."

He wasn't listening.

"Tell me!" Francisco begged. His mind was on that other time. He fell back against his pillow, exhausted. "Please! Tell me." He turned to Delores to plead for him. "Make her tell me. I've got to know who killed my Elena."

Carmen didn't know if it was crueler to

tell him or not to. Would it drive him mad to know he'd shot Elena? Would he remember what she'd already said? Surely somewhere in his addled brain, he must have realized the truth.

Francisco's voice was a slim thread. Carmen didn't ask about his condition, but a lot was going unsaid. Francisco didn't get his answer, but Carmen took the last word for herself.

"The whole secret in life," she said, "is to know when to be the mouse, and when to be the fox."

* * *

The two women stepped into the hall. They passed the room that would have been Mario's if Carmen hadn't taken him. All the infant paraphernalia had been taken away. It was outfitted as a guest room, as if there had never been a baby at all. As if Elena had never been mistress of this house. Delores flicked the light out as she walked past.

"What happened to the baby stuff?"

"I don't know," Delores said. "I only ever saw it like this. Maybe Segundo had the room cleared on the night..." Delores cleared her throat, staring at Mario, "on the night Elena lost her baby."

"You've been taking care of Francisco?"

Delores nodded.

"How long?"

"Ever since he came out of the coma. They said some gangsters shot him and your sister. He's been kind of crazy ever since he woke up. Not that he was ever sane."

"When wasn't he crazy?" Carmen asked.

"You got a point," Delores agreed. "It's funny. For a long time, the police thought you had been shot, too, and dumped in some shallow grave somewhere, or drowned. We had a funeral for you and everything. Then the police said it was all a mistake, you were off somewhere, with a job as a nurse."

"It's true. I'm a nurse."

"Me, too." Delores jerked her head back toward the back of the house, where Francisco was.

"Not that kind of nurse," Carmen said.

"I just deliver babies."

Delores looked relieved, as if she'd been worrying about Carmen taking her job. As if Carmen would ever accept that job. Never again would she work for Francisco. She'd starve first.

"Like your ma did? Like you used to, here?"

"Yep, except at a hospital. No more illegals."

Delores looked skeptical.

"Okay, no more except the ones the priests send me."

"I just came here because..."

"You don't have to explain yourself to me. I know how hard jobs are to find in this town."

"Yeah but...he doesn't have anyone else who gives a shit. Maybe Manuela, but Manuela's got a life."

Carmen shifted Mario to her other shoulder, then reached out and took Delores's hand. "I of all people remember how he was. How he treated you, too. How he was probably behind your husband's death. How can you help him? It must be because you always had the softest heart."

"I remember how he was," Delores said. "Maybe God's ways of working aren't that mysterious. It's hard for him, because inside, he's still the big, mean guy. Impossible for him to be like this, really. I...I feel sorry for him."

"You're a better person than I am," Carmen said. "I never could do what you're doing for him."

"The man you remember, that we remember—that one's dead and gone." Delores's face was shadowed. The years had not been kind to her, but somehow she had become the heart of kindness. She brightened and said, "At least you have your little Mario. I guess it's a family name. Francisco's kind of crazy on that subject. He doesn't always remember that Elena died along with their son."

"My mother's name was Maria. This...is my Mario."

It was true. He *was* hers. She'd taken care of him every day of his life. Whether he called her Mami or Auntie, she was his parent, and would be, as long as she had the breath in her body to keep him safe. Carmen felt a renewed desire to leave the darkness and evil of this house in her rear view window.

"We're going," Carmen said.

"I'll call the chauffeur. He's an okay guy. From Texas, I hear. Hired after the war. He's got a phone in the garage apartment. It won't take but a minute for him to come around. He's no Blasio."

Carmen only knew she had to leave and had to get Mario away from the influence of his father before something went wrong. "If he gets to you before I talk to him, tell Detective Oliver I know where his gun and car are. I don't know him that well, but I think he can be trusted to deal with whatever story you cook up."

Epilogue

Carmen returned to Los Angeles, to the cute bungalow with the picket fence and big backyard. It wasn't so cute any more. She walked through the doors of Moonie's house that was now hers, and it hit her that Moonie was dead. The wall of grief was like walking into a world of gray. All the light and color were gone. There was no more normal. Yes, Carmen had Mario back, with no fear of police—or Francisco—coming after her, but her sense of safety had been violated. Moonie had been the solution to a question Carmen had never realized she'd had, like her missing puzzle piece. And now the puzzle would never be complete.

It rained the day he was buried. Detective Oliver came to the funeral straight from the hospital. He was wrapped in bandages and covered in bruises. Carmen told him where to find his

gun and gave him the keys to his rental car, which
was in her garage.

Mario never asked where Moonie was,
because he remembered. Moonie's lifeblood had
colored a path in the carpet of the house from
the bedroom to the steps to the back yard. It
couldn't be washed away.

Moonie's absence left a big hole in their
lives that Carmen felt no urge to fill. Mario didn't
remember a world without Moonie. The house
was so full of memories and ghosts, there was no
room for living. There was no peace there anymore. Weeks after the funeral, Carmen accepted
the first offer on the place, banked it, and got an
apartment in Boyle Heights across from the park.
All that remained of her Nogales life was in a box
at the top of her closet. She might go through it
some day.

She'd had to downsize anyway. She lost
her job. The brouhaha that had brought down
Moonie had focused too much attention on her
and someone realized there was a problem with
her name. The head nurse had called her into the

office and broke the news that Carmen would be on unpaid leave until her nursing license was straightened out.

Her nursing career was at an end.

She had to sit through a panel review. All men. All stern. All judgmental. Had she gotten into school as Carmen Garcia or as Elena Garcia? Had she done the classwork? Would she be willing to provide proof, and retake the tests, and do a new internship here in California under their eyes, where they could be assured it was she who had done the work and earned the results? And they were concerned that she dealt with young people. She, a woman, unmarried, living in sin, with a child. They assumed he was Moonie's child. They had a copy of the boy's birth certificate from New York with no father listed. There was a moral issue at stake, and they had their standards. Maybe if she lied, and said she was the aunt...

The questions went on and on, until Carmen had enough. She didn't want them to look at her so closely that they could figure out who Mario was.

She found a factory job, returning to her least-favorite profession, bookkeeping for a factory that sewed uniforms. It wasn't what she wished to do, but it was a living.

Besides, before long, everyone in the new apartment building, then everyone in their new neighborhood, learned she was both an old-school midwife and a nurse wrapped in one. That she'd lost her job at the hospital only endeared her to the kind of immigrant clients she started to have again. Pregnant immigrants were fruitful and multiplied, and as the babies kept coming, so did her job of birthing them. Soon she fit in, again, her same old niche in a new location. She was back on the path she had been born to follow.

In the new apartment, Carmen made Mario promise never to climb on the roof. He still had nightmares. He woke up screaming, sometimes hysterical over a creak from the apartment next door, a random noise, a shadow moving in the window. Carmen would open the blinds and stand in the dark with him, looking out together, until he was satisfied that there were no evil men outside, no evil spirits, no gangsters lurking to grab him. The only thing in the little front yard of the apartment building was a big tree he played in during the day. At night, when it blocked the streetlight, its trunk loomed as a creepy silhouette on the shades. It was a long time before Mario made his peace with it. Only when he knew he was safe was he able to fall asleep, often on Carmen's lap as they rocked in the rocking chair. She would gently return him to his bed and click out the light. Sometimes she left the drapes and blinds open so, if he chanced to wake, he could see the tree itself, and not its shadow.

In the night as the moon peeked out from behind the tree, she had the feeling, as she noticed it, that it watched back. Memories flooded her, of a night two years before.

"Moonie," she whispered. "What am I to do without you?"

Of course, there was no answer, but the light that beamed down on her seemed something more. It embraced her. She basked in it, leaning her forehead against the glass, her palm against the casement, as if on the shoulder of a lover. She felt a little less alone.

There was another creak. Mario did not waken. Carmen decided she would not tell him the noises disturbed her, too. He had been brave, but it was time for him to be a little boy, not her protector. It was she who must protect him for as long as she was able.

The big tree waited like a sentry at her window. Shadows cast here were merely from trees, not memories, not evil. If there was evil out there, it was somewhere far away.

About the Author

George Hatcher is an entrepreneur with a gift for business and storytelling. Whether he's traveling the globe as a consultant for lawyers in high profile aviation crash cases, advising boxers, or at home with Molly in California, he's always got his eye on the next project. A longer bio is on his website at:

www.georgehatcher.com/bio/bio.html